HOODED

Book One of the Furix Rising Series

A NOVEL BY
A. A. Woods

Amonoux

ISBN: 978-1-951803-05-6

Cover art designed by Alrun Maget, Instagram @alrun.art
Map designed by Oscar Paludi (Exoniensis)

Books by the Author

The Furix Rising Series
Hooded (Book 1)
Severed (Book 2)
Bladed (Book 3)

The Scottstown Heroes Series
Vagabonds (Book 1)
Renegades (Book 2)
Runaways (Book 2.5)

Other Books
Project Recollection (The Affinity Book 1)
The Star Siren
The Face of the Universe: A Short Story Collection

GUIDE TO HOODED SECTS

Red Hoods (Cerise Tower) — Predators

Yellow Hoods (Oeil Tower) — Birds

Black Hoods (Scara Tower) — Insects

Blue Hoods (Requin Tower) — Undersea Creatures

Green Hoods (Tierre Tower) —Forest-Dwelling Mammals

Brown Hoods (Chevin Tower) — Beasts of Burden

Silver Hoods (Skin Smiths) — Specialized for human torture

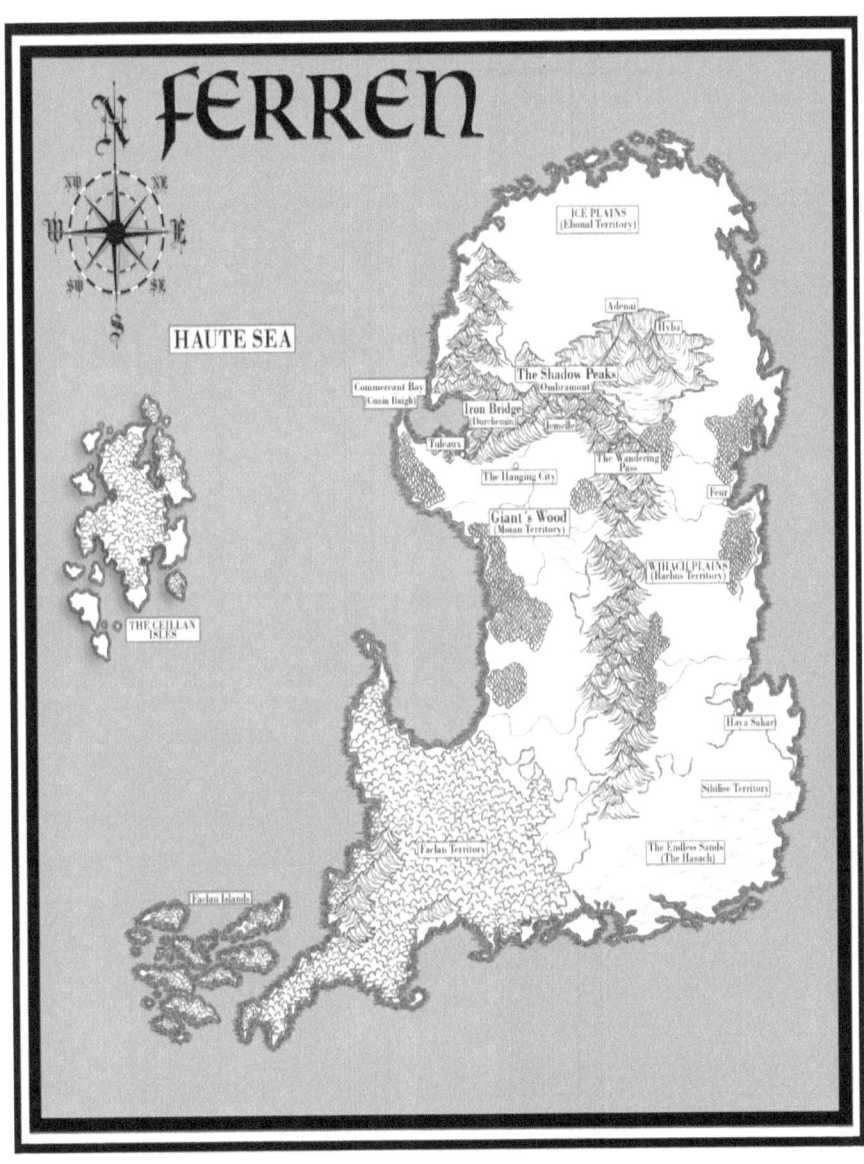

FERREN

HAUTE SEA

ICE PLAINS
(Elsonal Territory)

Adenai

Hyba

The Shadow Peaks
(Ombramont)

Commereant Bay
(Cuan Baigh)

Iron Bridge
(Durcleont)

Jemellet

The Wandering
Pass

Tuleaux

Feur

The Hanging City

Giant's Wood
(Monan Territory)

WHIACIL PLAINS
(Harbus Territory)

THE CEILLAN
ISLES

Hava Sahar

Sthilse Territory

Faelan Territory

The Endless Sands
(The Hasach)

Faelan Islands

Author's Note

This book has been in production, in some way or another, for almost five years.

It was one of the first ideas I had as a shiny, fresh-faced writer committing to the craft, eager to join the illustrious ranks of YA authordom. It was the fifth novel I finished, but the first one I really thought was *good*. Then, when I tore it down and rewrote it from the ground up, it got better. And now, after multiple beta reads, dozens of rejections, endless careful rewrites, and lots of blood, sweat, and tears, here it is, in your hands at last.

And I couldn't be more excited.

If you've checked out my other books, you'll know I like to create both funny, adventurous romps and dark, brooding tales of war and struggle. At the time of writing this introduction, I've published one of each type (*Vagabonds* being the former; *The Star Siren* the latter). *Hooded*, however, sits squarely in the middle, refusing to be slotted into either category. It's at once dark and adventurous; somber and snarky. The world you are about to enter is violent, dangerous, full of rage and pain and human malevolence. But (I hope) it is also exciting, romantic, and, most importantly, *fun*. In the blurb, I promise myths and monsters.

I did my absolute best to deliver.

All this is meant to say that I poured everything I had into making the book in your hands as awesome as possible. I know it won't be for everyone (nothing ever is), but should you end up enjoying this strange, ferocious, heartfelt voyage of a story, I'd love to hear from you! If you catch the hints of Little Red Riding Hood, love Carlette as much as I do, or appreciate the blend of *Revenant*-style bleakness and YA excitement, please reach out to me on my website, Facebook, or write a review to share your thoughts. I read everything readers say and will incorporate all of it into future stories to make more of what you enjoy!

Finally, I'd like to say *thank you*. Thank you for taking a chance and picking up this book. Thank you for reading this far (and hopefully further). And thank you, always, for getting excited about the weird stuff that comes out of authors' brains. If not for tolerant readers, we'd definitely all be insane by now.

You're the true magic here.

So, without further ado, here is *Hooded*...

PROLOGUE

✳ THE WOMAN IN RED ✳

Ina shivered against the cold stone of the mountain caves, knees aching from where the rebels had dropped her. She shuddered, cringed against the sound of bodies being dragged over rock. As the blindfold cut into the sides of her face, harsh voices chattered in the unintelligible languages of the Ferrenese tribes, words thrown over her like volleys of gunfire. Arguing, commanding, questioning.

Celebrating.

Something snagged on Ina's cape, yanking the coarse fabric tight against her neck. Suddenly, her nostrils filled with the pungent body odor of the Collector she had been assigned to defend, mingled with the crisp, metallic scent of blood. Ina cried out and tried to pull away, but her bound hands and feet slipped on mud and slush. Laughter echoed in the cave, cruel blades of sound cutting through Ina's courage like swooping raptors.

"Is the little *girl* afraid of dead men?" whispered a voice somewhere over her head. It was harsh and strangely hypnotic in its accented Delarese. Ina tried to roll away, but a sharp-nailed hand curled over her face, pressing it into the snow. "But that cannot be, for you leave enough dead men behind you to fill armies. Maybe you are just afraid to meet your gods, little girl, knowing that this island would have been better off if you'd never been born."

"That's fresh, coming from you," Ina spat.

The hand disappeared, leaving Ina to squirm away and sputter against the sludge coating the side of her face.

"This one has spirit," said the woman, her coarse voice harmonizing with shifting stone, padded footsteps.

She was greeted by the eerie chuckling of a bloodthirsty crowd.

Ina tried to control her breathing, but somewhere deep within the abandoned mining tunnel, she could hear a ragged, cavernous snarl. Fear twisted her gut, fluttering and wild.

Please, no, Ina thought desperately as one of the mountain stags whinnied. *Anything but that.*

"It is time," called the woman.

Silence fell over the cave, broken only by the clatter of hooves and the breathing of enormous beasts.

Calloused hands grabbed Ina's shoulders, yanking her to her knees. One jerked her crimson hood back as another held her upright. Cold steel pressed against her spine, a painful, silent threat in case she tried to use her power against them.

Ina lifted her chin to face whatever horrors these rebels had in store.

Gentle fingers removed her blindfold, even more terrifying for their incongruous tenderness.

As the fabric fell away, Ina had to fight the urge to shudder. She was surrounded by enemies—wild faces that glared at her with so much hate it felt like a physical force. Hair braided with leather and fur, tattooed faces painted in blood, surrounded by the rusting iron

10

contraptions of an abandoned mining cave, these rebels looked like the ghosts of a world that had passed them by.

Behind them, mountain stags tossed their heads and gnashed their fangs, straining to reach the corpses of Ina's traveling partners. Clumped into one corner were the five Raebus women Ina had been transporting over the Wandering Pass, their red hair wild and pale skin flushed.

And there, crouching in front of Ina, was the monster herself.

Ina had heard enough about the Bloody Paws ringleader to recognize the twisted smile and ice-white dreadlocks.

"You," Ina snarled, hating the tremor in her voice.

Yokan cocked her head, dreadlocks shifting to reveal the bleeding paw tattoo on her right cheek.

"My brothers and sisters say I should kill you. They don't believe you deserve a second chance, after serving as Delasir's pet dog. They think you half-breeds are a plague we must wipe from our home."

Ina clenched her jaw, shaking all over as she glared into the woman's eyes. They glinted with the kind of savage energy that Ina had only ever seen in beasts.

She saw no mercy in their depths.

"But I disagree," Yokan continued. "I think that all creatures in this world deserve a second chance."

"What about the others?" Ina snarled.

Yokan only smirked.

The bodies scattered around the cave pulsed with echoing violence. The Bloody Paws had hit Ina's convoy with no warning, silent as owls, malignant as a winter storm. The lookout had given them just enough time to assemble before the enormous fanged stags crashed into the Pass, killing their guards right away. Ina had stood before the stolen women, arms thrown wide, but there were too many and they were too vicious and Ina....

She had failed. In the critical moment when her mind had slipped into the hounds, one of the rebels launched a rock from her sling, knocking Ina senseless.

11

Grand Mera would have been ashamed.

Ina leaned forward, fighting terror as she glared at the Bloody Paw leader.

"You didn't offer my companions a second chance," she said, straining to keep her voice calm.

"They didn't deserve one," Yokan replied, gesturing at the bodies. "Colonists. Merchants. What need do I have for such worms? They are with Hyba now."

"What about the others you've killed? What about the other hoods who have magic in their blood, just like you!"

"Not like me, child," purred the woman, tucking a loose strand of Ina's hair behind her ear. There was blood caked under Yokan's nails. Ina fought the urge to retch. "Not like me. They are corrupted, bound by your laws. *Tame*. Do you think I am tame?"

Ina curled one lip. "You're a monster."

The woman shook her head.

"You people. Anything free and beautiful you call ugly. Dangerous. *Monster*. You don't even try to understand. But I will give you a chance."

Yokan rose to her feet, sinuous and graceful. There was a rustling as the Bloody Paws shifted. Ina's eyes were drawn to one young woman, short and dark-haired with a smile as malevolent as pain itself. The rebel's fierce eyes were arresting, the white ring around her pupils standing out in stark relief to her near-black irises.

Yokan threw her arms out and Ina's attention snapped back.

"I am looking for someone, little girl," Yokan said, her voice settling fog-like over the cave. "Someone important, who was lost to me when I was no older than you are now. My niece, in whose veins runs the blood of Voka, the great wolf-rider."

"If they had anything to do with that witch, they're long dead," Ina said, her heart skittering against her ribcage as she met Yokan's eyes. "The king assigns an entire battalion of hoods to hunt down Voka's descendants."

12

"Oh, I think not. Because you see, my sister was traced to Tuleaux. She made it beyond your walls right before her birthing time. And what do they do with babies ripped from their mother's arms in that seething pit you call a city?" Yokan lifted the edge of Ina's crimson hood, running it between her fingers with a leering smile. "They turn them into you."

"The baby would still have been killed," Ina insisted, as if she might talk sense into this wild creature in human skin. "Children with uncertain genealogies are destroyed."

A seething mutter whispered around the cave.

Yokan's smile didn't falter.

"You underestimate my sister, little girl," said the rebel leader, hand moving to Ina's neck where the anchor tattoo marked Ina as property of the king. Ina tried to lean away but Yokan's fingers pinched into the skin of her shoulder, holding her close.

Yokan's eyes were huge, the white ring around her pupils dancing with excitement.

"She would be about your age. And any descendant of Voka would never be less than a Prederaux," Yokan said, tugging on Ina's red hood again.

"I was born in the Convent," Ina said, voice breaking. "My father was a merchant from Beraselle. You can see for yourself I'm no Ebonal."

Ina tried to wrench her shoulder out of the woman's claws, but Yokan only tightened her grip and pulled the young woman closer.

"Prove you are my niece and I will spare your life."

"And if I'm not?"

"Then you are of no use to me."

A hum of hysteria was filling Ina's brain, clouding her thoughts. She tried to reach out with her mind, find a predator to bend to her will. To work the magic of *enhabitation*. But, with a gesture from Yokan, the steel pressed harder against her neck, making Ina's stomach roll.

13

"You can't do this! Who do you think you are?" Ina snarled, eyes watering with pain as warm blood trickled down her back. "I am property of the king!"

The woman peered down at Ina with a ferocious smile, teeth sharp, white hair reflecting the firelight and throwing her face into dark relief.

"And I am Yokan, blessed by Voka, leader of the Bloody Paws. Under my name, this land will become free once more." She straightened. "Bring her."

Strong hands dragged Ina toward the back of the tunnel. Ina threw out desperate, pleading looks, as if some scrap of hope might be caught against the jagged edges of the cave. But all she found were the hostile expressions of the Bloody Paws and the confused, frightened eyes of the girls she'd been assigned to protect.

Ina cried out as her bruised knees hit the rusted tracks of a mining car. She wriggled against the rebels' grasp, but it was no use. Their hands were as strong as Delasir steel.

As they turned a corner, that savage growling seemed to fill the air, a sound so deep and menacing it might have been the mountain itself speaking to them. It was rippling up from a black pit, a gaping maw in the rear of the cave. Ina stopped struggling, her mind stretching, finding a power so vast and beyond her control that to brush against it felt like holding fire.

She tried to catch a rock with her bound feet, to stop her inevitable path to the pit's edge, but she couldn't. The men yanked her forward and suddenly she was staring into an abyss, broken by the gleam of white fur.

Ina couldn't stop the whimper that slipped through her clenched teeth.

It was an Amonoux, a Great Wolf, the most fearsome creature of Ferren. Glowering up at them with all seven of its iridescent eyes, the wolf's white fur bristled as it bared its fangs. It was easily twice the size of a horse, maybe more, and the gray tip of its tail indicated that it was still a juvenile. Thick ropes were wrapped around its neck, caked with dried blood as they kept the beast half-strangled. Kept it from howling for its pack.

Ina would have felt sympathy if her fear had left any room.

She'd never seen an Amonoux before. She'd heard stories, of course, and she'd been a child when the pack had flowed down from the mountains, seeking food after a long, hard winter and finding easy prey outside the gates of Tuleaux. But now, seeing one of the giant beasts in person, Ina felt her chest constrict and her courage flicker like a blown candle. The people of Ferren claimed that each pair of eyes saw a different layer of the world and the seventh, a glittering jewel placed right between the creature's ears, saw souls. The ultimate source of the Amonoux power. Their true sustenance.

But, of course, no one had looked through the Great Wolf's eyes since Voka herself.

Yokan stepped aside, peering down at the slavering beast like a mother gazing at her child.

"This is my test," Yokan said as Ina tried to breathe against the iron bands of terror constricting around her ribs. "Prove that you are the Furix. Stop the wolf."

"I can't," Ina said, too frightened to keep the pleading out of her voice. "You know I can't. I've never been trained with one, I don't have a connection!"

"Make one," Yokan said.

"It's illegal! They would execute me for even thinking of it!"

"Do you think I care about the backwards laws of your city?"

"Please," Ina shrieked as the men pulled her upright, hoisting her into the air so that her numb toes barely brushed the ground. "I'm not a Furix! I'm not that powerful!"

"Then ask forgiveness, child, for soon you will face Hyba, and she does not forget."

Ina screamed and kicked out. Frantically, too desperate to worry about taboo, she tried to enhabit the rebels, to slip into their minds and stop this barbarism. But the knife pricked her spine. Distracted her. She fell against the men's defenses like water on rock.

15

For a moment Ina dangled over nothingness, a chasm filled by the ferocious, vibrating growl of the young wolf. Ina's breath caught; her frenzied eyes found Yokan's.

And then she fell, the air whistling against her cold skin.

Ina landed hard. Her knees crumpled. Her body fell with a heavy thud. Acidic pain pumped through her veins, aggregating around one shin. A snapped bone. Ina's breath flew out of her in an agonized rush, as if to abandon a doomed body.

A rock shifted.

Ina's head jerked up.

The Amonoux towered over her, its massive jaws dripping as it stalked forward. Ina threw herself backwards but found only the pit's black wall.

"Help," Ina whispered, her voice failing her. "Please, someone."

"Stop the Amonoux," Yokan repeated, her voice as callous and uncaring as the wind.

The wolf seemed to glow, its many eyes glinting with hunger.

The seventh eye fixed on Ina, sharp with starvation, greedy for a fresh soul.

Mentally clawing through tangles of pain, Ina reached out. Her mind stretched; her bound hands unfolded. Desperately, she tried to tap into the energy that binds all living things. She groped for the wolf, extending a tendril of thought the way one might hold a hand out for a dog to sniff.

Instead of the neat, orderly minds of her hounds, Ina found a power as enormous and unruly as a hurricane. Thick vines of raw energy lashed around the beast, knocking her aside with a thoughtless, instinctual strike. Ina tried to fight her way through. She could sense something beneath, something familiar.

But with another lancing attack, her reach was broken.

Ina scrambled backwards, gripping at the wall, pulling herself upright. Her heart hammered. Her brain panicked. Ina opened her mouth to scream.

The wolf's jaws closed with iron force around her skull.

High above the pit, Yokan's cold eyes narrowed as she watched blood burst over the pit's wall, hissing as it hit the stone.

"Too bad," said the short, black-haired rebel, leaning over the edge with an expression of gleeful distaste. "We could have used that hood."

Yokan turned away, fists clenched. She was running out of options. Her forces were strong, but Delasir was stronger. Without the Furix to bring the tribes together, the foreigners' hold on her island, her *home,* was only going to grow.

Yokan glowered at the black rock around her, wondering how long until the enemy crushed her Bloody Paws into dust.

"Feed the stags," Yokan snapped, ignoring the echoing sounds of ripping flesh. "And deal with the girls."

"What do you suggest we do with them?"

"Set them loose. We have enough mouths to feed."

"They might not make it over the Peaks."

Yokan scowled. "They will if they are strong enough."

The young woman nodded. Without another word, Yokan turned back to watch as the wolf devoured the hooded girl, blood clouding on its white coat like a gathering storm.

CHAPTER ONE

❄ GHOST EYES ❄

There was a rustle of uneasiness among the youngsters as the flying fox was brought out. Carlette watched them battle with the urge to step back, pride warring with instinct. A young boy—one of the few in the Prederaux red hood—wrapped the crimson fabric tighter around his shivering body, as if he could disappear into the shadow of his cape.

Carlette strode forward until she was positioned between the novices and the snarling predator. Cold seeped into her boots as she broke the crusty top layer of snow, but she ignored it. Her focus was reserved for the youthful eyes widening in awe as their mentor stood inches from a muzzled beast restrained only by flimsy ropes and laboring guards.

"This," Carlette said, addressing the gathered students, none older than thirteen, "is what the Moian tribe calls a *sionach*."

Carlette stepped back with a sharp nod to the guards. With a unified grunt, the men pulled the restraints tight. The sionach snarled, its growl reverberating off the mountains behind them, but it was powerless to stop them from pulling its limbs taut.

"See here," Carlette said, running a hand along the membranous skin that stretched between the fox's arm and leg. "This allows her to glide between trees and stay away from the beetles and forest spiders. To enhabit a sionach, you must learn what these feel like, or you won't be prepared to deal with her instinct to flee."

"But ma'am," piped up a small, steely-eyed girl with dark skin and braided black hair. "We aren't yellow hoods. Why should we master flying? Isn't that for the Tower of the Eye?"

"There will always be some crossover between schools at Jemelle," Carlette answered, patient and slow. Years of listening to Grand Mera had made Carlette the perfect mimic of the old woman's voice. "Bugs, for example, can often fly, and many birds swim beneath the waves. Ground animals can be predators and sometimes even a steed can be something else as well, like the carnivorous mountain stags the Ebonal people ride. Besides, one must always respect the other towers, for no member of the Order stands above any other."

The guards shifted, exchanging mocking smirks that seemed to say *but all of you freaks stand beneath* us. Carlette ignored them. She was used to their scorn, the derision that her tattoo brought. *Witch. Monster. Half-breed savage.* To them she was property, barely human.

But she wore the anchor tattoo with pride.

"Come on now," Carlette said, her voice militaristic but not cruel. "Touch her. Look in her eyes and form a connection. One at a time, line up."

Carlette expected the steely-eyed little girl to be first, but she had to swallow her shock when the frightened boy took a tottering step forward, red hood still wrapped tightly around his shoulders. Carlette schooled her pale features into an expression much like Grand Mera's, distant and nonjudgmental.

"Very good," she said, moving aside. "Now, just like we practiced with the hounds."

The boy stood before the flying fox, his white-rimmed eyes owlish. His body angled away from the beast, whose menacing growls had become a single, wicked note. But he didn't falter.

"Form a connection," Carlette said, her voice dropping into something kinder, soothing. "Once you've enhabited her, the rest of her kind will feel familiar."

"Yeah, they're basically family to you animals, aren't they?" called one of the guards. The rest of them snorted in response. Again, Carlette ignored them. Keeping her gaze firmly on the young boy, now reaching one quivering hand out toward the beast's muzzled snout, Carlette would not, *could not* let her attention waver.

The boy's fingertips touched flared nostrils, so gentle it might have been the brush of butterfly wings. His brow furrowed. The snarling, angry note the fox had been sustaining trailed off. The white rims around the boy's pupils glowed. Matching white rings appeared in the fox's black eyes. Their breathing synchronized.

"Very good," Carlette said, careful to keep her voice low. The boy's feelings were tangled with the fox's now. The creature's wild impulses would be almost inseparable from his own. "Feel her will mold to yours. You could ride her through the Giant's Wood or use her strength in a battle."

"She can smell me," said the boy in a distant, awestruck voice. "Even more than the hounds could."

Carlette smiled.

"They do have incredible senses, don't they? And they use each and every one to survive in the—"

Suddenly, one of the fox's limbs loosened. The boy cried out and toppled backwards, breaking the connection. With predatory grace, the sionach lashed out, its razor-sharp claws hissing through the air.

There was a rip and a shriek of surprise as the boy went flying into his classmates in a tumble of bodies.

Carlette's head snapped up.

"Why did you do that?" she growled at the snickering guard who had released his rope.

"Sorry, *ma'am*," he sneered. "Must have slipped. Sometimes when I'm around magic, I just can't control my hands."

The other guards chuckled, fighting to haul the fox backwards and away from the novices. Carlette's fists clenched as she fought the wave of hot power that surged through her, crashing against her self-control.

"Maybe I should make your hands do whatever *I* want," she said softly, stepping forward, her mind whipping out like a cat's tail. "How would you like that?"

"T-that's illegal," stammered the guard, fear crystalizing the amusement in his expression.

"Try me again," Carlette said, "and we'll see."

"Half-breed bitch," he spat, but scrambled away as Carlette stretched out her fingers. The other guards exchanged glances, free hands flying to their pistols.

Wrestling back her roiling, rabid magic, Carlette dropped her hand.

No.

Not again.

Grand Mera couldn't keep covering for her. She had to learn *control*.

"I think that's enough for today," she said, voice tight. "Bring her back tomorrow. Same time. Except you," she said, pointing at the now-pale guard. "Never come to this plateau again."

"Hoods don't give orders." said an older, more grizzled guard.

"Perhaps not, but my requests tend to make it to Grand Mera. If you'd like to explain to her why a member of the upcoming Prederaux class almost died today, be my guest."

Turning away with dismissive finality, Carlette crouched in front of her students. The boy lay sprawled in the thin snow, cradling one arm, face twisted with pain.

Carlette reached out. "Let me see."

She could already smell the wound, her raw senses prickling against his fear and the lingering scent of the Delarese men. The boy held out one shaking arm, revealing a clean slice that dripped blood on the training ground, gaping from elbow to wrist.

"It's just a scratch," Carlette said, ripping off a bit of the boy's tattered, fluttering cape and binding his sleeve tight. "Nothing to worry about. I've had far worse."

"W-why do they hate us?" asked the boy, the question small and vulnerable.

Carlette kept her eyes on the knots, unable to meet his gaze. His voice pulled at something deep inside her, the force of her power struggling to get loose.

She wrestled her answer into some semblance of Grand Mera's brusqueness.

"Because they fear us," Carlette said, helping the boy to his feet. "They have no power. They know that you could destroy them with nothing more than a thought."

"But we can't," said the steely-eyed girl. "We aren't trained to enhabit humans. It's illegal."

Carlette's lips twisted into a bitter smile as she wrapped an arm around the wounded boy.

"But the difference between a threat and an action is the difference between survival and the noose. You will all need to learn how to walk that line if you plan to graduate in one piece."

Satisfied that the boy would live and the other students were safely in Cerise tower, Carlette leaned against a pillar. The stone square between the six towers of Jemelle, jokingly referred to as 'the green', bustled with activity. As snow drifted down in lazy swirls, hunched-over hoods and guards hurried to get out of the cold, haul supplies to various sheds, and bring and send news to the appropriate people.

To her, the cold was a balm against what had almost happened.

Carlette watched silently as a cluster of guards wrestled with a gigantic mountain stag, a brood mare captured for the breeding stalls. A class of black hoods trotted past, on their way to the insect conservatory for practice. Beyond the towers, Carlette could just barely make out Jemelle's fences, a crown of spiked wood around their mountain base.

And beyond?

She sighed.

"Hello, dear," came a voice from her shoulder. "I heard there was trouble with the fox today."

Carlette froze, fighting the urge to curl her lip in disgust as her nose filled with the acrid scent of decay. A figure shuffled closer, his breath wheezy and strangely cold against her neck.

Erebus, Jemelle's Skin Smith, one of the precious few hoods allowed to enhabit a human being.

And they think I'm the monster.

She gritted her teeth.

"Nothing I couldn't handle," Carlette said, voice straining to stay polite as the Skin Smith's ancient fingers snaked over her shoulder, his silver hood fluttering against her arm.

"Why are you teaching them such advanced magic? It would be easier for them to master the hounds first."

"There aren't wild hounds in Ferren. Besides, they can't get better if I don't challenge them."

"But they are just children," said the nauseating, silky voice, too close to her ear. "As are you, beautiful child."

Carlette forced herself to remain still as Erebus's finger slid down her cheek, over the anchor tattoo on her neck. Power thrummed down

23

her spine, still coursing through her like a stampede. She made herself think about graduation this Gaulday, only a week away, when she might be presented to the Woodsman and join the King's Axe. Travel across the sea, fulfill her life's purpose. At sixteen years old she could be considered for the warfront if Grand Mera saw fit, and then she'd never have to deal with Erebus's unwanted attentions again.

But only if she could control her temper.

"What do you want?" Carlette asked through clenched teeth.

"So much anger, child. I am well-schooled in ways to... relieve such feelings."

"I'm sure you are."

"The Guerison taught me all the secrets of the human body."

Erebus's fingers slid to Carlette's skull, pressing into her ice-white hair the way one's hand might close over a piece of fruit. Carlette yanked herself free and whirled on the old man.

"Don't you have Nuri spies to torture?" she snapped.

Erebus's lips parted in a moldy grin. Carlette had met doctors trained in the Guerison, healers and battle medics and sea-faring surgeons. But this man was the only Skin Smith she had ever known, trained in the gruesome arts of suffering and cruelty.

"Oh, I have a few of them *simmering*," he said with a chuckle. "But I'm taking a rest. It's hard work, you know, serving our king in such a... messy way."

Carlette swallowed bile. Never had the Order's law of celibacy felt like such a blessing. The strict edicts to protect the purity of their power kept even Erebus at bay.

"I need to report to Grand Mera," Carlette said, pulling up her red hood and turning away. Erebus grabbed her hand and pulled her back toward him, an eel reeling in his catch.

"Someday, my young ghost, the laws will change. The Guerison scientists are already experimenting with what a quarter-Ferrenese child might be able to do. Perhaps you won't have to be so... lonely."

Carlette yanked her hand free. Her temper boiled, frighteningly close to slipping its leash.

24

Not again, she prayed desperately.

But she was saved by the piercing trill of a scream, echoing against the mountain, slicing through Carlette's anger.

Close by.

In a swirl of red, she ripped her arm free, spun toward the source of the sound, and set off running.

CHAPTER TWO

❋ LOVE LOST ❋

Carlette had to elbow her way through a crowd at the main gates of Jemelle, following the stuttering screeches that rose and fell in staccato beats.

"What's going on?" Carlette demanded as she skidded to a stop next to her best friend.

Aheya's eyes were wide, shadowed beneath the red fabric of her hood. She only shook her head, skin as pale as the fresh autumn snow.

An angry voice rose from somewhere in front of them. "Back off! Back away or I'll gut each and every one of you rogues!"

Carlette peered through the thicket of shoulders, dreading what she would see.

Crouched in the middle of the observing crowd was a half-dressed woman, one hand holding a pile of fabric against her bare chest, the other wielding the wicked, curved blade of a scout. She was short, eyes rimless and clear brown, and even Carlette was impressed at the level of ferocity in her expression.

A few guards laughed, but most had the grace to look serious.

"Who…?" Carlette whispered.

Aheya jerked her chin. Carlette followed her friend's frightened gaze.

"No," Carlette breathed.

It was Sindur, his hands now bound behind his back, yellow hood ripped away to reveal the anchor tattoo on his neck, surrounded by talon scars. Unlike the scout, Sindur's face was tight and controlled. He knew what was coming.

They all did.

"Thought you would whore around with monsters, eh Calixa?" jeered a guard.

"Touch me and you'll be fucking with an iron cock," she snarled, brandishing her knife in a wide circle as the guards made cautious grabs at her.

"Calixa, don't," Sindur said, but his plea was cut short by a brutal fist to the stomach. The boy bent double. Carlette winced, wishing for the spectacle to end.

Sindur was her age, one of the best in Oeil Tower. With any luck, he would have been recommended this year, joined the King's Axe and fought for Delasir in the Narrows. It seemed like only hours ago that Sindur was cracking jokes at dinner about how much trouble they were going to cause for Nurkaij in the war across the sea, how he would take on a stormrider brigade alone with a wave of enhabited eagles. Carlette had laughed at Sindur's impression of some theoretical Nuri airman, flapping his arms and clawing at his eyes in mock fear.

Now that laughter seemed very far away.

"Come on, we don't need to watch," Carlette said, laying a hand on Aheya's shoulder. Beneath her fingertips, the girl was shaking, vibrating like the warning of an avalanche. "Aheya," Carlette tried again.

But her friend's gaze flickered back and forth, from the scene in front of them to a tall, kind-faced guard standing back from the action, expression stony.

Dachen.

Of course.

Carlette had been so consumed in her own preparations for the upcoming Gaulday that she had chosen to ignore Aheya's strange comments and midnight absences. It was enough for Carlette to worry about Grand Mera choosing her to present to the Woodsman, enough to fret about having to stay in Jemelle for a whole year and watch her classmates go off to fight. Or worse, be chosen for an on-island assignment, like the Skin Smiths or Collectors.

It was selfishness, really, that had allowed her to turn a blind eye. Selfishness and willful misunderstanding.

"Aheya, we should go," Carlette said, injecting more force into her words. "*Now.*"

But a sharp voice rose over the crowd, as commanding as lightning.

"What's this?"

The crowd parted and a tall, imposing woman strode through the slush, her boots clicking against the cobblestones. Silence echoed, a stillness so deep that it seemed to penetrate the very mountains.

Grand Mera, the headmistress of Jemelle, the King's assigned commander to the Order of the Hood, stepped into the circle.

She walked like an inexorable truth. Tall and angular, collarbones as sharp as blades, the Delasir woman's gray hair was pulled back, as always, in an unforgiving bun. Her austere clothing was plain, adorned with none of the frills or baubles that the Delasir merchants loved so much. She was chiseled, her expression fixed as her steel eyes moved deliberately from face to face.

"What," Grand Mera repeated, "is this?"

"Lovers, ma'am," said an older guard as the scout, Calixa, tried to cover herself. "Found them in the stables."

"Is this true?" Grand Mera said, turning to Sindur.

28

The guards muttered, angry that their commander would ask a half-breed to verify their story. But Grand Mera's eyes didn't flicker.

Sindur's head dropped.

Even from this distance, Carlette could feel Grand Mera's disappointment. It was subtle—the slight dip in her shoulders, a decreased pulse—but Carlette could sense it. She had been around this woman more than half her life. She knew better than anyone how determined Grand Mera was that every child brought in from the Convent made it back to Tuleaux in one piece, ready to fight in the war across the sea. Carlette knew what this loss would mean.

But to the crowd, Grand Mera was unchanged. Her neck remained straight and tense, lips pinched in disapproval.

"You know the law," she said, her voice closing over them like a cell door. "To be hooded is to be celibate. To abstain from the pleasures of the flesh. To never bear children and weaken the power that has been carefully cultivated in you. You fornicated with this woman in full knowledge that it might deteriorate our forces, slowly erode our power until the word hooded means no more than the word soldier. Do you deny it?"

Carlette knew there was no point. The evidence was there, etched in the face of every watching guard. But Sindur raised his head and faced Grand Mera with a glimmer of rebellion in his eye.

"I do not."

Grand Mera's mouth pressed tighter. She nodded to the guards holding him.

"No!" shrieked Calixa, spinning toward her lover.

"Aheya, don't look—"

But it was too late. Before anyone could move, a guard pulled out his pistol and fired it into Sindur's temple. A haze of red exploded from Sindur's head. His eyes widened in surprise. Then froze that way. With a muddy thump, Sindur's body fell into the slush, brain and blood staining the fresh snow.

Calixa screamed.

"No, no, no" she sobbed, unable to maintain her fierce veneer as she watched the handsome boy, his face a web of training scars, twitch one last time.

"As for you," Grand Mera said, turning to the scout, whose blade was now pointed uselessly at the ground. "You are no longer welcome in Jemelle. A full force of guards will escort you to Tuleaux for immediate deportation to Delasir, where you will answer to the king's justice."

The old woman stepped over Sindur's body, leaning down until she was eye-level with Calixa.

"I will see to it *personally* that you hang for what you did here today. You are responsible for the destruction of Delarese property, the ruination of this boy's life, and the disturbance of my school's peace. Make no mistake, you will be punished accordingly."

Calixa's face twisted as tears streaked through the grime on her cheeks.

"Ignorant bitch," she spat. "If anyone's responsible for ruining his life, it's *you*. It's this place. It's every fucking law the Magistrate ever signed. You don't care about him. You don't care about any of them."

Grand Mera straightened, gaze as cold and closed as the Wandering Pass in winter.

"Take her away."

Carlette watched as the crowd broke up, her expression hinting at none of the turmoil she felt. Sindur's blood still trickled into the stone, filling the rivulets between cobblestones. His body would be hung on the wall, in clear view of all those coming into Jemelle on the Iron Road. A sign would dangle from his neck, warning travelers and hoods alike about the reality of life in Ferren.

Reminding them the cost of stepping out of line.

Straightening her cape, Carlette allowed the cold wash of training to clear her head. She was a tool, a weapon. This was her life.

Stay the path.

"Come on," Carlette said, putting an arm around Aheya. "Come with me."

"Carlette, what am I going to do?" Aheya whispered. "I can't... I don't..."

"Shhh, it's okay," Carlette said, trying to pull her friend away from listening ears. "Don't speak."

Aheya's eyes were huge as they turned to Carlette.

"How can they treat us like this?"

Carlette didn't know what to say. She had often wondered if they were monsters, as the guards so often taunted. If perhaps she *was* an aberration, an unnatural blight on the world as the Church of the Hand proclaimed. Maybe then such brutality could be justified. Carlette took comfort in the knowledge that they were necessary. Unnatural or not, hoods served a noble purpose.

But was it worth it?

"Come on, Aheya, let's go—"

"Carlette."

Grand Mera's voice cracked over them. Carlette straightened, pulled back her shoulders to face Jemelle's commander.

"Yes ma'am?"

"Come to my office. I have a matter to discuss with you."

"Right away," said Carlette, bowing her head.

Grand Mera nodded, her hard eyes flashing to Aheya. The woman didn't miss a thing—not the tears coursing down the girl's curved cheeks, not the way her shoulders shook with repressed sobs. But there was nothing to be done. If Aheya was digging her grave, there was no way to stop her. Carlette saw the pain deep in her mentor's eyes, the veiled ferocity that years of silent frustration had done nothing to quell.

And Carlette loved her for it.

"Very good," said Grand Mera.

With the tight shoulders of a woman trying to save the world all by herself, Grand Mera strode off, her boot prints staining the snow with blood.

CHAPTER THREE

❋ A DUTY TO THE ORDER ❋

When she first arrived in Jemelle, new to her power and learning about all the things that her upbringing hadn't prepared her for, Carlette had been terrified of Grand Mera's office. Situated between the Tierre and Requin towers, it was a squat stone building, austere and cold in every regard. Even the inside felt like an empty cave. No personal items, no embroidered blanket on the narrow bed, no maps or letters on the wall. Only one thing marked that a person even lived here—the stamped edict from King Asbel naming this woman head of Jemelle. It was such an old document that Grand Mera's name had been smudged into illegibility, but some of the older students used to claim they could read it. They would make up fantastical titles and spin long, drawn-out tales about their commander as if a history could somehow breathe warmth into her callous, creased face.

Carlette, though, had learned to see the warmth that was already there, the mercy that moved beneath layers of ice. She owed this woman her life, her future.

Everything.

Watching Grand Mera's quill scrape away on a piece of parchment, Carlette wondered about Aheya. How could she have been so stupid? Clenching and unclenching her fists behind her back, Carlette glared at the stone wall behind Grand Mera, as black and barren as a winter night.

Soon, it won't matter, Carlette thought. We'll be across the sea. Dachen will be here. The temptation will be over.

A nasty, uninvited voice in the back of Carlette's mind spoke up.

Can she wait that long?

There was a click as Grand Mera put her quill down and leaned back in her chair.

"You've been summoned by the Magistrate."

"Me?" Carlette asked, unable to keep the surprise out of her voice. Of all the hoods in Jemelle, the Magistrate was least aware of Carlette.

It was imperative that Carlette and Grand Mera kept it that way.

"Not you specifically," said Grand Mera, pushing to her feet and clasping her hands behind her back, a relic instinct of her military days. "But he demanded that I send my best Prederaux for a special covert mission. Everyone here knows that's you."

Carlette shifted. The old woman's voice was calm, but her words were a sharp reminder of their heavy, shared secret. Carlette had been born outside the Convent of Others. Her parentage was unknown. And with every passing year of her power growing and sprawling like a weed, Carlette wondered if Grand Mera regretted taking such a risk on her. Allowing an eight-year-old orphan to slip silently into Jemelle must have seemed safe at the time. After all, hooded men and, on rare occasion, Ferrenese natives were known to slip into the beds of lonely settlers. Sometimes a Tuleaux girl gave birth to a baby with white-rimmed eyes. It wasn't unheard of.

33

But, even with Grand Mera's warnings tied to her conscience like so many stones, even knowing that a single false step could end with both their bodies on the wall, Carlette couldn't hide the instinctual wildness of her power.

It had made her life in Jemelle like walking a razor's edge.

"What's the mission?" Carlette asked, gaze fixed on the empty wall, wishing there was something for her to stare at besides blank stone.

"Prisoner escort. They've captured a Nuri flight engineer north of the city, the only survivor of a crash. They want Erebus to work on him, see if he can help us locate Caika."

"The Nuri mountain base? They still haven't found it?"

"No, and their influence here is getting stronger," said Grand Mera with a sigh. "They've started taking captives, young women and children. It doesn't take an army general to figure out that they've begun their own breeding program."

Carlette didn't want to think about it. After almost a hundred years of Delasir claiming long-held Nuri territory—aided, of course, by magic—Nurkaij had finally discovered the secret to Delasir's success. Ferren. Driven by desperation and the resource drain of war, Delasir's southern and most hated neighbor had stumbled upon the remote island of strange beasts and white-rimmed eyes. Then, armed with their own understanding of enhabitation magic, Nurkaij had evened the odds. The war became a stalemate. And, to strengthen their hold on the island, the Nuri cowards had built their base high in the mountains, impossible to find, accessible only by their damn airships. Like spiders, they had used this headquarters to chip away at the tribes, thinning Delasir's source while building a foundation of their own.

The bastards.

"I'll do it," Carlette said, trying not to think about what *treatment* Erebus would have for the unfortunate Nuri engineer.

"Of course you will," Grand Mera said, her voice a crisp clip as she turned to face Carlette. There was something glittering there, a

34

restrained excitement that made Carlette stand taller. "Finish this mission and I will recommend you personally to the Woodsman for reassignment to the front."

Carlette's jaw fell.

"Close your mouth, you look like a simpleton," Grand Mera snapped, chucking Carlette under the chin. "It's for your own good. Every day you remain in this place is another day someone might ask the wrong question, and then where will we be?"

"Of course," Carlette said, bowing her head.

The old woman sighed, laying a hand on Carlette's shoulder.

"I've always had a soft spot for you, child. From the day my sister brought you here as a knobby-kneed girl needing a place to hide, I've been a fool."

Carlette bowed her head.

"I'm sorry."

"Sorry? For what, being born?" The weight of Grand Mera's hand lifted and Carlette looked up to see the headmistress back behind her desk, stamping the letter she'd been writing when Carlette walked in. "I care for you, but I will breathe easier when you're on the other side of the ocean. I don't fancy ending my fifty years of service to the King at the wrong end of a firing squad."

"No one knows," Carlette said. "I swear to you, no one suspects a thing. I keep our secret at all costs."

Grand Mera paused in her work, eyes slanting up with what could have been a sardonic glint.

"I am aware. You almost killed that boy last year. Joram, wasn't it?"

"He was asking questions."

"He was teasing you."

"About not knowing their secret handshake from the Convent. I needed to make an example."

"And you did. I imagine that none of Joram's fellows will ever linger in the same room with you again."

35

"I don't need to make friends," Carlette said. "I'm a weapon of the king, not a nanny."

Grand Mera straightened, folding the paper in half.

"I wish I could offer you a different life, Carlette. But we all must accept what the ancestors saw fit to give us." She held out the letter. "An edict of free passage and express permission to enhabit the prisoner, should he try to flee. Show that seal to anyone who gives you trouble on Durchemin."

Carlette took the parchment with tentative fingers. She'd never been outside Jemelle alone before. In fact, she'd only left its walls a handful of times since arriving with Mya eight years ago. To be trusted with such freedom, to be allowed to walk Durchemin without an escort...

"You honor me, Grand Mera," Carlette said, passing four fingers across her forehead in the customary sign of respect.

"You will repay me by surviving this mission and earning your place in the King's Axe. The road is more dangerous than it used to be. Bloody Paws have been attacking even the most defended caravans, and one of last year's graduates is missing."

"Who?"

"Ina," Grand Mera said, eyes flashing. "She was assigned to a group of Collectors coming back from Raebus territory. Didn't make it through the Wandering Pass."

"Rebels?"

"I imagine Yokan did this, although I have no proof. Those brutes have been sabotaging us every chance they get."

"The king will bring them to heel, just as he's always done."

Grand Mera's lips twisted in the faintest hint of a smile, withered with age and bitterness.

"The king is ten, Carlette. It's his generals we depend on. And unfortunately, a few Voka sympathizers on the edge of the settlements aren't exactly their priority."

36

"If Jemelle falls, they could lose the war," Carlette said, surprised and unnerved by the exhaustion in her mentor's voice. "They have to care about us."

"That is exactly why they choose not to." Grand Mera's expression was wry. "No one likes their life to depend on something else, Carlette. Especially not civilized people."

Carlette pursed her lips, holding her breath for a moment. Then she exhaled, releasing words with it.

"One of the guards almost set a sionach on my student today." Carlette kept her eyes on the ground as she spoke. "They're getting bolder."

Grand Mera sighed and rubbed a hand over her cropped hair. It was a sign of weakness that she only ever showed in front of Carlette.

"Idiots," she muttered, shaking her head. "Every few decades they forget what they're dealing with, forget why they're here. Do they imagine Voka's rebellion was one woman standing alone against the city? Less than forty years have passed and they make the same mistakes again."

"Do… do you remember Voka?"

Grand Mera raised an eyebrow.

"Careful, girl, or someone might think you're sympathetic to the rebel cause."

"I'm not," Carlette said with more force than she had intended. "I just wonder…" She wasn't sure exactly what she wondered. What was beyond the fences? What her mother's people were like? How Voka almost won?

"Of course you do," said Grand Mera. "Any child raised on fables wonders. But she was just a woman, just an Ebonal girl with a unique power."

"To enhabit the Amonoux," Carlette said, hating how childlike her voice sounded.

"Yes, to enhabit the Amonoux. But she was human, Carlette, and she died like one. And now countless women die every year for nothing more than a suspected heritage. If the Magistrate put as much

37

effort into defending the pass as he did to hunting Voka's descendants, I wouldn't lose any more of my students." Grand Mera's face chilled. "You leave at dawn. Keep your hood up and your gloves on at all times. Stay the path."

"Stay the path," Carlette repeated, bowing her head. She turned to leave.

"And Carlette."

She waited, hands frozen in the act of pulling up her hood.

"Don't fail me," Grand Mera said at last, dropping her gaze in dismissal.

CHAPTER FOUR

❋ LETHAL QUESTIONS ❋

Sunrise found Carlette in the kennels, crouched in front of a new littler of scrambling puppies. They squashed themselves against the bars, eager for the chance to lick her fingers. Shipped in from Delasir, the hounds were used to train young hoods and guard the caravans that plunged into the Shadow Peaks, hunting rebels and collecting fodder for the Convent. Most novices never spent any time in the kennels, too spooked by the eerie winds and distant growls to explore the abandoned mining tunnels beneath the school. But Carlette had spent her childhood here, her lonely free hours filled with the comfort of warm animal breath, surrounded by the simple thoughts of beasts. Sneaking out of her dorm in Cerise tower always reminded her of nights with Quaina, prowling around Tuleaux, two orphans invisible to the world.

Now Carlette was invisible to no one, her red hood and anchor tattoo marking her for what she was.

Carlette tried to smile as the bitch licked her palm, the lanky animal whuffling in excitement as her puppies tumbled over each other. Their simple consciousnesses brushed against her own like berries; cheerful and small and ripe for picking. It would be easy, comforting even, to stretch out her power. See the world through their eyes. Command their writhing, panting, cascading bodies.

But she was too distracted.

Her mind kept drifting to the path ahead of her. It was a long walk to Tuleaux. The possibility of attack on either leg of the journey was as huge and ominous as Grand Mera's trust, a crushing weight on her shoulders.

But no, that wasn't what had kept her up all night, brought her to the kennels before dawn to seek such primal comfort.

She was going to see Mya.

The round-faced matron of Tuleaux's orphanage was as different from her sister as it was possible to be. Where Grand Mera was straight-backed, thin, and stone-faced, Mya was rounded and warm, cheeks always ruddy and voice as constant as any law of nature; either booming in laughter or shouting at the children that trailed after her like an obedient flock.

As puppies licked her jammed-in fingers, Carlette thought of the orphans. Of the woman who had raised her.

Of Quaina.

She withdrew her hand with a sigh, ignoring the high-pitched, disappointed yips.

It had been eight long years since she'd been alone with Mya. Eight years since the decision that had linked three fates together with iron manacles. And now Carlette had to face Mya as a forged weapon of the king, an object of destruction and war.

What would she say?

A mind larger than those of the hounds brushed against Carlette's, accompanying the familiar smell of woodsmoke and dried lavender.

"I thought I might find you here," said a sweet, tentative voice.

40

Carlette didn't answer as Aheya paused on the final step of the ladder, red hair shimmering in the sunlight leaking through the open trapdoor.

"Couldn't sleep," Carlette said, rubbing her face and leaning against a crate filled with restraints for the larger, wilder animals that lurked deeper in the tunnels.

Aheya's feet were whisper-soft as she padded over to her friend. Even now, Carlette could feel the human mind, complicated and tangled and so very fragile. As easily crushed as a butterfly. If those guards knew how strong she *really* was, she would be hanging from the wall before sundown.

"Are you worried?" Aheya asked, sitting next to her.

Carlette's lips quirked.

"It's a dangerous journey."

"You're the best," Aheya said, wrapping long, sinewy arms around her knees. "Those rebels don't stand a chance."

Carlette snorted. "It's the traders I'm more worried about. The outpost will be filled with cretins on their final trips before winter. Remember what happened to Finn?"

Aheya shuddered.

"But you have those," she said, nodding to the armguards Carlette always wore, her gloves pulled on over the pock-marked, sculpted leather. A weapon of her own design. They were Carlette's secret, but Aheya knew her secrets.

Except one.

Carlette leaned her head back against the crate, watching the puppies tumble. "Let's hope I don't have to use them."

"I heard what happened today," said Aheya in a soft voice. "On the training platform. Damn fool deserved to be sliced."

"With any luck the Bloody Paws will do our work for us."

"*Carlette*," gasped Aheya, but Carlette was already on her feet, glaring down at the puppies who had become a squirming ball of excitement.

"Do you really want to go to the warfront?" she asked, voice low and careful.

"With all my heart," Aheya said. Her response was schooled. Practiced.

And a lie.

Carlette shot her friend a sad, knowing smile. "Really?"

Aheya shrugged. "It's what we were made for."

Carlette nodded, watching the dogs. They, too, were made for this purpose. For training and breeding and chasing off rebels.

Were they happy?

"Carlette?"

Aheya's voice was a sparrow's chirrup, filled with the coursing rivers of uncertainty and fear familiar to any in the Order.

"What?"

Aheya took a long moment to respond. In the strangled, stretching silence, Carlette could hear growls echoing from the tunnel's depths.

"There's a... a rumor." Aheya's eyes flashed up for an instant and Carlette caught a taste of something more than fear, something electric and desperate. "Of a man in Tuleaux... who can... cure us."

Aheya's voice trailed off. Her hands were shaking as they clutched her shins. There was so much longing in the implied question, an entire unlived life packed into two words.

Carlette straightened, looking away. "I've heard of him too. Some drunk on the docks who promises to end a hood's powers if they lie with him. Calls himself the Null. Aheya, it's just a rumor—"

"But it's not," Aheya burst out, shoving to her feet and grabbing Carlette's arm. "I heard a scout talking about it the other day. She didn't know I was listening, but they found a deserter. A blue hood who left her post on a merchant ship. They brought her before the Magistrate, but she didn't have the eyes anymore. The white ring turned red and she couldn't connect."

"And what happened to this woman?" Carlette snapped, pulling herself free.

Aheya hesitated. Said nothing.

"They killed her, didn't they? She's hanging on the fences, nothing more than bird food and a warning to *us*. Aheya, this is madness—"

"Please," Aheya whispered, "I have to try. If I can prove I don't have powers, maybe they'll let me go."

"And do what? Marry Dachen and make more half-breeds who won't even have enough power to fight?" Aheya took a sharp breath but Carlette plunged cruelly on. "Best case, they'll be killed at birth. But we both know you'll never get that far."

Finally turning to face her friend, Carlette wasn't surprised by the tears shimmering in the half-light, traveling down Aheya's cheeks like brave explorers looking for a new world.

Carlette took her hand, squeezing it. "You are a weapon. And weapons do not love."

Aheya's lips quirked. "This one does."

Carlette shook her head and pulled the other girl into a hug. She was grateful that fate had spared her such a choice. As an outcast among outcasts with only one true friend, Carlette hadn't had the luxury of fantasies. At that moment, she was glad for it.

Because none of them could have what Aheya wanted.

"Please, Carlette," she whispered, pulling back from the hug. "Please. Just see what you can find. If there's a chance, any chance…"

The bells above them began to ring, signaling dawn, morning training, breakfast.

And Carlette's chance at a better life.

"I'll ask," Carlette said, releasing Aheya and reaching for the ladder. "But you should forget all this. Move on."

Her smile, when she answered, was tragic. "There's a reason all the best tales are love stories. They're impossible to forget."

· · ——————— · ✳ · ——————— · ·

The Iron Bridge was a testament to Delasir's power, a wonder of iron and steel and ice. Jokingly referred to as *the cage*, Durchemin was the only safe way to travel between Jemelle and Tuleaux. A web of metal nailed into the mountains themselves, sloping and winding down until it reached the cliffside edge of the Magistrate's city, it hung like an ugly demon between the Shadow Peaks and the impossibly huge Goddeau trees of the Giant's Wood.

Carlette stood at Jemelle's gates, waiting for the guards to check her papers. Even though she saw it every day, Durchemin still had the ability to steal her breath. Awe and excitement pulsed through her. She took deep gulps of frozen air, relishing the feeling of purpose, the path of a mission laid out before her.

"You're clear to go," the guard grumbled at last, shoving Grand Mera's edict back into Carlette's palm. "You're expected back by midnight tomorrow. If you don't return on time, you will be labeled as a deserter and hunted down. Understand?"

"I do," Carlette said, pulling up her hood to cover ice-white hair, so pale it was almost indistinguishable from the snow dusting her shoulders.

"Very good," the guard said, voice gruff and disapproving. "Be on your way."

Smiling to herself, Carlette took a deep breath and stepped from the gate onto Durchemin's wooden slats. The guard turned away with a huff, the set of his shoulders making it perfectly clear how he felt about letting students leave Jemelle without escorts. But Carlette barely noticed as she took the steps two at a time, her legs, strong from years of training, pumping with the drumbeat of her heart. The wind whipped at her cape and the cold began to bite her nose, but it was all worth it for the feeling of standing alone on the steep mountain face, the forest below her and the mountains above. No guards to dismiss her, no Erebus to leer. As she wove through muttering traders and caravans of slow-moving donkeys, Carlette's smile unfolded into a full grin.

For the first time in years, Carlette felt free.

44

CHAPTER FIVE

❅ HIDDEN CLAWS ❅

Staring at the lodge that squatted between two boulders, nestled into the mountain face with iron braces stretching in both directions, Carlette listened to her stomach growl. Its rumbling was almost as loud as the wind whistling through the small, square opening in the fencing behind her, just wide enough for messenger pigeons to bring in news from Tuleaux.

Oh, how she wanted to keep moving, push through and reach the city where she could disappear into the crowds and get a hot meal without attracting unwanted attention. Even out here, she could feel the unwelcome eyes of mercenaries and scouts, eying her like a lost cow or worse, a slab of meat ready to be thrown to their dogs. With her chin held high and her white hair whipping in the wind, Carlette watched three burly men—Collectors no doubt—shove through the front door, voices loud and unwelcoming.

Carlette sighed, putting a fist to her belly. She'd missed breakfast when Aheya had come to ask for help, and she'd been too excited to eat anyway. Now, between the altitude and the exertion, Carlette was beginning to feel the muzzy haze of fatigue settle over her.

Thinking of the Magistrate and the other officials who might be there when she arrived, Carlette gritted her teeth.

She wasn't going to let a few mountain thugs ruin her chance to join the King's Axe.

As the door swung open beneath Carlette's gloved hand, an assault of noise and smell greeted her like a warning. Smoke, body odor, spilled beer, sweet mead, roasting meat, and wood varnish all splashed into a cocktail of trailside comforts. Every table was full. A scrawny, freckled boy played an upbeat jig on his fiddle, barely audible over the shouted laughter and orders for more.

Carlette pulled her cowl over her forehead, welcoming its shadow. The Collectors and scouts were already predisposed to dislike the Order, but Carlette's features were uniquely unpalatable in this crowd. White hair, pale skin. Ebonal traits, found only in the deepest mountain wilderness beyond Jemelle. Her mother's tribe was famous for their catastrophic violence and their unholy rage toward the settlers who had stolen their women, burrowed into their mountains, burned down their cities to build mining centers and military bases.

And, worst of all, the Ebonals had produced the most infamous rebel.

Voka.

Carlette gritted her teeth as a fierce, wild-haired scout glared at her. How many ways could she wear her differences on the outside? How many wedges kept her from the rest of society?

No matter, she told herself. At the warfront, I will be respected and honored. I will save all their sorry lives by keeping Nurkaij at bay.

As Grand Mera always said, a dagger doesn't need praise. It only needs to do its job.

Carlette settled herself on a bar stool, watching the fiddler. The music was a sweet tune, out of place among the men and women who had absorbed Ferren's savagery into themselves.

"What are ye doing?"

The bartender stood in front of her, arms folded, eyes merciless. He was a tall man, built like the mountains, with a six-barreled revolver on one hip. While the top of the man's head was bald, the rest of his face made up for it with a thick bush of dirty beard.

"I'm getting lunch," Carlette said. "And a pint, if you please."

"We don't serve deserters," said the man, glowering down at Carlette as if she was something dangerous and contagious. His fingers twitched toward the gun.

Carlette clenched her fists, feeling the tension in her leather armguards. The thongs around her middle fingers drew taut.

Not now.

With a hard smile, Carlette reached into the pocket of her hood and extracted Grand Mera's edict.

"I have been requested by the Magistrate for prisoner transfer," Carlette said through gritted teeth. "I am no deserter."

The man's eyes flashed to the other tables. Carlette saw them settle on a black hood in the far corner, surrounded by Jemelle guards. The poor boy looked miserable. Carlette wondered what had brought him to Tuleaux. A medical issue, perhaps, or discipline?

Nothing pleasant, that was certain.

"Sir," Carlette said, drawing his attention back to her, "I won't cause trouble. I only want to eat and drink and be on my way."

The man's eyes narrowed, and she could see him looking for a reason to refuse her. To him, she was just as bad as the barbarians beyond the cage, the wild folk of the land who picked off Delasir settlers as if they were forest grouse. A lone hood made him nervous. She was unleashed, uncontrolled by guards or soldiers.

Not that any of them could stop me if I wanted to kill you, Carlette thought, keeping that forced smile pinned on her face.

Finally, the bartender huffed and reached behind him, slamming a glass down and filling it with mead.

"Be quick about it," he grumbled, throwing a ration of dried beef at her.

"Thank you," Carlette said, almost choking on the words. Sipping her flagon, she felt the rage inside her burble and grow.

They have no idea what it's like. Any of them.

She had to believe that on the warfront, she would be valued. After all, as the Order was constantly reminded, before them the war had been at a stalemate. Delasir's canons would take down Nuri airships and the dead zone between the countries grew and grew. The old king could only watch as his people starved, the resources of the south eluding them.

But with the discovery of Ferren, Delasir's luck had turned. Their home nation pushed south like an rockslide, gaining land. Growing on it. And now, Delasir had a strong foothold on the continent, demanding respect from the countries that had once dismissed it.

Soon, the emperor's Ziggurat would fall.

Delasir would rule.

And then what? Carlette thought as she yanked off a bite of jerky. What happens to people like me when the war is over?

Her musings were interrupted by a hum of instinct. Carlette's mind zeroed in. Her ears perked as she sensed a shift, a sudden silence. The fiddle had stopped. A few tables rustled and shifted, but it was subdued. Waiting.

Watching.

A hand came down on Carlette's shoulder.

"What have we here?" said a raspy voice. "A mongrel that slipped its leash?"

Carlette's nostrils filled with the stink of dried blood and musk.

Bounty-hunter.

She shrugged off his hand and spun to face him.

"Move along," Carlette said, her white-rimmed eyes meeting the man's beetle-black ones. The hunter wore a thick fur hat and a belt of

48

weapons. A rifle loomed over his shoulder, slung across his broad back, and three handguns burrowed in his belt like ticks. But it was his face that drew Carlette's attention. Cruel, hardened, less human than her hounds, it was a thing of darkness, carved by the brutality of the world.

I'm not the only monster here, Carlette thought as the man leered at her.

"So you're traveling with a pardon, eh?" rasped the man, leaning so close that Carlette could smell his last drink. Whiskey. "Think that makes you clean? I caught one of your kind just the other day. Begged for mercy before the guards dragged him off."

Carlette scowled, made to turn back to her meal. But the man grabbed her shoulder, held her there.

"Uppity bitch, you think I can't kill you right here? I have a pardon too, and it lets me do whatever I want outside those precious fences. You look like the kind of ghost-girl who needs to be taught her *place.*"

He spat on the last word. Carlette flashed a look at the bartender, but the big man only frowned, arms still folded.

"My presence has been requested by the Magistrate," Carlette said, holding her temper with iron chains. She could feel this man's mind, a simple, bristling thing with one purpose. It would be so easy to reach out and squeeze the life out of him, letting his brain tissue starve until there was nothing left to hold.

Instead, Carlette clenched her teeth and allowed the man's laugh to wash over her.

"Of course you have," said the mercenary, spreading his arms to invite the rest of the bar to join in. "You're *special*, aren't you? You've been picked out?"

The black hood in the corner was sinking lower and lower in his seat, trying not to meet Carlette's eyes. She didn't blame him. If this escalated, she wasn't the only one in danger. But the refusal to help still stung.

Even in the Order, there was no one to depend on.

"If you'll excuse me, I need to finish—"

"You don't get to have *manners*," growled the man, his face suddenly inches from hers. His traveling companions shifted behind him, their grins flickering uncertainly. "You don't get to be *human*. You're only good for one thing, and that isn't eating *our* food and drinking *our* beer like you're one of us. Whoever let you out made a mistake. One I plan to fix."

The man's hand slapped against his belt, drunk fingers fumbling for a weapon. His eyes were filled with the ugly, greasy hatred that the guards of Jemelle tried, unsuccessfully, to hide.

And Carlette's temper snapped.

Anger crashed through her in a violent wave. Before she'd even decided to act, she had him pinned against a wooden beam, one arm against his bristly neck.

"You're right to be afraid of us," Carlette hissed, the man's fear leaking into her senses, injecting her with the razor-sharp high of the hunt. "Even now, I could take over your mind and make you do whatever I want. What do you think it feels like to die slowly under my hand, without even the freedom to breathe?"

"You can't," the man snarled, his breathing rough as Carlette pushed her arm into his windpipe. "It's i-illegal."

"So is threatening property of the king. That didn't seem to bother you before, now did it? But I'd rather fight Yokan herself than be in your disgusting mind for a single instant, so perhaps I should find another way to uphold Tuleaux law…"

Carlette jerked her hand forward, pulling on the leather thong wrapped around her middle finger. In an instant, her armguard bristled with spines, shimmering in the firelight and pressing against the hunter's skin, leaving a hundred tiny indentations.

"Do you know what these are?" Carlette whispered, her voice silky. "The frill-spines of a snow snake. Very poisonous. For some reason, the trappers don't keep them. They only care about the skins, something about fashion in Delasir, but I think they're missing the most valuable part. A single prick from one of these," Carlette pushed her arm closer for emphasis. The man strained to press himself into the wall. "And you'll be on the ground in seconds, every muscle in your body frozen. More than a prick and you'll start hallucinating. Your mind will fill with demons and monsters, more terrifying than anything in this world. They'll eat you alive while you scream, and no one will be there to help you because it's all in your *mind*. What do you think, *sir*? Does that sound like a good way to die?"

The bar was so silent Carlette could hear the wind shrieking outside, Howl's sign shuddering from side to side. The faces around her were like a painting, frozen, straddling that line between stillness and violence. Carlette knew that one wrong move could push the whole crowd against her.

Despite her strength, even she couldn't fight the entire lodge at once.

Carlette gave the hunter a final push, grazing his neck with the spines, before stepping back.

"Next time you think a girl in a bar looks like an easy target," Carlette snapped, "remember this. Remember me."

Tossing a single coin on the bar, Carlette turned and shoved through the door, returning to the blistering cold the way a girl falls into her lover's arms. It was comforting to be back outside, or at least familiar. Her feet slapped against the wooden slats and she forced herself to slow down. To breathe. Her rage was a molten thing, pulsing, demanding blood, and she was grateful to be so far away from all those people.

All those potential victims.

When she had reached a safe distance, Carlette stopped and jammed her gloved hand through the iron bars, hanging over nothingness. Ice crystals scratched against her face and the frozen metal numbed her forearm, even through the thick leather, but she didn't move. She hoped the chill could quell her temper… and her fear.

This had happened before, in Jemelle. The last time, instead of leaving a fear-soaked stranger behind her, it had been a guard. And he had died. Carlette remembered the storm that man had set off inside her, the tornado of emotion that she couldn't rein in. She was younger and more volatile, but the expression in Grand Mera's eyes had told her it was more than that.

It was a problem.

The headmistress had covered it up. Sent a few men away, told a few lies to the witnessing classmates. But Carlette had been pulled from general training. The use of her power had been restricted, oppressively controlled.

And she'd been reminded, again, to never reveal how she came to Jemelle.

Staring down at the trees that stretched up toward Durchemin, behemoths so huge that the Moian tribe built entire cities in them, Carlette thought about her mother. A lost girl, stumbling into a foreign orphanage. Eyes so pale that Mya had never been sure. No father named, no family to look for her.

Who were you?

Grand Mera's voice came into her mind. *Stay the path.* It was a comfortless piece of advice, but it somehow deflated Carlette's anger. Allowed her to exhale. Warm breath plumed around her face like smoke.

You are a weapon, not a wild creature.

You can control this.

Shoving away from the cage, Carlette glared out at the landscape. She had a job to do.

Turning her back on the sweeping forest, Carlette wrapped her cape around her and kept walking, ignoring the ache of her numb feet and the pain in her shoulder where the man's grimy fingernails had dug in.

But it was the soft, persistent rumble in her stomach that kept her anger simmering, waiting for a spark.

CHAPTER SIX

❅ TULEAUX ❅

As the edge of the city came into view, Carlette braced herself. Her numb hands clenched, the spines on her armguards rippling. She'd seen the fences before, returning every so often for a customary check-in with the Magistrate and the occasional holiday, surrounded by Jemelle guards and tight with fear. But no matter how many times she rounded the cliff's edge and saw Tuleaux draped on the hillside, a crooked, sprawling elbow of life around the glittering Commercant Bay, she never got used to the bodies.

There were more than a dozen today, drifting in the wind and bouncing gently against the wooden slats. Long hair—white, brown, black—whipped in the icy breeze, as if the spirits of their ancestors called them to the afterlife, leeching the remnants of soul from their bodies like cotton mopping up a spill. Signs hung around withered, frozen necks, their crimes scrawled in barbed Delarese.

Enhabited a settler.

Attacked a man in the Convent.

Tried to escape.

But right beside the cage, so close that Carlette could smell the last of her putrid, clinging fear, hung a muscled Moian woman. Her dark brown hair was a tangle of dried blood, crusting around the bullet's exit wound like ice around a riverbed. Animal bones decorated her torn furs and the bleeding paw tattoo stretched up her right cheek, claws curving over strong facial bones.

Her crime had earned her a place of distinction. The worst of the worst.

Stinks of Voka.

Carlette ducked her head, silently filing herself behind the line of people waiting to pass through the gates and into the city. She wondered what the woman had done to deserve such a label. Voka was a name still spoken in whispers, a face that the older settlers could still describe. Carlette had once heard a grizzled trapper tell the story of Voka's rebellion. She had listened with bated breath, surrounded by other round-eyed children as he described the wolf-rider who had united the tribes, marched against Tuleaux, burned down half the city before a traitor in her company stepped in and stopped the torrent of Voka's power. If not for that brave spy, Delasir would have lost the bay, lost their port in Ferren, and, likely, lost the war.

Had this Moian woman hanging on the fences enhabited an Amonoux? Or was it just the Bloody Paw tattoo that the Magistrate hated so much? Or maybe this native woman was just in the wrong place at the wrong time, her heritage in question, her paperwork incomplete.

Carlette passed four fingers across her forehead for the woman, careful that no one saw the gesture. She pulled out Grand Mera's edict and forced herself to stare ahead. A few bodies on the wall were worth the peace that Delasir brought, she reminded herself. The triumphs across the sea were more important. Carlette was a citizen of the King, loyal to the cause.

Sometimes it was hard to remember that.

54

"Papers?" demanded a guard, holding out one hand while the other rested on the two-barreled pistol on his hip.

It was a capital crime for Carlette to so much as touch a gun, much less shoot one, but their steely glint and shadowed purpose had always fascinated her, a pull as strong as the minds of predators.

Like all monsters, she had an affinity for lethal things.

She held out Grand Mera's letter and the guard flipped it open, eyes narrow and dubious. Carlette waited, examining the gate. It was crafted from two enormous iron slabs fitted into the stone and wood, etched with a history of scars.

"Traveling alone, are you?" the guard asked, eying Carlette as if she were a rabid dog.

"It's in the letter."

"So it is," he said, voice dripping with skepticism. "That woman risks a great deal, sending you without an escort."

"Grand Mera," Carlette said, enunciating the name, "has seen fit to send me without wasting time of those who cannot spare it."

"Aye, because it's so hard to keep a bunch of half-breed brats in line?"

"There are more dangers outside our walls than in, *sir*. Dangers that I would imagine you're keenly aware of."

Carlette gave the guard a once-over, unable to hold back her scorn as she took in the clean uniform and polished weapons. This paunchy man had probably never walked Durchemin or visited Jemelle. High enough in rank to be trusted with the wall but low enough to avoid actual battle, Carlette imagined him laughing at the men sent out into the wilderness, pompously dismissing those who guarded the crown's most valuable asset, never once wondering if he should see for himself the cold, danger-laced life he had been spared by either connection or bribery.

The guard's narrow mouth puckered. He thrust Grand Mera's letter back at Carlette.

"Be on your way. If I get so much as a sniff of trouble from you…"

He gestured at the bodies, his expression twisting into the malevolent brother of a smile.

Carlette slipped past, too angry to do more than nod her head. More men oversaw the influx of travelers, their scowls ominous as Carlette took her place. The travelers around her fell silent. She could feel their eyes settle on her hood like burning pinpoints of sunlight, so hot and unfriendly it was a wonder she didn't catch fire.

She counted down the steps as she trundled forward.

Four.

"Unnatural," muttered a settler behind her, a woman laden with as many pelts as she could carry.

Three.

The man in front of Carlette kept glancing back, his nervousness making him move even slower.

Two.

Carlette's fingers ached. Her blood pounded. She could feel the radiating heat from where the mercenary had grabbed her, spun her round. Every whisper seemed to make the handprint grow, until she felt like her whole body was being touched, prickled by the hissing whispers that she couldn't escape.

One.

The man in front of her finally slipped through the gates. Carlette followed, exhaling with relief as she stepped onto the staircase that would lead her down to Tuleaux.

Even in such a state, Carlette was soothed by the beauty of her home.

Tuleaux was built into the mountainside, its wealth concentrated on a high plateau overlooking the sea, the Geldrue, defended on one side by mountain and on the other by open air. Carved into the stone walls sweeping down from the Geldrue were a network of tunnels, easily shut, that made the ground beneath the merchant homes a maze of prison cells, storage chambers, and the protected, underground lattice of the Convent of Others.

At the bottom of the cliff, as organized as dumped pebbles, were the Slants. Less grand than the Geldrue, it made up for its lack of ornamentation in size and noise, wrapping around Commercant Bay like a welcome mat for the sailors who had braved the Haute Sea to reach it. Interspersed with sharp church steeples and trading squares—including the enormous Chantiere, where the Gaulday celebrations would be thickest and where, with any luck, Carlette might be presented to the Woodsman in a few days—the Slants were mostly made up of brothels, bars, restaurants, and other establishments made to serve the men and women disembarking their ships after weeks of travel.

And, of course, Mya's orphanage.

Overall, Tuleaux gave the impression of a lichen, immovable and stubborn as it clung to its rocky base. Sailors often lamented that the colony didn't compare to the stretching elegance of Beraselle or the bristling menace of Revinburg. But to Carlette there was a gut-deep comfort as she filled her lungs with crisp ocean air and watched the trade ships bob in the harbor. It reminded her of a time before she wore the anchor tattoo, before she'd even known she was destined to wear one. The smells of Tuleaux—so acute to Carlette's senses—brought back memories of stealing biscuits, of chasing stray cats through the docks, of sitting for hours with Quaina in their favorite spot and guessing what each ship held.

Her eyes prickled shamefully. Carlette took a deep, salty breath, marveling at how even the warmest of memories could cause pain.

Perhaps there was nothing in this world that didn't.

Reaching the Geldrue, Carlette let herself be funneled toward the Slants. The gaping tunnel network swallowed the poorer travelers as they ambled toward their destinations. She could have flashed her letter and joined the well-dressed merchants heading toward the Magistrate's home, a monstrosity of stone and steel overlooking the bay like a squatting demigod.

But she didn't want to give up her freedom so soon.

Following the crowd as it wound through the cliff, Carlette tried not to think. She tried not to notice the whispers, the thoughts, the *fear*. Tried not to think about why she was there and how much had changed. As the sun reappeared and she stepped outside, she tried not to see the tall, painted roof of Mya's orphanage. Cheerful. Bright. Welcoming.

Carlette swallowed and walked the other way.

Grateful for the throng of afternoon shoppers, she let the Rae du Ora swallow her, disappearing into the chaos of the city's main boulevard.

She wasn't ready to face Mya. Not yet.

So instead she took in the familiar establishments, each one accompanied by another jab of memory. Petibon, the sweetshop run by an enormous, kind-faced woman who gifted scraps to grinning orphans. The Elephant's Ear, a pub decorated with the huge heads of exotic creatures and the object of Quaina's favorite game, stealing the loose tusk from the bar's namesake mount. Bijoux, where the ruddy-faced jeweler would chase them halfway to the docks just to make sure their grubby hands stayed far away from his glittering silver and steel creations. It had been so long since she'd walked freely in the city, Carlette had almost forgotten the feel of it. The gritty, stubborn cheer that the settlers seemed to have adopted with single-minded purpose. These men and women had chosen a difficult life in a dangerous place and made the best of their situation.

She missed the days when she'd been a part of it.

Carlette wandered through the alleyways, toward the docks. Three ships were unloading, the sailors and seafaring hoods shell-shocked and ruffled. But Carlette drifted past them. She wove through the hive of activity with hunched shoulders, ducking a swinging crate, darting around a cluster of gossiping men, stepping over a hound's taut leash. Voices rose and fell behind her like the waves, but her attention was sharp. Steadfast.

Finally, Carlette slipped behind one of the dock's many lighthouses.

With a sigh, she sank to the ground, throwing off her hood and letting her boots hang over the water. Noise still babbled behind her, but she focused on the steady inhale and exhale of the ocean as it crashed into the dock's pillars, on the sun-kissed warmth.

She'd always found it strange that Quaina had loved to come here. Loud-mouthed and wry, Quaina was a creature of spotlight. She thrived in noise and bedlam the way Carlette thrived in silence. There was no place that Quaina could not infuse with her boundless energy. But at least once a day, Quaina would come here, Carlette in tow, just to stare out at the ocean.

Once, Carlette had asked her why.

"I like to dream of something else," Quaina responded, her face uncharacteristically serious. "Something better."

At seven, Carlette couldn't imagine anything better than exploring the city with her best friend. But now Quaina's words were weights around Carlette's heart. Better was infinite, endless, tantalizing. *Better* was a world without guilt, without the white rings around her eyes.

Without the heavy burden of the past.

Lost in memory, Carlette didn't notice the clumsy footsteps stumbling around the corner.

"Not every day there's a pretty girl waiting for me 'ere," said a deep voice, followed by a hiccup.

Carlette whipped around, fingers ready to clench. But her hands relaxed almost at once. A man stood behind her, face soft and veined, eyes slightly crossed. His tattered clothing was streaked with wine stains and bits of food, and the flask in his hand wasn't the only thing that reeked of stale alcohol.

But it was his eyes that drew Carlette's attention.

His murky, mud-brown irises enclosed not white around his pupils but *red*.

"Who are you?" Carlette asked, forcing herself not to wrinkle her nose as the man plopped down next to her.

"Name's Eylon," he slurred, offering her his flask. She shook her head. "Just as well, can't afford much more af'er last night."

Carlette watched Eylon take a deep drink, tipping precariously backwards. His neck pulled tight and she caught a glimpse of the anchor tattoo, harsh against his cracked, ruddy skin. As his rancid stink filled the air, Aheya's plea returned to her.

Please. Just see what you can find. If there's a chance, any chance...

Breathing through her mouth, Carlette steeled herself and pushed the question toward him.

"You're the Null, aren't you? The man without power?"

Eylon's head tilted, his bleary eyes fixed on his hand as if the flask there might refill by some magic.

"Aye," he said, dull and emotionless.

"And you were relieved of your duties?"

"Aye."

Carlette watched him for a moment as he hiccupped. "Is it true you can transfer it?"

Eylon turned to face her, his whole body moving as if underwater.

"You've got a lot of questions, don'tche?"

Carlette held his gaze. "Is it true?"

"Wouldn't know, would I? I 'ent allowed to try. All those rules about bein' pure and all. Still a member of the Order, y'see?" Eylon jabbed a finger at his tattoo.

"But you don't wear a hood anymore," Carlette pointed out.

"They took it when they found out. All the better for me. At leas' the mark I can hide."

Carlette frowned as she thought of Aheya.

"So it's a lie then? A rumor?"

The man lifted an eyebrow as he swayed toward her.

"Well, since you're such a fine gal, I'll give it to you for a bottle o' somethin'. Don't much care what."

Carlette leaned away, trying to hide her disgust. "How, exactly?"

The man's smile would have been lecherous if it wasn't so pathetic. "Only one way, s'far as I know. I 'ent exactly a girl's dream, but I figure it's better than being assigned one of those rich sods in the Convent. At least a girl gets to choose me, for what it's worth."

Carlette swallowed bile as she thought of being any closer to this stinking excuse for a man than she already was. But she schooled her expression into something as close to neutral as she could make it.

"I'll pass."

Eylon shrugged.

"Not desperate enough. Had a girl come to me last week, brought a whole case o' wine. Stole it off the ship she was assigned to, poor dear. She weren't happy about it neither, but the next day she was singin' my praises."

"What happened to her?"

Eylon shrugged, weaving precariously close to the edge of the dock.

"Dead. Caught tryin' to escape. Didn't even take the time to look at her eyes, 'else they would've known she wasn' no good to them anymore."

Carlette thought of the bodies on the wall and her blood ran cold. She'd heard stories, of course. The sea-faring hoods had it worst of all, surrounded by sailors, protected only enough to ensure their survival. She could imagine what the girl had been escaping well enough, and it made her shudder.

But to choose *this* with only the vaguest hope of being set free?

Who would accept such a risk?

Carlette could think of one.

"Thank you, sir," she said, rising to her feet, brushing the dirt off her cape. "This has been most... illuminating."

"Don't tell, will ya?" Eylon said, his eyes glassy and unfocused. "My life ain't much, but it's worth somethin' ta me. And I can' imagine the Magistrate up there bein' too happy if he found out what I can do."

"I think the Magistrate would be the least of your worries," said Carlette, thinking of the Nuri witch-hunters, trained for the sole purpose of killing those with magic. Rumor had it that the Emperor of Nurkaij had offered a person's weight in gold if they could cure 'the Ferrenese curse'. She didn't even want to think about how Nurkaij would react if they found out that the cure they sought was right here, too drunk to walk straight.

Carlette jerked her cowl back up, hiding her worry.

"I won't tell a soul."

And, knowing exactly what would happen if she told Aheya, Carlette fully intended to keep that promise.

CHAPTER SEVEN

❋ HOMESICK ❋

Six orphans were scrubbing the wooden floor of the orphanage's dining room, oblivious to the figure weaving through the rafters above them. Carlette waited for the gasp, the telltale thud of a dropped hand brush, but it never came. No one looked up.

Strange, she thought, settling herself in a shadowed nook and peering owlishly from the darkness.

In her day, not only would she and Quaina be glowering up at the roof, waiting for a water bomb or a dropped bucket of mud; they'd likely be up there joining the fun. But she could hardly blame them. With Mya's voice booming in from outside, they were probably just nervous to be caught in the crossfire. Slipping in through the metal vent in the building's façade, Carlette had almost given away her position with a laugh as the heavy matron shouted at a red-faced boy and his two friends, a stolen bag of oat cakes spilled at their feet. Mya's voice continued to gain momentum, as unstoppable as a steam engine, so Carlette settled in to watch and marvel at how much had changed.

The building felt smaller, somehow. Cramped. Where the rafters had once seemed as wide as the Rae du Ora, now they were more like the Shadow Peak's ribs, narrow and treacherous. Perhaps Carlette had grown, but it was more than that. Her memories were physical. Bloated. And this place filled them with them.

As a distraction, Carlette tried to examine the faces of the orphans below her. But they smudged and blended. Only one stood out, a girl who had followed Quaina on more than one of their illicit adventures. Mileen, an orphan several years younger than Carlette, scrubbed the mantle of the fireplace with vicious, jerky movements, her eyes dark and angry. Like so many of them, Mileen had been born in a local brothel to a drug-addicted woman who died soon after giving birth. Unlike the other orphans, however, Mileen wore the damning evidence of heritage on her face. Her perpetually dark Nuri skin proclaimed to the world that her mother had slept with either a slave or a spy.

Carlette wasn't sure which one was worse.

A huge glop of soap suds hit the back of Mileen's head, spritzing the mantle. She jerked around, eyes raking the room for a culprit.

One boy grinned lazily, wringing his rag into the bucket at his feet.

"Dirty water suits you, bronzie," he drawled, flicking the soapy rag like a whip. "It matches your skin."

Mileen's face colored, turning a deep red that made her tan cheeks glow. Carlette leaned forward as the girl's fists clenched. Even from the rafters, Carlette could smell the girl's wrath, the resentment that had brewed into a toxic, hazy mire. Carlette wanted to leap in, slap the boy for his insolence, comfort the girl who had once been her friend.

But she could only grip the Goddeau wood and watch, breathless, as Mileen marched up to him.

"If you have something to say, say it," Mileen spat.

64

"You know, someone really should tell the prince we've got another traitor in the city. Maybe the Pirate Queen can have some company on the gallows."

"I'm no traitor," Mileen growled.

"Your father was a Nuri rat."

"And your mother was a whore. My blood is no dirtier than yours."

The boy's smirk twisted into a snarl. "Tempted to spread your legs for coin, Mileen? Maybe you'll get a good price. Every soldier wants to fuck their enemy."

"Well if they want to fuck a little girl, I know where to send them," Mileen responded, shoving him back.

Carlette watched the interaction, teeth clenched. It was one thing for the world to torture *her*. Perhaps it was even a fair exchange: extraordinary abilities and obsidian-sharp senses in exchange for misery, derision, enslavement. She was a weapon. There was reason for it.

But Mileen?

She'd simply drawn up short in the cosmic gamble of childbirth. And the fact that such a stroke of bad luck had left her brown eyes hard and her brown fists quick made Carlette want to rip apart the wood under her fingernails.

The boy was swelling, his chest expanding like an airship balloon. "One of these days, I'm going to teach you a lesson."

"I've always wanted to learn to kiss my own ass."

The boy growled.

His arm swung back.

Every face in the orphanage turned, wide-eyed and expectant.

"What's this?" boomed a familiar voice.

Carlette marveled at how the two sisters could say the same words but have completely different effects. Where Grand Mera's whip-crack tone demanded silence, Mya's galvanized activity. Every orphan in the room returned furiously to their scrubbing, heads

65

ducked, faces innocent. Mya stalked inside, eyes immediately finding the trouble.

"What's going on, you two?"

"Mileen was threatening me," said the boy, his pale Delarese skin still flushed.

Mileen only glared, daring Mya to take the boy's bait.

The matron grabbed a nearby girl by the scruff of her threadbare tunic.

"What did you see?" she said, voice a rumbling threat. Carlette bit back a chuckle, watching the terrified little redhead shake under those smoldering, dangerous eyes. Poor thing. It was a terrible choice, between snitching and lying to Mya. Carlette had faced it on more than one occasion, and, no matter what she chose, she always came away with bruises.

"H-he instigated, ma'am," the girl stammered. "C-called her a bronzie. Threw soap."

Mya released her with a disgusted look. The tiny redhead scurried away like an insect in the light.

"Chamber pot duty for three days," Mya said, pointing a sausage-thick finger at the boy. "And I'll speak to *you* later," she said, swiveling on Mileen, whose face was stony and defiant. Carlette recognized the set of Mileen's shoulders. She saw it in the mirror every day. It was a trembling that reminded her of a kettle about to boil over, a barely contained inferno. This girl would see blood before the season turned.

Carlette could only hope there was enough strength to support that rage.

Mya's eyes flickered around the room, taking in the hunched shoulders and furtive grins of her orphans. No one wanted to attract her attention, not in this state. Satisfied, Mya whacked the bully on the head and pointed at the floor.

"Back to work. I want this place shining by Gaulday. Prince Dirlen would be ashamed to see it in such a state."

"It's not like he's gonna come *here*," the boy grumbled, rubbing his head.

Mya grabbed his ear, yanking him close.

"There is a member of the royal family in this city for the first time in almost twenty years. I will *not* have my orphanage looking like a pigsty. Now back to work."

Shoving the boy away, she threw one last stern look at Mileen and swept toward her office.

Carlette followed.

Leaping silently through a narrow opening between the roof of the wide dining room and Mya's tiny bedchamber, Carlette slipped into the relative darkness and waited for Mya to close her door. There was a click, a sigh.

"Get down from there before you start giving the children ideas."

Carlette dropped with a quiet *thump*, her padded boots soft against the polished wood.

"How did you know?" she asked with a sheepish grin.

"You think I'm not used to your tricks? It's been eight years, Carlette. Nowhere near long enough for me to stop looking up every time I enter a room."

Carlette straightened, chuckling. "They ought to send you into the forest. You'd have the tribes mending the fences by lunchtime."

Mya was unamused as she settled in behind her weathered wooden desk.

"Sit," she said, gesturing to a narrow chair.

Carlette's lips twitched at the rush of nostalgia. How many times had she sat in that seat, squirming against the pain in her rear, red-faced with embarrassment after whatever punishment Mya had assigned? At the time, this chair, this room had been the worst place in the world. But Carlette had learned that there were far worse things than a spanking and going to bed without dinner.

Mya faced her prodigal orphan with a tight smile.

"How are you?" Carlette asked, trying not to fidget under the stare that somehow managed to be both piercing and warm. It was this expression that made the resemblance between Mya and Grand Mera obvious.

"Getting by. The Magistrate has been busy planning this year's Gaulday celebration, so I'm afraid he's let a few things... slide."

"Are you getting enough provisions?"

"We'll make it through winter." Mya sighed. "Although with the blockade, it's going to be a hard one."

"Blockade?"

Mya offered a wan smile. "News on the street is that a group of bounty hunters captured the Pirate Queen. They brought her in this morning when it was still dark out, but it's all over town. Her fleet is anchored outside the bay and their damn birds are taking down anything that moves. Three freighters were destroyed this morning."

"By all the ancestors," Carlette breathed.

"I haven't let the children out all day. Called it a cleaning day, but I'm afraid. They do seem to find trouble." Mya eyed Carlette. "I'm assuming you haven't lost that particular penchant for mayhem."

"I'm here on official business, I swear. Just wanted to stop in and... check on things."

"Of course."

Carlette's heart ached. "I'll be across the sea soon. You won't need to worry about my surprise visits anymore."

Mya's mouth pressed tight enough to sap the color from her lips. She rubbed her face with thick fingers, expression melting into one of remorse.

"I'm sorry, dear. I'm so sorry. But you know why I worry. It's not just about you, these children... without me, who would care for them? There are kind souls in this city, but not enough. Never enough."

"I haven't told anyone," Carlette said, hating the endless secrets. She remembered a time when her love for Mya was pure. Back then, Mya's booming voice had been stronger, affectionate power rolling off her in ferocious waves. Now, the older woman seemed shrunken by fear. Crushed by the burden of a choice made eight years ago, a desperate flight through the darkness. Carlette could smell the unease saturating the room like a rotting animal. Just like Grand Mera, Mya lived waiting for the dam to break, for the juggling act to end.

"I know," Mya sighed at last. "I trust you."

"After this week, it won't matter. Grand Mera is going to present me to the Woodsman herself. I'll be on the first ship to Delasir."

"If those pirates are still out there, it won't be a very long trip."

"The Magistrate will deal with them."

"And then what? You go to war? You die on a battlefield hundreds of miles from home?"

Carlette's gut clenched. "I have no home."

Mya slammed a hand down on her desk.

"Don't you *dare* say that," she stormed, a flicker of her old self coloring her face. "I have fed you, clothed you, punished you for wrongs and praised you for rights. And I taught you to be more grateful than that."

Carlette's smile was a sad, weak thing. "How is it a home if you can never go back?"

"Here you are, back."

They both lapsed into silence.

Carlette forced herself to roll her shoulders, clenching gloved hands.

"I look forward to fighting in the Narrows. I'll be among my own kind, fighting with the skills Grand Mera has given me." Carlette's eyes flashed up to Mya's face. "And no one will care where I come from, so long as I fight well."

Mya chuckled once. "You always did." Her smile faltered. "Your mother did too, before she died. She was strong. Stronger than I've ever seen before. She would have lived, if I had called a doctor…"

"Neither of us would have lived if you had done that," Carlette said.

"No, I suppose not." Mya's eyes were lost in memory, drifting toward the wall as if drawn to some spot that, years ago, had held more than empty air.

"I should go," Carlette said, breaking the stillness. "I was supposed to report to the Magistrate as soon as I arrived. He'll be expecting me soon."

Mya pursed her lips at the rule-breaking, but Carlette could see her gratitude. Despite the danger, she was secretly glad for Carlette's visit.

"One thing…" Carlette swallowed, hating to admit weakness. "Take care of Mileen. She has a good heart."

Mya nodded brusquely. "An undervalued thing these days. The poor dear has a hard life ahead of her, but she's learning. With any luck, she'll find her place in this world. Or make her own." Mya's cheek twitched, but whether in a frown or a smile it was impossible to tell. "Reminds me of Quaina sometimes."

Ignoring the mention of her friend, Carlette rose to her feet. "I'll go out the back. You shouldn't be seen with me."

Carlette waited for Mya to deny it, to offer the words what would smooth her pleated temper. She wanted so badly for this woman, as close to a mother as she had ever known, to say that perfect thing to make the events of the day melt, the harsh colors of anger blur into softer hues of comfort and belonging.

But Mya said nothing, her lips a familiar hard line that Carlette had seen so often on the other side of the mountains, on a different face.

There was nothing more to say.

Carlette didn't belong here. Not anymore.

"I'll try to visit again before I go."

"We'll be watching the ceremony," Mya said. "The orphanage has been specially invited by the Magistrate. We'll be right in front."

But not allowed to speak to her.

Carlette nodded.

"I'll see you soon then," she said, and leapt back into the rafters.

Carlette fled, her feet carrying her along the familiar escape even as her heart yanked backwards, pleading a return to comfort. She tried to remind herself that she didn't need *comfort*. She was a soldier, ready for war. A weapon. She'd grown beyond such things.

If only, Carlette thought, dropping into a side-alley and disappearing into the crowd of Ave Maisan.

With a heavy heart, Carlette allowed the flow of people to guide her back up the hill, toward the Magistrate and her mission and the life she couldn't escape.

CHAPTER EIGHT

❋ PRINCES AND QUEENS ❋

Carlette had always thought the Magistrate's house looked like a perched eagle about to swoop down and feed. It swept along the entire length of the cliff's edge, flush with the rocky drop, its pillar-supported arms stretched over the city like a mother hen's wings. Multiple guards stalked the wall at all times, scanning the sky for pirates or Nuri airships, tiny moving figures in a castle full of secret affairs.

As children, Carlette and Quaina had snuck up through the tunnels to explore the Geldrue, darting through shadows as they flitted from mansion to mansion. They gaped at the finely dressed merchants and visiting nobles, giggling as they scampered away from patrolling soldiers. There wasn't much wealth in Tuleaux, but what little there was clumped on the hilltop like a tumor, as different from the world below as Tuleaux was from the wild tribal cities. Inevitably, their trips to the wealthy sector ended with them being carried out under the arms of grumpy guards, tossed back into the Slants like bags of potatoes. But it never deterred them. Quaina was infatuated by wealth and luxury as much as Carlette had been obsessed with the Giant's Wood.

She paused in front of the Magistrate's front gate, an intricate work of wrought iron inlaid with an overlapping design of anchors. It was strange for her to be standing in the open, surrounded by painted walls and fine, imported gardens. She felt the itching urge to run, duck into the shadows, disappear like the ghost they thought she was.

Carlette took a deep breath and shook herself.

She had a mission here.

Forcing her feet to step through the monstrous iron doors, she tried to empty her mind. The men protecting the front gates examined Grand Mera's edict of free passage, watching her as if expecting a Bloody Paw rebel to leap out from beneath her hood. She ignored them, keeping her face still and her eyes down. She was a tool, sent for a purpose, not a tourist here to gawk at the sights.

But when the men finally waved her in and she entered the main hall, Carlette couldn't help but gasp.

Ferren had originally been discovered by Delasir after they'd run through their own iron ore. Desperate for more metal, the hungry nation had stumbled upon this island. And the city of Tuleaux was born, as they now said, between the anvil and the hammer. For many years, iron was Ferren's only export, hard-won and precious. Then the tribes began to attack the settlers with strange powers and instinctual gifts. Magic. The founder of the city—Micros Gaul himself—was the first to realize that this extraordinary new place could be far more valuable than just a glorified mine.

Despite his discovery, Gaul's once-home and statehouse was a testament to the power of iron. Obsidian stone columns were wreathed in twisted metal that had been shaped into leaves and flowers, soft but somehow still threatening. The tiled floor was outlined with hammered steel and the monstrous main hall – large enough to fit the entire population of Jemelle and have room to spare—seemed like one of the Moian gods, vast and grand and echoing of violence.

Carlette paused in the doorway, gaping. She had never felt smaller.

No wonder Voka's rebellion had failed. Any culture that could create something like this must be unstoppable.

She was glad to be on their side.

"Move along," snapped a voice behind her. Carlette started and forced herself to walk forward, following the welcome mat of light at the back of the entrance hall. It was the Magistrate's office, placed carefully like a prized jewel overlooking the glittering sea.

As Carlette approached the open door, three figures appeared, silhouetted against the sunset. Carlette blinked. Her eyes adjusted as they moved toward her.

It was two guards in full Tuleaux regalia, hauling a slumped woman between them. Carlette stepped aside, bowing her head so that she disappeared into the shadow of her hood. But her eyes strayed curiously to the figure in the middle. The woman was tall and narrow, with a vaguely stretched quality. Long neck, long legs, long arms, swathed in dark prison clothes. A blindfold was tied tight around the woman's eyes and her hands were bound in Iron Gloves, the locked metal blocking her magic.

As the guards strode past, barely acknowledging her presence, Carlette saw tiny tufts of what she was sure had once been feathers woven into the prisoner's black braids. And even dragged along, barely keeping herself upright, this creature radiated authority like a stink, her face etched with the lines of an arrogant grin.

The Pirate Queen, Carlette thought, thinking of Mya's news.

As if hearing the thought, the woman's head pulled up. Carlette felt a surge of nameless things as her mind touched the woman's, as she smelled the streak of blood on her lip and the distinctly avian scent beneath the haze of pain and captivity. Carlette found herself thinking of blue skies, wide open water.

Freedom.

74

The woman's lips quirked in a brazen smile and then she was gone, dragged to the side and toward the cliff cells below their feet.

Carlette could only imagine the security that would surround that cell.

It was an unprecedented victory, for Tuleaux to hold the Ceillan leader, head of the pirates who had destroyed so many of their shipments. The Featherhands, they called themselves. The Pirate Queen's crews had pecked away at Delasir's defenses like patient birds, and she herself had become infamous, an indomitable force of nature that bent all men to her will and rode a raptor like a man rides a horse.

Suppressing a chill, Carlette adjusted her hood and handed her letter to one of the men guarding the Magistrate's office. She could see an additional six guards inside, backlit against the glass that overlooked the sea. According to gossip, the old Magistrate used to keep only two personal guards for protection. But after Voka and the sweeping restlessness that had followed her rebellion, his replacement had tripled that number.

The guard peered at her, yanking her hood back and examining her face as if treachery would be written across her forehead. Then he nodded and escorted her inside.

"She won't break," said a deep male voice as Carlette's eyes adjusted to the room. It was cold, metallic, and comfortless, filled with an enormous table—Goddeau wood rimmed with iron. Maps and edicts papered the walls. And there was Magistrate Luis Zingal, standing by the window, hands clasped behind his back as he stared out at the sea. Like Grand Mera he was vine-thin, salt-and-pepper hair brushed back from his forehead and brown Delarese eyes. He reminded Carlette of a fox.

On the left side of the table stood three other figures—two hoods, blue and yellow, hovering behind a broad-chested giant with rippling muscles and a bearded, oddly kind face.

The Woodsman.

Carlette swallowed bile. She hadn't expected to run into the man himself, her future commander. She kept her eyes on the table, wondering what she should say. Could she prove herself to him now? Try to earn his favor before facing him on Gaulday?

"I thought you were supposed to have experts in this sort of thing," drawled another voice to Carlette's right, the snide tone instantly unlikable.

Jerking her head up, Carlette saw the source of the noise and felt herself shrink even more.

It wasn't obvious by his look. Brown hair, brown eyes, tall and pale from years of pampered Northern luxury, he could have been any other Delasir merchant come to try his luck at a new life. But his clothing gave him away. A finely cut coat with a sash of embroidered anchors, pinned together by a gilded iron crown. Only commanders and generals could wear that pin...

Commanders, generals, and the royal family themselves.

It couldn't be anyone but Prince Dirlen, illegitimate son of the king's mother, older brother of King Elan.

"Our Skin Smith is currently needed in Jemelle," the Magistrate responded. "And sending the brat away would be unwise, what with half her fleet bobbing right outside Commercant Bay."

"We need a way to scatter them," said the Woodsman, his voice earthy and comforting, like a warm cider on a cold winter night. "And soon. I fully intend to return to the front after the Gaulday presentations."

"Be my guest, Commander," drawled the Prince, his expression infuriatingly indolent. "Although it does seem a waste to lose half the new recruits to pirates before they even see battle."

The Woodsman's gaze snapped to the Prince at then back to the Magistrate, unable to hide his irritation.

"This is not a good time to be stalled, Luis," he growled, bear-like in his intensity. "Nurkaij is using magic. In battle. We defeated their first battalion of Ferrenese recruits recently, and by a thin margin at that. If we don't find Caika soon, if they manage to start a breeding program—"

"We are doing everything in our power, I assure you," said the Magistrate, turning away from the sunset to face the men. His eyes passed over Carlette as if she was part of the décor.

"What of the spy? The Nuri mechanic?"

"I'm sending him to the Skin Smith tomorrow." Carlette stood up straighter. "He will be broken by the time the scouts return and will show them the way. We should be able to deliver Caika to the king by the next full moon."

"Don't think you'll be delivering much of anything with those pirates at your front door," said the prince.

"Perhaps I should put *you* in charge of questioning our captive, Prince Dirlen," snapped the Magistrate, eyes flashing. "After all, weren't you sent here to learn how your father's empire works?"

Prince Dirlen's face shifted. Carlette caught the pungent scent of anger.

"Among other reasons."

"She won't break," the Woodsman repeated. "I've seen her kind before. She will die before she agrees to help us."

"Then we must find another way to get the pirates to behave. Perhaps the threat of a public execution?"

"They know we can't kill her. She's our leverage."

"Pain can be motivating," the Magistrate said, eyes drifting over the papers scattered on the enormous table. "A finger, perhaps? A gift to her fleet to remind them of our intentions?"

The Woodsman pursed his lips but said nothing.

"Gentlemen," came Prince Dirlen's voice, infused with bored disinterest. "Not that watching you two flounder to control this place isn't *fascinating*, but you do have company."

Carlette flushed as all eyes fell on her.

"I am aware, Prince," said the Magistrate in a tight voice. "I sent for her. She's here to escort the Nuri spy to Jemelle."

"Ah yes, the beginning of our great Caika adventure," said Dirlen with a half-smile. "Do you intend for her to stand there all night, listening to the details of your plans?"

Dirlen's expression was apathetic, but Carlette could see the glimmer of cleverness in his eyes, hidden but not well enough. She'd heard from the soldiers about the bastard son of Queen Aenna, born before she'd married King Asbel. Somehow the clever youth had managed to win the king's heart at only five years old. He was adopted, given rank and trained in the best schools while young Elan was raised to rule.

And now he was here, no doubt sent by General Gulon, who had taken over the war after King Asbel's death.

He didn't look pleased about the change of scenery.

The Magistrate seemed to be holding his breath so he didn't commit an executable offense and punch a prince. Carlette kept her eyes down. Finally, he addressed her.

"You're late."

"Apologies, sir," Carlette said, biting her tongue to swallow a defensive retort. She wasn't late; in fact she was early. The sun had not yet set, hovering above the ocean behind the Magistrate like a Gaulday bauble. "I was held up at the gates."

"I don't want excuses. You're Grand Mera's best?"

Carlette's cheeks reddened even more, but she kept her expression schooled and emotionless, fighting the urge to look at the Woodsman.

"I honor my country as best I can, sir," she said.

"Well, I expect you to do more than your *best* tomorrow. It is critically important that the young man we've captured makes it through the mountains quickly and quietly. Do you understand me?"

"Yes, sir," Carlette said, bowing her head.

"Isn't it, er, *unusual* to put so much trust in one of *them*?" Prince Dirlen interjected.

"They are our front line," the Woodsman said in a dangerous tone. "I trust them with my life every day."

78

"Perhaps the war has affected your logic," Dirlen answered carelessly. "With the Bloody Paws so active, it seems foolish to entrust our one hope of finding Caika in the hands of a girl with more attachment to this land than our home."

Carlette straightened, biting her cheek, holding back her anger. Luckily, the Magistrate spoke first.

"Prince Dirlen, you are new to Tuleaux so I will explain things to you. Without the Order, we would have lost this city decades ago. Our hoods have proven themselves invaluable assets both here and abroad. While your suspicion is understandable given your... new understanding of how things work here, it is unwelcome in this room. As is your pessimism. We will find this base, rid Ferren of Nuri soldiers, and we will do it with Jemelle's continuing assistance. There is no need to worry the king."

"Oh, my brother isn't worried about much," Dirlen said airily. "I get to do all the worrying for him."

The Magistrate's face twisted into a frown. He waved one hand at Carlette. Taking the dismissal, she retreated into the great hall, all but grinning to herself.

The Magistrate had called her the best, in front of the Woodsman. She couldn't have asked for a better first impression. Her feet all but skimmed the ground as she was led to the Order's barracks beneath the statehouse and locked inside for the night. She wasn't even bothered by the dampness of her bed or the bone-deep chill of the room, carved from the mountain itself.

If she succeeded tomorrow, if she proved herself capable of this task, she would join the King's Axe. She would graduate, earn her battleaxe tattoo, and take her place among her brothers and sisters fighting for Delasir.

All she had to do was escort one man across Durchemin without anyone noticing them.

How hard could that be?

CHAPTER NINE

❋ THE MAN FROM THE SKY ❋

The Nuri mechanic was nothing like Carlette expected. While standing in the cavernous entrance, waiting for guards to return with the prisoner, Carlette had pictured an older man, dark skin tanned from the hot Nurkaij sun. She imagined dusted black hair, eyes sly and calculating. In her mind, the spy was cold and undaunted, as sharp and inhuman as a loosed arrow sent to penetrate their lands.

But when the echoes of a struggle made Carlette turn, she found herself trying to hide her surprise at the figure being dragged up, bucking and fighting the Magistrate's men with every step.

He was young. No older than seventeen. Her age.

And terrified.

His skin was brown, but it wasn't the bark-like leather Carlette had seen in the older Nuri prisoners. No, the spy's face was creamy, a smooth walnut that matched his eyes. She could see laugh lines etched around his mouth, the beginnings of a kind history written on his face. Dressed in a tattered aviator uniform, complete with fur-lined cap and scratched leather gloves, he didn't look like the villain of the sailor's breathless stories.

He looked too... human.

Carlette straightened her spine, watching impassively as the guards punched the young man in the gut. He doubled over, manacled hands digging into his belly, breath escaping his lips in a whoosh. She could smell the prison and sweat on him, layered upon a foundation of fear.

"You think you can handle him?" growled one of the guards, throwing the mechanic down in front of Carlette the way one might toss a rotting carcass.

"Of course," Carlette answered.

The boy scrambled to his feet. He swung around and made to lunge at the guards.

Carlette yanked off one glove and felt the nerves of her fingers tangle in the air, wrapping around the prisoner's will like strangler vines. The white rims around her pupils glowed. The mechanic froze, his body shaking as it tried to defy her. As his mind tried to throw her off. But holding him was as easy as breathing mountain air.

To Aheya and the other hoods—even other Prederaux—enhabiting a human mind for any length of time would be catastrophically exhausting. Humanity's complex will was a rearing horse, violent and unruly. But to Carlette, slipping into the brain of anyone, even a fellow hood, was like sliding into a cold river, a breathless exhale.

The boy's eyes were wide, panicked, silently pleading. She forced her hand to shake. Frowned with apparent effort. And then dropped her hand, making a show of panting as her eyes darkened, iridescent to dull white.

The young man, though, was shaking in earnest. Carlette knew what he was going through, since it was part of the Order's training to be enhabited. Carlette could still remember when Aheya had dominated her mind, her friend vomiting from the struggle. It had felt like a raging wildfire was climbing up the back of her neck, up her spine, into her brain. Grand Mera told them it was tissue dying, that the natural instinct to struggle cuts off blood supply and slowly drains the body of life. It was why their training was so intensive. They had to grow accustomed to the feel of a creature dying in their mental hands, learn to shrug off the nauseating shock of death and leap to the next mind. Continue fighting.

And they had to learn the limits of enhabitation for situations just like this.

Carlette didn't so much as wince when the boy fell to his knees and retched on the marble floor. The guards leapt back with disgust.

"We need to be going," Carlette said, grabbing the prisoner's arm and yanking him upright. "I apologize for the mess."

Ignoring the heat of their glares on her back, Carlette guided the staggering Nuri out of the statehouse, winding her way toward the city gates.

"I suggest you don't try to escape again," Carlette said as they began the long ascent up the stairs, her hand on his elbow. "Next time, I will hold longer."

"Witch," he spat, eyes wild as he tried to yank his elbow free. Carlette dug her nails in, one hand still ungloved.

She would not engage the prisoner, would not personify him. This was a man who had helped fly soldiers over the mountains, a talon in the reaching claws of her enemy. His people were a plague that threatened to destroy everything Carlette knew and hated everything Carlette was.

Despite the laugh lines.

The entrance guard had changed. Carlette waited as a new woman examined Grand Mera's signature with squinting, suspicious eyes, her frown roving from the paper to the dark-skinned boy breathing hard beside her. Carlette could understand her hesitation, but it no longer made sense for prisoners to be transferred with a whole relief of guards. The Bloody Paws hovered on the edge of Durchemin, their birds watching, their mountain stags posed and ready to attack. If they saw a group of uniformed men dragging a prisoner through the cage, they were sure to pounce, if for no other reason than to disrupt the Magistrate's plans. However, two travelers, alone and unguarded, were less likely to attract rebel attention. And only a near-fully-trained hood could control a man on the road to his death.

"What's this one doing?" called a man from the guardhouse, leering.

Carlette's gut twisted.

"Sanctioned mission," the woman answered.

"Nothin' sanctioned about him," said the guard, striding up to her prisoner and getting in his face. "I lost six men to one of your airships," he growled, grabbing hold of the leather jacket. He yanked out a slim dagger, pressing it against the boy's dirty cheek. "I should cut you down right here."

"Do that, and I'll have every reason to throw your body off the fences," Carlette said, matter of fact.

The guard threw her a dismissive look. "You wouldn't dare."

"This spy has valuable information. He will reach Jemelle and he will reach it alive. Do you really think that the Magistrate would prioritize your vengeance over finding Caika?"

The guard's anger flickered. Carlette took the prisoner's arm, yanking him away.

"He is under my protection," Carlette said, leaning forward. "I wouldn't challenge that, if I were you."

The woman glanced between them, unsure. But the guard's eyes were fireballs of hate, glowering like evil suns.

"You're just as bad. I'd cut down the whole lot of you and sleep well that night."

"Well, you wouldn't sleep well for long," Carlette said with a forced, sharp-toothed smile. "You'd be overrun by rebels before the sun next rose. Now, may I please be on my way?"

The man looked like he wanted to slice his blade across her throat. But Carlette's patience had reached its limit. She turned to the woman, lifting her eyebrows.

"Stay the path, girl," she ordered, thrusting Grand Mera's letter of free passage back with an ungracious scowl, as if this trouble was Carlette's fault.

"I always do," said Carlette, yanking the Nuri with her as she stepped through the massive iron gates.

For several moments, Carlette allowed the chill wind to swirl around her. Her temper sizzled against the cold. *Every single fucking time.* She was so frustrated, so *exasperated,* that she almost didn't notice the change in the mechanic's posture, the slight softening of his features.

"I didn't think you'd stop him," he whispered, voice almost drowned by the howling wind.

"I've been assigned to protect you," Carlette said.

He lapsed into silence. After a moment of their boots thudding against the wooden slats, Carlette felt him pull against her, stopping. She paused and glanced back at him.

"Caika is growing stronger, you know," he said. "Soon we'll have the power to destroy this city. You don't have to die for those ungrateful bastards."

With a flick of thought, Carlette prodded him forward.

He gasped but didn't move.

"Caika won't last until the next full moon," she said.

"You think I'm going to help them find it?" he spat back, planting his feet. His voice might have been intimidating if he wasn't so frightened. "You really think I'll betray my people for that scum?"

Carlette grabbed his arm and pulled, making him stumble.

"Our Skin Smith is a talented man," she said. "He could make a rebel sing the Delasir anthem if he wanted."

"I won't break," the young spy insisted.

"Yes you will," Carlette said, too tired to hold onto her anger. She hated the Nuri as much as any hood, but it was impossible not to picture him in Erebus's hut, screaming as that awful man did whatever unspeakable things he had been trained to do behind closed doors.

She shuddered.

When Carlette had first arrived at Jemelle, she was shocked at how often agonized shrieks echoed out from Erebus's obsidian shed, filling the school with the inhuman noise. The other students were used to it. The Convent of Others, of course, had its fair share of unspeakable rooms. But to Carlette, the screams were fingernails running down her spine, shredding the curtain of comfort that had swathed her childhood.

Quaina used to insist that orphans were the bottom of the social ladder. But Quaina had been wrong. There were several rungs below them, and, as Carlette learned how much worse life could be, she was grateful she had taken only one step down. This mechanic, born a Nuri, captured a spy... he was truly mud. Condemnable and condemned.

They continued in silence, minutes stretching into hours. Carlette could feel his mind searching, scanning the cage, desperately looking for holes in the iron bars. But the road fulfilled its purpose—keeping danger out, keeping prisoners in.

After several hours of walking, the Nuri couldn't take it anymore. He gasped, manacles clanking as he gripped his knees and bent double. Carlette paused, letting him catch his breath.

"The mountains take their toll."

"I fly an airship," he spat. "I'm used to altitude."

Carlette shrugged, but she'd heard of this problem before. In the cabins that hung below the camouflaged balloons, the Nuri men and women grew accustomed to the sun-warmed air of Nurkaij, or at least the humid ocean breeze. Up in the crisp chill of the Shadow Peaks, the air was different. Cold and raw and painful.

In Jemelle, it was all they knew.

"We will stop to rest soon," Carlette said. "The halfway point is coming."

She didn't plan to enter Howl—that had been enough of a fiasco the day before. But Carlette had thought ahead enough to grab a few biscuits and a packet of dried meat from the barracks. They would drink snowmelt from Howl's spring, sit on the benches outside and take in the view of the Giant's Wood spread out below them. At least Carlette would. She didn't much care what the Nuri did, so long as he didn't go near the hole reserved for messenger birds.

"Come on," Carlette said, grabbing his manacles and pulling. "We need to make it back before sunset."

"Or what? You turn into smoke?"

Carlette leveled him with a glare.

"Or we are attacked by rebels and we both die."

The boy spat on the ground, his saliva freezing instantly on the metal.

"At least that's something."

As Howl came into view, Carlette marveled that the grimy tavern never seemed to change. The men and women filtering through the doors were almost identical to yesterday's—Collectors, scouts, bounty hunters. It's rancid, body-odor stink still wafted toward her like an unwelcoming fog, familiar and disgusting.

And, just like yesterday, Carlette felt the same distinct sense of unease, her instincts prickling like goosebumps.

"Sit," Carlette ordered, shoving her prisoner toward a roughly hewn bench.

Glaring at her, he sat, manacles jangling. Carlette scanned the mountain above them as she unhooked a canteen from her belt. Yanking off a glove with her teeth, she made to fill it at one of the twin troughs lined with braying donkeys and pack mules.

Her mind hummed as water trickled into the canteen.

"Here," she said, thrusting the water at the Nuri spy.

He took it, eyes bleak.

"What a miserable life," he said, shaking his head as he raised the canteen, "to walk over the mountains when you could fly."

Carlette wasn't listening. Something was wrong. She felt it buzzing in her nerves, vibrating up her bare fingers. The mental tang that filled the air was different, tainted with something wild. It was more than just the brutal men and women in the tavern.

Something was out there.

"I can't imagine you've ever been to Nurkaij," the boy said as he wiped his mouth, gazing out at the snow-tipped trees. "Anyone who's seen Vaijan would never tolerate living in a place like this."

Carlette flexed her fingers, feeling the leather thongs pull tight, hidden spines rippling.

"Really, it's amazing humanity ever settled here. Our scientists think the first Ferrenese people came over on a southern land bridge, which would make your ancestors the same as mine. But that's just a theory—"

"We need to keep moving," Carlette cut in, her voice sharp, echoing against the mountain. "Quickly, get—"

But her order was broken by a keening howl, the throaty human imitation of a wolf. Carlette's gaze snapped up, squinting against the sun. She heard the mechanic's sharp inhale.

Cascading down the steep mountain face like a rockslide, a herd of stags tumbled toward them, swarmed by birds, their roaring riders brandishing stolen rifles. Carlette lunged aside as a bullet pinged near her, close enough to sting.

"Attack! We're under attack!" Carlette shouted.

Her hands snapped forward. Spines sprung up just as Howl's doors slammed open. Bloody Paws careened toward the hanging cage.

And, unseen by Carlette, a tall, wiry, dark-skinned young airman made his break for the small gap in the iron bars, eyes frantic with hope.

CHAPTER TEN

❄ TRUST FALL ❄

The Bloody Paws crashed against the grated ceiling of Durchemin in a tidal wave of noise. Bullets rained down on Carlette as she threw her arms over her head. Hunters fired. Masked rebels crawled over them like swarming cockroaches. A dirty scout crashed into the ice, blood spurting from her shoulder. A Bloody Paw jerked and toppled over the side, sliding along the scraggly cliffside, leaving a crimson trail in his wake.

Carlette's eyes glowed as she slipped into one of the stags. She could taste old blood on the beast's fangs, feel the weight of its enormous antlers. As her real body lunged for cover beneath one of the benches, Carlette launched the stag off the mountain face, head down.

Antlers snagged on clothing.

Two figures fell with the flailing beast, shrieking as they scrambled for a hold.

Carlette cut her tie with the stag's mind, entering one of the Bloody Paws like a monkey jumping to the next tree. She cringed as the oil of the rebel's mind coated her thoughts. It was a young woman, sharp with vitriolic hatred. This was a powerful mind, kinked with energy, teeming with feather-light connections to the world around her. For the first time in her life, Carlette struggled to hold this girl, felt her gaze go blurry as she saw through other eyes.

At the edge of the rebel's vision, Carlette caught a movement.

A contrast.

Brown skin in sharp relief against blue sky, the Nuri rebel glancing backwards as he ran toward the opening in the grated Durchemin bars.

Carlette tossed the rebel's mind aside as violently as possible. If she was lucky, the girl's attention would be thrown. But she couldn't think about that now. Scrambling upright, she sprinted after the mechanic. Saw his brown jacket flutter. Watched his manacled hands pick up something gray and shining. He was only twenty feet ahead of her, but he'd gathered a desperate kind of speed. His toes were digging in, his body hunched against the hail of gunfire, the stray bullets from both sides. Carlette's senses zeroed in, blocking out the shouting settlers, the ululating howls of the Bloody Paws.

She reached out, stretching her power toward the prisoner.

The rock next to her exploded and her attention split like a lightning-struck tree.

The world swirled for a moment. Her ears rang. She blinked, desperately trying to clear her vision.

She was too late.

Launching himself off the wooden slats of the path, the Nuri tucked in his arms, ducked his head, and leaped through the opening.

Carlette lunged.

Her body slammed against the cage, fingertips grasping. Her hand brushed the edge of his jacket as he twisted, his body sinuous as water. He grabbed at the lower bars of the Cage in a practiced, acrobatic movement, something only a man used to open air would learn.

Carlette's breathing was sharp, panicked as she felt the cage shudder with the boy's sudden weight. She tried to reach out, her mind brushing his. But it was lost in the melee, in her own horror, in the swirl of consciousness pounding around her. It was like trying to catch a butterfly in a rainstorm. She couldn't see him, couldn't reach him.

And then he was gone.

She glimpsed his dark shape below her feet, sliding down the mountain face, feet scrabbling against the steep rock. He would be in the Giant's Wood in moments, send some signal to his comrades soon after. Maybe the Moian tribe would pick him up, execute him for the crimes of his people. Maybe he would be saved.

Either way, Carlette had failed.

She would never go to Delasir, would never fight alongside the Woodsman. She would be assigned to guard Tuleaux, or worse, the merchant ships. Carlette could picture Grand Mera's shame. Mya's worry. They would never be free of her secret, crushed forever by the burden of what Carlette was.

She couldn't let that happen.

Carlette put one foot on the opening. The words of her training echoed in her mind. *Stay the path.* It went against every instinct, every rule of Jemelle. For a hood to leave Durchemin, to enter wild territory on their own, was tantamount to treason. She could be labeled a deserter, executed for nothing more than *considering* what she was about to do. Her chances of being accepted into the King's Axe after leaving the assigned road were laughably low.

But if she didn't finish this job, she had no chance at all.

Taking a deep breath and feeling like a wingless bird about to leave its nest, Carlette leapt.

The ground came up fast. Carlette threw her arms out, spines facing the rock. She braced for impact.

It was still enough to make her bones shudder.

Her forearms scraped against the stone with a raw, grating squeal. Carlette's boots slipped against sleek ice. Her body began to pick up speed, the sounds of attack fading beneath the thud of her own heartbeat.

She needed to slow down.

Glancing beneath her, she saw the mountain's ribs approaching, layers of obsidian eroded by time and the elements, sharp as daggers. The teeth of the Shadow Peaks.

Carlette dug her toes in, pushing with her forearms. Black rock rose suddenly beneath one thigh, slicing open her trousers. She rolled to the side, one arm parting with the mountain. She slid faster. Her back slammed against a boulder and she gasped, swallowing snow and ice dust. Frozen air clouded around her.

Gritting her teeth, Carlette spun her body back, slapping against the mountain. Her fingers dug into a crevice. Ripped free. She felt the pads of her hand tear open, but she tried again. With one arm slowing her descent, snow snake spines snapping and breaking under her weight, Carlette's other hand scrabbled at the rocks.

She slowed.

Skidded.

Finally, her foot found a hold. With a bone-jarring halt, she came to an abrupt stop. Carlette glanced below her.

The base of the mountain was a maze of thin obsidian walls and snow-filled valleys, peppered with abandoned mining tunnels, leveling out to where the Giant's Wood shadowed all. Carlette breathed, her exhale fogging the view. She could hear the fight above her still echoing off the peaks. A body tumbled past. But she was far away from it now, as distant from the world she'd always known as she was from the clouds themselves.

Something moved below her.

Carlette leaned out, keen eyes scanning the snow.

There!

A dark shape was sprinting between two black plates, leaping through knee-deep powder. His elbows jabbed out, wrists bound by black metal.

Carlette shoved off from the mountain, her feet moving as if by magic as she sprinted down the incline. Where before speed had been her enemy, she now embraced it with a recklessness Grand Mera would have slapped her for. Rock layers as lethal as blades flew past her, but she couldn't stop. She pumped her arms, threw herself forward.

The airman glanced back just as she entered his crevice. His eyes widened as he saw her barreling toward him. He made to leap aside, but the snow was too deep.

His foot caught.

Carlette hit him like an avalanche, knocking them both down in a puff of white.

For a moment, nothingness filled Carlette's vision. Her lungs screamed as she inhaled snow crystals. Her joints protested the abuse.

And then she felt the mechanic scramble beneath her, clawing around for something.

Carlette grabbed his knees. He twisted like a fish. She reached out with her mind, but something hard slammed against one cheek. Stars burst in her vision. Her grip loosened. Instinctually, she rolled to one side. A gunshot echoed, bouncing between the two black slabs of stone like a rubber ball.

She glanced up.

He stood above her, a stolen pistol gripped in both hands. His face was twisted, determined.

But his arms were shaking.

Carlette barely had time to register the panicked look in the boy's eyes before he fired again. She dove to the side, hood rippling like blood. The boy fired again and Carlette felt a bullet sing her shoulder, whistling in the cold.

Enough!

Gritting her teeth with concentration, Carlette snapped her gaze to the mechanic. Her mind sprung around him, caging him, holing him still. His limbs locked halfway through their arc of turning to face her.

Finally, everything fell still and silent.

Carlette took a deep breath. Her body felt like one big bruise, every inch of her pounding. Her leg was bleeding where the rock had sliced it open and she knew that an impressive bruise was forming on her cheekbone. Worse, her hands were shredded, her remaining glove tattered and bloody, her other hand dripping red in the snow.

But she focused on the young man, her mind tightening around his like barbed wire.

"I could kill you for escaping," Carlette said, making the words resonate in his head. "No one would blame me for it. Tell me, why shouldn't I let your brain starve?"

She loosened her hold to allow him to speak while keeping his body stock-still, shaking violently as he tried to buck her control.

"Kill me then. We're both going to die anyway."

Carlette didn't respond.

Standing there, heartbeat slowly returning to normal, she felt the true gravity of their situation sink in. Leaving the assigned path and breaking eight years of faithful service had felt so monumental to Carlette that she hadn't considered what came after. To her, the choice had ended with her leap from Durchemin. In that instant her life had shifted like continental plates. She had broken a cardinal rule, disobeyed the strictest of orders. Her attention had been only on recapturing the prisoner and begging for Grand Mera's forgiveness.

But what if they never made it that far?

Now, knee-deep in snow, shadowed by the monstrous Goddeau trees, reality crept in, unwelcome and venomous. A whole valley separated her from Jemelle, a valley filled with the most dangerous creatures known to mankind. Forest spiders, giant beetles, snow snakes, sionach. Not to mention the hanging cities filled with Moians who hated the Order of the Hood more than they hated Nuri soldiers.

Everything around them wanted them dead, and Carlette had nothing but her own power and the Nuri's stolen gun for defense.

It would be a miracle if they survived the night.

Carlette reached out and yanked the pistol out of the boy's grip.

"I'll take that," she said.

The mechanic didn't know it was illegal for her to carry the weapon, and she had no intention of informing him. She feigned confidence, checking the bullets the way she had often seen the guards do.

Three left.

She swallowed.

"I will get you to Jemelle," Carlette said at last, tucking the gun into her belt as if she did that all the time. She planted her hands on her hips, facing the prisoner. His face was blanching, eyes watering with pain. "I will not kill you. And I will defend you in this forest to the best of my ability. In return, I ask for your help."

"Why would I help you?" he gasped.

She released him.

The Nuri crashed to his knees, vomit hissing as it hit the icy ground.

"Because I'm the only chance you have," Carlette said, watching him retch with emotionless eyes. "You might survive torture. Perhaps you can even escape. But without me, you won't make it one day down here."

Carlette watched his shoulders heave. She waited, dreading another snarl, another rejection. To him, she was a monster, but she hoped at least to be a necessary one. If she had to watch her back every step of the way, their chances went from slim to none.

Finally, he tilted his head up. Carlette hated his wry resignation, but the Nuri boy sighed.

"Well then," he said. "I guess I don't have much of a choice."

CHAPTER ELEVEN

❋ IN THE SHADOW OF TREES ❋

The forest was a thing of shifting light. As they wove their way through trees as thick as Durchemin itself, awe filled Carlette's chest. She could feel life pulsing, thick and viscous and thrumming in the dappled afternoon. The consciousness of a thousand beating hearts swirled around her, a vortex of thoughts and movements. Insects scrambled up the trunks of Goddeau trees, weaving through cracks in the deep red bark. Enormous shapes rustled overhead, leaping, soaring, disappearing in a flutter of leaves. The very air seemed to breathe, as if the trees themselves were conscious.

She had expected the forest to be dark, dreary, dripping with spiders and insect traps and wild natives. But she was wrong.

It was beautiful.

As they passed through a clearing filled with infant saplings, fingerlings of wood stretching for a distant, filtered light, Carlette remembered the last time she was in the Giant's Wood. Even though the trees around Tuleaux were smaller, dwarfed by the thin seaside soil and the settler's history of chopping them down, Carlette had felt the same deep recognition that she did now. A pull to this place, a thrilling excitement that was marrow-deep. It was like walking through the halls of Mya's orphanage, only more intense.

Here, under a roof of branches, pounded by life on all sides, Carlette was home.

"Do you know where we're going?" the Nuri asked.

"I can track Jemelle based on the position of the sun."

"I'm surprised they taught their precious prisoners how to navigate outside the school."

Carlette ignored him as they climbed over a massive root system.

He stumbled and she grabbed his arm before he could crack his head open on the nearest obsidian boulder.

"Thanks," he said.

Carlette didn't respond.

"Stoic, aren't you?"

"I don't fraternize with prisoners."

"Yeah, well I'm not supposed to speak to a witch." He shrugged, glancing over his shoulder as Carlette prodded him onward. "But we're both having a weird day."

Carlette rolled her eyes and shoved the mechanic with her bandaged hands, now wrapped in fabric ripped from her undershirt. "Keep walking and stay quiet. We don't want to attract attention."

Carlette held her breath, listening to the noises of the forest, hoping he would stay silent. But after a few more crunching steps, the airman spoke again.

"Am I the first prisoner you've transported?"

"I said stay quiet."

"Because you seem new at this."

"Will you shut up?"

"Is it because you've never been outside the school? Or were you in another unit before, hunting down native virgins or something?"

Carlette growled to herself, wishing she could just gag him and be done with it.

He tilted his head back, staring at the canopy. The Goddeau Trees were so tall, it felt like the tips of their branches must brush the very sky.

"I've never seen them from below," he said in a thoughtful voice. "They look a lot bigger down here."

"They're also much more dangerous," Carlette said, trying and failing to hide her frustration.

He shrugged. "I'm a dead man anyway. Might as well enjoy the views."

Carlette ground her teeth. "There are few deaths less pleasant than being eaten alive by forest spiders."

"What about having your fingernails pulled out by a Skin Smith?"

Carlette had no answer. The boy crawled beneath a thick webbing of shrubbery, jumping as a gigantic Norjay leapt from the bushes with a scolding caw.

"Do you have a name?" the airman asked after another too-short silence.

"Not one that concerns you."

He stopped in his tracks. Carlette was so focused on watching the forest around her that she almost knocked him over. Her hand flew to the pistol, waiting for the attack. But the Nuri's head was cocked, and his eyes lacked the hostility she had come to expect. Instead his gaze was curious. Probing.

"Why do you hate me so much?"

Carlette's growl fizzled out on her tongue. The innocent question slithered beneath her armor, struck her very core. It was too familiar, too recent. He could have been the hooded student she had saved, his arm bleeding, his wide eyes panicked.

Why do they hate us so much?

Carlette swallowed.

"Your people hunt mine down for sport," she said, trying to reignite her anger. "You fight King Elan at every step, attack our Collectors, execute hoods for nothing more than existing."

"And your kind kill mine by the thousands," he said, eyes hard. "I've watched entire airships go down under enhabited birds. I've seen villages crushed by stampeding buffalo and elephants turn on their own riders. But I've never killed a hood and I don't think you've ever killed a Nuri soldier."

"You don't know anything about me."

"No, I don't. But I do know we're both stuck out here together. And I, for one, would like to know what to call you."

Carlette glared at him. But she couldn't think of a reason to hold back something as simple as a name.

"Carlette," she said at last. "My name is Carlette."

"I'm Tuk."

"I don't care," Carlette said, shoving him forward and trying to convince herself that this didn't change anything.

After hours of walking, Tuk stumbled, his boot catching on a protruding root. As Carlette reached down to haul him to his feet, she smelled the blood before she saw it, pooling in the Nuri's sliced glove.

"Damn," Tuk swore, clenching his injured hand.

"We need to clean that," Carlette said. She tugged his fingers back, peered at the wound. "Goddeau bark is poisonous. You'll lose the hand if we don't get the pieces out."

"Well aren't you a considerate witch?"

She ignored the jab as she let her mind relax, her senses filtering out the chittering of birds and swishing of leaves.

There.

An opening, around which the animals gathered.

"This way."

She pulled Tuk with her as she picked her way down a long slope, filled with crooked trees. Using the trunks for support, she guided them toward a crashing river, overflowing with snowmelt and ice. The water churned and bubbled as it flew over rocks, crashed into stones, beat against the riverbank. In the distance, Carlette could hear a waterfall, filling the air with a persistent hissing.

"Be quick about it," Carlette said, giving the boy a push.

"You know, I thought I would get used to the cold here," Tuk said as he pulled off his ripped glove and plunged his hand into the water with a grimace. "Can't say I have quite yet."

Carlette ignored him, scanning the clearing like a fox hound.

"If you ever came to a city in Nurkaij, you'd realize what you've been missing out on," Tuk said as he swirled his injured hand in the water, rubbing the last of the wood out with jerky movements. Carlette listened to the jabbering of needle-nosed Norjays and the distant territorial shrieks of a sionach. "This place feels like someone took the color out of the world. But in Vaijan—"

"If I came to Vaijan, I'd be executed before I could step off the ship," Carlette snapped as her ears strained for whatever threat might catch them unawares at the water's edge.

That silenced Tuk for a moment as he clenched and unclenched his hand.

"I can't imagine what your life here is like," Tuk said.

"It's fine."

"Is it?" he asked.

Carlette hated his questions. What right did he have, to ask things like that? It's not as if he could change things, go back and give her different parents. A different bloodline.

A different life.

After a long, tense silence, he shrugged. "Well, it certainly wouldn't be good enough for me. I'd take a sunny day on the beach over this weather any—"

"Shhh!"

Carlette jerked out a silencing hand. The skin on her neck was prickling. The hairs on her arm stood up beneath her gauntlets, tiny warning sentinels. Carlette bent her knees before her brain even registered the hush growing near, the sudden absence of sound.

"We need to go," Carlette said, voice tight.

"But—"

"We need to go *now*."

She grabbed Tuk's leather jacket, hauling him up. She spun them away from the water, her body coiling as she prepared to break into a sprint.

When her gaze returned to the shadowed forest, catching on a glimmer of white, Carlette felt her heart drop out of her chest.

They both froze.

Standing in the shaded darkness were three huge Amonoux. Larger than any animal Carlette had ever seen, they hovered between the Goddeau trees as if the forest had been made for them. Shoulders as wide as the Tuleaux gates, at least twenty-five feet tall, they were ominous and eerie and horrifyingly beautiful. Tuk might be awed their size, the iridescent, jewel-bright glimmer of each wolf's seven eyes. But Carlette swallowed as she felt the minds of these creatures' brush against her own. A vast and kinetic power haloed each of the Amonoux, and wrapping around it felt like trying to hold lightning. Surrounded, shielded by the kinked and woven souls of every animal they had ever eaten, the minds of the wolves were impenetrable. Unenhabitable.

Unstoppable.

Flanked by two smaller pups, the gigantic she-wolf padded forward, silent as a wraith. Carlette stepped in front of her prisoner, mind reeling. She could sense anger, an insistent prodding. They were questioning her without words, *looking* for something. Carlette reached out and winced as a power so much greater than her own slapped her mind aside.

But there was something familiar tangled in that mesh around the she-wolf.

Carlette had seen her before.

The Amonoux prowled toward them, nose twitching, hackles rising. How did she know this animal? Where had they met?

Then she remembered.

The eyes, the glittering white fur, the obsidian-black claws.

Carlette's mind tumbled, falling back into a day eight years ago. The worst day of her life…

Tuk was reaching slowly into her belt and Carlette felt him step around her, as if from a great distance, her mind flickering in and out.

"Quaina?"

She was a child again, searching for her friend. Laughter filled the woods around Tuleaux as silence pressed in on the Goddeau trees around them.

"Quaina, where are you?"

Tuk was lifting something. Carlette couldn't breathe. The she-wolf curled her lips, the deep growl almost cosmic in its reverberating power.

In her memories, Carlette heard the same growl, laced with hunger instead of rage. Filling the forest with a different kind of need

In the haze of a dream, Carlette saw the she-wolf stalk forward.

Saw the Nuri mechanic cock the stolen gun.

She blinked.

"No!"

But it was too late. The bullet ripped into the she-wolf's flank. Blood sprayed over the riverbank, tinting ice the same color as Carlette's cape. The Amonoux snarled, snapped her jaws. The two others threw their heads back and howled.

"No, wait!"

Tuk fired twice more into the she-wolf, but the bullets were wasted. Even Carlette, who had never held a gun in her life, knew that nothing but a point-blank shot could penetrate an Amonoux's hide. Inches of thick, wiry fur covered layers and layers of muscle. He couldn't kill her from here, not without a canon or a military-grade spear-gun.

But he could make her very angry.

"Move!"

Tuk leapt to the side as the wolf swiped out at him, her razor-sharp claws barely missing. Carlette surged after him but was stopped when one of the other Amonoux grabbed her hood in its fangs, yanking her back. Snapping her hands forward, Carlette cut out with her spines. She felt them make contact, heard a whine of pain.

She rolled away, trusting the neurotoxin to stop the creature... at least for a little while.

Tuk sprinted down the riverbank, away from Carlette, followed by the two remaining wolves. He tried to fire over his shoulder, but the gun clicked empty. So he threw the pistol at the she-wolf. She leapt over the projectile with all the grace of a snowfall.

Carlette was chasing after them, but she wasn't going to make it. The boy was cornered between a swiftly narrowing bank and the tumultuous water. Ice had piled up on one side, blocking the prisoner's escape.

Clenching her jaw, Carlette scrambled over the bank, reaching out with her mind. It was instinctual, uncontrolled, something Grand Mera had always berated her for. This automatic lashing out was a native trait, exactly what the Convent of Others bred out of their genetic lines. But with adrenaline singing through her veins and fear clouding her thoughts, she couldn't suppress the tendrils that shot from her like skeins of wool.

As her body stumbled through the mud, Carlette's mind dove into a whirlpool of energy. She felt it slice her, a mental storm of razor blades.

Don't hurt him! she projected, hurling the thought at the wolves like throwing knives. *Don't hurt him!*

She didn't care that he was her enemy. To her panicked mind, Tuk was Quaina. He was someone else who was in the Giant's Wood because of her.

Someone else who would die because of her.

102

As Carlette beat against their massive, gargantuan power, both animals froze. The smaller of the two bristled, his breath one continuous stream of deep-throat snarls.

But the she-wolf turned, lips settling around glistening fangs. All seven iridescent eyes focused on Carlette. She felt their power, sizing her up. Measuring her.

"Don't hurt him," Carlette said aloud.

Her head ached from the effort of holding the she-wolf's attention. One of the woven strands of her power brushed against Carlette, not unlike an outstretched hand. Carlette's mouth fell open. She felt tears prickle, spilling over. Her breathing caught, sobs building in her chest. The forest stood still as Carlette felt the glow of a soul she had felt so many times. A spirit she knew almost as well as her own. Perhaps better.

Quaina.

And then something slammed into her. Metal cracked against her face. Strong arms circled her chest, her breath rushed out.

She hit the water.

Ice chunks scraped her throat as she swallowed, tried to inhale. Her hood was a tangle of fabric, drowning, dragging. A foot kicked her shin. The arms around her ribcage tightened.

"Put your feet downstream!" Tuk yelled, adjusting his own body.

She tried to shift, but the water slammed her against a rock before she could change direction. Her ribs screamed in pain. She couldn't breathe, couldn't move. Her fingers and feet were already numb with cold.

"Stay with me!"

Tuk's grip on her arm was loose, slipping, as they both cascaded over an outcropping, plunged into a deep basin, were held under as water crashed down on top of them. Carlette kicked out but she didn't know which way was up.

Darkness and light spun like living things.

She was going to die.

Panic filled her lungs in the absence of air.

A sharp tug on her arm, and a body slammed against hers. Her head burst into the air like a popped cork. A spray of water glittered in the evening sun.

"SWIM!" screamed a voice in her ear, earsplitting over the thrum of steady water.

Two realizations struck Carlette in quick succession.

First, they weren't churning anymore. The water was thick and lazy here, tugging them along, approaching an edge. A haze of mist blotted out the sky.

And two, the waterfall's distant noise wasn't so distant anymore.

Throwing back the wet, clingy edges of her hood, Carlette kicked frantically toward shore. One hand clawed forward, the other caught by Tuk's solid grip. She couldn't feel her fingers, but she stretched them out anyway, desperate for land. The water towed them, unstoppable, greedy. But they were close. Her hand hit something, slid off. Tuk yanked on a tree root before it snapped in his grasp.

With a final, shivering push Carlette managed to grab a low-hanging sapling. She gripped it with a numb hand, pulling them both in. Tuk shoved her forward before yanking himself out of the water, his feet sliding against the slippery edge of the waterfall just as he managed to pull himself free.

For a moment they both lay draped over the sapling, swallowing gluttonous gulps of chilly air. Carlette was shaking all over, as frozen as she'd ever been in her life.

"Come on," Tuk said at last, shimmying down the tree trunk toward shore. "We need to make a fire."

Carlette's numbness went deeper than cold as she stumbled after her prisoner, letting Tuk lead them to a sparse area of foothills peppered with old mining caves. When he pulled her into a narrow tunnel, barely big enough for them to stand upright, she just waited there, pulsing with shock. She couldn't muster even a perfunctory curiosity at the half-full iron cart rusting in the corner or the dusty, blackened firepit piled high with disintegrating wood. On the other side of the pit was a stack of old furs, so rotted that they barely resembled animal hides anymore.

She only blinked at them.

Her mind was a towel that had been brutally wrung dry and beaten with horrible understanding. The grueling experience of touching the Amonoux's mind, of finding Quaina there, left her so empty and hollow that she could have curled up and died right at the mouth of the cave and hardly noticed. How does one continue with the burden of knowledge like that?

Why would one bother?

"Help me build a fire," Tuk said, his teeth chattering.

Carlette didn't respond. She could feel sleep splashing against her mind, pulling at her the way the river had pulled them toward the waterfall. How lovely would it be to just drift into that nothingness, let it all wash away with the dark?

"Carlette," Tuk snapped, grabbing one shoulder with a manacled hand. "Stay with me, aye? You're supposed to be the fighter here."

Shaking herself, Carlette blinked away the nimbus shape of the she-wolf imprinted on her eyelids. She let the world rush back in, vivid and painful and demanding.

Right.

She was a fighter. She was a weapon.

She had to focus.

"Let go of me," she said, pulling her arm free. But she joined him in the slow work of gathering kindling.

They were trembling so much it was almost impossible to pick up the branches and leaves around the cave entrance. But somehow Tuk managed to build a small pile of tinder. Carlette dragged in larger branches, barely conscious as she watched the young man try to light the damp wood, his tongue poking out between blue lips.

He struck the flint once.

Twice.

On the third try, the dead leaves caught.

Tuk let out a whoop of victory and blew on the little flame. His voice echoed. Carlette knew she should be worried about cairogs and spiders living in these abandoned caverns, but she couldn't bring herself to care. Her mind was still spinning, still reliving the encounter.

"And they said I was hopeless at basic survival," Tuk said with a grin.

Carlette stared at the tiny flame. It wasn't enough. They both knew it.

She glared at him through tear-filled eyes, needing to know. "Why did you save me?"

Tuk looked at her, his body vibrating with cold.

"You were right," he said with a shrug. "I can't survive here without you."

Carlette could sense more brewing beneath the surface of that statement, a change in the boy's eyes. But she dropped her gaze.

"Back there... you looked like you'd seen a ghost," Tuk ventured.

Again, his question struck right into the red middle of her pain.

"I did," Carlette said.

Her cheeks were wet. She curled herself into a tight ball, swallowing convulsively.

No. Not in front of him.

She couldn't allow this to undo her, couldn't fall to the memory. She thought she had learned to mash things down until there was only the scythe of function. Her hood. Her mission.

You are a weapon.

But Quaina's soul brushing against her own, tangled into the she-wolf's power, had been enough to smash Carlette's foundation like a battering ram. Tuk lingered by the entrance of the cave, free to stay or flee or kill her. And she didn't care. The pain was too much, eating her from the inside out.

Quaina was trapped in that creature's power, her soul imprisoned, and it was entirely Carlette's fault.

She dug her face into her knees, gasping for air.

Instead of running, Tuk plopped down next to her, yanking over one of the putrid skins. Heavy fur fell over her, curling around the drenched hood. Carlette breathed through her mouth, shivering inside the makeshift canopy. There was a moment of calm, almost companionable silence. And then Tuk's arm alighted against her shoulder like a timid songbird.

Her head jerked up. She stared.

He was smiling.

It was cautious and resigned, the smile of someone just as confused as she was. But friendly.

"This is foolish," she rasped, her throat raw.

"What? Being human?" He snorted. "Even witches can't avoid that, aye?"

An unwilling chuckle escaped Carlette's numb lips.

"Look, I don't know what happened back there. But if there's any way I can help—"

"There isn't," Carlette said, too quickly.

Tuk withdrew his arm. Carlette felt a strange surge of… loss? But it evaporated as the mechanic began to untie his jacket, a shy smile wrinkling his eyes.

"Well, miss Carlette," he said, shedding wet layers, "it looks like we're going to get to know one another pretty well if we want to survive the night."

She swallowed, wishing she could argue, knowing she could not.

It's just another duty, she told herself, clenching her jaw. Just a way to get home.

She glared up at Tuk with iron eyes.

"Can you keep your witchcraft to yourself for a night?" he asked, shoulders hunched with the awkward weight of their predicament.

"No promises."

Tuk laughed and Carlette found her lips curving without her permission as the boy's face lit up like the harbor at night.

She turned away.

Stay the path.

CHAPTER TWELVE

❈ DIVERSION ❈

Carlette woke to a hand covering her mouth.

"Shhh," Tuk hissed in her ear, pressing damp clothing into her hands. "I hear voices."

It was disorienting to wake up next to him, especially considering that Carlette had spent half the night struggling to stay conscious, keeping a prim distance between their almost-completely-naked bodies. It had been a challenge, when she was so cold and Tuk's body seemed to radiate, ludicrously generous in its dispersal of heat. Carlette had listened to his breathing, tense first and then ebbing into soft exhales. She'd thought she would lie there all night, shivering, waiting for him to roll over and strangle her.

But somehow, she'd slept.

Now, she yanked a damp coat and fleeces on over her underthings, trying to ignore the rancid stink the decaying furs had left on her skin. Tuk was already dressed, crouching at the mouth of the cave.

"They're coming down the gully," he said, peering up the rocky trail that wound through an ancient riverbed, long dried up.

Strapping on her forearm-guards, Carlette joined Tuk at the mouth of the cave.

"Collectors?" Carlette asked.

Tuk shot her a wide-eyed look. "I hope not."

Before she could answer, Carlette heard whoops and hollers bouncing between the foothills. Animal sounds from human throats. Cawing. Shrieking.

Howling.

These weren't traders.

"Bloody Paws," Carlette muttered, clenching her fists.

Tuk's face went white. "We can't stay here. Their beasts will smell us."

"If we move, they'll be able to track our footprints."

Carlette's gaze was razor-sharp, staring at the bend as the group came into view.

Twelve. She counted twelve rebels, seven on mountain stags, a handful of prisoners stumbling along behind. Even from this distance, Carlette could see the bleeding paw tattoos on their necks, claws reaching up almost to their cheekbones. Every one of them had braided their hair with leather thongs and bird feathers. Faces painted with animal blood. Furs matted with gore.

But none were as intimidating as the woman riding at the front of the pack. Her face was made of angles, as if carved from the very slate beneath the hooves of her stag. On the woman's collarbone rested a corded necklace of human teeth. On her head perched a tiara made of snapped femurs. The bladed bow that hung from her shoulder was strung with vertebrae and her boots were stitched with various small bones. She sat tall on the back of her stag, her expression even more vicious than the fanged beast below her.

"Yokan," Carlette whispered.

110

"Who?" Tuk asked.

"She leads the Bloody Paws. Our soldiers have been hunting her for years."

The woman was yanking her prisoners forward. Two of them were hoods, one red, one blue. Carlette couldn't see faces beneath the thick wool of their cowls, but her fists clenched in anger.

She leaned out.

If she could bring back Yokan's head, the Magistrate would forgive anything. The Bloody Paws were the scourge of Tuleaux, of the mountains. For months the long walk between Tuleaux and Jemelle had been almost too deadly to make.

She had to act soon. The Bloody Paws caravan was closing in, growing nearer with each whoop and caw.

Carlette's muscles coiled.

"Aye! You can't go down there," Tuk said, throwing his bound hands out to stop her.

She rounded on him. "If I kill her, it would crush the rebels. We might be able to wipe them out for good."

"Do you really think you can get past *those* by yourself?"

Carlette followed his finger.

Her stomach clenched.

Following the parade of Bloody Paws and their prisoners, slinking along the ridgeline like the shadows of clouds, were several cairogs. Like everything in the Giant's Wood, they were enormous and lethal. At least as long as three fully-grown men and peppered with legs, they moved sinuously, flowing over rocks. Due to the color of their grey-black exoskeletons, the cairogs and their painted riders blended in with the obsidian mountain so much that Carlette might have missed them, had Tuk not pointed them out. Only flickering shadows and the patches of scattered snow gave away their many-legged movements.

"You'd be eaten alive before you ever reach her."

Carlette's fingers tightened, the spines in her gauntlet rippling. What she wouldn't give for a crossbow or even a good throwing knife. She could end this right now from their invisible vantage point.

"We need to go deeper into the caves," Tuk said, pressing himself back. "We have a better chance of surviving if we hide in the mountain."

But Carlette wasn't listening.

Because at that moment, Yokan yanked her prisoners forward. One stumbled, foot catching a sharp piece of slate. With a flutter of crimson, the hood caught the wind. Pulled back. Auburn hair shimmered in the sunlight. The girl's face—bruised and bloody—glared up at her captor.

"Aheya!" Carlette gasped.

Tuk grabbed her arm but she strained against him.

"They. Will. Kill. You." Tuk said, panting with every word as he tried to hold her back. "And then I'll be wolf-food!"

"That's my friend!"

"And those are Nuri soldiers," Tuk hissed back, jerking his chin at two of the other captives. "You don't see me about to commit suicide."

"We have to do something!"

"Like what? We have no weapons, no advantage—"

"I could enhabit her stag," Carlette said, breath coming quickly. "Cause chaos. They might get away."

"That's a terrible idea."

"You have a better one?"

"Yes! Stay *here*!"

"Tuk, why do you think they're bringing those men and women back alive. To torture them. Their last moments will be spent screaming for mercy, and that's *if* they're lucky enough to *have* last moments."

Tuk narrowed his eyes, clutching the chain between his wrists as if for balance. "Since when do Ferrenese witches care about Nuri soldiers?"

"They're people, Tuk. Human beings. The Bloody Paws... even your men don't deserve such a fate."

"And the fate that awaits me in Jemelle? Is it any different?"

Carlette's words caught in her throat. She stared at him for a moment, her lips a pursed line. Tuk didn't break eye contact.

She straightened.

"If I had been caught by Nuri soldiers and our roles were reversed, what would they do to me? They would experiment on me, wouldn't they? Tear me apart looking for the source of my magic. You tell me there aren't breeding halls in Caika. Tell me there aren't places where the screaming never stops. Because I don't think your hands are any cleaner than mine."

Tuk's thick eyebrows pulled together into one solid line.

"You think I'm a witch," Carlette continued. "Maybe you're right. Maybe I am an aberration. I don't know what to think anymore. But I *do* know that my friend is down there. Your *men* are down there. And I refuse to leave them to the savagery that the Bloody Paws have in store."

Tuk glowered at her for a long minute.

Then, finally, his face broke into a grim smile.

"A Nuri airman teaming up with a Delarese hood? No one will ever believe it."

Carlette didn't answer. Her eyes were already scanning the Bloody Paws and prisoners. She was silent for a long moment, every muscle tense and waiting for a cairog to appear in the mouth of their tunnel or an enhabited bird to fly past and see them.

Tuk peered out next to her, his shoulder warm against her own.

"So? What did I just sign up for?"

"I have a plan," she said at last. "But you're not going to like it."

Carlette felt exposed without her hood as she picked her way down the slope, careful not to leave footprints. She itched to pull red fabric around her body, the shield of her position protecting her from unwanted eyes. But here, with the Bloody Paws prancing through the gully below them, her hood would stand out against the stone like blood on snow.

Carlette's feet slid and there was a resonant crack as a pebble tumbled down below her. She ducked behind a rock, curling herself into a tight ball as the rough edges of strange minds brushed against her own.

She had been found.

Yokan called for a halt, the guttural Ebonal words scraping against the mountainside.

"I think we have a rat hiding somewhere close," Yokan said in gleeful Delarese. "Come out, little rodent, and we might not kill you."

Carlette worked quickly, slicing her still-raw hand open with the tiny dagger she kept in her boot. With grim determination, Carlette smeared the wound over her neck, covering her anchor tattoo, wincing at the protest of the inflamed flesh. She could hear the stags rustling below, their growling neighs rising as they smelled blood.

Yokan barked another command in Ebonal. Carlette heard rocks shift, both above and below. Cairogs clicked over the stone face of the gully.

Heading toward her.

Come on, Tuk, Carlette thought, palms aching as she clenched her fists. Her mind was already reaching out, probing for Yokan's mount. Yokan held the beast, but with only a distant, delicate touch. The trusting connection of a long-forged bond. A partnership, in which there was no need for the stranglehold of a full enhabitation.

"I smell a *girl*-mind," Yokan crowed in her accented Delarese. "How weak and cowardly, hiding from my brave soldiers. Come out of your hole, little girl. Face us in the light."

Carlette's body was a study in tension, every muscle braced, her mind a reined-in horse. She kept her mind ready, waiting, gently

114

brushing each of the stags. It would sap strength quickly to hold them all at once...

A cairog appeared at the corner of her vision, skittering closer. Carlette felt the proximity of two stags, their wide nostrils humming as they sniffed her out.

Suddenly, a mighty, metallic *crash* echoed down the gully.

The rebels froze.

"Landslide!" one captive screamed.

Just on time, Tuk shoved the mining wagon out of their tiny tunnel, heaving the cart and all its contents down the hillside. Rocks tumbled into bigger rocks. Dust rose in clouds.

And, in the distraction, the Bloody Paws' hold on their animals slipped.

Carlette's mind was a steel trap, closing around every one of the beasts in the gully at once. She leapt on top of her rock, clenching her fists, snapping out her spines. But the rebels who had been inches away from her were now tumbling down the rock face, tossed from their panicked beasts like sacks of meat.

All but one black-haired Moian girl, whose cairog shifted nervously but made no move to throw her off.

From her vantage point, Carlette watched the mountain stags stampede into Bloody Paws. Bodies were everywhere. Blood ran, but Carlette had no idea whose it was. Yokan drew her bow, aimed it at the fleeing blue hood.

Carlette pulled the mental reins of Yokan's steed.

The creature reared, sending Yokan tumbling into the melee of falling rock.

Cairogs were swarming down the mountain, six of them, their eyes white. Twice as many as Carlette had counted. She couldn't hold them—their minds were too foreign, too strange—so she focused on the nearest stags, launching the antlered beasts into the insects. The cairogs rolled, their movements synchronized and controlled.

There was a powerful insect enhabiter here.

115

Prisoners were disappearing like voles into the caves. Carlette could sense Tuk sliding toward her with her hood tucked in his shirt.

Her mind was weakening, assaulted by the rebels, spread thin by the animals. Everything beat against Carlette like waves against a ship, threatening to pull her down. Other minds were trying to shove her out of their beasts, working individually, but if they coordinated their attacks...

She had to get out of here.

She scanned the scene but couldn't find Aheya anywhere. Yokan screamed orders in Ebonal. Carlette couldn't understand the words, but she saw the rebel leader pointing at her. Then at a stag.

An arrow punched into it, hitting true.

It died.

Carlette gasped.

Sick, slippery nausea gripped her belly. Her hold slipped. Two of the beasts fell away from her mind like sand through fingers.

"Come on!"

Tuk's voice, in her ear.

Carlette sent a final pulse of power, scattering the Mountain stags.

And then Tuk yanked her backward, into a different tunnel.

Her line of vision broken, Carlette could only sense the animals distantly, as if through a haze. She blinked, her mind returning to one place, one set of eyes. It was always disorienting to go from multiple minds to one.

Tuk sprinted beside her, their footsteps echoing in the wide mining cavern. A pair of rails guided their mad escape, snaking deep into the mountain, a trail that Delasir men had once walked. Carlette's breath plumed in the cold, dry air. Tuk's exhales were ragged next to her, his fear a physical weight. They passed a pile of pickaxes and an ancient campsite. Old tin cups were knocked over, half-filled with dust.

Carlette wondered what had happened to the miners who once toiled here. Had they fallen to rebels? Died in some creative and

116

horrible way in Moian tree-cities or Ebonal mountain caves? Or had they simply evacuated, fallen back when iron became the second most valuable export of Ferren?

As the air began to thicken and the tunnel grew so dark that Carlette couldn't even see her own hand in front of her face, they slowed to a jog. Then to a walk. Tuk released her. Carlette smoothed down the spines on her arms.

A crash echoed down the tunnel.

"What was that?"

"Sorry," Tuk said, panting. "Fell over."

Carlette listened for a long moment but heard nothing. Sensed nothing. There was a fuzziness to her thoughts, an exhaustion that went beyond just the fight. There were too many minds, the insects of the mountain swarming her, battering her senses.

She couldn't think.

"We should stop," Carlette said, her hands shaking as she felt for the wall.

"This feels like wood... Ouch!" Something jerked. "Splinter," he explained.

"I'm not sure if it's safe to make a fire," Carlette said, her mind abuzz.

Could there possibly be this many insects living in the mines?

Were they... getting closer?

She tried to reach out, to expand her senses, but something was blocking her. A strange, cultivated emptiness.

She'd never felt anything like it before.

"Well, we either make a fire or fall into a crevasse somewhere," Tuk said, his voice interrupted by scrapes and clicks. "As an airman, I have no intention of dying *under* the mountains."

Carlette leaned against the cave wall, her head pulsing. She had stretched too far, that must be it. Enhabited too many strong predators at once. No other Prederaux in Jemelle could have done what she did, so of course it had been too much. She simply had to recover.

She listened to Tuk grapple with the wood for several moments, his curses and mutterings flowing over her. Comforting.

"Thank you," she said at last.

Tuk paused.

"For what?"

"For helping save my friend," Carlette explained.

He chuckled. "Least I could do for the girl trying to kill me."

Carlette bit her lip, her thoughts as hazy as a disturbed riverbed. She sighed and tilted her head back.

"I wish things were different," she said, almost to herself.

Tuk didn't respond. His manacles clinked as he shifted.

"There must be something better," Carlette said. Then smiled to herself. "That's what my friend used to wish for. A better way."

"I don't think our world takes kindly to that. My dad used to say he'd rather live a soldier than die a martyr."

Carlette winced. A father. Tuk had a father. A mother too. She folded her arms against the chill as Tuk snorted.

"Of course, the dumb fool didn't take his own advice," Tuk muttered, hitting rocks together.

"What happened to him?"

"Died saving a ship full of prisoners."

"Sounds like a good man."

"Would have been a better man if he'd stuck around," Tuk said, but Carlette sensed a softness in Tuk's words. A pride.

"I'm sorry. I know how it feels to lose someone."

Tuk struck the flint again. "Would this have anything to do with those Amonoux we saw?"

Carlette didn't answer.

"I mean, you looked like you'd seen a ghost. You were pale before, but when that she-wolf turned on you—"

"It's not important," Carlette snapped.

Tuk took a breath before speaking again.

"It's strange, but I always figured that the first hood I met in person would be some evil beast. Everyone in Nurkaij is always going on about what unnatural monsters you are." He paused. "And then I saw you cry. Commander Invitas never said anything about that."

Carlette listened to him struggle with the damp wood, her thoughts a muddle. What he was saying should make her angry, revealing a weakness she didn't want to show.

But she wasn't angry.

She was tired.

Light bloomed in the cave, a spark illuminating the space between Tuk's hands.

"Yes!" he whooped, manacles clanking as he pumped the air. "I am the king of this mountain!"

"I'm afraid," said a voice from above him, "that we don't recognize kings here."

Carlette froze. Her throat constricted. Her exhausted mind flickered out and she sensed, even through the dense confusion of a million assaulting minds, a human being. Tilting her head back, she saw their infant fire reflected in the pitch-black exoskeleton of an enormous cairog, hanging upside-down over their heads. It's pincers, each as thick as Carlette's thigh, chittered and snapped. Its long hairs shimmered, fluttering beneath thick chittenous armor.

A tiny black-haired girl clung to the insect's vast shoulders, peering down at them with an impish, malevolent smile.

"Hi there," she said.

Tuk's voice caught in a strangled shout. Carlette's hands snapped forward, her instincts honing in on the monster before them, on the girl. She couldn't enhabit the insect, didn't have the experience. But perhaps the Moian warrior...

She made to move away from the wall, grab Tuk, run. But one of the cairog's long, twisted feelers shot out. The fire snapped off, a candle being blown out.

And then something thick and slimy was curling around her neck, pulling tight as a hangman's noose.

CHAPTER THIRTEEN

❄ BEETLESPEAKER ❄

Carlette's world was a blur of sound and panic. She couldn't breathe. The cairog's scaly leg jerked her through the darkness, smashing her body against every corner as the gigantic insect zipped along the ceiling. Pincers clicked. Loose stones tumbled down the tunnel's edges. Her head hit a rock. Her ribcage smashed against a wall. Unconsciousness sloshed around her like water. The deep-seated magic in her mind scrambled, grappling for the human consciousness entangled with the insect's, both of them dangerous and sharp.

She was powerless to enhabit either as her brain starved.

Her back hit another wall. Carlette's raw throat tried to release a scream. It came out as a strangled gurgle. Tuk's foot kicked her thigh; a spasmic movement. She could hear his breath whistling, struggling.

They were going to suffocate.

Suddenly, the darkness broke. Carlette tried to make sense of the moving shapes, but her eyes wouldn't focus. There was a human howl, a responding snarl that she felt in her very bones. Firelight flickered in her vision, distant and dim. Pillars of stone passed like sentinels, and she could make out shorter, moving columns.

People.

Rebels.

The insect's grip loosened, dropped her. Her kneecaps shrieked in agony as they hit the stone floor, but she didn't cry out. Instead she gulped air, swallowing breaths as if they were her last. Maybe they would be. She coughed, her eyes watering as she teetered on all fours, ready to collapse.

But she was given no such privilege.

Hands yanked her hair back and someone tied a blindfold over her face, painfully tight. Her hands were swathed in fabric, bound behind her back.

"What have we here?" said a voice that seemed entirely made of sharp edges.

Yokan.

Carlette heard a scuffle next to her. Tuk's manacles clanked and he spat something in Nuri, followed by a meaty thud. Tuk groaned. Carlette heard a body hit the ground.

"I think Byrna Beetlespeaker found the source of our *disruption*," said the Bloody Paw leader, her voice lilting strangely, drawing emphasis in unexpected places. Carlette heard feet shift next to her. The metallic tang of dried blood filled her nostrils, along with animal skin, campfires, body odor, freshly dug earth.

Carlette cringed as she sensed someone kneel in front of Tuk.

Yokan smelled like death.

"Are you a troublemaker then?" Yokan hissed.

"Get off me," Tuk snapped.

There was another thud, another punch.

"Iron-bound hands. Fingers stained with rust. Perhaps you thought it would be fun to scatter our prisoners. Kill our beasts. Work for our *enemy*." Yokan's voice was silky and dangerous. "But never fear, bronze boy, the fun will be repaid in full."

"I don't know what you're talking about."

"And who are you, playing with Nuri scum?" Yokan said, pulling Carlette's head back with vicious strength. Fingernails scraped along Carlette's neck, where blood had dried over her anchor tattoo.

Yokan was silent for a moment. Carlette's throat worked, her starved lungs trying to breathe despite the angle of her neck.

"A Delasir slave working with a captured Nuri spy?" Yokan's voice was incredulous. Amused. She cackled once. "Our children will sing songs about this! How unnatural, like a dog befriending a viper."

Malevolent laughter filled the cave. Carlette tried to sort through the voices, count their number. But the echoes made it impossible. It sounded like a thousand men and women were crammed under the Shadow Peaks, mocking her.

And beneath it all was that choked growling that made Carlette's hair stand on end.

"So tell me, child," Yokan said, rotten breath washing over Carlette's face. "What tower birthed you?"

"She's not a hood!" Tuk broke in, his voice raspy. "She's a turncoat. Was helping me track down Jemelle."

"The anchor speaks for itself," Yokan said.

"Every half-breed child gets one. Not all of them make it to Jemelle."

"And yet she enhabited our beasts."

"I saw a red hood among your captives," Tuk insisted. "You didn't bother to blindfold her, so why were you surprised when she took over the predators in your midst?" He snorted. "Of course she'd take the opportunity to escape. She'd be a fool not to."

Yokan released Carlette's hair. She gasped, toppling forward. With her hands tied behind her back, she couldn't stop her fall and collapsed against the stone, her chest scraping against sharp rock as she inhaled.

Why was Tuk lying to Yokan? Carlette knew a Nuri spy was unlikely to find mercy among these rebels, but to lie to them, to pretend that Carlette wasn't exactly what Yokan accused her of being…

They would search him, find her red hood tucked in the front of his tunic, and then what? He would be a liar as well as an enemy.

Yokan moved, her footsteps almost silent as she shifted.

"It would take a hood of great power to cause such trouble," Yokan said, almost to herself.

"Well, looks like you lost a powerful captive."

Yokan chuckled. "Nothing in this forest is lost to my hunters. She simply gave our riders something to chase."

Carlette felt a chill whisper down her spine. She shivered and someone kicked her.

"Stop it!"

Tuk's voice echoed. There was an ominous silence.

"It is fitting, though," Yokan continued as if there had been no interruption, "For you to fall so *fortuitously* into our midst."

Tuk's breath came out, sharp and pained. His body shifted, as if being pulled upright. Carlette struggled against her bonds.

That's my prisoner, you bitch, she found herself thinking.

"You see, the men we captured were just soldiers. Useful only to feed our hungry stags. A foot soldier does not know how to fly a sky-ship or build a fortress… or find a secret base."

Carlette's heart sank.

They knew about Caika.

"But I've seen other men like you fall to the ground. They die first, stabbed in the back by their own men. Now why would that be?"

Tuk's teeth clicked together. Carlette could feel terror rolling off him in waves, his familiar consciousness the only thing she could even vaguely sense with her vision cut off and her palms covered.

"My thinking," Yokan went on, "is that the one who controls the ship must know where to fly it, eh? And could tell us all about the toys such a place would have."

Yokan made a sharp movement. Tuk cried out. Carlette kicked, scrambled, trying to find purchase, but a boot collided with her ribcage.

She wheezed.

"Tell me, little boy. Will you help us find your secret base?"

Images bloomed into Carlette's head. Bloody Paws on airships, armed with guns and crossbows. If Yokan found Caika before Tuleaux did, it would be catastrophic. She would rain down a reckless fire, destroy both the Nuri and Delarese settlements. Tribes would flock to her brutality, follow her lead.

The island would become a living hell.

Tuk laughed.

"You wouldn't make it within twenty leagues of Caika."

"Ah, but with your help..."

"Think again," Tuk said. Carlette heard him spit.

Yokan laughed. "They're always so *spirited* in the beginning. Until the screaming starts."

Carlette swallowed, thinking hard. What could she do? Could she surprise them, kick out in a certain way, perhaps knock Yokan down?

But claws curled around the roots of her hair, interrupting her pathetic plans.

Jerking her upright.

"I'm thinking you like this girl, yes?" purred the rebel leader, running a fingernail along Carlette's tattoo. "You seem to care about her. Perhaps for that we won't kill her." She paused significantly. "Yet."

Carlette could almost hear Tuk's heartbeat, harmonizing with that deep, mysterious snarling.

"Or, if you'd rather, we feed her to our little pet," Yokan said. Carlette cried out as she was hauled over rock, Tuk beside her. The growling got closer. The rebels were dragging them somewhere, approaching whatever was making that horrible noise.

Carlette's knees found a sharp edge. A deep-tunnel breeze whispered over her, lifting her clumped, dirty hair and rustling the

124

edges of her still-damp furs. She shivered. Someone was shoved down next to her, someone who smelled like the Giant's Wood and open skies.

Manacles clinked. Something snarled. There was a swish of fabric.

"No," the mechanic whispered.

A knife was pressed to Carlette's neck as her blindfold was ripped off. It was the unspoken understanding that if she tried to enhabit anything, her end would be swift and unforgiving.

Carlette's eyes adjusted to the dark. She felt her stomach clench.

Below her, in a sunken pit of carved obsidian, was an Amonoux. But unlike the vast, graceful creatures she and Tuk had met out in the Giant's Wood, this one was matted, shrunken, its once-thick fur hanging off bony ridges like a pelt on tent poles. It was so huge that it barely fit in the wide hollow, but still the beast cowered from them, its seven eyes roving the surrounding rebels with a frantic, terrified anger.

The creature's head swung around, following a cairog that skittered over the cave's ceiling with one black-haired rider hanging on like a bat. When it looked up, Carlette saw warm blood on the beast's neck, crusted around ropes that had dug so deep it was a wonder the animal was still alive.

It can't call for its pack, Carlette thought, pity rushing through her. With her eyes uncovered, she could feel the wolf's pain, smell the stench of agony and fear. It was a juvenile, a pup. Even beneath the sustained, almost endless snarl she could sense its longing for home.

"If you will not help us," Yokan was saying as she tilted Carlette over the edge of the pit. "Then your partner is of no more use than a herd animal."

The wolf's eyes rolled up, fixing hungrily on Carlette. The seventh eye, usually a jewel-bright glimmer, was dull and starved.

They had been feeding the wolf dead meat. Its power had shrunk.

But not enough.

125

Carlette had touched the Amonoux in the Giant's Wood. Distracted them. It was more than any of her classmates could hope to do, but even she couldn't *enhabit* one of these gods of the mountain. To stop an Amonoux, to actually reach through its web of power and *control* it... only Voka had ever managed such a feat, and her line was long dead.

Which meant that if they dropped her in that pit, there was no way to stop the wolf from devouring Carlette, body and soul.

Fear clogged her veins.

Was this what Quaina had felt with the starving she-wolf bearing down on her?

"Don't," Tuk said, his voice level. Forceful.

But shaking.

"Tell me where Caika hides, little Nuri boy?" Yokan asked as Carlette pushed back, trying to shove away from the pit's edge. The cairog that had captured them was right overhead, its tiny rider holding on with nothing but her knees. She was dark-haired, Moian, young, with a smug face partially hidden by a black scarf pulled over her nose. Carlette met the girl's dancing eyes, felt the cruel amusement.

This rebel, at least, would enjoy watching her die.

Carlette wriggled, but Yokan only shoved her out further. She was dangling now, her entire torso hanging over nothing but air. The Amonoux below her drooled, thick ropes of saliva dripping from dirty, blood-matted jaws.

"I can give you information about Tuleaux," Tuk said, his eyes snapping to Carlette and then back to Yokan. "I was there as a prisoner. I can tell you where the jails are. The prince is there, and the pirate queen. She was in the cell right next to me—"

"I have freed over twenty of my warriors from their prisons," Yokan said as Carlette tried to throw herself backwards. "I know Tuleaux almost as well as I know these mountains."

Tuk was breathing heavily now. Carlette felt Yokan's nails slide against her tunic. If she let go, Carlette would fall head-first. Her skull would strike rock and the last thing she saw would be the red dust of iron ore and the dark brown blood that had turned the wolf's coat the color of autumn leaves.

"I don't know how to find it on land," Tuk said, his voice pleading.

"What mountain is it on?"

"I... I can't..."

Yokan's fingers opened. Carlette fell forward, cried out. Fingernails closed over her shoulder, piercing her skin, stopping her fall.

"I will not ask again," Yokan said.

Tuk pursed his lips.

Met Carlette's eyes.

"It's on Adenai," Tuk said, casting his eyes to the floor. "Above the cloud-line."

Yokan cackled.

"How fitting, that such a place would sit on our life-mother." She pulled Carlette back, grinned down at her. "See, you were useful after all."

Yokan threw Carlette aside, gesturing to her warriors and releasing a stream of orders in twisted Ebonal. Carlette's gaze fell on Tuk. She saw his worry, his sick relief.

And then another blindfold was tightened around her head.

CHAPTER FOURTEEN

❊ RED LOST, RED FOUND ❊

The Bloody Paws tossed Carlette into a dusty corner of the enormous cave. She hit hard, breath whooshing out of her as she rolled onto her side. Fabric cut into her sore hands and forehead. She pushed with bound feet until her back found a wall and curved herself against it, rubbing her fists against the ragged stone.

One finger wormed loose of the swaddling.

Finally.

Information flooded into Carlette as she tasted the life in the cave.

Another body landed next to her own as the sounds of a campsite rose around them. Carlette listened to pots clattering, voices shouting in strange languages, animals snorting and clicking. She sensed Tuk's familiar mind next to her.

"Are you okay?" she whispered.

Tuk snorted and shifted. "Of course I am. A bunch of wild monsters don't scare me."

His voice was quivering.

"Thank you," Carlette breathed, her voice low and soft.

"For what? Keeping you alive was purely selfish, I assure you."

"Still," Carlette said. "I'm grateful. You could have let them kill me."

"And you could have let me get eaten by those things in the forest. We're even."

Carlette was silent for a moment. Boots thundered past, toward a commotion somewhere beyond their feet. Carlette widened her senses, tried desperately to touch the minds of those around her, to find out what was going on. Her bare finger prickled as she wove herself into the chaos around her, felt the excitement, violence, bloodlust.

But with her eyes covered and her head still throbbing from the cairog's attack, she couldn't possibly hope to enhabit anything.

"Did they search you?" she said when the footsteps had gone by.

"Very rudely."

Carlette swallowed, slumping. There it was. Soon they would question her, do whatever they did to captured members of the Order. And worse, her edict of safe passage would be in Yokan's slimy claws...

"I dropped your hood on the way here," Tuk said. Carlette jerked upright. "No idea where—it was impossible to tell anything with that *creature* manhandling us. But they didn't find it."

Her breath caught. "Why did you do that?"

"There was a rumor in Caika. Something a rebel confessed to us. He told us that the Bloody Paws are hunting down red hoods. Specifically. Killing them in a particularly awful way. He wouldn't say why—died during the interrogation process—but we did manage to understand that their leader is looking for someone. A long-lost relative or something. And everyone who's *not* that person... she kills."

129

Carlette didn't know what to say. This man, a prisoner she had fully intended to hand over to the worst fate imaginable, had saved her.

Twice.

She swallowed again, inhaled smoky, blood-tinged air.

"Tuk... why are you helping me?"

She felt him shrug.

"I never really believed that hoods were evil. I mean, I saw what they did to Kammunuk. And I heard the stories. But whenever I saw one captured... they were just... people. Sold and traded like animals. Forced into service." Tuk shrugged again. "I guess I can understand what that feels like."

Carlette didn't know what to make of that. He was like no one she'd ever met.

Suddenly, there was an explosion of noise nearby.

"What's going on?" Carlette hissed, trying to shoulder her way into a seated position.

"They've just brought in two more prisoners," Tuk said. Then he hesitated. "I think one is your friend."

Carlette's heart sank as she heard a new voice, high and panicked.

"Let me go! Hands *off* me, you barbarians!"

Aheya.

The Amonoux's growling intensified as the struggle reached a painful climax. Aheya screamed. Tuk stiffened.

"It's not often," came Yokan's oily voice, "that we catch a red hood sneaking through the mountains at night. All alone, unguarded. You made it easy for us."

Aheya cried out and Carlette heard the horrible sound of a blade being drawn.

"We've been watching Durchemin for months, looking for your kind. Berries on the vine, ripe for the plucking."

So that's why they attacked when I was at Howl, Carlette thought. They saw my hood.

And now they see Aheya's.

Carlette ached as the scene played out in her mind. Her friend, sneaking out of Jemelle, trying to find Eylon in some doomed and hopeless quest for normalcy. Desperate enough to be careless.

Aheya was silent. Tuk shifted. Carlette reached out, touched his mind. It was familiar, inviting, easy, even with her eyes covered. He tensed for a moment, protective walls snapping into place. Carlette floated a soft, unspoken question.

Please?

After a breathless moment, Tuk let her in.

She could see.

It was almost worse.

Aheya was on her knees in the middle of the cavern, held by a woman with silky black hair and tanned skin. The Bloody Paw rested a scythe against Aheya's neck, grinning at Yokan, eyes glittering with white-rimmed malice. Black, angular tattoos coated her bare shoulders, the marks of a Sibilese warrior.

Aheya's whole body was shaking as Yokan brushed her head in a gentle caress. Carlette kept her touch on Tuk's mind gentle and unrestrictive, painless.

She felt his heartbeat quicken as if it was her own.

"What do you want?" Aheya spat.

"What do I want?" Yokan asked, thoughtful. She released Aheya's head, addressed her gathered troops. "I want my land to be free. I want you settlers and half-breeds to stop invading *my* forests, punching through *my* mountains. I want the women of my tribe to grow up without the fear of ending up in your evil Convent, under your worthless men. Little girl, I want your kind *dead*."

The Bloody Paws jeered. The Sibilese warrior's mouth curved in a vicious smile.

"Then kill me and be done with it."

"Not so easy, child. No, I'm going to give you a chance." Yokan paced around Aheya, a predator circling a kill. "You see, I'm looking for someone. Someone who has been lost to me for many years."

"I don't know what you're talking about," Aheya snapped.

131

"You see, my ignorant friend, there is an enhabiter out there in whose veins runs Voka's blood, and mine. Your people would call her my *niece*."

A significant pause filled the air, thick with hatred.

"Many years ago, my sister and I were given to the strongest man in our tribe. The last of Voka's line. He was brutal. Some would say savage. But then, people say that about me."

Through Tuk's eyes, Carlette saw Yokan's smile spread, the midnight unfolding of a grotesque flower.

"Seventeen years ago, my sister's monthly blood stopped. The tribe rejoiced; our leaders celebrated. We had hope again." Yokan's grin spread, if possible, even wider. "That was, until she disappeared."

Carlette's pulse was quickening, almost deafening as it thudded in her ears. She had to act, and fast.

"My sister," Yokan continued, "was powerful. We scoured the forest, searched everywhere. But by the time we tracked her to the walls of Tuleaux, it was too late. We found her body, hidden in a shallow grave beyond the wall. And when we opened her belly… she was empty."

Aheya's face was disgusted, but the leering smiles of the Bloody Paws around her made Carlette realize they'd all heard this story. Many times. To them, it was exciting. The beetle-speaker stood behind Yokan, short and dense with muscle, her black hair chopped boyishly short. She smirked as Yokan went on.

"Don't you understand yet? Somewhere in Tuleaux, a child was born. A child of great potential, with wolf-rider blood and Ebonal strength. The strongest our kind can produce. If such a child was born a girl, able to inherit Voka's great gift, she would survive. She would rise to Jemelle's highest tower."

Yokan took Aheya's red hood between her fingertips, lifted it in front of Aheya's waxen face.

"She would wear this."

Aheya's chest heaved, her panicked breath fogging the air. The Sibilese warrior held her tighter.

132

"My mother was a Raebus clanswoman," Aheya snarled. "I was born in the Convent."

"Then you are of no use to me," Yokan said with a helpless shrug. "Either way, we will soon know." Yokan nodded to the woman holding Aheya. "Bring her."

Aheya struggled, kicking out as the warrior yanked her upright. The Sibilese woman's inky black braid swung like a pendulum, ticking away Aheya's last moments. Carlette watched with a horrible sinking sensation as her best friend was dragged to the edge of the pit.

The Amonoux's snarls were thick and hungry.

"My test is simple," Yokan said, as if this were nothing more than a morning exercise. "Stop the wolf and you will be spared."

"We have to do something," Carlette breathed as Tuk shifted beside her.

"I can't!" Aheya said, her voice a wail. "No one can! Amonoux are too powerful, their strength—"

Yokan grabbed Aheya's hair, brought the girl's face up to hers with a sudden, savage intensity.

"Voka could," Yokan said, in Aheya's face. "Voka *did*. And somewhere out there is a girl that can end this war, lead us to victory. I hope that girl is you," Yokan's eyes swept down Aheya's skinny frame, wasted from months of terror and secrecy. "But I doubt it."

"Tuk, help me," Carlette said, leaning into the Nuri mechanic.

"How?" Tuk whispered back.

"Please!" Aheya shrieked as she dangled over the pit's edge. "Please, I'll help you! I don't work for Jemelle, I was trying to escape!"

"None of us can escape our debt," Yokan sneered. "Any more than a beast can escape its nature. You are what you are, child. If you wanted a different life, you should have chosen better."

"I didn't have a choice! Please, I'm just like you!"

"You're nothing like me," Yokan said, jerking her chin in a nod.

Carlette struggled against her bonds.

The Sibilese warrior opened her long fingers.

133

Aheya disappeared into the pit with a gut-wrenching shriek.

"Tuk! Take off my blindfold! *Now!*" Carlette hissed, rolling on the stone.

Tuk threw himself to the side. His hands brushed Carlette's face. He fumbled with the tight fabric.

And then Carlette could *see*.

Her senses flew open like balcony doors. She absorbed the rush of Aheya's terror, the bloodlust of the crowd, the hunger of the wolf. Carlette didn't care if she was giving away her position, didn't care that the Bloody Paws were looking for someone *exactly like her*. All she cared about was her friend screaming in the pit.

Carlette let instinct be her guide.

She reached out, following familiar threads.

With a tentative touch, she brushed against the Amonoux's mind.

She couldn't possibly enhabit such a creature, could she? All her life, she'd been told it was impossible. Illegal. Only Voka had done it. Only Voka *could* do it. And the rebel leader had been a monster of catastrophic proportions. A ghost of the mountains, a nightmare.

Aheya's scream filled the cavern.

"Please! *Please!*"

Yokan's story had awoken something in Carlette, unleashed a swarm of questions. Why had Mya slapped her when she had asked questions about her mother? Why had Grand Mera done worse? The subject of Carlette's birth was a gaping hole in her life, a tender spot that she wasn't allowed to touch.

But now she found herself wondering.

Was her mother Yokan's long-lost sister?

Was her father the last living descendant of Voka?

With the recklessness of a child diving into a shallow pond, Carlette shot a spear of power toward the Amonoux, knowing that if she couldn't penetrate its defenses, she would be smashed against them. At best, she would pass out.

At worst, she would lose her mind.

134

Thinking only of her friend, of dear Aheya who wanted nothing more than to follow her own heart, Carlette flung herself at the Amonoux's mind…

And entered it.

CHAPTER FIFTEEN

❋ THE FURIX ❋

It was power beyond anything Carlette had ever known.

Even in its weakened state, this behemoth of a creature was wrapped in life-force, swathed in souls. Energy crackled in the wolf's blood, a repressed, subdued majesty that the rebels had kept chained and starved. Through the Amonoux's eyes, Carlette marveled at the swirls of consciousness that lapped against the cave. The eddies of life. Each pair of eyes saw something different—Carlette could only understand a portion of what the wolf's brain experienced—but through that seventh and most mysterious eye, she could see the woven magic of the world, tighter where humans and beasts stood, looser in the empty space between, but always there, surrounding them.

All at once Carlette understood. These wolves were a link in the chain of Ferren. Like a snowstorm or a wildfire, the Amonoux were neither good nor evil but an integral part of this land. These were the mainstays of hooded power, the guardians of the island's magic.

Carlette had only an instant to marvel at the Amonoux's vast and terrifying mind before it sensed her presence. The wolf snarled, sharp slices of mental energy striking Carlette. She tightened her hold. Her eyes glowed. The wolf shook, its massive shoulders quivering.

The Bloody Paws fell silent.

Aheya, cowering against the side of the wolf pit, clawed at the wall, hauling herself up.

Carlette held onto the Amonoux with everything she had, absorbing its pain, coaxing it to trust her.

Let her go, she pleaded. Let my friend go.

For a moment, everything was still.

Then Yokan broke the silence.

"Bring me a torch!"

Tuk swore. Carlette shook all over from the effort of holding the Amonoux back. All it would take was a single rebel torch, an unlucky glimmer to reveal the bright white rings in the Amonoux's eyes.

And hers.

Leaning against the cave wall for support, Carlette used the last reserve of her mental strength to slip into the black-haired girl on the ceiling. Byrna. It was a bristling mind, teeming with foreign magic.

Carlette sliced through the girl's defenses like a knife through animal fat.

Everything hurt.

She felt Tuk's shoulder against her own, keeping her upright.

With a single swift command, Carlette forced Byrna to pull out a dagger and drop it into the pit. The knife clattered against the stone. Watching through the Amonoux's eyes, Carlette saw Aheya turn toward the sound.

Carlette sent an exhausted arrow of thought into her friend.

Cut the ropes!

It had to be enough. She didn't have the strength for more. But Aheya, to her relief, lunged forward. The steel glinted in her hand.

With the wolf's multifaceted vision, Carlette could see colorful threads around Aheya, curling like tendrils of smoke.

"Stop her!" Yokan barked.

But Aheya's hands were already in motion, one pulling, the other slashing.

The tired ropes snapped open.

Carlette felt the agonizing tingle of release, the Amonoux's raw throat opening. Its collar fell away, mangled, matted, revoltingly cruel.

And she could hold on no longer.

The juvenile wolf shook her off with an ecstatic rumble, rolled its shoulders, threw its head back, and howled.

There was an instant of silent shock, louder than any scream.

Here we go, Carlette thought, half-delirious with exhaustion.

Yokan began to shout orders. Men and women ran for their steeds. Prisoners were thrown aside as a distant, eerie howl answered.

"We need to get out of here," Tuk whispered. Carlette's head lolled against his shoulder. "Carlette, stay with me!"

She couldn't form thoughts. Her mind was like pulverized meat.

How had she done that? It shouldn't have been possible, *couldn't* have been possible. She'd never trained with an Amonoux.

But she had seen them before.

Her mind flashed back to that night, Quaina's last, out in the forest. She could remember the smell of the spring leaves, the crisp scent of melting snow. They'd both heard the rumors about beasts stalking down from the mountains, hunting food after a long and desperate winter. But Carlette had been too eager, too youthful and naïve.

And Quaina never turned down an adventure.

Images flashed through Carlette's mind even as the Bloody Paw campsite erupted into chaos. She remembered Quaina's bobbing, straw-colored hair. The first intoxicating taste of the woods. Carlette had thrown her hands out, her laughter echoing against impossibly

138

large trees, cutting off when she saw the massive shapes moving in the shadows.

She'd heard a cry of surprise.

Seen the she-wolf, gaunt and fierce, looming over Quaina.

Carlette had screamed. Sprinted toward the monster. Her fingertips had brushed against thick fur, ruffled the wolf's pelt.

Don't, Carlette could remember thinking.

Had the she-wolf paused?

The memory ended there.

That's where the guards had found her, alone in the clearing with only a spatter of blood to mark Quaina's death. They had marveled at how lucky she was, wondered how a little girl could have survived an Amonoux attack.

But what if it hadn't been luck?

Carlette's head jerked upright with a clatter of manacles.

"Stay with me!" Tuk snapped, shaking her again. "We need to get out of here!"

Carlette's thoughts were like murky water. She could sense the wolf pack crashing through the Giant's Wood, an avalanche of force. They would be here in moments, led by the unforgiving she-wolf with Quaina's soul tangled up in her great mind.

The sound of a crossbow cut off the wolf's howling.

In a distant world, Aheya's scream was silenced.

"Please, Carlette, I need you," Tuk said, his face close. Carlette could smell his breath and it reminded her of fresh-baked oat cakes.

She blinked.

Bloody Paws swirled around them, preparing for battle.

Carlette took a deep breath…

And caught sight of Byrna. The tiny beetle-speaker was staring at her upside-down, head cocked. A coy, knowing smile played over her features.

Carlette felt a chill.

As three huge rebels sprinted by, wielding spears as they leapt on their mountain stags, Byrna opened her mouth, about to reveal Carlette's great secret.

Like a striking snake, Carlette smashed into the girl's head. Blinding pain shot up Carlette's spine as her exhausted body protested, but she fought through it. With every scrap of her training, she clenched a mental fist around Byrna's mind and dominated the girl's powers.

The cairog skittered over the ceiling, ignored by shouting rebels. Feelers shot out, wrapped around Tuk's torso, Carlette's waist. He thrashed against them but Carlette sat statue-still. Byrna was fighting against her hold, trying to drive Carlette out with the undisciplined defenses of a thunderstorm. But where this girl's mind was a force of nature, Carlette's was a weapon. Honed and trained.

She conquered the girl easily.

Tuk cried out as the cairog's feelers lifted them into the air. Carlette, touched his arm, her entire body screaming in agony.

"Be still," she groaned.

She would hold. For him, she would hold.

As the rest of the Bloody Paws scrambled to defend against the approaching Amonoux pack, Carlette bent Byrna to her will. The cairog skittered along the cave's roof, bearing them away.

As they passed over the pit, Carlette caught sight of her friend's body, draped over the corpse of the Amonoux like a discarded doll. A crossbow bolt stuck out from the wolf's seventh eye, feathers still quivering. Tears pricked Carlette's glowing eyes, and with a deep chill she realized she wasn't sure which life had been worse.

There must be a better way.

Passing four fingers over her forehead to salute a fallen sister, Carlette let the cairog carry them deep into the mountain, wrapped in the cover of darkness.

CHAPTER SIXTEEN

❋ SIGNALS AND STORIES ❋

Carlette held as long as she could, but Byrna's mind was decaying under her stranglehold, fighting her exhausted power like a spitting cat. It wouldn't be long before the girl's brain gave out, and, with Carlette's attention on escape, she hadn't tracked the twists and turns of the tunnel. Worse, she had the impression that, should the beetle-speaker die, the chittering black mass carrying them wouldn't hesitate to turn on them for food.

"We'll stop here," Carlette rasped. Her exhaustion was a squirming, writhing thing inside her, demanding to be felt. "I think we're safe."

"Say that to the subject of my next nightmare," Tuk said, leaning away from the insect's many skittering legs. He'd managed to grab a torch from beside the Amonoux pit and its flickering light made the mining cave seem ghostly and ethereal. Carlette could almost imagine the men and women that had toiled away in here, fighting against all odds to carve their mark on this strange new land.

Grinding her teeth, Carlette sent a jab of command through Byrna. The cairog slowed. Twisted down the wall of the cave.

Released them.

Carlette immediately collapsed, gasping. Tuk was at her side in an instant, but she waved him away.

"The girl," she panted, body vibrating. "Secure her."

Tuk stared at her for a moment, mouth open in question. With shaking fingers, Carlette pointed at the dagger hilt protruding from the girl's boot. Tuk's eyes widened, but he scrambled to obey.

Carlette watched blearily as Tuk eased the small, dense body from the cairog's shoulders, careful to stay away from the insect's clipping pincers and beady eyes. He slid the knife out with a quiet *snick*. Finally, when he had the blade pressed firmly against Byrna's neck, Carlette let go.

Twin retching sounds filled the tunnel.

For a moment, Carlette's world was nothing more than the curdling of her stomach, the pounding in her head. Even the dim light of Tuk's torch pulsing against the rock was enough make her cringe.

A harsh, guttural laugh filled the darkness, followed by the splash of more sick.

"So much for you being just some Tuleaux-bred bitch," Byrna said, wiping her mouth with the back of her hand.

Carlette's only answer was to retch again, an unproductive, painful clench of the torso. Tuk was glancing nervously at the cairog clicking back and forth in a strange dance, anxious for its master.

Byrna chuckled again.

"And I thought today would be boring."

"What's wrong?" Tuk asked as he watched Carlette continue to dry-heave, holding the knife against Byrna's spine. "What happened to you?"

"Any Moian child knows better than to reach too far," she drawled. "It seems you have less sense than a larva."

142

"Well aren't you pleasant," Carlette gasped, leaning against a boulder. The tremors wracking her body were violent, exhaustion a venom coursing through her bloodstream.

She met Tuk's eyes.

How were they going to get out of this?

They were trapped deep in the mountain with a violent rebel and her carnivorous insect, surrounded by the terrors of the Peaks, all but powerless to defend themselves. They had no guns, one knife, and a hood who could barely stand.

Carlette leaned her head back.

"Let's rest for a while," she said, staring at the amber-tinted ceiling.

"I don't think you have much of a choice, larva-girl," Byrna sneered as Tuk pushed the rebel down into a seated position. "I've seen whores at dawn with more energy than you."

"That thing's looking at me like I'm lunch," Tuk muttered, eyes fixed on the gigantic beetle looming at the edge of their tiny circle of light.

"How do we get out of the tunnels?" Carlette croaked, too drained to face the Moian warrior.

Byrna's laugh echoed around them. The hair on Carlette's neck stood up.

"With my help, that's how," she said. "And why should I help you?"

"So we don't kill you."

"Kill me and your Nuri friend will be right about Tabis. I've trained her to eat my enemies." She smirked. "Alive."

Carlette didn't think she was exaggerating.

With colossal effort, Carlette managed to lift her head and meet Byrna's fiery eyes. Black pupils, white rings, deep brown irises the color of Goddeau wood. "Perhaps you're eager to starve to death?"

"We'll die of thirst first," Byrna said with a blade-sharp grin.

"I have no intention of entombing myself under the Peaks."

"You should have thought of that before you ran like a frightened cockroach. You might have had more luck in the forest. But I doubt it."

Carlette glanced to Tuk for support, but his gaze was still fixed on the insect.

"What do you want, then?" Carlette asked, turning back. "Do you want me to go back? Turn myself in? Let Yokan kill me?"

Byrna's grin widened. Her teeth glowed in the darkness like a legion of pale ghosts.

"You don't know who you are, do you?"

"I don't know what you're talking about," Carlette snapped, even as her stomach clenched.

"Clearly." Byrna cocked her head. "Let me guess; you're the best in your class. Strongest hood in your tower, probably in all of Jemelle. Even the instructors were surprised by your ability to enhabit animals you weren't trained in. Complex beasts. Predators. *Humans*."

Carlette didn't answer. Tuk was watching them, eyes wide and flicking every so often toward the beetle.

Byrna went on.

"Haven't you ever wondered why the settlers use half-breeds for their defenses? Why they don't just steal our children and train them as their own?"

"Your power is unstable," Carlette answered. "It needs to be tempered by Delarese control."

"Words from the Convent itself, eh?" Byrna said, her tone chilling. "But not the whole story, larva-girl. It's because they're afraid of us. They know we can't be contained."

"There is no *we*," Carlette snarled.

"We're stronger than they can ever imagine."

"Stop referring to me like I'm—"

"You're a Furix."

There it was.

The words seemed so small and innocent. So simple.

But devastating.

144

Tuk's mouth fell open. His gaze flashed to hers. But she ignored him.

"I... I'm just a hood. Loyal to Grand Mera and—"

"I thought you'd already spouted enough shit for the night," Byrna sneered, jerking her head at the puddle of vomit beside Carlette. "Don't make it worse."

"What does it matter to you? Yokan was going to kill me."

"Yokan didn't know."

"And if she had?"

Byrna only grinned.

Carlette pressed her fists to her forehead as her world tilted dangerously, an unstable mass of shifting planes. It was unacceptable. She couldn't be a Furix. She had followed every law, kept to the path like a perfect cog in Delasir's war machine. She was hooded, a member of the Order, a weapon trained and honed to fight Nurkaij in any way possible. It was what she had always wanted...

But no, that wasn't right. Before the white rings had appeared in her eyes, she'd dreamed of exploration. Of setting out on the seas with Quaina.

Of learning about the Giant's Wood.

Carlette thought of her mother, of all the conflicting images accreting into a single person. A pregnant Ebonal girl who had run away from her duty. A desperate child who had appeared on Mya's doorstep, her eyes too pale to tell. A virginal offering to a descendant of Voka, a man of great power.

Why did her mother run away?

And why, of all places, had she fled to Tuleaux?

Carlette shook her head. Exhaustion pounded against her, making it difficult to think straight.

"We can't do anything more without rest," Carlette said at last, dropping her fists into her lap and leaning against the stone wall. "Tuk, can you keep watch?"

"You think I'm sleeping with that thing around?"

Byrna snickered.

145

But Carlette was already slipping away. She was exhausted, overwhelmed, and wanted more than anything to shut her brain down. She could deal with these questions another time, after rest and food. Maybe they'd make more sense in the daylight.

Maybe not.

Either way, she was in no shape to do anything about it now. So, releasing her hold on the physical world, Carlette allowed fatigue to drag her at last into that thoughtless, blissful oblivion of sleep.

When they finally left the caves, it felt like stepping out of hell.

After hours and hours of total darkness, gambling on a mining cart track in the hopes that there was a coin-toss chance of survival, struggling to keep panic at bay after Tuk's torch burnt out with a fatalistic sizzle, Carlette had wondered if death might actually be a relief. Between Byrna's snide comments and the cairog's nervous clicking, fear had become their constant companion, crawling up their skin, settling at the base of their necks like a tick.

But now, throwing an arm up against the blinding sunlight, Carlette's heart was swamped with giddy relief.

Even the Giant's Wood didn't scare her after *that*.

She leaned against the tunnel wall, gulping fresh air and waiting for her eyes to adjust.

"I never thought land could look so beautiful," Tuk said.

Suddenly, Byrna clicked her tongue. Carlette jerked around. They had tied a blindfold around the Moian girl's eyes, swaddled her hands with what was left of Carlette's jerkin. But the cairog had followed them like a trained dog, too close for comfort. Its many legs sounded like a constant tumble of stones as it skittered over the roof. Every so often, a scaly feeler would brush Carlette's shoulder in a probing, malignant question.

But at Byrna's signal, the cairog flowed over the cave's ceiling, twisted around the entrance, and skittered into gully.

"Stop!" Carlette called, reaching out a hand. She stumbled forward, her instincts humming. She couldn't let the insect escape. Somehow, Byrna had sent a message, even without her magic. She had to keep the monster from leaving.

Carlette stretched out her mind, felt for the strange, alien body. But she couldn't grasp it. It felt like trying to grab a seashell and finding only sand. The cairog was less a consciousness than a system of moving parts. Machine-like. Efficient. Cold and cruel with only a hint of the familiar. Carlette squeezed with all her might, but the cairog's mind crumbled through her mental grip and disappeared over the foothills, leaving them alone at the edge of the Giant's Wood.

"That can't be good," Tuk said at last.

Carlette rounded on Byrna. "What did you do?"

"You hoods are all the same," Byrna said with a lazy grin. "You think of the beasts you enhabit as servants to take orders. You treat them the way Tuleaux treats you."

"What," Carlette repeated, grabbing the front of Byrna's tunic, "did you do?"

Byrna just smiled at her. "I suppose we'll find out, won't we larva-girl?"

Carlette thrust Byrna away from her in disgust, glaring out at the Giant's Wood.

The only way to reach Jemelle was through those trees. Trees now teeming with potential danger.

"We've seen worse," Tuk offered.

Carlette's lips twitched. "Not much."

"Well," Tuk said. "I trust you."

Byrna let out an explosive sigh. "Could you two just fuck and get it over with? You're like virgins on promise-day."

Carlette ignored her.

"Let's go," she said, grabbing Byrna's arm and hauling her forward.

Entering the Giant's Wood, Carlette felt like her nerves were on fire. Every time a branch snapped or a bird cawed, her pulse quickened. Even Tuk was silent as they waited for Byrna's trap to spring.

Byrna, on the other hand, was no help at all.

"Would you stop that?" Carlette hissed as Byrna began to whistle.

"Why? Unlike you, I'm welcome here."

"I swear to all my ancestors…"

"You know what I can't figure out," Byrna said in a loud, carrying voice. Carlette swung around, growling as Tuk pulled them up short. His manacles clinked. Byrna's mouth was curved like a strung bow beneath her blindfold, tangled black hair floating in a paradoxical halo. "Which side you're on. You have a Nuri airman in cuffs, yet you let him keep watch. You claim the Bloody Paws are monstrous enemies, yet you keep me alive."

"I need you."

"That's a lie," Byrna purred. "I think you're not sure, larva-girl. I think you're realizing the world is as murky as a well of shit and you're not liking it."

"Shut up."

"It's always been strange to me that you hoods clutch to your understanding of things like babies with their toys. After all, why would you *want* things to stay as they are? Who would choose to be slaves, when there are other options?"

"You don't know what you're talking about."

Byrna spat. "Seems to me like you've got it backwards."

Carlette stepped up to her, getting in Byrna's face. Not that it mattered, with the other girl blindfolded, but Carlette's senses were humming, her muscles stretched to the breaking point. Something was wrong and she couldn't tell what, but it had to do with this obnoxious, self-satisfied, vulgar Moian girl.

"Be. Quiet."

Byrna showed her teeth. "Or what? You kill me?

"Yes."

"You're not the first idiot to threaten my life. And you sure as hell won't be the last." Byrna leaned back, tilting her chin in the general direction of Carlette's face. "Besides, I want to see your expression when you realize I'm right."

"You're a murderer."

"And?"

"There's nothing right about that."

"Depends on who you're killing, eh?" she paused, cocking her head as if to listen. "Anyway, if I were you, I'd take a moment to think things over. You might not have much time left to decide."

Byrna grinned.

The hairs on Carlette's neck prickled.

She took a step back as her drained mind stretched and snapped like a sail in the wind.

"Um, Carlette?"

Tuk's head was tilting up, eyes wide, hand beginning to shake.

Carlette followed his gaze to see Tabis curled around the nearest tree, pincers quivering. And, above the cairog, the thick Goddeau branches bowed beneath the weight of a dozen mounted sionach, riders glaring down at them over black bandanas.

Carlette swallowed.

Byrna's trap had sprung.

CHAPTER SEVENTEEN

❋ THE HANGING CITY ❋

Carlette stumbled, her knee cracking against the wooden slats of the swinging bridge. Vertigo threatened as she gaped down at the forest floor, impossibly far away.

"Move," growled the Moian man behind her, shoving her forward.

Sionach filled the trees, flowing past the bridge at speeds Carlette could never have imagined. Jaws snapped, claws scraped, and their whole entourage moved closer to the massive central tree sprinkled with glittering lights.

Carlette glanced back at Tuk, who was yanking his shoulder out of a thick Moian woman's grip. Their eyes met briefly before Carlette was forced to move again, trying to ignore the wild swinging of the suspended bridge.

One misstep and she would be nothing more than a smear of blood on the giant tree's root system.

Byrna guided them into the Hanging City, marching with impudent glee as Tabis scuttled along beneath the bridge, making everyone nervous. Byrna was by far the smallest of the Moian hunting party, but the men and women watched her the way they might watch a spider, eyes flickering nervously to the slingshot hanging on Byrna's belt. She was like a stranger in their midst, wilder than the rest. Carlette was reminded of how the other Jemelle students looked at her during training sessions. Respected. Admired.

But different.

They were afraid of her, Carlette realized with a jolt.

Her attention was drawn away from Byrna Beetlespeaker as the shadow of the enormous city fell over them. Lanterns hung in the branches, a million tiny lights illuminating carved wooden homes that looked so natural it was almost as if the tree had grown that way. It was like something out of Mya's bedtime fairy tales: stairs twining around the behemoth trunk, decks and bridges forming a lattice with the surrounding branches.

It would have been an overwhelming sight if she hadn't had a knife pressed to the back of her neck.

Eyes peered out at their ragged convoy as flying foxes soared past. Children dangled from branches, staring at Carlette and Tuk as if they were creatures in a menagerie. Carlette looked up, head tilting painfully to follow the endless wooden spiral.

The Moian warrior jabbed his knife, making her wince.

"Take them to the hammock cells," growled a man standing at the end of the bridge, his shoulders corded with muscle beneath cairog-scale armor.

"They will go to my father," said Byrna in a light voice, lifting one eyebrow to peer up at the man.

He glowered. "You've been gone a long time." The guard's fingers curled around his own slingshot.

Byrna only folded her arms. "And now I'm back."

He responded in Moian, the words like the sigh of wind through trees. It sounded urgent, questioning. Bordering on angry.

"I am no Tuleaux spy," Byrna said with a lazy smile, her voice loud as she spoke in accented Delarese. "I have been with the Bloody Paws, doing the work you are too cowardly to accept. But I am back with a gift for my father." Byrna leaned in as if she planned to whisper a secret to the enormous city guard. "And I suggest you get the fuck out of my way."

The guard didn't look happy about it. But, with a quick glance at the man holding Carlette, he stepped aside.

The sionach riders disappeared into the gargantuan tree. Carlette swallowed. She could sense the vast arrangement of humanity around her, a city teeming with life. It was like Tuleaux but a different flavor. Instead of resigned order she tasted wild pleasure. These people belonged here, were not displaced and rugged settlers but a part of this land, as much as the beasts they rode and the trees they lived in.

It was enough to make her head spin.

The knife jabbed into the back of her neck and Carlette gasped. Something warm and wet trickled down her spine. She withdrew her power like a broken rubber cord, closing her defenses.

"Careful," growled her captor, yanking on Carlette's white hair to hiss in her ear. "Byrna may speak for you, but put on so much as *ant* skin and I slice your neck and see you try to breathe."

"Leave her alone!" Tuk called from behind, struggling to reach her.

"It's fine," she said, letting the man propel her onward.

Byrna turned around to walk backwards along the edge of a wooden deck with no railing. The sight made Carlette queasy.

"You two are quite a curiosity," she said. "But then, with all that repressed instinct, I'd imagine you're dying for a good romp."

Byrna winked at Carlette.

"Where are you taking us?" Carlette asked as they began to climb the stairs. Tiny homes appeared like squirrel holes, filled with eyes. Women watched with folded arms, pushing the smaller children behind their legs.

Byrna cackled. "Still think you're in charge?"

"This is pointless," Carlette said, her neck throbbing. "I'll never help you. You should kill me now and get it over with."

"The men and women of this city want you dead," Byrna said, not bothering to keep her voice down as they approached a landing— a wide, triangular viewing deck attached to a boxy home hanging from one of the Goddeau tree's largest branches. "The Bloody Paws want you dead. Nurkaij wants you dead. Every man, woman, and child in Ferren wants you dead, dead, dead." Byrna stopped in front of the carved wooden door, her eyes sparkling. "It would be easier than taking a shit, killing you. And I have every reason in the world to do it. But here I am, about to save your life. You should be kissing my damn boots."

"I'll pass," Tuk muttered, yanking himself free of the woman holding him with a clank.

Byrna's eyes danced with impunity. "I've seen your kind before. All pure and straight until the clothes come off."

She grabbed her crotch in a rude gesture and then spun, laughing, to hammer three times on the carved wooden door. Carlette held her breath, trying to ignore the shell-shocked expression on Tuk's face.

Tabis clicked behind them.

For a single heartbeat, there was silence in the forest, broken by the shuffling of gigantic shapes in the canopy and the raspy breathing of the man holding her hair.

And then the door flew open.

Byrna's father was a short man, barely reaching Carlette's shoulder, but he was built like a boulder. Years of climbing trees and hunting forest spiders had made him more frightening than any war veteran. A jagged scar lifted one edge of his mouth. Another snaked up his neck where one ear was missing, leaving a crater of scar tissue. His clothing was rich and elegant, but Carlette could see beetle-black armor and a saddle hanging by the door.

"Byrna?"

The man's voice was soft, unexpected in its gentleness. Ripples of disbelief flowed from him.

"Father," Byrna said, bowing her head. "I've come back."

The man moved suddenly, quickly, his arms wrapping around his daughter and yanking her into a hug.

"Byrna."

Carlette exchanged a look with Tuk. He shrugged.

"What happened? We thought you'd been taken to the Convent. We sent a whole hunting party out after you."

Byrna's face was tight, her amusement gone. For the first time, Carlette could see what was hiding beneath the smirks and bravado: a wound that no amount of time could heal.

"I escaped," Byrna said emotionlessly.

"But it's been almost two years. Were you in Tuleaux all that time?"

Byrna's mouth quirked, but it couldn't quite be called a smile.

"Not quite."

"Here, come inside. We can talk."

"Father," Byrna said, jerking her head toward Carlette and Tuk. "I have something to discuss with you." She glanced back. "In private."

"Of course, child, anything."

The guard holding Carlette gave a disapproving sniff.

Finally, Byrna's father seemed to notice the prisoners. His eyes hardened and Carlette caught a glimpse of the man who ruled the Moians. Commanding authority radiated from him even with tears drying on his cheeks.

He gestured at the two hunters.

"Secure them inside."

· · ———————— · ❋ · ———————— · ·

Carlette caught a brief glimpse of the home before cloth was tied—again—around her face. The cabin was simple, with hints of stone in the wood. A long table dominated the main floor and a balcony ran along the top. She assumed the bedrooms were up there.

And then her sight was cut off.

Trying to breathe evenly and not wonder what Byrna was telling her father to do with them, Carlette listened to the mumbling exchange of words she couldn't understand. The guards' heavy footfalls faded. Byrna's father whispered, soft and gentle.

Questioning.

"I don't want to talk about that," Byrna snapped in Delarese, her voice sharper than Carlette had ever heard it. "I want to talk about *them*."

"We haven't heard from you in nearly two years. Your brothers have been scouring the forest, shooting down every raiding party they can find. We just want to know what happened."

"I spent time in the Convent and then escaped. That's all you need to know."

"Except that you joined the Bloody Paws."

She was silent.

"Damnit Byrna, that woman is making everything worse! Did you know she killed seven of our girls in one of her 'salvation missions'? We found their bodies, half-digested by Fethidi. She didn't bother to try and get them home."

"At least she's doing *something*," Byrna snapped back.

"We're doing something too. Trying to make peace."

Byrna snorted. "Peace. Since when do you expose your privates to an enemy's knife?"

"Delasir isn't going anywhere. If we keep fighting them, we'll only lose more of our people. The war is over."

"Not. Anymore," Byrna growled.

Footsteps paced over to Carlette. Someone grabbed her by the hair.

"I brought you the cure to our foreign infection."

The Moian chief sighed. "How is a half-breed from Jemelle supposed to—?"

155

"She's a Furix."

Silence met Byrna's statement. Carlette tried to pull her head free, but Byrna's fingers curled into unforgiving claws. Next to her, Tuk shifted with a soft clink.

"That's impossible," the chief said after a long pause. "Her heir died. He was hunted down years ago…"

"He had a child."

"I never heard about—"

"Yokan only told her most loyal soldiers, but there was another girl who was given to him. Yokan's younger sister. She escaped, but he had already planted a seed in her belly. They tracked her to Tuleaux and found her body outside the city's walls." Byrna jerked Carlette's head. "*This* is her daughter. *This* is Voka's heir."

There was another silence. Carlette struggled to breathe.

"Why didn't you bring her to Yokan?"

"She doesn't know her own strength," Byrna said, releasing her grip. Carlette leaned forward, gasping. "And she won't work with the Bloody Paws."

"Smart girl," he said in an acrid tone.

"But you could train her. Show her how to be one of us."

Carlette spit on the ground. "I'll never be one of you."

There was a rustle of clothing, a tug around her face. Suddenly, her blindfold whipped away. The man—a lethal, legendary Moian chief—was crouched in front of her, smiling kindly. Carlette was surprised to find a deep empathy in his eyes, the kind of warmth she had been starved of since leaving Mya's orphanage.

"Do you value your life, child?"

Carlette narrowed her eyes. "I will not be threatened."

"Oh, I'm not going to kill you," he chuckled. "Although apparently I can't make promises for my daughter here. I simply ask if you value your life. I know what they do to children in that place they call a school. We've all heard the stories. Whippings. Executions. Forced celibacy." He shook his head. "It doesn't seem like an existence worth having."

156

Carlette glared at the man. He sighed, closed his eyes.

"I do not hate the men and women of Tuleaux, my friend. Unlike Yokan and her rebels, I do not wish to wipe them from our land. I want only to give my people a better future, perhaps one without so much bloodshed and misery." He looked at her. "Maybe even one without war."

Carlette glanced at Tuk, who was frowning beneath his blindfold. Before she'd met him, she would have snapped something about there being no better future until Nurkaij was defeated. About her being loyal to Grand Mera and not to them.

But now?

Carlette met his gaze, her heart tearing itself apart. Grand Mera and training were the pillars of Carlette's upbringing. The anchors of her life. She remembered what Grand Mera always said when fate took a horrible twist.

We can't change the way things are.

But what if they could?

Carlette leaned forward, almost touching the man's scarred nose. "Show me," she said.

CHAPTER EIGHTEEN

※ OPPORTUNITY ※

Yokan ignored her whimpering prisoners as she waited on the hilltop, glowering. The Shadow Peaks loomed behind her, the silent gods of a burning world. Black and unforgiving, they stood by as Delasir continued to pierce into her forests, rape her lands. Adenai, the mother of life. Hyba, the rider of death. Twin peaks in the middle of a sweeping range that snaked down the middle of this island.

Her island.

Aed shifted below her, hungry. Yokan reached down to pat her huge flank.

"Soon," she said in Ebonal as Aed snapped at a nearby prisoner, making him jump.

The re-captured men and women—half of what they'd originally brought in—cringed away from her. Yokan despised them for it. These sniveling worms had tarnished her perfect world. They were a slow, steady poison that leeched into Ferren's groundwater. And still they had the gall to bleat for mercy, whine for Yokan to spare them. The Nuri soldiers had almost fallen over one another to be the first to offer what little information they had.

Cowards.

Yokan would relish feeding them to the stags.

Another wave of rage crashed through her. That Nuri airman had been the key to everything. With him, Yokan could have overthrown Caika, hijacked their weaponry, used it to burn Tuleaux to the ground. And that girl, that half-breed slut who had opened her legs to Nurkaij…

She would have been a good dinner for Aed.

Yokan growled, knuckles pale against black leather reins.

Somehow, the Nuri had managed to untie his little slave-girl's blindfold. And the bitch had been more powerful than expected. Byrna was one of her strongest recruits, a survivor of the Convent with a delicious thirst for violence. Yokan had welcomed her with open arms. Fed the flames of her rage. It was rare to find a beetle-speaker with so much power, not to mention someone with the anger to wield it.

And yet the slave-girl had stolen her.

Surprising, but not altogether unheard of. In the panic of adrenaline, even the least gifted of Yokan's tribe had been known to slip into the minds of much more powerful creatures. Perhaps the girl was more than Yokan thought she was.

Perhaps not.

Either way, they must have had help.

Because someone had enhabited her captured Amonoux.

They'd lost twenty Bloody Paws to the wolf pack. The giant she-wolf alone had consumed twelve, no doubt to feed the pup who trailed behind her, deadly even before being weaned. Yokan mourned for her fallen comrades. Their stolen souls would never find Hyba.

But if she took the time to wail about every life she had ever seen snuffed out, Yokan would be as weak as the sniveling prisoners behind her.

159

Denaya rode up to Yokan, her stag panting heavily. The woman's black braid was frayed, her dark skin scratched and dirty. One of Denaya's hands rested on the scythe at her hip, a Sibilese weapon.

"Your report?" Yokan asked.

Something red fluttered in the mountain breeze. With the instinct of a wild thing, Yokan caught the object Denaya threw at her.

It was a hood.

Yokan stared at it.

"Where did you find this?"

"In the tunnels," Denaya answered as her stag shifted restlessly. The southern warriors had never quite mastered Ebonal mounts, and a nervous, questioning distance still separated Denaya and her steed.

Yokan ran the wool of the hood through her fingers.

"Check the inner pocket," Denaya said, jerking her chin.

Frowning, Yokan fished out a slim letter, folded in half. The paper was creamy and white as snow, marked in graceful swirls of high-quality ink.

Yokan ran a finger around the seal.

It was the mark of that bitch who ran Jemelle. Yokan had seen it before, on the letters they had intercepted when raiding Durchemin.

Yokan leapt off Aed, keeping a firm hold on the letter and the red hood. Denaya watched impassively as she grabbed one of the prisoners, yanking the man forward.

He was a Collector, the slimiest of all Delasir settlers. One of Yokan's raiding parties had captured him transporting six Ebonal virgins through the mountains, destined for the Convent of Others. Yokan had taken great pleasure in giving him the open slash that ran down one side of his face.

"Read it," Yokan said, thrusting the letter at him.

"Suck my cock," he growled, spitting on Yokan's boots.

For a moment, she just smiled. This man's arrogance had been fueled by power, by the fear of frightened little girls taken from their homes. With the armed support of Delasir soldiers and a red hood and her pack of dogs, it was true that this Collector was likely a force to

160

be approached with caution. Once. But now, without all those fancy weapons and obedient slaves, this man stood in front of her as if he had nothing to be afraid of.

She grinned.

Slowly, languidly, Yokan pulled the man's bound wrists toward her. With her free hand, she drew a tiny, slender blade from her belt buckle, its bone handle decorated with flecks of obsidian. It was a strange knife, shaped like a snapped reed. Yokan had requested it specifically. Designed it herself.

Holding the man's hands tenderly in her own, Yokan tilted her head. Still he glared at her, waiting for her to ask again so he could refuse.

But polite negotiation was a thing of *his* world.

And he was in her territory now.

With a single, smooth motion, Yokan jammed the knife beneath the nail of his middle finger, all the way up to the hilt.

The man's shriek echoed through the gully. A flock of birds exploded out of a nearby Goddeau tree. Yokan twisted the knife and his scream echoed again. Behind him, one of the prisoners fell to the ground, heaving.

"Every time you refuse," Yokan said, offering him the letter again. "I will hurt another finger."

The man was still screaming, staring at his hands as if surprised they could cause him so much agony.

She smiled wider.

This pampered creature from across the sea knew nothing of pain. But it was a language she spoke fluently, one she relished teaching to others. Grabbing the knife to get his attention, she held the letter up to his face.

"What does it *say*?"

"I-It's an edict of free passage," he panted, breathless. "Signed by Grand Mera!"

"And that means…?"

161

"It means that you can go anywhere," the man said, his words tumbling out. "It allows whoever is carrying it to go in and out of Jemelle without being arrested."

"It was found in a dropped hood. What does that mean?"

When he didn't answer, she jerked the knife. The man screamed again, throwing his head back.

"Pull it out! Pull it out!"

"I imagine there are girls who say that in your Convent," Yokan growled, pressing even harder. "Do you think anyone listens to *them*?" She clucked her tongue as the man's voice began to tear.

"It was probably given to whoever wore it!" the man cried, his eyes watering. "It's a way for them to travel without an escort! Please, that's all I know!"

"So whoever wears this can enter Jemelle without questioning?"

"I think so! I don't know, just please, stop!"

Yokan yanked the knife free. Blood spurted from the man's finger as he collapsed into the snow, snot and tears streaming down his face in rivers. Yokan didn't look at him, her attention instead on the letter, the hood.

A plan was moving into place like shifting ice plates.

Was it possible that so much could be solved by such a little thing?

"Tell me, Denaya," Yokan said, stepping up to the edge of their vantage point, gazing toward the ocean where she knew Tuleaux bulged like a fat insect, "When is their holiday? That festival to honor the first settlers?"

"Two days from now," Denaya answered.

"Well then, my friend," Yokan said, her lips curving into a smile as wicked as her blade, "we have work to do."

CHAPTER NINETEEN

❄ WHAT COULD HAVE BEEN ❄

Carlette rubbed her wrists as she watched one of the Moians struggle to pick the lock on Tuk's manacles.

"Dirt," said the man, gesturing at the lock hole. "Much dirt."

"Yeah, well, we haven't exactly been strolling through the park here," Tuk muttered.

The Moian shook his head, shrugging.

"He doesn't speak Delarese," said Byrna's father, who had now introduced himself with a long, complicated Moian title that loosely translated to Roland Cloud-Death. When Carlette had asked him what the name meant, he had simply shrugged and said, "Reputations seem to make themselves, don't they?"

"How did you learn to speak it?" Carlette asked. Byrna watched them from the other side of the platform, arms crossed, smirking as Tabis's feelers played with her dirty hair.

"Missionaries," Roland said, signaling to someone in the trees. "The Church of the Hand is very generous with their lessons. For a while at least."

"It's illegal for them to be out here alone," Carlette said.

"That's illegal for you as well," said Roland with a sly smile. "And yet here you are."

Carlette bit her lip. "Are the preachers still in your city?"

A darkness passed over Roland's face.

"No," he said, his voice a deep rumble. "They are no longer welcome."

Carlette wasn't listening, though, because at that moment six huge sionaches landed on the deck, their huge claws scraping against the wood. Carlette swallowed a gasp as Tuk scrambled out of their way.

The Moian's flying foxes were marvelous to behold; three times the size of anything bred beneath Jemelle, their fur gleamed and their limbs were strong and sure. On each fox sat a warrior, knees gripping the edges of molded leather saddles. Black bandanas were tied around their mouths and from their belts hung slingshots, throwing knives, and poisoned darts.

Carlette exchanged a look with Tuk, struggling to hide how impressed she was.

The man who was supposed to be picking Tuk's lock threw his hands in the air, shaking his head at Roland.

"Well, son," said the Moian leader with a half-laugh. "It looks like you're stuck in those for the time being. We'll visit our blacksmith later, but he's on ground level. Can't have him lighting fires up in our trees, eh?"

Tuk stood, grinning up at the nearest towering sionach. "Do we get to ride those?"

Roland laughed.

"Airmen," he said, patting a flank as its rider leapt to the deck. "Always ready to leap into the skies."

Tuk shrugged, his smile sheepish, but Roland had turned away to give orders, gesturing at the six riders. Byrna strode forward, her knees bouncing.

"What's going on?" Carlette asked, gaze pointedly avoiding the bleeding paw tattoo.

Byrna's eyes glittered.

"You wanted to see what we fight for. Now stop picking your ass and get on."

· · ———————— · ❄ · ———————— · ·

The foxes moved like blowing clouds, almost silent as they leapt from branch to branch. Carlette had to swallow a cry every time the one beneath her spread its arms, coiled its muscles, and soared to the next tree. But the trip was as smooth as a dream and soon she began to relax, enjoying the wind in her face and the gentle rustle of leaves each time they landed.

Tuk shouted behind her, "This is amazing!"

She fought the urge to laugh.

Ahead of them, Byrna rode Tabis, the gigantic cairog keeping an impressive pace as it skittered through the canopy. Carlette caught glimpses of the glistening black exoskeleton through the branches, and every so often a cluster of birds would burst out, spooked by Tabis's pincers.

Roland led them deeper into the forest, riding his own sionach with an easy, majestic grace. But where were they going? What could they show Carlette that would convince her to abandon everything she'd ever known?

She wasn't sure she wanted to know the answer.

Suddenly, they were rising. Gliding into the vast canopy of a beastly tree, all knots and whorls. Carlette watched Byrna's cairog vanish into the thick foliage. And then they were plunging in behind her. Trees scraped at Carlette's face, but the borrowed bandana kept her mouth safe. The sionach launched up, into a wide opening nestled in the heart of the Goddeau tree.

Carlette leaned out to get a better view.

On a wide deck, built into the tree's open palm, was a building. It was open, airy, and hung with woven reeds and brown leathers that fluttered in the breeze. Movement caught Carlette's eye, and she realized that the platform was teeming with small bodies. Children laughing, playing, tumbling over one another. And, all around them, infant sionaches rolling between the children's legs. Carlette watched one little boy reach out and touch the nose of a striped fox, happiness radiating from both bodies.

The whole forest seemed to envelop this place, holding it like a treasure.

Carlette's rider pulled up short at a lowered area of the platform. It was an unloading area, with built-in steps to make it easy to dismount the massive beasts. Carlette stumbled off, ignoring Roland's offered hand and Byrna's knowing smirk. She knew her mouth was open, but she couldn't close it.

Tuk eyes darted between the children and Carlette's awestruck expression, but he couldn't see what she did. Couldn't *feel* what she did. Because to Carlette, who was woven into the world like thread in a tapestry, it was so much more than just children, more than young Moian warriors being trained to ride.

It was magic.

Roland stepped up to her as the instructors called out, organizing the chaos with nothing more than a smile and a touch. One cackling youngster made a run for the edge of the deck, his sionach bouncing along behind him, only to get scooped up by a laughing woman.

"What do you think?" Roland asked with a sideways glance.

"They're… happy," she said, hating the tremor in her voice.

Such a simple word.

In Jemelle, students might have bouts of happiness, moments of joy. Snowball fights, mud pits, playing tag in the main square. But these brief reprieves were broken by sneering guards, interrupted by

166

brutal training sessions. Tainted, always, by the bleak architecture of their lives.

Here, though, there was no undertow of fear or loneliness. No thrum of noxious hate. Just children, playing with their friends, cared for by people who *loved* them.

She fell to her knees.

"I imagine this feels a bit different than where you grew up," Roland said in a gentle voice, crouching next to her.

"A school's a school," Tuk said from somewhere very far off.

Carlette was drowning.

A hand came down on her shoulder.

"This is why we fight your Collectors," Roland said, gesturing to a tiny girl as she giggled, toddling toward a grinning warrior. "This is why my people hate yours. We do not seek bloodshed, only the means to stop it."

"All the settlers know is blood and death," Byrna broke in, sitting on the railing as Tabis nuzzled her elbow. "We must speak their language to be heard."

"Anyone can learn a new tongue," Roland said.

Stay the path.

Did Grand Mera know about this? About the stark contrast between Jemelle and *this*? Did she know that there was another way to live?

Suddenly, options burst in front of Carlette like lightning strikes, one right after the other. Delasir could *trade* with the natives, contract their help for the war. Imagine what could be accomplished; Delasir's technological might paired with Ferrenese magic. Finding Caika would be easy with the help of Ceillan pirates. The Wandering Pass could be secured with mountain stags. Everything could be so much *better.*

And the war itself?

If Roland had given her a new view of Moians, Tuk had done that and more for Nurkaij. He was nothing like the soldier she'd expected.

He was kind. Brave. Loyal. She knew in her soul that she couldn't hand him over, and if she wouldn't do that…

Carlette glanced at him, emotion welling.

Maybe there was another way there too.

She shook her head. These ideas were foolish, dangerously naïve. But how could she ignore them? Maybe the only way to bring about a better world was to believe, stupidly, that it was possible, to be a fool.

She shoved to her feet.

"What would you have me do?" Carlette asked unsteadily.

"I would have you join us," said Roland with a smile. "Learn our ways. And help us try to speak with the leaders of your city. Perhaps they will listen to you."

Byrna released an explosive breath.

"Father, that's pointless," she said, throwing out her hands. "You know the Magistrate won't listen to a *hood*. If we come to them whining for peace, they will fuck us to death."

"Violence will only ever create more violence," Roland said, facing his daughter.

Byrna grinned, a savage expression. "Exactly."

"Glad she's on our side," Tuk muttered under his breath. "I think."

"I serve Voka," Byrna went on.

"She's dead."

"No she's not," Byrna said, her eyes shifting to Carlette. "Not yet."

"I need to think," Carlette cut in. "Please."

Roland paused and then, at last, nodded. Turning to the six riders, he said, "Take them home. And *leave them alone*." The last order was directed right at his daughter.

Byrna leapt onto her cairog, face twisted in a scowl.

"These whelps will know war, father," she said, gesturing at the children. "They'll know that we failed them. Unless we act soon."

"Go home, Byrna," Roland said.

168

But, as Carlette mounted behind her own rider and the sionach carried them away, she allowed a private thought to bubble inside her, a thought she would never speak aloud.

What if Byrna was right?

· · ———————— · ✳ · ———————— · ·

When they landed back on the deck around Roland's cabin, two burly figures were waiting for them out front. As tall as Tuk and twice as wide, the Moian men were identical in every way except for the color of their bandana—one forest green, the other murky brown.

Byrna leapt from her cairog and hit the deck running, sprinting toward them.

"You fuckers!"

Carlette's eyes widened as the two men tackled Byrna to the ground. She disappeared under their massive bulk and for a moment Carlette wondered if they'd killed her. Then, suddenly, her head popped free and the three of them were hugging and laughing and pulling down their bandanas. All three jabbered away in cheerful Moian as Carlette dismounted.

"Is that how they greet each other here?" Tuk said, massaging his wrists. They'd been rubbed raw, the skin beneath his manacles pink and bleeding.

"Maybe they're... related?" Carlette answered, eyeing the tangle of arms and legs.

"I just hope they don't do it to one of us. They'd crush you flat."

"I'm tougher than I look."

"I know *that*," he said, rolling his eyes. "But look at those two. They could bring down any of our airships just by grabbing hold."

"I'd like to see that," Carlette said with a smile.

Tuk glanced at her, his brown cheeks pink. And she felt a change in the air. A thrilling, intoxicating, bone-deep thrum, almost imperceptible but for the way it changed everything.

Dangerous.

Carlette shifted her body away from Tuk.

"I'm sure airships are amazing to behold," she said in a stiff voice.

"The most beautiful things in the world," Tuk said, rubbing his neck with a rueful expression. "Damn, I miss flying."

Carlette wanted to ask more, to learn about Tuk's past and how he could possibly *enjoy* being so high in the air, but they were interrupted by Byrna shoving toward them.

"These two mammoths," Byrna said, punching one on the arm, "Are my brothers. And they'll be guarding the house."

"Thank you," Carlette said.

"For what? You try to escape and they'll rip your guts out," Byrna said with a grin, as if relishing the idea. "With their hands."

"I thought you were loyal to Voka," Carlette said.

"I'm loyal, not stupid," Byrna said. "Now get inside. I'm bored of you, and when I get bored, I tend to kill things."

Tuk snorted.

"I pity the man who catches your eye," Tuk said as the two hulking men led them inside.

"Oh, don't worry." Byrna waggled her fingers. "I don't like Nuri. Sand in the bloodstream, ruins the taste."

And with an echoing cackle that made Carlette's hair stand on end, Byrna shut the door and locked them inside.

Carlette found a shaped bit of wood protruding from the wall and sank onto it, rubbing her face.

"Well… damn," Tuk said, plopping down at the table and resting his heavy manacles on the wood.

Carlette exhaled.

"Yeah."

"What do you think? Gonna sign up and be their little mascot?"

Tears beaded at the corner of her eyes. "I don't know what to think. I don't understand any of this."

170

She scrubbed her cheeks. Took a breath. For the past eight years, she had concealed everything; her fear, her solitude, her anger. But something about sitting in this warm, wooden home had undone all her defenses.

Tuk leaned forward, eyes bright and sympathetic, and Carlette struggled to inhale.

"I'm sorry," he said, low and sincere. "I'm confused too. When you grow up being told that everyone on this island is an evil witch, you expect horns and tails. But you're... well, you're certainly not an evil witch."

Yet another thing that didn't make sense, this enemy who didn't feel like an enemy. Carlette's gut knotted. She couldn't bear for him to say that, not after so much.

Not after Quaina.

"No, Tuk," she said to her hands. "I don't deserve your sympathy."

"Come now, that's not how this goes. I'm supposed to be calling you a monster, and you're supposed to say something about me being Nuri scum and we both get all angry and righteous. You're ruining the game."

Carlette coughed a laugh, but tears continued to bubble from her eyes, staining her face with fresh weakness.

"Why do you think you don't deserve my sympathy?" Tuk asked, the lightness gone.

Carlette's gaze roved over the Moian home, her fingers running along the wood. It was so strange to be back in the Giant's Wood this way. So wrong. She shouldn't feel comfortable here, didn't *deserve* to feel at home.

"When I was eight years old," she started, her voice a whisper, "I snuck out of Tuleaux. There was a shipment coming in from the forest. They were opening the ground fences, just for an hour. Guards were everywhere, but my friend and I... well, we were experts at breaking the rules."

Tuk was silent and Carlette silently thanked him for it.

"I had always been… *drawn* to the forest. I just wanted to see it. To smell it. I had dreamed of going into the Giant's Wood for so long that I stopped believing it was dangerous. When the rangers told stories of spiders and insects and foxes, I listened in wonder, not fear. And my friend… Quaina… she wanted to help."

Carlette swallowed and stared at the tips of her boots. Blood had smeared over one toe and she wondered who it belonged to. So much had happened in the past few days, it was impossible to know.

"It was spring. The winter had been hard. That's what the shipment was—food scavenged from the forest. The city was desperate. Quaina and I were so skinny… we slipped right between the soldiers and they didn't even see us. Everyone was scanning the woods, watching for the wolves. We'd heard them howling in the night. Just as desperate as we were."

Carlette sighed and clenched her fists. The burden of this story, this horrible memory, was a rock around her heart.

"Quaina and I didn't think, we just sprinted into the trees. I remember laughing. We were so proud. The trees are smaller by the ocean—thinner soil—but they were the largest things we'd ever seen. Quaina tried to climb one and fell. She twisted her ankle. But still we laughed."

Tuk was motionless. Carlette was beginning to shake.

"The Amonoux pack showed up without warning. One minute we were alone in the shadows and the next... They were like ghosts. Quaina told me to run. She always told me to run, was always protecting me, keeping me safe when we got into trouble. It was our way."

Carlette turned her blurry gaze to the ceiling.

"So I did. I thought she was behind me, but when I turned back, she had fallen. Her ankle, I think, or a root. I'll never know. The largest wolf was on top of her, about to bite down." Carlette took a deep breath. "Something happened. I didn't understand it at the time. But I reached out and…" Carlette clenched her fists. "She died anyway."

Finally, terrified of what she might find, Carlette lifted her head and met Tuk's eyes.

"It was just the beginning. I started to lose control, enhabiting other orphans and guards. Mya, the orphanage matron... she got desperate. If anyone found out that she'd taken an unregistered child, she would lose her funding. Maybe even her life. So she brought me to Jemelle and left me there..."

Carlette fell silent, not really sure what she was trying to say anymore. She felt like a bucket that someone had emptied and abandoned.

"It wasn't your fault," Tuk said. "Things happen. Wolves eat. You couldn't have stopped them."

Carlette shook her head.

"It was my fault we were outside Tuleaux's walls. And my power drew the wolves, I'm sure of it now. I left her, Tuk. Ran away when she needed me most, when I was the reason she was there in the first place." Carlette's eyes snapped up. "I deserve everything that school has done to me."

Tuk pushed to his feet and came to her. Before she knew what to make of it, he was next to her, gripping her hand.

"Carlette, you can't blame yourself for everything. You were born this way because your mother was Ebonal. You wanted to go into the forest because you were a curious child. And your friend died because it was a hard winter and the Amonoux were hungry."

Carlette felt Tuk's words burrow into her, worming greedily into her soul. Oh, how she wanted to believe him. She'd gone over that moment in her head so many times that sometimes it felt like it was still happening, that she was still grabbing hold of the wolf's leg and reeling at the catastrophic storm inside her brain. She'd never told anyone the whole story before. Even Grand Mera, who heard Mya's version and hadn't spoken of it since. And so Carlette had lived it, held it, carried it around.

But aloud, something about the memory changed.

"You do deserve happiness, Carlette. We all do."

173

"Tuk…"

What she was going to say was lost as Tuk leaned in.

Frantic, panicked thoughts flashed across Carlette's brain. They could both be killed for this! If anyone found out, Carlette would be executed. Tuk would face worse than torture. Grand Mera's pinched face bloomed in Carlette's mind, disapproving, disappointed.

Carlette jerked her head back, hitting the Goddeau wood with a thump.

Tuk's eyes widened, almost in surprise.

But before either of them could figure out what to do, a horn reverberated the air, accompanied by the distant sound of screams.

174

CHAPTER TWENTY

❋ NURKAIJ STRIKES ❋

The door burst open and Byrna rushed in, followed by her brothers.

"What's going on?" Carlette demanded as she and Tuk leapt to their feet. She tried to ignore the way Byrna's eyes flashed to her still-damp cheeks, the curve of Tuk's arms that hinted where they had just been.

But Byrna's snide smile didn't come.

Something was very wrong.

"Nuri soldiers," Byrna said, grabbing Carlette's arm. Carlette yanked herself free.

"I'll follow," Carlette said, voice biting.

Suddenly, Byrna's nose was inches from her own.

"You caused this," the Moian girl snarled, breath smelling of copper and fury. "I don't know how, but I swear to the Fethidi demons, I will find out."

"What are you talking about?" Carlette said.

But Byrna wasn't listening. She was already shoving outside, the door swinging in her wake. Carlette glanced at Tuk before they hurried out after her.

The forest outside was unrecognizable. Thick, viscous smoke wafted toward them on a wind of shrieks. A distant crash echoed. Panic and shock braided together in a toxic haze, filling the emptiness that had been serene less than an hour ago.

"What happened?" Tuk whispered.

Byrna was loading her slingshot, Tabis shifting nervously at the edge of the deck.

"I should ask *you*," she growled without looking up. "A Nuri fleet is bearing down on this city. Three outlying villages have already burned and they're pushing toward the capital." Byrna's eyes flashed up. "Why do you think that is?"

Tuk paled, the rosy flush on his cheeks vanishing.

"I didn't do anything," he said, lifting chained hands, shaking his head. "What could I have possibly done?"

"No one could have followed us," Carlette added, trying to keep her voice reasonable. "I don't even know where we are."

Byrna snarled and grabbed the front of Tuk's jacket.

"Hey!" Carlette said, trying to get between them, but Byrna had the iron strength of a climber, the unbreakable grip of a girl raised in the trees.

"If I ever find out you had *anything* to do with this, the spiders will be the only ones who find your body."

Tuk didn't balk. He leaned into Byrna's face, his nose less than an inch from hers.

"I didn't. Do. Anything."

Byrna threw him away. Tuk stumbled but Carlette grabbed his arm, keeping him upright.

"Are you okay?" she whispered, but was interrupted by the thundering footsteps of Byrna's father sprinting toward them.

"They've taken the northern guard tower," he panted. He already had a bloody gash on one cheek.

"What do they want?" Carlette asked.

"What the Nuri always want," he said, voice strangely calm among the whorls of chaos. "To burn witches."

Tuk tugged on Carlette's elbow. Pulled her ear close.

"I know what's happening," he hissed. "They brought over our new ships from Vaijan, the city's latest invention. Zanburs, Commander Invitas called them. They must have located the Hanging City just in time to test them out."

"Tuk," Carlette said with a swallow as Byrna helped her father strap on his armor. "Did they follow us here?"

"I didn't do anything," Tuk said. "I swear."

Carlette wanted to say more but she was interrupted by Byrna throwing her a bandana.

"Your hair might as well be a beacon," Byrna snapped. "Cover it up."

"Where are we going?"

"*We* are going to fight," Byrna said. "*You* are going to climb down the tree and escape on your own. With any luck you won't get crushed under a flaming airship."

"We can help," Tuk broke in, shouldering past Carlette. "We can fight."

"You?" She snorted. "I doubt it."

"I'm no more loyal to Caika than Carlette is to Jemelle," he said.

Carlette's gut twisted.

Byrna opened her mouth, but Roland put a hand on her shoulder. "Let them."

Byrna pursed her lips. Folded her arms. And then, with a whip-quick movement, she threw a dagger at Carlette. Carlette snatched it out of the air before it punctured her leg.

Byrna smirked. "Maybe you aren't useless after all."

Roland stepped away from them, into the gathering circle of warriors. His low voice rolled like thunder. Carlette couldn't understand the Moian words, but their grave effect was clear.

She knew what this kind of invasion meant.

If Nurkaij had found the city, the Moians would have to move. It would mean the end of this beautiful place. Their only hope was to escape, to flee deeper into the forest.

Carlette's heart pounded. She clutched the dagger, pathetically useless against Nuri airships. Tuk shifted next to her, hands chained, even more defenseless. And besides, he was no warrior. He was a mechanic, trained to keep his head in battle and ensure that his ship stayed in the air.

Stayed in the air...

An idea struck Carlette.

"Tuk," she whispered as Roland addressed his men, clapping them on the shoulder one by one. "If we could get you onboard one of those ships, could you sink it?"

Tuk's expression was blank for a moment. *Sink it*? he mouthed.

And then his eyes grew wide.

"Of course," he said in a babble. "It's a lot easier to crash them than it is to fly them. But there will be too many for us to do much..."

Tuk's eyes grew distant. He stared at the treetops, at the surrounding soldiers.

"The resupply ship," he said at last.

"What?"

"The resupply ship!" Tuk exploded. Roland's voice trailed off as everyone turned to look at them. "The little ships in the forest are like bees. Their number and speed will make them hard to defeat, but they can't reach Caika on their own." Tuk was shifting his weight, almost bouncing. "If we damage the resupply ship, protocol will force the others to abandon their mission to save it. It would give your people plenty of time to escape."

Byrna's eyes narrowed.

"And how can we be sure this isn't some cowardly Nuri trick?"

178

Tuk shrugged. "I suppose you can't."

"It's your only chance," Carlette cut in, trying to infuse her words with strength.

Another distant crash ricocheted off the Goddeau trunks. Screams rolled toward them, a crashing wave of panic. Roland's expression was cold and grim, but he smiled, and for the first time since meeting the kind-faced man, Carlette could see Byrna's resemblance.

"Very well, young man. What do we do?"

Carlette perched on a branch, one hand on the tree's thick bark, the other on Tuk's shoulder, waiting for the signal. Fear pounded in her belly as she went through the endless myriad of things that could go wrong.

They could fall to their deaths.

Carlette's power could fail.

The Nuri fighter in the Zanbur could react too quickly.

But somehow, despite all her misgivings, this fight felt... clean. Unlike the greasy uncertainty she'd had transporting Tuk or listening to prisoners scream in Erebus's shed, this was the war she craved: an unsoiled fight against an enemy that was slaughtering innocents. Carlette had long ago accepted that she was little more than a blade to be wielded, but for the first time she felt happy to be swung.

How strange that it was a Moian chief holding the hilt.

Tuk shifted beside her. The men in the trees waited patiently, but Carlette could sense their burbling anger. Shrieks and cracks filled the air, growing closer. Who knew how many had already fallen to their deaths or perished under gunfire.

"There," hissed Tuk.

Below them, a tiny airship zipped around the edge of one tree, coming into view. Two men and a woman sat in a basket hanging below the long, thin balloon. One was in the back, his arm churning as he pumped the engine. The woman in the middle fed fuel to the contained inferno that kept the ship in the air. In front was the gunman, one hand on a mounted rifle, the other on a flamethrower, delivering death with both.

Carlette reached out with her mind, brushing against the gunman. She flinched. Tuk glanced at her.

"It's hard when the mind is… unpalatable."

"No surprise," Tuk muttered, narrowing his eyes. "That sack of dung was the worst in the corps."

But Carlette was already gathering her power. Two more Zanburs appeared behind the first, flying toward them in a bird-like formation.

She had to act quickly.

Like a spider reaching along its web, Carlette unfurled her power in wispy tendrils. She could feel the minds of foxes and Moian warriors nestled in the trees, the rodents on the forest floor scampering away, the birds frantically escaping the spreading smell of death.

Drifting down to the ship, Carlette let her mind circle around the three men.

It had to be simultaneous.

She had to be strong.

"Ready?" Carlette whispered.

"Yes," said Tuk. His voice cracked.

They leaned out.

Carlette's magic snapped around the soldiers' minds, silencing their protests, freezing their bodies. She felt the exertion, but it was just like climbing the stairs of Durchemin—at once exhausting and enthralling.

"Go!" Carlette said as she focused on the pilot.

The Zanbur shifted to the side, closer to their tree. Tuk took a deep breath.

"If I die, don't let Byrna do anything horrible to my body," Tuk said.

And then he jumped.

180

Carlette held her breath as Tuk's body arced, nothing but open air between him and the forest floor. He was graceful, fearless, fierce, a Nuri mechanic in his truest form, a creature of the sky. Tuk's fingers reached out, brushing along the top of the balloon. He grabbed hold of a railing that ran along its edge. A rope stretched, dug into the balloon, and suddenly Tuk was swinging along the ship, shimmying quick as a squirrel into the basket. He grabbed a mooring line and threw it to Carlette.

She swallowed. Looked down.

And leapt out to grab it.

Fear clawed her chest as her fingers clawed the air. The rope was nothing, tiny, an almost-invisible thing in the vastness of the forest, but she managed to grab hold. It pulled taut. She swung beneath the ship, biting down a scream as the healing skin of her palms rubbed raw.

Into the fire... she thought frantically, taking deep breaths.

As she began to climb, a war cry rose around them.

The signal had been given.

Carlette yanked herself up the rope, trying to ignore how far away the ground was, how much her hands hurt. Her body swung as darts and stones rained down. But the Moians aim was as good as legend.

A sionach soared past, its rider blowing a dart.

Clinging to the line beneath the airship, Carlette felt the Nuri soldiers die. She had been trained to brush off the nauseating, gut-jerk feeling of a life being snuffed out. A life she was holding. But it was never comfortable, and, as Carlette dangled over nothing, she had to remind herself to hold on. To breathe evenly. Her stomach heaved.

A body fell past her.

Carlette swallowed again, harder this time. She was almost there.

The second body tumbled to the forest floor as she grabbed the edge of the Zanbur. Strong fingers wrapped around her forearm. With a breathless pull, Tuk yanked her into the basket. She rolled onto the wooden slats and relished the simple rise and fall of her chest. Her life. Tuk grinned at her, but Carlette couldn't relish their victory as the feeble struggling of the Nuri woman's mind beat against her mental grip like butterfly wings.

She shoved to her feet.

The final soldier in the Zanbur was taller than Carlette, more rounded. Carlette could feel the strength of her mind beneath blind terror and pain. This woman was filled with the intoxicating passions that Carlette had never known; a love of food, a taste for men. Carlette took an instant liking to her, despite the snake-spear emblem on her vest.

Thump.

Blood spurted onto the deck. Carlette stumbled to one side and vomited over the edge of the airship, reeling from the sudden, shocking absence.

When she turned around, she saw a rock-sized indentation in the woman's forehead.

"Get going!" Byrna shouted, reloading her slingshot and diving into the melee behind them on Tabis.

Carlette wiped her mouth. She watched the chief's savage daughter disappear into the battle. Nuri soldiers screamed as Tabis bore down on them, a creature of their worst nightmares.

"C'mon," Tuk said, his tan skin pale. "We'd better hurry."

With shaking hands, Carlette began to undress the Nuri woman, wondering how much death she would endure before this was over.

CHAPTER TWENTY-ONE

✳ THE RESUPPLY SHIP ✳

The trees seemed to reach for them, intent on knotting the wires of the basket and scraping along the balloon. Carlette watched one sharp branch leave a long mark along their side, threads fraying in its wake.

"Untangle the forestay," Tuk shouted from the back of the ship.

"The what?"

"That rope in the front!"

Carlette had to scramble to stop a thick Goddeau branch from ripping the rigging to shreds. Leaning out over the edge of the basket to thrust leaves and twigs aside, she felt a rush of vertigo.

The ground was so far away it may as well not have existed.

"Carlette, I need you to feed the fire!"

She hurried to the middle. Her fingers fumbled as she carefully turned the knob on the fuel line. The flame leapt into the balloon in a spurt of fire.

"Careful!" Tuk shouted as the ship bounced upwards.

Carlette bit her lip, turning the knob back.

"This is more complicated than enhabiting," Carlette grumbled.

Tuk grinned. "Flying is a delicate art."

Something exploded behind them. Carlette couldn't see what it was through the dense foliage.

"This is unnatural," she said.

Tuk's laugh rang out, echoing off the thinning leaves.

"For you, maybe," he said as Carlette pressed her back against the inner wall of the basket, fingers clenched around the knees of her strange new uniform. She was grateful for the Nuri woman's size—it had allowed her to keep her own Jemelle clothing on underneath, giving her the comforting impression of being well-padded.

Not that it would help if she fell.

"And for you?" Carlette asked to distract herself.

Branches scraped against the underside of the ship. Tuk stared ahead, his gaze razor-sharp as he guided them toward open sky.

"I was born to it," he said, although his tone made Carlette think there was more to the story. Tuk flashed her a sad smile. "Perhaps it was destiny."

"I don't believe in destiny."

"You don't believe in much, do you?"

Tuk asked the question lightly, laced with sarcasm. But Carlette frowned, pressed herself harder against the basket's edge.

What did she believe in?

Suddenly, they burst through the canopy. Blue sky filled her vision, broken only by the massive, black shape hanging in the sky like a bloated moon.

The resupply ship.

It was giant, a nesting bird of prey perched on nothing as it waited for its children to return. The balloon could have been something out of a native legend, painted black with the golden sun-spear of Nurkaij on its side. The emblem had three snakes twisted around a triangular symbol, representing the Tribunal of Nuri deities: past, present, and

184

future. Carlette watched as more Zanburs floated from the gaping maw of the resupply ship like demons being born.

Is this what the King's Axe fought when they marched into battle? Is this what the Ceillan pirates hunted in their sky chariots? Carlette found herself marveling at the world she lived in, all the strange and fantastical things that existed beyond the ludicrously small circle of her own experience.

She glanced back. Tuk was frowning at the ship with a strange set to his eyebrows, resolve etched in the slash of his mouth. Carlette shimmied over to him.

"I do believe in some things," she said in a soft voice. "I believe in doing what's right."

Tuk's lips twitched. "That's not always a straight path to follow."

"No," she whispered, turning back to the ship, "I suppose it isn't."

Carlette remained silent as they floated toward the resupply ship. Zanburs drifted in and out, the returning vessels leaking smoke like blood. Gunmen perched on the edge swung from side to side, defending their mothership.

On the prow stood a man, his braided black hair pebbled with gray.

"Who's that?" Carlette whispered, keeping her hands on the fuel gage and checking to make sure her bandana hadn't shifted. She might be wearing the right uniform, but her skin and hair were more than enough to label her an intruder.

"Commander Invitas," Tuk hissed back, careful to keep his manacles hidden. "He's the leader of Caika. He almost never oversees missions…"

Shrieks and explosions echoed up as they drifted into the shadow of the resupply ship.

Carlette frowned. "I suppose he wanted to see the genocide of a people for himself."

Tuk winced but Carlette didn't have any interest in softening her statement. In this man, she could see everything her people hated about Nurkaij. Cold, calculating, expression unmoved by the screams of dying Moians, this man had seen death, had *caused* it, and felt proud.

This was the kind of creature who enjoyed war.

Tuk guided them into the enormous hangar and Commander Invitas disappeared from view. Carlette ducked low, face hidden as her eyes adjusted to the shadows.

It felt like being inside a whale. Wooden boning and ropes made up the ship's interior, the ribs of a living machine. Men and women scurried in the rigging, hauling wounded Stormriders out of their Zanburs, tossing around boxes of fresh ammunition, plugging in fuel lines. Carlette gaped at the iron tools, the polished guns, the *order*.

She was forced to admit, if just to herself, it was impressive.

But she had to be careful. To these soldiers, Carlette was a witch. An abomination. The Nurkaij emperor had offered a price for her head, for the head of anyone with the slightest bit of magic.

Any Nuri soldier would be glad to put a bullet in her brain.

Two workers swung overhead like monkeys, shouting something at Tuk. Carlette dropped to the ground, rolling beneath the engine. Tuk said something in rapid Nuri that Carlette couldn't even hope to understand. The two workers were out of her line of vision, but even so she sensed their trained efficiency, their controlled frenzy. They didn't let Tuk finish before one snapped out a brief, clear order.

Carlette felt them leave.

"What did you say?" she whispered when they were alone again.

"I said we fell under attack and I was the last survivor, barely managed to save the ship. They sent me to a docking bay. Stay low, we're passing under the viewing deck."

The engine was hot, this close to her face. She felt flushed and humid, overdressed. A part of her longed for the simplicity of her cowl and cape, her shield. Who knew what had happened to it, and with Grand Mera's letter inside? It was probably deep in the tunnels, draped over cold obsidian where it might remain forgotten until the end of time.

Something nagged at the corner of her thoughts, the feeling that she was missing something.

But a rumbling bump knocked her out of her thoughts.

She peered out to find Tuk grabbing onto a mooring line, speaking to the nearest soldier in rapid Nuri. Carlette could imagine what he was saying. *Leave me, I can handle the ship. Go and help the others.*

It was exactly the kind of selflessness people love in chaos.

"Ok," Tuk hissed. "They're gone."

Carlette shoved out from beneath the engine and followed Tuk as he leapt into the rigging and began to climb. Sparing a single glance down, where the floor of the hangar was open to the burning forest, smoke curling toward them like cairog feelers, she shuddered.

What kind of warrior is afraid of heights? she thought in disgust as she tangled her hands into the rope, swallowed the pain, and pulled.

Tuk led her up, toward a long, narrow chamber that traced the spine of the hangar. As they approached, Carlette reached out to touch the minds inside, stealing their senses in brief flickers so that no one would notice the telltale white eyes or the mental weight of her control.

The room was huge, dominated by a gigantic flame that filled the ship's balloon. Bodies milled around thick, snaking fuel lines. Kegs of oil lined the walls. Shouts rose and fell in harsh volleys, unintelligible to Carlette.

"What are we going to do?" she asked when Tuk paused.

He glanced around.

"It should be... there!"

He pointed at a thick tube that ran up the side of the ship.

"That's the main line that goes to the smaller ships. It comes from this room, but if breeched it could light the whole bay on fire."

187

"*What?*"

Tuk pointed into the fuel room, where flames hissed and spit.

"It isn't a perfect system. Some of the fuel ends up in the air. In a small ship, it's not such a problem, but for the amount going into that fire..."

"You're going to light the *air* on fire?"

Tuk grinned.

"But... those men..." Carlette murmured.

"We'll get them out. I don't feel like becoming a murderer and a traitor in the same day."

Carlette frowned. "This seems dangerous."

"We will have to get out of here fast."

"How fast?"

Tuk dropped his gaze to hers. "Really fast."

Carlette gulped, unable to respond.

"Can you enhabit all those men?" Tuk asked. "Get them to jump out?"

She twisted, looking at the shapes in the fuel room, backlit by the enormous bonfire.

"I'd need to get closer," she said.

He nodded. "Follow me."

Moving as gracefully as a sionach through the Goddeau trees, Tuk swung from rope to rope. When he caught the one closest to the fuel chamber, he began to pull himself up, Carlette scrambling along behind him. Together, they curled their fingers over the harsh, wooden edge of the deck, Carlette cringing as her hands oozed and bled. She forced herself to hold on.

"They're talking about the attack," Tuk hissed at her as he listened to the jabbering voices. "Apparently, the Commander was worried about an intel breach. They accelerated their plans."

"They must mean you," Carlette said.

But Tuk's eyes widened as he continued to listen. Carlette saw something strange in them—Pity? Fear? Horror?

"Carlette," he said, voice low. "They're talking about Jemelle. It sounds like an informant told them that Yokan is marching on it, and this time she has a way inside."

Carlette's heart fell into her stomach.

Like a spear of light breaking through the clouds, she realized what she'd been missing all along.

"The edict of safe passage..." Carlette said. "My hood!"

"SHHH!"

But it was too late. Faces appeared above them. A shout rang out.

"Carlette, stop them!"

A bell tolled, deafeningly close. Carlette shoved her terror aside, compelled herself to *concentrate*. It took everything she had, but she managed to quiet her mind enough to enhabit every Nuri soldier in the fuel room...

And make them jump out.

The entire airship shifted with the sudden redistribution of weight as engineers leapt from the chamber, grabbing at the hanging ropes. One man slipped, fell, silent and white-eyed as he tumbled out of Carlette's reach and into the enormous Goddeau trees.

She felt him die.

Carlette lifted her head, flushed with guilt and exhaustion. But Tuk had already dragged himself to the top of the hangar.

"I need your knife!" he called.

Soldiers and technicians were flying toward them as if they had wings. Carlette threw herself upwards, stretched out her hand, offered Tuk the blade.

He slashed through the fuel line with a single, vicious swipe. The air filled with an unsettling hiss. Someone grabbed Carlette's ankle and she kicked out, looking down to face the oncoming Nuri soldiers. The closest ones saw her hair, her skin, her tattoo. Eyes widened in recognition.

She couldn't let them see Tuk. If they realized who had betrayed them, he would lose everything...

"I need a spark!" Tuk shouted.

As she enhabited the soldiers around Tuk with sweeping, uncalculated strokes, Carlette used one foot to flick a gun out of its holster. She caught it in midair. Threw it over the deck's edge to Tuk.

"Brace yourself!" he cried out.

And fired.

Flame bloomed around them, superheated and ferocious.

Tuk was blown backwards.

He fell in an arc, eyes half-closed.

"No!"

Carlette released her rope and dove after him. But he was moving away, too fast, too uncontrolled. The Goddeau Trees below them seemed to reach up, eager to accept another bloody offering.

Carlette grabbed Tuk's arm. With her other hand, she snatched at a rope. Screamed as it ripped open her palms. She grabbed another rope, hooked her leg around one of the ship's ribs. Her body pulled taut, slammed into the side of the hangar. She heard the crackle of snapping wood. Filled with panic, unable to do more than hold on for dear life, she clutched Tuk's wrist and gritted her teeth against the ache of her leg around the beam.

It bowed out, lowering them inch by inch, before giving way entirely.

Carlette released a breathless scream.

And then it was knocked out of her.

The flat protrusion of a loading bay had caught their falling bodies. Abruptly, painfully, they came to a halt, crumpling into a tangled heap of limbs. Carlette groaned and rolled over. Her mind was an island of pain in a sea of noise. Tuk's breathing was shallow, his hair smoking. His aviator cap had been blown away. But, thank the elders, they'd stopped.

They were alive.

Color swirled around her, smudged and smoky. Alarms rang, reverberating in Carlette's addled mind. One bell rose above the others, a deep gong that could only mean one thing.

Retreat.

Tuk stirred. With a whimper, Carlette rolled upright to face him. She waited for someone to shout at them, for soldiers to slide down and take revenge on the arsonists.

But they were just two shapes, lost in a fresh and frantic chaos.

"I can't believe that actually worked," Tuk said, coughing. His face was streaked with oil and soot, but his eyes glittered like jewels.

Carlette opened her mouth to respond, but she was interrupted by a hum of noise. Black shapes rose from the forest, returning to their mother's call. Leaving the Moians to escape.

"Now what?" Carlette said, barely managing to stay upright.

"Now we get off this flaming wreck," he said with a snort, "And I return the favor."

"What?"

He looked at her, eyes unnervingly sincere.

"It's time to save Jemelle."

CHAPTER TWENTY-TWO

❋ A LONG WAY TO TRAVEL ❋

It took every bit of Carlette's discipline to accept the folded bit of cloth that Tuk had called a 'parachute' and trust it with her life. To her it was madness, a strange new kind of magic that she didn't understand. But Tuk's nimble courage convinced Carlette to strap on the harness, clip herself to Tuk's belt, close her eyes, and tumble out into thin air with him, screaming. She'd thought she could hold it in, but the ground rushing up, the cruel branches yanking at slender threads and thin fabric, was more terrifying than she could handle. They were tumbling, buffeted, unwelcome.

After what felt like an eternity of falling, they hit a thick branch.

Tuk grunted.

Something ripped.

Suddenly, Carlette was alone, the cords of the parachute wrapping around her limbs like a spider web. She flailed, hit another branch, knocked into the trunk.

And stopped.

Tangled in the branches of a massive Goddeau tree, surrounded by the carnage of the Nuri attack, back in dangerous territory, Carlette relished the wonderful sensation of being still, even dangling this high in the air. For a long moment she just hung there, breathing.

And then she realized she was completely and thoroughly stuck.

"Shit," she muttered, tugging on the knotted cords, swinging wildly.

Her mind began to fill with unhelpful thoughts. Would she be eaten by crows? Dragged away by cairogs? Would the spiders find her? Would the Moian warriors come back for survivors?

To her relief, Tuk appeared, walking along the narrow branch she hung from as if it was solid ground.

He crouched over her head.

"I didn't know you could scream like that."

"It was a long fall," Carlette grumbled.

Tuk only laughed.

Now, having made the endless, harrowing climb down the Goddeau tree with only a knife, the leftover parachute, and her gauntlet of spines to help them, that laughter felt very far away.

The forest floor was a bloodbath.

Bodies littered the ground, viscera splattered on the fallen leaves, unable to stay whole after such a plummet from the sky. Carved wood, still smoking, had broken off from the cities above and exploded into splinters. The sloping shapes of crashed Zanburs could be made out in the haze of the smoldering forest, as still as sleeping beasts.

Carlette was silent as Tuk descended the last stretch of the tree, his arms shaking. She curled her own arms around her torso, mind stretching out, trying to find life.

All she could taste was emptiness.

"This is not right," she whispered, her eyes falling on the broken body of a dark-haired child.

"It's war," Tuk said, his voice hoarse as he folded the parachute.

Carlette touched a burn on the nearest tree. "It always sounded so exciting in the stories. But this… there's nothing exciting about this."

Tuk kicked a nearby root, causing a hound-sized rat to scurry away. Carlette could feel the creature's hunger, the ecstasy of so much *food*.

It made her stomach roil.

"You haven't seen enough of war," he said in a bitter voice.

"And you have?"

Tuk flinched.

"Tuk," Carlette said, unable to stop herself. She had to know, *had* to understand, or else she'd always wonder if the airman she'd risked her life for was just another one of *them*. She turned to him with tears in her eyes. "Why did you join the army?"

Tuk rubbed a hand over his black hair. Carlette wondered if he missed his aviator cap as much as she missed her hood. Without their symbols they were just a girl and a boy, just two people standing in the burning skeleton of a place that had once been alive.

It made her understand why people loved their chains.

"I didn't have a choice," Tuk said at last. He started to walk. Carlette followed, the distant shadow of the mountains their guide. "I was born in Vaijan. My father was a trader with an established route through Kamora. With six ships to our family name and more than enough work, I pretty much grew up in the air." A nostalgic smile tugged at the corner of Tuk's mouth as he helped Carlette over a root. "He always used to say I was part eagle. Said I belonged on his airships, and that one day I would fly across the whole nation with him."

Carlette was silent, giving him space to continue. She had a feeling his story wouldn't end well. Not much in their world did.

He sighed, staring up at the sky.

"One day, he left with half his ships for a secret mission in the middle of the Continent. It was for the Emperor himself, or so my mother liked to claim. You see, my father had risen in Vaijan society enough for his family to live in the Ziggurat, an incredible honor. To tell the truth, I missed our life on the docks. Ziggurat life was too stiff and formal for my tastes. But my mother… she drank it in. When my father left, she waved him goodbye with a gold-trimmed scarf." He chuckled. "And he never changed out of his jacket."

Tuk's head dropped. He glared at the trees around them.

"That mission, the one for the emperor… my father never returned. He disappeared halfway through Kamora, shot down by the mountain folk. No one knows exactly what happened, but all three ships burned. They found no survivors."

"I'm sorry," Carlette whispered. Her fingers twitched, itching to reach for Tuk, to comfort him. But she held herself back. Such instincts should not be encouraged.

Tuk gave a weak laugh.

"Not as sorry as my mother was. Without a proper business, she had to bribe the Ziggurat to let us stay. She was addicted to high-story life, obsessed with family honor. To her, the worth of our name was tied to our ability to stay where we were, to not 'slide backwards' as she put it. I was only eleven when she sent me out to start working for the ship mechanics, using the skills my father taught me. I didn't mind, really. It helped me forget what had happened. But every night I got home to more parties, more finery, more lies."

Tuk sighed. Ruffled his hair again with that clink of manacles that had almost become familiar.

"My darling mother ran through our savings in less than six months. Soon she was borrowing, wheedling money out of our friends and family. In her effort to preserve our name, she ended up destroying it better than my father's death ever could. Soon, no one would deal with us. We were on the brink of ruin."

Tuk flashed Carlette a sad smile.

"I think, in some way, she had begun to hate me. I was a burden, you see. A reminder. A boy with his head in the clouds."

Carlette waited, holding her breath.

"She sold me to a recruiter. The war with Delasir had become desperate and our army was paying good money for healthy youths.

195

It was brilliant, aye? Nurkaij got soldiers to defend our homeland and the money paid out kept that homeland alive. Part of the Emperor's master plan. So when my mother caught wind of it..."

There was a moment of silence so bitter Carlette could almost taste it.

"I remember her haggling for me. Sitting next to Commander Invitas, she looked like a tropical bird. All colorful silks and shimmering jewels. She could have paid our rent by selling the lavish furniture and costumes... but then how could she throw her parties?"

"That's horrible," Carlette whispered.

"She got what she wanted," Tuk said ruefully. "Commander Invitas agreed that she could stay in the Ziggurat if I joined the air corps. There was a special job the Emperor needed fresh engineers for, one that would send me far away. She would probably never see me again, maybe never learn what happened to me. My mother told Commander Invitas to make sure she was properly compensated for her loss."

Carlette could see tears beading in the corner of Tuk's eyes, jewel-bright, more beautiful than any finery. But he scrubbed them away, his expression wry.

"No use getting sentimental about it now, aye?" he said, almost to himself. "Besides, I found a kind of family with Invitas. He's a tough commander, very demanding. But fair. And he never asks anything of you that he wouldn't do himself. It was an honor to serve under him."

"*Was* an honor?" Carlette said softly.

The forest around them stood silent, watching. Tuk flashed her a weak smile.

"Are *you* planning to go back and follow orders again like nothing's changed?"

Carlette hesitated. "I don't know."

"I've been told my whole life that hoods are wicked monsters and the native people of Ferren are aberrations of nature and that all of it should be destroyed. But the first time I find myself alone on this

196

island, I am saved by a hood, treated like a visiting guest by a Moian tribe that *my people* attacked, and witness a true act of savagery that came from above the forest, not below. I don't know about you, Carlette, but I'm starting to feel like a bit of an idiot."

She wrapped her arms around her belly again, around the stolen Nuri uniform. Was she still a hood, loyal to Grand Mera? Would she go back to Jemelle and be property of the King once more? And if not, then what? Who would she fight for?

"I do know one thing," Carlette said to the ground. "I have to save them. The other students. Maybe I won't stay, maybe I will, but I'm not going to let my mistake be the death of all those children. If the worst happens, the guards won't bother to help them." She looked up. "So I have to."

Tuk nodded. He was silent for a long moment.

"And me?" he asked at last.

"You're free to do what you want."

"The ice queen melts."

Carlette rolled her eyes. "Did you really think, after all you've done, that I would hand you over to be tortured?" She snorted. "And I thought mechanics were supposed to be smart."

Tuk grabbed Carlette's arm, forcing her to stop.

"I'm smart enough to understand what will happen if you go back without me. They'll kill you."

"Only if they catch me."

"I can't let you go in alone."

"And I can't let you come. You'll slow me down, especially with those." She jerked her head at the manacles. "I'm only going to warn Grand Mera. I trust her. She'll listen to me."

"And then what? She'll let you run free?"

Fear clawed at Carlette's belly, but fear was easy. Fear was normal.

She straightened.

"Yes," she said.

They both knew it was a lie.

197

Tuk seemed to be gathering, emotions swirling around him in a storm. When he finally spoke, it was halting and whisper-quiet, as if the very trees might spy on them.

"Carlette, come with me. I can find us an airship. We can run away from all this. Go to Raebus territory, maybe even the Sibilese deserts. There must be a way."

An image bloomed in Carlette's mind: the two of them walking through the lush green Raebus hillocks. Digging out an underground home. Starting a garden. She would have laughed, if her throat hadn't clogged up so badly. The idea of her, a trained killer, a living blade, being *domestic*? It was like trying to imagine an Amonoux as a house-pet.

She placed a hand on Tuk's. "If I abandon them, it makes me no better than the Bloody Paws."

"Then when we reach Jemelle…"

Carlette knew what he was asking.

Was it goodbye?

She knew what she *should* say. What Grand Mera would have her say. Cut ties, rip off the bandage, be done with it.

But instead, she dropped her eyes.

"I don't know," she said, and it felt like the new mantra of her life.

I don't know. I don't know. I don't know.

CHAPTER TWENTY-THREE

❊ GOODBYES ❊

They were perched on the mountainside, camouflaged by the long shadows of craggy peaks. As Carlette peered out at the gates of Jemelle, conflicting emotions cut through her like an ice storm. Hatred. Affection. Loss. Longing. She didn't know who these feelings were directed at, or even really what they meant.

But, staring down at the tiny forms of children moving off one of the training platforms, Carlette knew she had done the right thing coming back.

"It's uglier than I imagined," Tuk said, crouching next to her as guards marched along the high walls, the wood stained red by oxidized Goddeau toxin.

Carlette exhaled a laugh. "It's designed for function, not comfort."

"Sure looks like it," he said in a dubious tone. "And you grew up there?"

"I spent eight years of my life there," Carlette said, careful to make the distinction.

She had *grown up* in Tuleaux, with Mya and the sailors and the wild orphans. With Quaina's laughter and the baker's burnt oatcakes and the comforting hush-hush of ocean waves. Jemelle may have stolen half her life, commanded her loyalty, shaped her into the killing object she had become.

But she would never think of it as home.

"What are you going to do?"

Carlette pointed at the back gate, where ragged traders and Collectors returned from the Wandering Pass. Jemelle was their first stop on the return to civilization, the first link in Delasir's iron necklace.

"The front entrance is heavily guarded, but caravans come in and out the back all the time. I'll find one with a cart and sneak under it. The hounds will recognize my scent. I should be able to get in without trouble."

"I don't see any hounds."

"They keep them out of sight so they can't be enhabited all at once. It's the only way to protect ourselves from attacking rebels."

Carlette's gaze roved over the school, skimming the tiered spires. Oeil Tower of the Sky. Tierre Tower of the ground. Requin of the sea. Chevin of the steed. Scara of the beetle.

And tallest, most prominent of all was Carlette's home, painted bright red.

Cerise Tower of blood.

Tuk's hand touched her elbow. "Carlette, tell me true, if they catch you what will happen?"

She didn't turn to face him. She couldn't, not knowing what she would see. Liquid empathy, a concern that was both comforting and terrifying.

And below that, the kind of heat the Tuleaux guards would cheerfully kill her for.

200

"They will put me on trial as a deserter. If I'm lucky, I'll be pardoned and assigned to a ship or caravan, kept in chains until I have earned their trust back."

"Has anyone ever earned trust back?"

Carlette glared at Jemelle. "Not to my knowledge."

"And if you're not lucky?"

"I'll be hung from the wall as a warning to others."

"Carlette—"

"I can't abandon them," she snapped, whirling on Tuk, her voice harsher than intended. "I can't," she said again, softer.

"I understand. But let me help you. Let me *do* something."

Carlette swallowed hard.

"Go back to Caika," she said at last. "Help me stop this. Maybe if you talk to someone, get them to see reason... I don't know how, but there must be a way to make peace."

Tuk looked doubtful, but he nodded. "How will I find you?"

Carlette grinned, a brazen, cocky expression that hid everything else.

"You seem to have forgotten, Tuk. I'm a witch. I'll find you."

Tuk grinned back. "You better."

They clasped hands, comrades in arms, partners against a world that would see them both die and not even blink. For an instant, Carlette believed what she'd said. She believed in a future with no war, no enemies. Peace between Nurkaij and Delasir. Perhaps even the hoods could be free, their tattoos nothing more than a memory of a different time.

It was a childish dream, but Carlette clutched it to her chest like an ember. Her old life was done. She'd committed treason a thousand times over. All she had left was this one burning hope that perhaps her life could mean something. Achieve something.

She drew back, hating the moment their hands parted. But she would be damned before she saw Tuk executed for her mistakes.

"Please be careful," Carlette said.

Tuk snorted.

201

"I'm not the one breaking into a guarded fortress."

"Still," she said, "these mountains are patrolled. And I can't imagine your next escort will be as kind as I've been."

"Despite your horrendous first impression."

"Doesn't seem to bother you now."

"No," said Tuk, blushing. "No it doesn't."

· · ———————— · ❋ · ———————— · ·

Carlette discarded the stolen Nuri uniform. If anyone saw her with it, she couldn't even hope for a trial; any soldier would shoot her on sight. So instead she shivered in the frigid autumn air, crouching by the road, waiting for the telltale clatter of wagon wheels. Winter's bite was growing stronger and Carlette had to clench her jaw to keep her teeth from chattering.

A caravan had to be coming soon. The sun was sinking behind the mountains, casting streaks of gold and red into the sky like streamers. These last few hours of the day were always the busiest at the gates, with travelers making their final push into the safe belly of Jemelle before nightfall.

She just had to be patient.

When Carlette had first taken her hood and become a member of the Order, she'd been put on rotation with the patrol guards to learn the lay of the land. And the experience had appalled her. Snow snakes and infant auroks weren't the problem—after all, she'd always had a kinship with dangerous things. No, it was the Delarese traders who'd filled her with dread. Leering creatures that stank of treachery and mold, their very presence felt like a toxin. A taint that Carlette's newly awakened power couldn't ignore. And seeing them with the girls, with their *shipments,* had been the most chilling thing of all. Moian, Ebonal, Raebus, sometimes a Sibilese or the odd Ceillan. Once even a Faclan teenager with a bone piercing through her nose and blue tattoos almost completely obscuring the skin of her shaved head. The captured Ferrenese natives had varied in age, in height, in weight, in ferocity.

But all of them reeked of fear.

The other young hoods shrugged it off. When Carlette asked, they would say that the Convent wasn't that bad. They'd been well-fed and allowed to play together. The children, at least, were led above ground once a day to experience the light and chaos of the real world.

But once they entered the Convent of Others, the women would never see sunlight again.

The thought, even now, gave Carlette chills.

How had she missed this sickness, this *wrongness*? Was it because she'd escaped the worst of it? Or because she'd wanted approval? It seemed impossible now, wearing a Moian bandana and reeking of airship smoke, to believe what she used to accept so blindly. There was no honor here. The Delasir people built this place, this school, to suit themselves. They didn't care how much unhappiness it brought. Tuleaux was a machine, created to feed the war, to spin the wheel. And nothing would change.

Until someone stood up to change it.

She swallowed, forced herself to pay attention.

All she could do tonight was save the children. The young hoods still trapped in Jemelle were innocents. They wouldn't be for long, of course, but maybe she could change the paradigm before they were pushed into a life they did not deserve.

The noise of an approaching caravan reverberated around the corner. It was too far away for common settlers to hear, but Carlette's senses zeroed in. Over a dozen humans, six hounds, four auroks, and *there*. A cart. Heavy with something—women or pelts or food—but perfect for what she needed.

Crouching lower and trying to control her shivers, Carlette settled in to wait.

· · ——————— · ※ · ——————— · ·

Tuk was staying put until darkness fell, when he'd make his next move. While the worst of the Ferrenese predators were nocturnal, at least the hunters Jemelle sent out would have retreated behind the safety of its walls. So he sat, leaning against the mountainside, watching the goings on inside Carlette's old stronghold. It was an austere place, almost boring, so different from the assaulting noise and color of Vaijan. To him, it seemed cold enough to be a part of the mountains.

A group of younger students trained in the main square, whacking one another with sticks. Tuk chuckled, remembering his first day as a soldier. They'd put a gun in his hand, pointed him down the rifle range. He'd turned, looking for orders, and accidentally pointed the weapon at the cadet next to him.

The slap Commander Invitas had given him left him sore for days.

A small group of people were moving through an opening, led by a figure in a red hood. Tuk found himself wondering if that person knew Carlette. Had they shared a room or teacher?

He smiled wryly to himself. Look how far he'd come, from an angry young recruit forced into service to wondering about the enemy. Caring for a hood.

Falling in love with a witch.

He shook himself. There was no point. Carlette had gone off to do her duty and, in all likelihood, he'd never see her again. The thought made his chest constrict. *How foolish.* But he couldn't help picturing her white-blonde hair, her icepick eyes, the way her mouth quirked when he said something amusing. Carlette was a study of opposites. Light and dark. Beauty and danger. Control and instinct.

Tuk watched the main gates, wondering if he should look for her. But he knew that was a pointless exercise. She'd be well-hidden. After all, this was her game.

But something caught his eye.

Tuk leaned out.

There! Movement by the gate. A guard fell to his knees in front of the open doors, convulsing. The man next to him surged forward, hand stretched out. And then fell, struck down as if by magic.

The guards above them marched on without so much as glancing down.

Tuk squinted.

Having felt the effect of it himself, Tuk knew what an enhabited man looked like. Stiff. Unwilling. Movements jerky and sharp.

The fence guards were enhabited.

And the two at the gate had just been murdered.

Shapes emerged from beneath the bridge leading into Jemelle. Tuk bit down on his fist to stop a gasp from escaping. The small group of figures might be dressed in stolen hoods, but Tuk would recognize their leader anywhere. It was that Bloody Paw woman, the tall rebel with the sleek black braid who had pushed Carlette's friend into the Amonoux pit.

They were attacking.

But no, that wasn't right. They couldn't have enhabited all the guards on the wall. Someone would have sounded the alarm, seen the white rings and stopped them. This was a rear-guard, coming in after something had *already* happened.

Tuk remembered the red hood who had run through the main square. Too tall, too broad to be a child...

Yokan.

Tuk swallowed.

Carlette was too late. Jemelle had already fallen.

CHAPTER TWENTY-FOUR

❋ RETURN TO JEMELLE ❋

Carlette hung under the wagon, her agonized fingers gripping the rumbling axle. The cart, mercifully, had been packed full of aurok pelts. They smelled awful but, as Carlette dangled inches over the cobblestones, she knew anything was better than sneaking in under a wagon full of captives.

The caravan paused at the gates for the briefest of moments. Carlette heard fence guards wave the traders through, voices bored and strangely stiff. She didn't care. So long as the caravan went deep enough into the fortress for her to roll out and find cover, she would make it to Grand Mera's obsidian hut.

She snorted to herself as they trundled through the main gates.

If only Grand Mera could see me now.

Carlette counted buildings by the shadows they threw on the cart. Her hands screamed, inflamed and throbbing against the solid wood.

Leather boots stepped into puddles, splashing her face. But she held steady, waiting.

There.

Carlette shimmied herself to the edge of the wagon. With a flicker of thought, she enhabited the aurok pulling her. The beast tossed its massive head, reared back, making the traders shout. Voices rose. Footsteps thundered to the front of the caravan.

And, unseen in the sudden commotion, a quick-moving figure with ice-white hair slipped out from beneath the stacks of pelts.

Carlette dissolved into the shadows beside the one pub that Grand Mera allowed in Jemelle, called Steppingstone. She paused, taking a deep breath, but the hairs on her neck prickled without warning.

Something was wrong.

The tavern was quiet, the air in the streets still and heavy. Besides the shouting traders and the rumbling aurok, Jemelle was almost silent. Carlette could sense people all around her, but the flavors were different. More primal, somehow, as if caught in a storm. Was there a new visitor or officer causing this strange tension?

She shook her head, dispelling the thoughts.

It didn't matter what was going on in Jemelle. All Carlette needed to think about was reaching Grand Mera without being seen. Even now, Yokan could be on her way, mobilizing an attack. If one rebel got inside, opened the gates, the Bloody Paws would flood through the school and murder every student inside.

She couldn't let that happen.

With the graceful practice of someone who had grown up on the streets, Carlette crept from shadow to shadow, sneaking around doors and lights as she wound her way through Jemelle's austere buildings. Every time she saw a patrol she turned, doubled back, took another route.

But her instincts continued to whine.

She climbed onto the roof of a barracks, peering toward the inner wall that kept the young hoods separate from visitors. Shapes moved along the edge, more guards.

At least some things didn't change.

Carlette pursed her lips, watching two hoods sprint down a narrow side-street and duck through Jemelle's entrance. Heading to their dorms, perhaps? Or delivering a message?

But why were they alone?

Only one way to find out.

Carlette crawled down the side of the barracks and crept up to the wall. It was far too dangerous to go through the front doors—who knew where more guards could be hiding—so Carlette snapped her fingers forward, made sure her remaining spines were straight.

And began to climb.

Even as a child, Carlette had never exactly enjoyed heights. Where Quaina would scamper along rooftops and dance around the rims of lighthouses, Carlette would edge carefully along, making some excuse to keep both feet on the ground when she could. Carlette could face dog packs or climb into aurok pens. But when it came to this kind of thing, Carlette was a reluctant pupil.

Thinking of Aheya, of Tuk, she dug the spines of her gauntlet into the wood and began to lift herself up. Her feet scrabbled against solid wood, slipping on the snow-dampened wall. There were no holds, but the wood was thick and her spines were strong. Arm by arm, with jerking lifts, Carlette dragged herself up.

Her breath clouded like a hood made of mist.

Fear pounded in her belly, in her ears.

At any moment, a guard could look over the edge and sound an alarm. Carlette was helpless, exposed. A street patrol had only to glance up and see the dark shape moving to know she was there. How ironic that they might shoot her down when Yokan was about to waltz in with no more resistance than the Collectors.

Carlette panted. Gripped the edge of the fence.

And, straining, pulled herself over.

This was the tricky part, getting off the ramparts without being seen. With swift, silent feet she ghosted along the wall. It took precious seconds to find a ladder and a more to scurry down it. When her boots splashed down on the school's main street, she felt a surge of satisfaction. A heady feeling of invincibility swept through her, that pure and simple joy of breaking the rules.

Quaina would be proud.

Wiping her hands on her pants and wincing at the cuts and tender skin, she ducked into the stables. Looked out.

At least Erebus's workshop was quiet tonight, Carlette thought with a shudder. She wasn't sure she could handle the screams, not when Tuk had come so close to being dragged inside.

When she was sure no guards were hiding by the doors, Carlette padded her way inside. Her steps were lithe, dancing, avoiding puddles and loose stones with cat-like leaps. In the black clothes she usually wore under her cape, she may as well have been part of the scenery, melting into the darkness as if it had claimed her.

Maybe it had.

Twisting through the buildings, listening to the distant whuffle of hounds, she felt a strange sense of detachment. This entire place could collapse, fall down the mountains in a rockslide, and Carlette would only mourn the lives lost in the fall.

How strange.

She'd reached the main square. Crouching in the shadow of a pillar, she realized that only a few days ago Erebus had come to her here, stroking her cheek, his decaying breath too close for comfort. It seemed like a lifetime had gone by since then.

Firelight sputtered in Grand Mera's windows, alluring, comforting. She'd know what to do, how to deal with Yokan. She alone would understand, would hear Carlette's full side. Without the watchful eye of the guards or the looming danger of the Magistrate finding out, Grand Mera would let Carlette speak.

Reckless and intoxicated by the freedom of moving alone at night, Carlette ducked through the columns that surrounded the green. Snow glimmered. Candles flickered in tower windows. There was dread all around, a concentrated sense of fear. But that was normal, wasn't it? Jemelle was a hive of frightened children, raw iron ore being beaten into swords.

She had always felt unease in this place.

Hadn't she?

Carlette reached Grand Mera's window. She glanced inside to find her mentor, her commander at her desk, stock-still and rigid.

Just like always.

With the gentle fingers of a thief, Carlette slid the window open. Leapt in.

"Grand Mera, it's me, don't sound the—"

But Carlette's voice trailed off. Her skin crawled. The old woman was staring at her, face in shadow, eerily dark.

"Grand Mera?" Carlette whispered.

"It's good of you to come back," she answered, voice raspy and strained.

"What's going on?"

"I've been waiting for you, ever since my lookouts told me you'd entered the city."

Carlette froze, hand still on the window-frame. She should run, right now. She might still escape.

But loyalty to the leader of Jemelle kept her rooted.

"I wasn't aware anyone saw me."

"Oh, you wouldn't have noticed them. They're very good at staying *low*."

It sounded like an inside joke, something she should understand. But she didn't. Carlette faced her mentor, wishing she could see those familiar, hawk-sharp eyes.

"Grand Mera, there's something I need to tell you—"

"I already know, dear."

Carlette frowned. Never, in all their years together, had Grand Mera called her *dear*.

"Jemelle's in danger—"

"Jemelle has *always* been in danger. It *is* a danger, of the most disgusting kind. You must have known Hyba would claim it one day."

210

Carlette's breathing stopped. "You're not Grand Mera."

The old woman's torso leaned forward, allowing the fire to illuminate her eyes.

A ring of white glowed around the pupils.

Carlette leapt on the window ledge, ready to dive back out into the night, but hands shot out of the shadows. Strong arms dragged her back. Someone was chuckling, the sound echoing from two mouths.

And then one stopped.

Grand Mera collapsed on the desk, face-first.

Carlette snarled, lashed out with her magic. But they had covered her hands, bound them behind her back with rough efficiency. A blindfold yanked her head to one side, pulling out hair. She tried to scream but someone shoved a wad of fabric between her teeth, almost choking her.

"Well done, child," came that other voice, the voice that had been Grand Mera's twin.

Yokan.

"I must admit, I didn't expect to see you again. Byrna tells me you escaped the Moians in short order, but who thought you'd actually *return*. What a well-trained little dog you are."

Anger and fear zinged through Carlette as she pieced together what had happened. *They're very good at staying low.* It was Byrna. *Byrna* had watched her through the eyes of the insects that lived in Jemelle, eating their trash, nesting on their animals.

Byrna had betrayed her.

Carlette growled, tried to yank herself free, but a clawed hand grabbed her by the chin. Forced her face up.

"You're a conniving little whelp, I'll give you that. Under different circumstances, you might be useful. But I'm afraid all things must end. You see, girl, I have a *plan*." Yokan's face was close, her breath putrid. "And you do seem to enjoy disrupting them."

Carlette tried to pull loose, spit out the gag. If she were free, she could lash out, wrap Yokan in a web of power and slowly squeeze the life out of her. A part of her wondered if she'd even enjoy it.

But Carlette was the prisoner. She was at their mercy.

And they were going to kill her.

She heard the sing of a blade being drawn.

Her heart thundered.

Had Byrna not told them who she was? That Carlette was the very person Yokan was hunting? Perhaps the beetle-speaker had decided that a new Furix would be too much trouble. Or something else had happened. If her family had been hurt in the battle…

A knife pressed against Carlette's convulsing throat.

"I wish you were more… *flexible*. But my experience has proven that hoods can rarely be re-trained for our purposes. May Hyba greet you with open arms and grant forgiveness for your existence."

Carlette tried to scream. Tried to roll her body away. It was no use. In that last moment, knowing the knife was about to bite down, she sent a wild prayer to whatever god was listening that Tuk would survive the wilderness of the Shadow Peaks.

Crash.

The window shattered. Summoned like a demon, Tuk's voice shouted something from outside. The knife lifted. Carlette blinked beneath the blindfold, wondering if she was imagining things.

And then the cabin exploded.

CHAPTER TWENTY-FIVE

✳ INTO DARKNESS ✳

Chaos bloomed. Flames licked at Carlette's sides. She wanted to scream, but the gag filled her mouth. She'd fallen, been dropped right in the middle of the melee, and could do nothing to defend herself. There was the thud of metal against flesh and a woman cried out. Tuk grunted. Manacles clanked. Yokan's voice rose in a scream, shrill and panicked.

"Forget him! Don't let her burn!"

Strong hands gripped Carlette's shoulders. She smelled singed hair. She struggled, threw her body against this new force.

"Stop wiggling, aye? It's me!"

Someone was sawing through the ropes around her hands. They broke. Carlette yanked out the gag, pushed up the blindfold.

And Tuk was there, holding out a hand to pull her up.

"Are you okay?" he asked.

Carlette could only gape at the pandemonium growing around them. Somehow, Tuk had managed to send a wave of fire over Grand Mera's desk. Now flames were licking up the walls, swallowing the mattress and sheets, curling the papers. Burning her hair. Yokan and her rebels were furiously swatting a crown of fire on Grand Mera's iron-gray head. Carlette took a shaky step forward, torn between her desire to save Grand Mera and her instinct to flee.

Yokan's head snapped up, white-blue eyes immediately finding Carlette's. She barked an order in Ebonal, a single word. Two Bloody Paws turned on them, weapons drawn.

"Umm, this was the end of my plan," Tuk said.

"Follow me!"

Carlette grabbed Tuk's chain and they burst through the front door into the square. The snow was thick but Carlette's terror drove her forward. They sprinted across the unbroken white, leaving smoking footprints in their wake. Power slammed into her mind like battering rams. Two rebels, chasing them. With a flicker of thought, she sent both to their knees, vomiting into the snow.

Faces appeared in the windows of the towers around them. Carlette wondered how many of the young hoods had guessed that something was wrong. But if Yokan had the guards under her thumb, if her Bloody Paws had already managed to take over…

Something brushed her mind and Carlette thrust the worries away. *Survival first.* Tuk stumbled. His chain pulled free just as Carlette felt a shift in the air.

She turned to grab him, tell him to hurry.

But before she could speak, the young mechanic launched himself at her.

Tuk tackled her into the snow. His fists were already swinging as she rolled away, clawing at the cobblestones beneath the powder. She could see the glow of his eyes, white rims terrifyingly stark against his normal dark brown. Carlette drew her knee in to kick him off. He hardly reacted as her foot collided with his belly, launching him. She rolled over, made to crawl away, but metal collided with the side of her head. Tuk's manacles, whipped sideways with ruthless force. Her eyes crossed. She collapsed, blinking as the world doubled, as the towers seemed to swim in an ocean of stars.

Tuk's fingers curled around her throat, squeezing hard.

Somewhere nearby, Yokan's laugh rose over the square.

"You thought you could escape *me*, little girl? I who fight in Voka's name?"

Let's see about that.

With a savage surge of power, Carlette drove into Yokan's mind, forced her open. The woman shrieked. Even as Tuk's fingers tightened around her windpipe, Carlette plunged into her enemy's head, recklessly fast.

Her eyes burned.

Her body ached.

It took a few precious moments to find what she was looking for. And then, with a slicing thought, she severed all of Yokan's connections.

Including the one to Grand Mera.

Tuk blinked. His eyes focused and he frowned, drawing his hands away.

"What—?"

"Later," Carlette wheezed, scrambling to her feet and dragging Tuk with her.

There was no way they would make it to the fences. They needed a place to hide, *now*. Carlette thought briefly of Cerise tower, but that was no good, not with a Nuri in tow and bloodthirsty Ebonal warriors on their trail.

An idea struck her.

With a swell of adrenaline, she yanked Tuk through the last of the snow and threw them both into an alleyway. They sprinted through the narrow avenue between the Scara and Requin towers. Her heart thudded in her ears like a war drum. If anyone followed them, if so much as an *ant* witnessed their flight…

When the trapdoor came into view, she dropped to her knees to slide toward it. With one hand, she flipped the wood over. The other jabbed down.

"Climb!"

Thankfully, Tuk didn't hesitate. Glancing over his shoulder, he dropped his legs into the hole and all but fell into the tunnels. Carlette jumped in after him, pulling the hatch closed over her head. The hounds were stirring, whining in pleasure at the surprise visit. She could sense a few of them inhaling, ready to bay with excitement. With a soft mental swoop, she pushed them back into sleep.

"We need to go deeper," Carlette said, trying to keep her ragged panting quiet.

"What's down there?"

"The larger animals. They used to bring them in through the mining tunnels before they collapsed the entries."

"Collapsed the entries?"

"It's our only chance," Carlette said, unable to keep the desperation out of her voice.

They both knew escaping into the tunnels would only prolong the inevitable. In the labyrinth network of mines beneath their feet, they would either starve or be hunted down.

Carlette met Tuk's eyes, not knowing what to say.

"Look at the pampered princess," came a voice from above them, "so lost without the protection of her tower."

Carlette's stomach clenched. Her head jerked up.

Byrna hung above her, knees gripping Tabis's black spine, face covered. Coal-black hair fanned around her face, framing glowing white-rimmed eyes.

Tuk shoved Carlette behind him, but Tabis's feelers were already stretching toward them. Hopelessness filled her chest. Twice this girl had tricked them. Twice Byrna had beaten her.

They wouldn't get lucky enough to escape again.

But, to Carlette's surprise, Byrna released her knees and fell, twisting in the air like a panther. She landed lightly, knees absorbing the impact, and pulled her mask down.

In the dim light, it took Carlette a moment to realize she was grinning.

"Not sure if I want to work with a Furix who hides behind her man," Byrna said with a smirk, folding her arms. "I might die of shame."

For a moment, Carlette only gaped. And then Byrna reached into her belt, pulling out something shimmering and metallic.

She offered it out on one palm, cocking her head.

"No more excuses, larva-girl," Byrna said with a wink. "I'd hate to think those chains are holding back your first romp in the hay."

On Byrna's hand, catching the torchlight like a precious jewel, was the tiny, glittering key to Tuk's manacles.

CHAPTER TWENTY-SIX

❋ ENEMY OF MY ENEMY ❋

Deep in the belly of the mountain, Carlette was in total darkness. Byrna's cairog clicked somewhere nearby and every time she heard the rocks shifting beneath its massive legs alarm rushed up her spine. Tuk's silent discomfort twined with her own, at gross odds with Byrna's amusement. To the beetle-speaker, traversing the utter blackness beneath Jemelle was as easy as walking. But for the rest of them it was like trying to stagger through the underworld.

When they paused at last to catch their breaths, Tabis keeping watch and Tuk struggling with the dirty keyholes of his manacles, Carlette was the first to break the stillness.

"Why did you save us?"

"I'm a creature of impulses," Byrna answered from somewhere to Carlette's right. "Do I need a reason?"

"If we're going to trust you, yes."

"Isn't it enough for me to serve the Furix?"

"Like you served Yokan?"

"She's not a Furix."

"And I'm not a fool." Carlette folded her arms even though no one could see it. "I want to know why you would turn against the Bloody Paws. You had no reason to."

Byrna was silent for a moment and Carlette risked a tendril-stretch of power. Conflict swirled in her, and something deeper. Almost like... guilt.

"I've done many things," Byrna said at last. Her voice was different now, serious for the first time since Carlette had met her. "I've killed men and women and left countless more to die. It never bothered me before."

Carlette was silent. Tuk shifted beside her, the grating of metal on metal fading as he paused in his efforts. They could both feel the weight of Byrna's words, the unnerving sincerity. They were at the beetle-speaker's mercy, and yet Carlette felt like this obstinate, violent, reckless Moian girl was pleading for *their* acceptance, asking *their* forgiveness.

"However," Byrna went on. "I've never, *ever* killed a child."

"Byrna," Carlette said after a moment. "What is Yokan planning to do?"

The girl was quiet for so long that Carlette wondered if she'd changed her mind about helping them. When she did speak, her voice was grave.

"She's going to bait the Amonoux pack into Tuleaux. During the festival. The she-wolf has a pup right now and Yokan has already sent a hunting party out to capture it, alive. In the chaos, they're going to kill the Magistrate."

"How will they get through the fences?"

Byrna shifted but didn't answer. The cairog made a clacking sound.

Suddenly, jarringly, everything slotted into place.

Carlette's blood went cold.

"They're going to use the students," she whispered.

219

That was why Yokan hadn't killed the guards. That was why she was keeping the young trainees alive. That was why she had jumped to defend Grand Mera before the fire could claim her best ticket into Tuleaux. Between Grand Mera's presence and the festival, no one would look too closely when the entire school of Jemelle came for Gaulday. The prince was there, the Woodsman visiting, and the Pirate Queen was in chains. There was much to celebrate. Plenty of reasons for Grand Mera to bring the entire Order on a visit to the harbor city.

Yokan wasn't going to sneak into Tuleaux.

She was going to march through the damned gates!

"She'll kill everyone," Carlette said, voice hollow. "If they put the Amonoux pup in the harbor…"

The series of events rolled out in Carlette's mind as if they'd already happened: an infant wolf howling for its mother from a fishing boat, the tangy scent of its blood carrying over the open water; the Amonoux pack crashing right through the center of town, down the Rae du Ora, into the docks. They would rip through everything, tear apart anyone in their way.

And who would be in their way?

Jemelle's students. Mya's orphans. Sailors and vendors and merchants and whores.

Everyone.

"By the elders," Carlette whispered, pressing the heel of her hand against her forehead.

"That's barbaric," Tuk said, his voice a grimace of disgust.

"And your people's attack on my city?" Byrna snapped. "The Nuri's attempt to wipe out an entire Moian tribe in one move? What was that, *mercy*?"

Tuk didn't answer.

"Yokan is no more or less barbaric than *anyone* on this island," Byrna said, her ferocity back in full force. "She was made by *your* war and she won't stop until it's over."

"And you?" Carlette cut in. "What's your intent?"

Carlette could almost feel Byrna's smile, the steel-edge blade of it.

"My *intent*," Byrna purred, "is to kill as many settlers as I can before they get me."

"What if I don't want that?" Carlette said, dropping her hand. "Tell me, Byrna, what if serving the Furix means putting aside your vendetta? What if I want to make something better?"

"There is nothing better," growled Byrna.

"My father used to tell a story," Tuk broke in, thoughtful and calm. "About two brothers."

"Yes, because everything can be solved by a Nuri fable," said Byrna with derision.

But Carlette waited for Tuk to continue.

"The two brothers were as different as night and day. One brother, the older one, found fault with everything. He would complain that his silk shoes were too tight, that his handmade clothing was scratchy, that his fine bread was too coarse. But the younger brother could find nothing wrong with anything. If someone stabbed him, this brother would claim it to be an honest mistake."

Byrna heaved an exasperated sigh. Carlette shushed her.

"One day," Tuk continued, ignoring them both, "the boys' father decided it was time to test their natures. The man, a rich trader from Ayurai had purchased a new stallion. A great beast. And the father decided to give it to the older brother as a gift, to try and make him happy. But he didn't want the younger brother's incessant pleasantness to ruin the surprise, so the trader gifted the older boy a stall with the most gorgeous stallion from the Hisanan Planes and gave the younger brother a stall full of manure.

"When the morning came, the older brother found his gift and wept. When the father asked why, the boy said that it was so much work to care for a horse and that he would never have the time or skill to do such a magnificent beast justice. The boy mourned that he was not a very good rider and would look ridiculous on a stallion like this one. And of course, when he failed to do right by the animal, his father would be forced to sell it.

"Frustrated, the father went to the other brother, eager to see if at least one of his sons had some sense. But all he found was his youngest child, eagerly shoveling through the horse manure. When the trader asked the boy what he was doing, he replied 'well with this much shit, there must be a horse in here somewhere.'"

Byrna snorted. "And that's supposed to teach us that gift horses are a burden?"

Tuk chuckled.

"What I'm saying is that perhaps the shit we're in depends on how we look at it," he said, chains clinking as he shifted.

Byrna was silent for a long moment.

"You really believe in it, don't you, larva-girl? This better future of yours?"

"I have to," Carlette whispered.

Byrna snorted again, even rougher this time.

"Byrna," Carlette went on. "Join me. I swear I will never ask you to murder innocents or kill children. We'll find a way through this that doesn't require us to become monsters. What do you say?"

"I say you're raving mad," Byrna laughed. "But luckily, so am I."

"I'm glad," Tuk said with a chuckle. "Because I don't want to face *you* on the battlefield."

"And I don't want you at my back. What kind of pathetic rescue was that?"

"How *did* you get into Jemelle, Tuk?" Carlette asked, breaking in.

"I used the parachute," he said in a sheepish voice, almost inaudible.

For a moment, neither girl spoke.

And then they both broke out laughing.

"Maybe you're not so useless after all," Byrna said with a cackle.

"I saw the Bloody Paws at the gate and I knew you were in danger," Tuk said, voice thick with embarrassment.

Byrna gagged.

"Urg, I'm going to be sick."

Carlette was glad the beetle-speaker couldn't see the flush spreading on her pale cheeks.

"Thank you," she said to Tuk, and meant it.

"If we are going to *thank* each other every time danger strikes," Byrna drawled, "go ahead and slice my throat."

"We need a plan," Carlette said, ignoring her. "We have to stop the hunt."

The return of the harsh scraping indicated Tuk was wrestling with his manacles again. Byrna spoke over the sound.

"You want to go into the Shadow Peaks and stop Yokan's best Ebonal hunters from doing exactly what they want to do?"

Her question was incredulous… and maybe just a little bit admiring.

Carlette's brain hummed with ideas, each more foolish than the last. "We'll need mountain stags."

"Oh no, I don't ride anything that has less than ten legs."

"Who's the coward now?" Tuk grumbled.

"They'll be tied outside Jemelle," Carlette said, thinking aloud. "I can find them. We'll only need two; Byrna's small enough to ride with me. Once we get them, we should be able to catch up to the hunting party."

"Yeah, because *catching up* is the easy part."

"Do you want to help or not?"

"Just pointing out the obvious."

Carlette was ready to snap back, but there was a click and a rustle and then Tuk whooped with joy.

"Yes!" he cried. A flung hand struck Carlette's shoulder. "Sorry."

"What do you think?" Carlette asked, turning toward him.

"I'm with you," he answered. She could picture his grin, imagine him rubbing his raw, bare wrists. "And I'll be a lot more helpful from now on."

Carlette's adrenaline was pumping. Her plan unfolded like a rope bridge, wavering and unstable but holding firm.

"If we can stop them from getting the wolf pup, will Yokan back down?"

"I don't know," Byrna said. "She can't take Tuleaux on her own. But even if the pack never shows up, she'll still be inside the city walls."

"Which could cause damage," Tuk said.

"Not nearly as much," Carlette said. "Stop the hunt and we'll ruin the worst of her plan. We might even reach Tuleaux and warn someone."

"I should have known I'd signed up to *save* settlers." But Byrna didn't sound overly bothered.

Carlette rubbed her face, a giddy kind of terror welling inside her. "Ok, so we track the Ebonal hunting party down on stolen mountain stags that I've only enhabited once before, save the Amonoux pup without being eaten by the she-wolf, and then try to reach Tuleaux before Yokan arrives, all while somehow avoiding arrest and execution. Did I miss anything?"

Byrna's cackle filled the cavern, making her cairog snip disapprovingly.

"Count me in."

CHAPTER TWENTY-SEVEN

❋ OLD STORIES ❋

Riding a mountain stag through the stark white landscape felt like flying. Carlette's hair whipped out behind her, blending in with the hills. The enormous stags moved like wraiths, hooves churning, mist pluming from their wide nostrils in thick bursts. With effortless grace the beasts floated over snow so deep it would have swallowed Byrna whole.

Beside her, Tuk cried out in surprise as his mount cleared a boulder that was almost the size of Grand Mera's hut.

"I know how he feels," Byrna grumbled behind Carlette. The Moian girl's arms had been vice-tight around Carlette's waist since they'd set out, leaving two stunned Bloody Paw guards and the rest of the mountain stags scattered in their wake. At the edge of the Wandering Pass, Byrna had clicked a command to Tabis and the cairog disappeared into the mountain, absorbed by the morning shadows

Carlette had been too afraid to ask Byrna what she'd said.

And now, holding the two stags with loose mental tethers, Carlette drove them hard. She could feel their massive, pumping hearts, their long, confident limbs and quick, savage eyes.

It was the kind of freedom she'd never known, had always secretly wanted.

Byrna and Tuk, however, felt quite differently.

"You're crushing my ribs," Carlette said, trying to shift forward on the shaped leather saddle, decorated with bones.

"Too bad," Byrna growled, squeezing tighter as they cleared a wide crevasse.

"If I die, nothing will stop the stags from eating you."

Her grip loosened.

Carlette felt herself grinning against her will. It was treacherous to feel such pure and unadulterated joy when Grand Mera's brain was being starved and the children of Jemelle were in imminent danger. But, as her stag clicked over a rocky outcropping and launched them over a ditch, she couldn't help it.

"How are you?" Carlette called over.

"Just. Fine," Tuk said between gritted teeth.

She laughed, the sound as fluttery as her loose hair.

"I hate blood-hunters," Byrna muttered.

"What?"

"Those who enhabit animals."

"Aren't they common among Moians?"

"You expect me to share the secrets of my people?"

Carlette blew out a frustrated breath. "How are we supposed to work together you if you don't trust me?"

Byrna mumbled something distinctly offensive. Carlette guided their stag into another ground-eating leap, making Byrna yelp and burrow her face into Carlette's back.

"Fine, fine, what do you want to know."

Carlette was silent for a moment. The icy wind whipped at her cheeks.

At last she said, "Tell me about Voka."

"You've heard the stories."

"Only what I've been allowed to hear," Carlette said, guilt squirming in her stomach like worms. "I want to know the truth."

Byrna chuckled into Carlette's back.

"The *truth*?" Carlette heard a snort. "Spoken like a true settler to believe such a thing even exists. You think I met Voka? Shook her hand and cleaned her chamber pot?"

Carlette frowned. "I know your people have their own stories. I want to hear them."

For several thick heartbeats of the mountain stag, she wondered if Byrna was going to ignore her question. Irritation grated the edges of Carlette's euphoria.

"Voka was magnificent," Byrna said at last, her voice muffled as she kept her face buried. "They say she stood as tall as any man, taller than most. She painted her white hair with blood and was first to wear the paw tattoo. My father met her once, when he was just a boy. Said she was the kind of warrior who could face down an aurok and win."

Carlette breathed in time with the stags, absorbing the image. Somehow, this woman was in Carlette's family tree, in *her*. Was Voka her grandmother? Great-grandmother? Aunt or cousin?

Carlette wondered if she'd ever know.

"Voka's rebellion started with her own people," Byrna continued. "The Ebonal tribe was the fiercest, the most violent. When they struck, blood ran from the Delasir mines in rivers. Her war began in summer and, by the fall, she'd taken the mountains back. Even before she was wolf-rider, Voka killed more soldiers and settlers than the rest of them put together. Or so they say."

Carlette held her breath, remembering the exaggerated campfire stories about a wild creature on the back of a wolf, half-beast herself. In those fire-lit nights, Voka had been a demon out of Carlette's nightmares. Feral. Ghostly. But Byrna's Voka was different.

This felt *real*.

"When Tuleaux retaliated for the loss of their mines, Voka lost. Her tribe was turned back and scattered. She and one of her blood-sisters disappeared for three months. To this day, no one knows what happened during that time. But when Voka returned with the thaw of spring, she returned alone and on the back of Sairan. Her Amonoux."

Carlette only knew a few words in Ebonal, but this one she recognized.

Freedom.

"While news of her power spread, the tribes united behind her. Sibilese nomads came on their rock lizards. Raebus clansmen marched over the pass. Ceillan chariots dropped from the sky like rain. Even the Moians joined. Every warrior who could reach the Peaks, by land or air, declared themselves for Voka. My father said it was a grand showing, a final stand against the Delasir invaders who had corrupted our home."

Carlette felt a surge of sadness. She knew how this part of the story ended.

"Voka had a handpicked group that she kept close. They called themselves the Riders of Hyba and painted their hair with blood, like her. They were first through the gates of Tuleaux when the city fell. But the Magistrate at the time was a clever man. He waited for Voka to plunge into the city so he could cut off her retreat. When he gave the signal, Voka and her blood-sisters were surrounded."

Byrna's voice became heavy with disgust.

"One of the riders stabbed her in the side with a poison-tipped blade. Not enough to kill, but enough to stop the battle in its tracks. She lost her hold on the wolf. Her other blood-sisters were shot down. And, with the head of her army cut off, they lost."

Carlette swallowed. She knew the rest. Voka was executed in the most brutal and public way the Magistrate could think of. This was where the sailors always stopped, blushing as they realized that the eyes drinking in their every word were those of children. But Carlette knew all too well what kinds of horrors Delasir could come up with.

"What happened after she died?"

228

Byrna laughed.

"Everyone went home, larva-girl. The Sibilese slunk back to their deserts. The Raebus clans rode over the pass and tried to close it behind them. And us…" Byrna hesitated. "Well, we've been limping along ever since."

"And no one's risen up? Tried to take Voka's place?"

"What do you think Yokan's doing, picking daisies?"

"She's no leader," Carlette snapped. "She's a rabid dog."

"At least she's trying."

Carlette bit back a sharp reply. She used to think that Yokan and her Bloody Paws had brought violence to Ferren. But Carlette was beginning to understand that violence was already here. It was a topsoil that Delasir had spread. A poison she'd been a part of.

As she listened to the thump of hooves on snow, almost inaudible over the deep, resonant breathing of the stags, Carlette tried to put the pieces of her life together. She was like a shattered clay pot, dropped and then fired. Her pieces weren't the same shape anymore. She couldn't slide them into place.

"Bit of a different story than you're used to, huh?" Byrna asked.

"If the Furix came," Carlette said, thoughtfully, not quite in answer. "If she re-appeared, then what? What would the tribes do?"

"Well I suppose that would depend on how much of a dainty little bitch she was."

"Will it always be a woman? Couldn't there be a man out there who can enhabit an Amonoux?"

"You'd love that, wouldn't you? An excuse to let a *man* take over?"

Carlette didn't dignify that with a response.

"No," Byrna said when it became clear Carlette wasn't going to answer. "Power follows the female line. A man, no matter how strong, could never lead us to freedom."

"And a hood?"

The beetle-speaker's hands shook, clutching at Carlette's stolen overcoat, but when Byrna spoke her voice held no sign of weakness.

229

"If a Furix came along with strength enough to unite the tribes, no one's going to wipe their ass about what she's wearing. Only a Delarese idiot would think a piece of clothing matters."

Carlette nodded, but she couldn't help but wonder if Byrna was wrong.

The midday sun found the three of them straddling a narrow ridge. Byrna, black hair dusted with snow, crawled along the top as Carlette kept a firm hold on the two stags. Tuk was clutching his knees to his chest, taking deep, pluming breaths.

"How are you?" Carlette asked, not liking the blue tint of his lips.

"I don't think I've ever been this cold," he said with a shudder.

"Here, move closer to Nea."

"I'll stay over here, thanks," Tuk said, eying the towering stag. Nea's muscles bulged, her long fangs as white and deadly as the snow. Carlette laughed, careful to keep her voice low.

"She won't hurt you, not with me here."

"Still," Tuk said. "I'll keep my distance."

Byrna slid down the side of the ridge, cheeks red with windburn.

"They're here alright. Trap's being set as we speak."

"What's the trap?"

"Gunpowder," Byrna answered, brushing off snow. "I was supposed to help. The plan was to dust tree-beetles in gunpowder and use them to control the explosions. I guess they must have found another way."

Carlette's stomach twisted. "They're going to cause an avalanche?"

"Several," Byrna said, blowing on her hands. "Right up against the ridge. It'll be easy to separate the infant and make sure the mother can't follow them."

"Will it work?"

Byrna's black eyes glinted. "It did before."

Carlette clenched her fists, feeling the spines ripple beneath the thick gloves she'd grabbed from Jemelle's stores.

"I thought the Bloody Paws were trying to protect this place," Tuk said, shaking his head. "What does killing puppies have anything to do with saving Ferren."

"We all make sacrifices," Byrna snapped. "But maybe a pampered Nuri prince wouldn't understand that."

"Stop it," Carlette said. "We need to think. If we're going to save the pup…"

"We'd have to stop the avalanche," said Tuk.

"Or stop the wolves from coming through the pass," Byrna cut in.

"Or incapacitate the hunters when the avalanche starts," Carlette added.

She rubbed her forehead. It all seemed so impossible. They were just three teenagers; what chance did they have against fully trained Ebonal hunters, men and women who had lived their lives in this bitter landscape, breathing in its power?

"What we need," Tuk said in a thoughtful voice, "is a distraction."

Carlette turned to him, unnerved by the determination in his expression.

"Carlette, if we can give you an opening, do you think you could enhabit the she-wolf? Turn the pack around?"

Carlette swallowed. The she-wolf would be the toughest of all, her power dense and armored after years and years of consuming souls. Carlette couldn't even imagine the pain of trying to withstand such fortifications.

But she remembered that day by the river, Tuk sprinting away, the wolves chasing after him.

And Quaina's familiar soul, inviting her in.

"I think so," she said with more confidence than she felt.

"Good," Tuk said, beginning to pace. "So if we keep the hunters busy, you can stop the wolves from walking into their trap."

"Slow down, little daisy," Byrna said, folding her arms. "What kind of distraction did you have in mind?"

Reaching beneath his heavy coat, Tuk pulled out the tattered, crumpled remains of the parachute.

Carlette's eyebrows shot up.

Byrna snorted, shaking her head. "I would slice open my own asshole before I trust my life to *that*."

Tuk grinned at Byrna, a taunting, devilish smile that Carlette recognized as bait.

"Who's the daisy now?"

CHAPTER TWENTY-EIGHT

❋ RED SNOW ❋

The true insanity of their plan didn't hit Carlette until she was crawling along the upper ridgeline, holding the molded mountain stag saddle to her chest, scanning the gulf below for the massive shapes of the Amonoux.

By that point it was too late to turn back.

Swallowing her fear, Carlette crouched low, carving a moat through the white powder as she scuttled along a sharp crest of obsidian. She could sense the Bloody Paws below, their owl-like silence ominous and wrong, a scar on the otherwise beautiful vista. She soaked it in. From this vantage point in the clouds, the world fell open below her like a storybook. The Peaks snaked away on either side, reaching for the coast on one end and curling south toward The Hasach on the other. Adenai and Hyba—the tallest mountains— loomed above them, impossibly huge. It was no wonder the natives had named these two, sisters in size and shape, after their gods.

Or was it the other way around?

Carlette was shivering, damp cold leaking through her stolen overcoat. As she settled in to wait, she wondered idly who had last worn this jacket. A trader, perhaps, or a Collector? It made Carlette cringe to think that she was wearing anything that might have touched one of those loathsome brutes.

We all make sacrifices.

For the umpteenth time, Carlette checked on Byrna and Tuk. They were in place, on the other side of the gigantic V between the mountains. She could sense Tuk's exasperation, Byrna's acidity, and their total mismatched antagonism even through the feather-touch link.

She shivered again and wished she was over there with them. At least then she wouldn't be freezing to death by herself.

For endless, frigid minutes, Carlette squatted in the snow. All her senses were open, the doors to her mind thrown as wide as Mya's windows on a warm day. She could feel the Snow snakes burrowing deep in the crevasses, waiting for unsuspecting prey. A herd of mountain stags picked their way south for the winter, fleeing the cruel winds of the ice plains the Ebonals called home. The natural world around her moved like clockwork, a silent march that never stopped.

Cocooned in a palm of rock, surrounded by infinity, Carlette felt impossibly small. No matter what happened to her, this cycle would continue. It was an endless orbit of life and death, indifferent to the squabbles of mankind.

The thought was strangely comforting.

Her musings were interrupted by the brush of a gigantic power against her mind.

She twisted, peering over the ridgeline. The Ebonal warriors below her had disappeared. Even their stags were nowhere to be seen. Carlette could sense the hunting party, crouched in dug-out holes behind mounds of snow, but their minds were carefully blank and empty.

Carlette leaned out further, holding her breath, eyes adjusting to the painful brilliance. She clutched the saddle closer to her chest, trying not to shiver.

There.

Moving with the confidence of apex predators, the Amonoux pack emerged like a part of the landscape. Their fur was as white as the snow around them, their eyes glittering even from this distance.

No matter how many times she saw them, she would never get used to their *size*.

Once, Carlette had overheard a Delasir veteran telling stories about the war, about how Nurkaij met them in battle. He'd spoken of airships, of course, but also of the elephants. For months after, Carlette and Quaina had pestered every sailor and settler they could find for a better description of the continental monstrosities. Their young minds were electric with the idea of lumbering beasts the size of houses with armored tusks and beady eyes. According to what little they'd gathered, the size of these animals made them slow. Their feet—each one at least as wide around as a wagon wheel— moved with a plodding certainty that made Carlette think of glaciers.

The Amonoux were nothing like that.

They hinted elegance and speed with every twitch of the tail, every ripple of musculature. Even though the she-wolf matriarch was easily as large as a Nuri elephant, Carlette knew which one would be more terrifying to face in battle.

No wonder Voka's name is still spoken in whispers, Carlette thought as she stared at the she-wolf and the pup trailing behind her massive tail. *No wonder people are still afraid.*

Carlette prodded for Tuk and Byrna. She could taste the beetle-speaker's terror as Tuk strapped them both into the parachute. Through Byrna's ears, she heard Tuk hissing frustrated reassurances that the snow was thick, the wind was steady, they weren't going to die, no they *probably* wouldn't break their legs.

Through Tuk, she felt Byrna elbow him in the gut.

235

Carlette swallowed a half-hysterical laugh before it could betray her.

The she-wolf moved into the shadow of the mountain, her pack close behind. For a moment, everything was silent, quiet.

And then the Ebonal hunters burst from the snow like dolphins.

"BYRNA, NOW!" Carlette heard Tuk shout, felt Byrna's gasp.

Carlette watched as they launched from their vantage point, leaping into the open air with a battle-cry. The sound echoed. Snow broke off, tumbling into the gulf. Screaming like a demon from the underworld, Byrna lifted her slingshot and fired. A Bloody Paw cried out and fell. The Amonoux were rearing. Gut-deep, bone-shuddering snarls reverberated in the very stone.

It was Carlette's turn.

Praying that her death would be more dignified than a sledding accident, Carlette dug her toes in and threw herself on top of the snow, jamming the saddle between her body and the powder. Almost immediately, she was rocketing down the mountain with the speed of a loosed arrow. Snow sprayed up like ocean mist, coating her eyelashes. She couldn't see.

But she didn't need to.

Turn back! Danger! Run into the mountains!

Carlette threw the messages like daggers, but they fell uselessly against the she-wolf's power, the impenetrable barrier wrapped her mind. Too far down to reconsider, Carlette continued to batter against that cairog-thick shell as she hurtled onward, hoping the wolves wouldn't see *her* as the threat and decide to meet her halfway.

Danger! This is a trap! A trap for your baby!

Carlette picked at the kinked wires of magical defense, but each one sliced her. Kept her back. She couldn't get through, couldn't meet the wolf in a way she would understand.

Stop!

And then Carlette's mind brushed against a wire she knew. A familiar essence, braided into the wolf's.

Quaina.

All at once, Carlette understood Voka's story.

She and one of her blood-sisters disappeared for three months. To this day, no one knows what happened during that time. But when Voka returned with the thaw of spring, she returned alone...

But Voka hadn't returned alone.

Not really.

Carlette didn't stop to think. She was more than halfway down the mountain. The other wolves were growling, snapping at the rebels.

Twining herself into that familiar mental thread and blinking against the frozen tears on her eyelashes, Carlette followed Quaina's soul into the recesses of the Amonoux. The she-wolf was ten times more powerful than the juvenile Carlette had enhabited in the Bloody Paw cave, but, as Carlette went deeper, she was overcome by that same sense of otherness. She saw through seven eyes, felt the ground through paws larger than her whole body. The wolf's bond with her pup became Carlette's bond; the ironclad command of her pack heavy and somber in Carlette's human hands.

Go back, Carlette said, plucking Quaina's thread. Please, there's a trap here. They're after your pup. Go back or they'll kill him.

The she-wolf's essence curled out toward her like smoke. It was majesty. Wilderness. Both cruel and kind, wise and wild. Carlette fought the urge to cringe away from the size of it.

Quaina bubbled up to her, offered by the she-wolf like an apology.

Carlette had almost reached the bottom. The she-wolf was turning, her snarls so low that Carlette could only hear them through the Amonoux's own ears. Time slowed. Tuk fell, Byrna howled, the Bloody Paws collapsed under bulls-eye attacks.

And then, without warning, the mountainside exploded.

The force launched Carlette's body across the gulf. She slammed into the snow on the other side of the valley, sinking in so deep that for a moment she didn't know where the sky was. The ground seemed to pop and crackle.

No!

Clawing her way out, Carlette scrambled to reach the air. But the cracks of breaking snowdrifts were already vibrating like the battle-cry of Hyba herself.

Carlette reached the surface, scrubbed snow off her face.

The scene before her had shifted, dizzyingly fast.

Ebonal hunters chased the Amonoux pup on their steeds. The snow above them loosened and toppled, ominously slow. The she-wolf snapped out, jaws clamping around a stag. Ignoring it's piercing, equine scream, she tore it in half, slamming its rider into a pile of rocks. With a whip of her giant head, the she-wolf sent the remainder of the stag flying, knocking two other hunters off their mounts.

But the pack was surrounded.

What could she do?

Byrna and Tuk had landed in the snow. The beetle-speaker continued to fling chunks of ice at the Bloody Paws, undaunted by the avalanche gaining speed as it raced down the mountain. Tuk wrestled with an Ebonal man almost twice his size. With a flash of power, Carlette knocked the warrior unconscious.

She made to wade forward, to help her friends.

But the Bloody Paws were converging.

They'd isolated the pup.

With a breathless struggle, Carlette managed to extract herself from the snow and somersault gracelessly down the mountain.

She had to stop this.

Her power stretched out, enhabiting two Bloody Paws at once, holding them still. A snarling Amonoux leapt close and bit off one's head.

Carlette gagged at the death.

She swallowed, plunged on.

Snow fell like a herd of horses, thundering down the mountain.

I'm too far, she thought as Tuk called out after her. *I'll never make it.*

Stretching her magic to its very limits, she tried to enhabit all the Bloody Paw warriors at once. But there were too many, her view too chaotic. The avalanche crashed into the gulf, controlled explosions funneling the full brunt of it right on top of the Amonoux pack. Two wolves disappeared under the onslaught. The she-wolf backed away.

The sun disappeared.

Carlette coughed as she inhaled ice crystals. A wave hit her in the chest, knocking her to the ground. For a moment of insidious terror, Carlette thought she was buried, that she had misjudged the slide.

But someone was wrapping an arm around her neck, hauling her backwards.

"Of all the stupid, prissy things to do, you had to run *into* it, didn't you?" Byrna growled in her ear.

"Are you okay?" Tuk asked, helping Byrna dislodge Carlette from the snow. Her feet scrambled against the loose ground. She couldn't see, couldn't breathe. Fear pulsed in her, but it wasn't her own. Something was scratching against her mind like a cat against a door, frantic with desperation.

Carlette coughed, spitting out snow.

"No!" she cried out, pulling free of her friends. She stumbled forward. "*NO!*"

The snow was settling, and with it the sick reality of what had happened. The Bloody Paws—their hunting party only half what it had been that morning—were standing around the horse-sized infant Amonoux, gloating over their prize. The pup's muzzle was tied, legs bound like a warthog. Carlette could feel its pain and fear, its innocence.

She fell to her knees.

"Come on, we need to move," Tuk hissed, tugging on Carlette's shoulder. "It's not too late, we can still—"

But he was interrupted by a thud. Carlette spun around just in time to see him fall, eyes crossing. Byrna twisted, slingshot already loaded, but the three Bloody Paws who had snuck up behind them were too fast. Too brutal. A stolen rifle butt slammed Byrna across the face, leaving a horrible *crack* in the silence the avalanche had left.

Byrna collapsed in a puff of white.

Carlette surged to her feet and lashed out with every last bit of her power, with every scrap of her strength.

She would not allow this.

She couldn't.

Biting, kicking, screaming, Carlette felt them fall around her. One to her magic. Another to her fist. But the third managed to grab her around the throat, choking off her battle cry.

The last thing she felt was the Amonoux she-wolf slamming desperately against her mind.

And then she was gone.

CHAPTER TWENTY-NINE

✳ TO DIE WITH HONOR ✳

Even Carlette had to admit that things looked hopeless. The Ebonal warriors pulled the three prisoners behind the mountain stags, cruel and impatient. Carlette walked when she could, but with her eyes covered and her hands wrapped in front of her, she was lucky if she stayed on her feet for three paces. Every so often, she felt the prod of a spear, heard a harsh command, but that didn't bother her as much as the whispers.

"Byrna," Carlette murmured when they stopped for a moment, the voices of the hunting party rising in argument. "What are they saying?"

"They're debating if they should kill us," Byrna hissed back. "We're slowing them down."

"They could just let us go," Tuk grumbled, and Carlette could hear the strain in his voice. Tuk wasn't a soldier. He wasn't used to drawn-out pain and bone-deep exhaustion. It had been at least a full day since the capture of the Amonoux pup and they'd been moving the whole time, stumbling—or dragged—through the snow and rubble.

"The woman is saying they should throw us off the mountain," Byrna went on, voice low. "We're close to the cliff's edge. They could just drop us over the side."

"That means we're over Durchemin. Maybe we could find help."

"Don't be stupid," Byrna snapped. "It's leagues below us. We'd be lucky if our bodies stayed whole after such a fall."

"What about the other side?" Carlette asked. "We could make a run for the ocean…"

"The blackstone would rip us to shreds."

Carlette was silent.

"Too bad we lost the parachute, eh?" Tuk said with a half-laugh.

Byrna muttered something rude.

There was a sudden *thump* and Tuk cried out in pain.

"No talking!" barked one of the Bloody Paws.

Carlette's lip curled in a snarl, but there was nothing she could do. They were at the mercy of this hunting pack, and it didn't sound like they were feeling very merciful.

She felt as if her heartbeat was counting down, ticking off her last seconds of life.

One of the warriors shouted and Carlette's rope pulled taut. They were moving again. She stumbled, trying to keep her feet beneath her. But the snow was determined to trip her. She fell. Her knee ripped open on a jagged spear of obsidian. When she tried to cry out, her mouth filled with ice and she wheezed.

Tuk grabbed her elbow.

"You okay?" he whispered.

There was a resounding crack as the warrior hit him again.

Carlette swallowed a curse. If they died, she vowed to herself that whoever that was would go down with them.

The wind whistled around her head, and she tried to picture where they were—high above Durchemin, avoiding the hunting trails that

242

the Amonoux might take to reach Tuleaux. The Bloody Paws would march over the peak, pick their way down the cliff on the other side of the Magistrate's home, and then what? Take a ship into the harbor? Enhabit a whale and swim?

Whatever their plan, Carlette knew she wasn't going to stop it as their prisoner.

An idea bloomed in her mind, a desperate and wafer-thin thread of hope.

"Are they making up their minds?" Carlette hissed when Byrna's shoulder hit her own.

"Afraid so, larva-girl."

"Wait for my signal."

"To do what, beg for our lives?"

"Just pay attention."

Carlette tried to gather her strength, but she was waning. A full day without food or water, dragged behind a beast with legs as long as she was tall, was enough to deplete anyone's energy.

I have strength enough for this, she thought to herself, picturing Tuleaux, Tuk, Byrna.

Mya.

So many lives on her shoulders.

She could not fail.

The hunting party stopped. Carlette stumbled into the rump of her stag. The rider shouted at her, smacking the back of her head. An argument exploded nearby.

"No, wait!" Byrna shouted.

Carlette felt a knife slice through her bonds. A strong hand yanked her backwards, where the wind's voice was a lethal howl. She took deep breaths. Forced herself to stay calm.

Now or never.

Carlette raised her voice. "At least let me die with my eyes open."

She felt all eyes turn to her, felt Tuk's surprise and Byrna's coiled tension.

"A mountain death is mercy," growled a woman's voice nearby. "If we bring you back, Yokan will kill you slow."

"Then kill me," Carlette said, trying to remember everything she knew of the Ebonal tribe. "But let me die with honor. Allow me to face Hyba."

Carlette's demand was met by a deep silence. She tried to stay strong, keep her spine straight. Everything hinged on a half-informed guess.

Were these the honorable Ebonal warriors of legend, soldiers who would already feel revulsion for their monstrous act? Would they respect the traditions Carlette had learned about?

Did those traditions even exist?

Her life dangled in the balance of that question.

"If you bodywalk," said a voice in broken Delarese, "We kill your friends and bathe you in their blood."

Carlette nodded.

Rough hands yanked off her blindfold.

For an instant, the sun blinded her.

And then details came at her like diving birds.

Byrna and Tuk tied to a stag, her blindfolded, him staring at Carlette. Tall men and women with layered furs arrayed around them. A howling, horrible cliff on one side, a steep slope on the other.

But only one detail mattered.

At the end of the convoy was a hulking white shape. The Amonoux pup, more than half the size of the stags pulling it. It was panting through its muzzle, eyes wide, lashed to a toboggan.

Perfect, Carlette thought.

"Tell Yokan I send my regards," Carlette said.

And then the pup was rolling, tilting the runners dangerously high. Commotion stirred and the Bloody Paws spun, sprinting to the pup, hands reaching for the edges of the sled.

But the woman holding Carlette's arm didn't move.

This keen-eyed huntress missed nothing. Her gaze lingered on Carlette's face, on the glowing white rings. She'd lifted her dagger in

244

the moment of chaos, ready to act. But realization was dawning on her clever features.

"You…"

At that moment, Byrna lunged forward and dug her nails into the haunches of their stag. The creature reared, screaming.

The woman's attention flickered.

Carlette dove into her mind and snuffed her into unconsciousness.

The pup had rolled the toboggan and was beginning to slide away, making the rest of the hunting party panic. Carlette felt a surge of guilt as the small white body began to accelerate down the ridgeline, upside-down, but she couldn't afford to dwell on its pain. Byrna had managed to grab a dagger from her stag's saddle and was already sawing through her bonds. Carlette grabbed the woman's knife and hurried to cut Tuk free.

"What now?" Byrna shouted over the commotion of screaming stags and warriors.

Carlette cast around for something, anything.

Her gaze fell on another, smaller toboggan, filled with supplies.

"Here!" she said, using the stolen knife to slice through the ropes.

"You're joking!"

Carlette tilted the sled, letting the supplies tumble down the cliff face. She spun it to face the slope.

Byrna opened her mouth to protest, but one of the Ebonals was notching an arrow, pointing at them.

"Go!" Carlette shouted, shoving them both, twisting to stop the man from firing. She flicked out, but he was ready for her, shielding against her.

The arrow missed them by inches.

The man moved fast, nocking another arrow. Two others were sprinting toward them, shouting.

Time to go!

Byrna was on the front of the toboggan, Tuk holding its rear, waiting for her. Carlette lunged. With all the force her legs could muster, she slammed into the Nuri mechanic. They hit Byrna's back with a breathless thump, tipped the sled over the precipice.

And suddenly, they were flying, barely skimming the snow as they careened down at a catastrophic pace.

"Hold on to something!" Byrna shrieked.

They bounced off a rock. Carlette's body lost contact with the sled but Tuk grabbed her waist, hauled her back. She gripped the frayed ropes with white knuckles, hands still bound. Hard wooden slats dug into her chest, her ribs, her hips, every bump painful. Tuk's body was heavy around her, holding her down.

"Fucking shit!"

They swerved.

Carlette glanced up. Byrna's fingers were curled in a death-grip around the antlers built to guide the sled. It was working. Fingerlings of black rock reached for them, sharp as knives, but Byrna navigated through them.

A ridge appeared, calamitously fast.

"Look out!" Carlette screamed.

Byrna threw the antlers to the side. The sled turned so quickly Carlette felt one runner rise out of the snow. Her chin hit the wood and she tasted blood.

"The cliff's coming!" Tuk shouted.

Carlette coughed, spraying blood onto the sled. A whine of panic filled her ears. Tuk had flown over these mountains enough to know what lay ahead of them.

Nothing.

"Byrna! We have to stop!"

"Any suggestions?" Byrna screamed back as she wove through the mountain's ribs. They were *gaining* speed. Carlette knew that at any second an invisible rock or crevasse could end them. And if not, then the long drop to the ocean would.

Their escape would be for nothing.

"We need to jump!"

"Are you crazy?" Byrna shrieked.

"It's the only way! Try and find some snow to—"

But Carlette never got the chance to finish. Their right runner caught on something hard, bucking one side into the air. The sled fishtailed, twisted, slammed down.

And ejected the three human bodies like a slingshot.

For the second time that day, Carlette entered a snowdrift at a near lethal speed. Her bones shuddered. The sled tumbled over her and pain erupted along her shoulder. A scream filled her ears, not her own. She was rolling, sliding, grabbing out. Her wounds reopened, spilling pus inside her gloves, but she held onto whatever she could. She tumbled, lost purchase, grabbed something else. Bit by bit, her descent slowed to a crawl.

With a final tumbling roll, she came to a stop.

For a moment, all she could do was breathe. Her entire body was on fire, each nerve and bone protesting the abuse. Her shoulder had been sliced open by the sled's runner and her hands were raw and bleeding *again*. She had broken at least one rib and her neck was stiff.

Even so, the mountains had smiled upon them.

It was pure luck that she had hit a snow drift and not a pile of rubble or worse, an obsidian rib. Her plan had worked. They still had a chance.

With shaking arms, Carlette wiggled toward daylight. She coughed, spat out snow.

"Tuk?" she called. "Byrna?"

"We have a problem," Tuk said from somewhere nearby.

The fear in his voice made her blood run cold. Surging out of the snowdrift, Carlette stumbled toward the two dark shapes in an ocean of white. The powder grabbed at her feet, its sticky fingers trying to tempt her exhausted body to stop, to rest in its cushioned arms.

Adrenaline alone kept her moving.

Finally, she reached them.

"Oh no," Carlette breathed, lurching to a stop.

Byrna's leg was twisted at a nauseating angle, bent in like an elbow. Her face was whiter than the landscape, her breathing low and

247

shallow. Tuk crouched at her side, apparently unhurt. But his expression was somber.

"I'm fine," Byrna said between clenched teeth. "Only a pampered Nuri prince would worry about a little thing like this."

But Carlette understood.

Byrna couldn't walk on a leg like that, no matter how they splinted it. Even if she could hobble along, the cliffs that would lead them to Tuleaux were steep and slippery, treacherous for even the most able-bodied, not to mention far away. They both knew Byrna would never make it, certainly not fast enough.

Which meant that Carlette had to choose between abandoning her new friend and leaving Tuleaux open to the Bloody Paw attack.

CHAPTER THIRTY

❋ DISCOVERY ❋

Carlette couldn't help but marvel at the beetle-speaker's strength. Byrna glared at the sky, jaw clenched so tight that muscles jumped in her cheek, face as white as Carlette's hair. But still she didn't scream as Carlette splinted her leg with the wooden shards of their shattered toboggan.

"Almost done," Carlette said as she tied ripped shreds of Tuk's undershirt around the makeshift cast.

"I could... do this... all day," Byrna said, her breath coming in shallow pants. She hissed as Carlette tightened the final knot.

Leaning back, Carlette prayed she had done everything right. Her medical knowledge was spotty at best. In Jemelle, she'd learned about the human body: what it looked like on the inside, how to cause the most amount of pain with the least amount of damage, and, in rare cases, how to heal injuries. She could staunch bleeding, tie a tourniquet, treat arrow and gun injuries, and recognize a fatal wound.

Once, very briefly, a Tuleaux medic had mentioned something about setting bones. She'd been nine at the time, still fresh to Jemelle and shocked by the very concept of war. But Carlette had dragged up the memory anyway, struggling to visualize the healer's hands as he tied saplings to a dummy's arm.

Now, looking at Byrna's leg, her chest tightened. What if she'd just made things worse?

Not that it would matter if they all died in the mountains.

"You should go," Byrna said through gritted teeth. "You can still save them."

"We're not leaving you here," Carlette snapped, looking around for Tuk.

He had sprinted off almost an hour ago, muttering something about the landscape looking familiar. Carlette suspected that the angle of Byrna's leg had made him woozy, but he should have returned by now.

"Worried about your boyfriend?"

Carlette flushed. "It's not like that."

"You hoods," Byrna scoffed, wincing as she shifted her leg. "Closed up tighter than a virgin's legs. It's not that scary, you know, to be ripe for someone."

"It is for me," Carlette snarled, temper snapping.

Right this minute, Yokan was marching on the place she called home, approaching the fences that protected Mya and Mileen and all the other orphans. Young hoods were being used as shields and here she was, talking about *this?*

Byrna snorted. "If you're going to be a traitor, might as well enjoy the perks."

"I can't do this right now."

"Now is the perfect time," Byrna said, leaning back on her elbows. "You have to decide where you stand, else Yokan will eat you alive."

Carlette kept scanning for Tuk, but she couldn't help the answer that bubbled to her lips, against her better judgement.

250

"They'll kill him," she whispered.

"They will anyway," Byrna pointed out. "Especially after everything that's happened."

It was more than that, though. Carlette could handle Tuk falling in battle, maybe even his execution. But to think of Tuk dangling from the fences, a sign on his chest telling hoods and Nuri spies and everyone else what he'd done, what *she'd* allowed to happen…

"Life's not all battles and wars," Byrna said with a grimace. "Sometimes it's enough to have a fire, a pile of furs, and someone to share them with."

Carlette snorted. "That's fresh, coming from a reformed Bloody Paw."

Byrna was silent for so long that Carlette turned to look at her, only to find her staring at the anchor tattoo on Carlette's neck.

"Some things are only skin deep." Her eyes lifted, drilling into Carlette's. "It's your decision to make them more than that."

"I don't have that kind of luxury," Carlette said, sitting back on her heels, trying to puzzle through their predicament and not think about what it would feel like to be with Tuk, to feel his fingers on her skin and see what he looked like beneath his uniform.

"Is it a luxury to be human?"

Carlette glared at Byrna's leg. "Yes."

Byrna sighed. "You're worse than those dried-up old raisins in the Convent," she said, falling back into the snow with a muffled *whump*.

Carlette hesitated for a moment, prodding the snow. But this conversation had gone well past the point of shyness.

"How did you escape?" she asked.

Byrna lifted her head, eyebrows high. "Looking for tips?"

"No one ever gets out of there. How did you do it?"

Byrna let her head fall back. "I got lucky."

Carlette waited silently, her breath forming small clouds as the cold seeped in through her legs. Finally, Byrna continued.

251

"I had been in the Convent almost a year when Yokan attacked. It was her fourth time raiding it. Found out later she was looking for you. I remember hearing the explosions and gunshots. The screams. Yokan's warriors were ruthless coming down the tunnels. I'd never seen so much blood..."

Byrna's voice trailed off. She coughed before continuing.

"When Yokan came to my cell, I thought she was Adenai herself, come to rescue me. Her face was painted with charcoal and her eyes were white. I renounced all the Moian gods right there and pledged myself to her."

Byrna took a deep breath. Carlette kept perfectly still, as if Byrna's story was a wild animal that would spook at the slightest movement.

"I don't know why she took me in. Maybe she could tell I was like her. Another demon born in the belly of the world. Whatever the reason, she opened my cell and said I had one chance to prove myself to her. To earn my freedom. The guards were fighting through the blockade she'd set behind us, getting closer. Yokan unlocked my gloves." Byrna chuckled darkly. "Let me tell you, those buffoons who guard your precious city are rather hilarious when they're covered in ants."

Carlette couldn't suppress a shudder. "That sounds... difficult."

"Not really. Threading the Weave is the greatest release in the world. Better than sex, sometimes."

"What's the Weave?" Carlette asked to keep the subject from sliding back into uncomfortable territory.

Byrna laughed outright. "What do they *teach* you in that school?"

Carlette didn't respond, knowing Byrna would fill the silence if she waited long enough.

"The Weave is everything. It's the threads of life that bind us together. It's the tapestry we reach for when we hold the mind of beasts." Byrna sighed and Carlette watched the mist rise from the girl's head, a tendril of smoky air. "My father told me it has something to do with this land. That in Ferren, people were created differently.

252

The power we hold… concentrates in our hands and eyes somehow. The settlers feel the physical world through their fingers. We feel the Weave."

Carlette thought of the chinked power around the she-wolf, the way the world seemed *thicker* around her. Dense with souls.

"Woven energy," Carlette muttered, tracing shapes in the snow.

"Energy, life, power. Call it what you will," Byrna said. "That's the Weave."

"Thank you," Carlette said, the words clumsy in her mouth. "I… never knew that."

Byrna snorted. "That and a million other things."

But Carlette wasn't listening. She felt like an untethered balloon, trying to process what Byrna had said.

The Weave.

The Convent.

Tuk.

So many moving parts. It was easy to understand why soldiers followed orders without question, why guards held onto their blind hatred. Some deep, insidious part of Carlette longed to return to a world that was simple, sliced into discrete pieces and given to her in calculated mouthfuls. Everything was so much larger and more complicated than her mind could possibly hold.

Still, she had to try.

Tuk's consciousness brushed against her own, ending her reflection. She rose, trying to shake off the heavy weight of unanswerable questions as he jogged into view.

Carlette opened her mouth to ask where he'd been. But her question cut off when she saw his face. It was alight with energy, eyes infectiously bright.

"I found it!" Tuk panted, clutching Carlette's shoulders so that he didn't topple onto Byrna. "I found it!"

"What, your balls?" Byrna asked, smirking.

Carlette shot her a warning look, but Tuk hardly seemed to notice. He was radiating the kind of energy that left Carlette light-headed, face stretched in the same grin he'd worn when they'd thought of hijacking the Nuri airship.

"I found my ship," Tuk said, the words falling out of him in a rush. "I thought I recognized this place, and I *did*. This is where I crashed, right before I was captured."

"Wait, did you say *crashed*?" said Byrna, whose face had gone, if possible, even paler.

"It's in no shape to reach Caika," Tuk said, almost bouncing on the tips of his toes, "But if I can light a fire, I should be able to glide it along the sea. With any luck, they may not notice us until we reach the harbor. We'll fly low and fast. Worst case scenario, we end up getting a little wet."

"No," Byrna said. "Worst case scenario, we're shot down and eaten by sharks."

"Well yeah, that too," Tuk said with a blush.

"I'd rather starve here, thank you very much."

"You'll freeze to death first," Carlette pointed out.

"At least I'll die on solid ground."

"Look," Tuk interrupted, "It's our only chance. It's not perfect, but I can do this. I can fix her."

"Of course it's a *her*," Byrna muttered. "What else would a high-flying bitch—"

"We'll do it," Carlette said, slicing a look at Byrna. "We trust you."

"Speak for yourself, little Furix, I trust nothing but my beetles."

"I'll carry her on if I have to," Carlette said, meeting Tuk's eyes. "Fix up your ship and we'll get on it."

Tuk's smile was brighter than any sunrise Carlette had ever seen.

CHAPTER THIRTY-ONE

❋ A SHARED HORIZON ❋

Carlette had lost count of how many times Byrna had vomited over the side of Tuk's ship, the sound of her retching audible even over the wind.

"I think your paint might be ruined," Carlette shouted, her own bandaged hands twisted in the rigging.

Tuk cackled. "I'll get her to clean it later!"

Byrna made a rude gesture without pulling her head back from the edge.

It had taken Tuk six hours to rig his vessel into some semblance of a functional airship. As Carlette half-supported, half-carried an acerbic, agonized, *angry* Byrna through the mountains, following the trail of Tuk's deep footprints, he'd bounded off ahead. It was as though nothing thrilled him more than flying a patched-up balloon over the mountains, down the cliffs, and into the turbulence of an incoming ocean storm. Tuk's energy only seemed to grow as the afternoon went on. By the time he and Carlette carried his basket to the nearest ledge, he was almost vibrating with anticipation.

They'd all made a point of ignoring the frozen, broken bodies of Tuk's old comrades.

Now, they were drifting over the edge of a cliff face, leaving the obsidian mountains behind. The surf boomed below them, hungry, waiting. Carlette's hands were numb but she refused to release the ropes, even for a second.

Somewhere up ahead, Delasir soldiers would be peering out of guard holes dug into the mountain. If Tuk wasn't careful, their trip would be cut short by a volley of gunshots tearing through their balloon and a long fall into unfriendly waters.

Carlette swallowed, concentrating.

Maybe she could help.

Even from this distance, she could feel the celebration, the rare happiness that spread from Tuleaux like fungal threads. She knew what the city would look like—every surface festooned with the gilded Delasir anchor or the Magistrate's knotted chain. Mya's orphans, faces scrubbed clean, would be sprinting down the Rae du Ora begging for the scraps of fresh oat cakes and popovers. Merchants would wear their best garments and vendors would present their wares on polished tables. It was the only day of the year that Tuleaux did nothing but celebrate, so the settlers did it with gusto.

This Gaulday, of course, would be that and more. After the capture of the Pirate Queen, the sailors would be drunk on victory. Carlette could imagine them catcalling the prettiest whores and dancing over cobblestones. Guards would shout obscenities about the Featherhands and insult Yokan in loud, carrying voices. The prince would give a speech, with special attention to the poor and needy. Mya would gather her hoard in a place of honor, right at the front, her children's eyes wide with admiration and yearning.

If Carlette failed, their eyes would be wide with something very different.

The ship dropped several feet.

256

Carlette's stomach seemed to fall out of her.

Byrna groaned.

"Sorry," Tuk called, not sounding remotely apologetic. "Caught a downdraft."

"Do that again and I'll cut off your prick and feed it to you," Byrna shouted.

Tuk only laughed, a wild, carefree sound that made Carlette's heart spark like flint.

Carefully, each hand placed as if she were putting together a mosaic, Carlette inched her way to Tuk.

"How long until we reach Commercant Bay?" she asked.

"Should be there within the hour," Tuk said with a grin. "And totally intact."

"Why didn't you fly your ship away when you crashed? You could have avoided all this."

Tuk shrugged. "It wouldn't have made it to Caika. The leak in the main balloon is why we're dropping. It doesn't matter for this mission, but if I'd tried to fly *up*, I would have flat-lined and crashed again even higher in the peaks." Tuk's smile widened. "Besides, if I hadn't been captured by Delasir guards, I would have missed all the excitement."

A surprised *ha* burst out of Carlette.

"Excitement? You've been condemned as a spy, betrayed your people, almost died *more than once*. Should I go on?"

"Beats boring fly-over missions."

"I'm not so sure. It seems like you'd be happy flying for no reason at all."

Tuk's laugh was a balm on Carlette's soul, like a coating of warm butter on freshly baked bread. "Probably. The Commander caught me sneaking away for a pleasure-trip once. I'd just gotten into a fight with my bunkmate and wanted to feel the open air. Breathe freely, you know? Caika isn't exactly roomy."

"What did he do?" Carlette asked, thinking of the kinds of punishments she'd seen her classmates receive. Whippings. Beatings. Locked in dark cells for days at a time without food or water.

"Oh, he gave me triple watch. I didn't sleep for three days." Tuk grimaced.

Carlette balked. "That's it?"

Tuk frowned. "Of course. No one survives the air corps unless they love flying. Half the boys I was bunked with took ships on joyrides, and the other half didn't only because their fathers or brothers were in the service, keeping an eye on them. The wind is in our blood, Carlette. Why do you think Nurkaij built the Ziggurat? Our people have always wanted to be closer to the sky."

Carlette sat back against the edge of the ship, clenching her teeth as they dropped again. Byrna was muttering inaudibly in the front of the basket, her forehead pressed to the railing.

"Did you enjoy it?" she asked after a minute. "The air corps?"

Tuk hesitated.

"Yes… and no. I love flying, always have. But I never really believed in the cause. Sure, I hated Delasir. They were invading our country and killing our people. I would have given anything to be on the front lines at Kammunuk, shooting down the King's soldiers. But this…" Tuk's eyes were fixed on the ocean fog, on the near-invisible horizon that threatened rain. "To kill someone because they were born different?" He shook his head. "I've watched my men gun down tribes and burn villages. You saw what they did to the Moians. And for what? So their power can't feed Delasir's war effort? So those kids can't be turned into weapons and used against us?" Tuk sighed. "Never made sense to me. It's like burning a forest so your neighbor can't build a house."

"Would you have Nurkaij create their own half-breeds?" Carlette paused. "Like me?"

Tuk's smile was sad. "I'm afraid they already are."

"And you support that?"

"No, but isn't it better than killing them? Aren't you glad that Jemelle at least gave you a chance?"

Carlette had no answer. She swallowed, tipped her head back. "All I know is I'm glad to be free of it."

He opened his mouth to respond, but at that moment, the sun disappeared. There was a horrible ripping sound. The airship shuddered.

"Duck!" Tuk shouted, shoving Carlette's head down and yanking the rudder to the side. The ship swerved, swinging wildly in a sudden wind. With deft expertise, Tuk rode it, launching them up and to the side. An angry *caw* rang out, too large, too close.

Carlette lifted her head.

By the elders…

A Ceillan raptor wheeled in the misty air, coming around for another strike. The bird was massive, iridescent feathers glimmering with sea mist. On its back, face painted, feathers braided into their hair, was the crouched shape of a man.

Pirates.

"It's the Featherhands!" Tuk shouted as the raptor cawed again. "He's calling for support."

"What do we do?"

The raptor soared toward the basket, twisting in midair as it disappeared below them. The ship bucked. Carlette's body jolted, her legs slipping through a tear in the woven reeds.

"Hold on!" Tuk shouted.

She tightened her grip in the rigging. Nothing but empty air separated her from the crashing sea. Carlette swallowed, pulled herself back into the ship as Byrna shouted obscenities at the pirate. Instinctually, she stretched her mind out for the hulking beast. But the bird was too strange, moving too fast, twisting in and out of her line of vision in erratic swoops. Her power couldn't grab hold.

There was another ripping sound from somewhere above them.

"They're going to tear us apart!" Tuk said.

259

Carlette twisted toward him, frantic. "Tuk, we have to reach the bay."

His expression hardened. He jerked his head in a nod, as if coming to a decision.

"You'll need to jump. I'll draw them away."

"We can't just leave you!"

Tuk's face was pale but determined. "I'll get you as close as I can and then you and Byrna will have to swim for it."

"But if they capture you—"

Tuk grinned at her, not entirely convincing. "I've charmed my way out of trouble before."

Carlette opened her mouth to respond, but Byrna interrupted her.

"What the fuck are you two doing back here?" she asked, shimming past the torn hole in the basket. "And what the fuck are we going to do about *that?*"

"He wants us to jump!" Carlette shouted over the noise of the waves.

"What?"

"Look," Tuk said. "Either you jump now and reach the city, or we all go down and Tuleaux is destroyed. Carlette, they are going to capture this ship. I can't out-fly a raptor, not in this state, and we don't have the weapons to fight back. Even you can't enhabit all the Featherhands at once. It's this or nothing."

Shards of fear cut through Carlette. She couldn't breathe, couldn't think. The idea of leaving him behind, allowing him to be captured by pirates, was nauseating, unpalatable. But their ship was dropping fast, air leaking from the puncture wounds the raptor had made on its first pass.

And two more raptors had appeared over the skyline, fast approaching.

"Ok," Carlette said, hating herself.

"At least we'll be out of the sky," said Byrna.

Carlette wrapped an arm around Byrna's waist, pulling them up to the edge.

260

"Wait for my signal!" Tuk called.

And then the pirates were on them.

It felt like a hurricane. Raptors sliced in from all sides. Bits of the balloon flapped in the breeze and their ship dropped again, harder this time. A tiny shriek escaped Byrna's lips. As they rounded the edge of the cliff, Carlette saw Commercant Bay sweeping out before them in all its sprawling glory; the Magistrate's home, the ships in the harbor, the floating Ceillan chariots penning them in.

Carlette's gut twisted at the lights and distant music.

Despite the blockade, Tuleaux would still celebrate.

Water sprayed Carlette, making her sputter, stopping her thoughts. They were skimming the waves now, barely above them.

"GO!" Tuk shouted.

Snatching one last glimpse of the Nuri airman who had changed everything, Carlette wrapped her arm around Byrna's waist, sent a brief, desperate prayer to whoever was listening.

And threw them both into the inky black sea.

CHAPTER THIRTY-TWO

❋ OCEAN EYES ❋

Hitting the water felt like an explosion in Carlette's brain. The cold struck first, knocking the wind out of her. And then she was assaulted by the concentrated life of the sea, sharp and painful and more potent than anything she'd ever known. It was distilled magic, an acid-bath of raw existence that threatened to swallow her whole. Sensation submerged her mind and body. Her limbs convulsed. Byrna's arm slipped out of her grip. How did the blue hoods control this? How did they cope with the *noise*? So strong was the feeling of being in a hailstorm, of being surrounded by a thousand hungry minds, that Carlette almost didn't notice the spreading numbness and rapid leeching of warmth.

She tumbled, helpless against the powerful waves.

She tasted salt.

Her eyes burned.

Where was the sky?

Focus.

Doing her best to block out the uproar of her magic, Carlette swiped out with a hand, caught a bit of fabric, pulled Byrna back to her.

They had to reach the surface. She could already feel her nerves losing precision, frozen muscles batting uselessly against a chaotic sea.

She kicked toward the wavering daylight.

Almost there.

Their heads burst through the surf only to be thrust back down by a wave. It took everything she had to keep a firm grip on Byrna, to avoid the beetle-speaker's frantic kicks. Carlette was trained for this, had been taught to stare down death without flinching.

Stay the path.

She waited. The wave passed. Their bodies stopped rolling. Her lungs screamed for air, but she gritted her teeth against the reflex to inhale. Looping an arm around Byrna's chest, Carlette dragged them both up.

This time, mercifully, they surfaced on the top on a crest. Sweet, icy air filled Carlette's lungs. Byrna was coughing. Carlette ignored it. Her eyes scanned the horizon.

There!

Over the roaring waves, losing altitude with every moment, Tuk's airship bumbled along like an intoxicated bird. The basket below his balloon was nothing more than tattered reeds, Tuk's long shape all but dangling from the ropes. Raptors swooped down on him. One grabbed at the balloon.

The airship fell.

She heard Tuk shout, followed by a massive splash.

Would he survive the fall? Was he tangled up in the balloon, unable to kick free? She squinted, her breathing harsh and panicked, her imagination wild.

Please don't let him drown…

The raptors swooped in and, with a graceful twist, snatched the deflated balloon out of the sea. They wheeled off, carrying the ruined airship toward the armada of floating sky chariots.

And there, tangled in the rigging, kicking to free himself, was Tuk.

"Stop!" Carlette screamed, throwing an arm out.

"W-what are you going to do, *s-swim* after them?" Byrna said through chattering teeth.

"They took him!"

"Yeah, w-well I d-don't think he'll t-thank you for pissing all o-over his sacrifice."

Carlette floated there a moment, Byrna bumping against her side. The cold was setting in. They had minutes, maybe seconds before their limbs froze and the autumn sea claimed their lives.

Carlette swallowed. Nodded.

"Let's go," she said, making herself turn and kick toward shore.

Byrna tried to be helpful, but her good leg tangled in Carlette's, dragging them backwards. After a few moments of frustrating progress, Carlette ordered Byrna to *stay still*. Flipping the beetle-speaker onto her back, she took over their rescue, limbs jerky as she fought the crashing waves and inched them closer to the looming cliff.

"Aren't. There. Any. Bugs. In. The. Sea?" Carlette said, teeth clicking with each word.

"N-no," Byrna said, shivering. "Not that I t-t-trained with. But t-there are p-p-predators."

Carlette clenched her jaw. There was no way she could pick out individual minds in the whirlpool of life below her. It was like trying to extract one ingredient from a soup. She could sense ferocious sharks and sleek seals, echoing up like voices from the back of a cavern. But she was powerless to enhabit them. Carlette had been trained to *see* her target, to touch the air.

Here, in the middle of the ocean, she was worse than useless.

She'd always taken for granted that the Prederaux were the best of the Order. They were certainly the most valued. But now, Carlette

264

wondered if she'd been wrong. Maybe it was the blue hoods who were the true masters at enhabitation.

Or, if they were anything like Byrna, the black.

A shudder wracked Carlette and she doubled her efforts. Her brain was beginning to fog, to drift away like wood on the tide. Byrna's breath against her neck was the only warm thing left in the world, and even that was chilling fast. The shore was tantalizingly close.

Carlette kept moving.

She could see the cracks in the cliff face, the algae stains at its base. The dark haze of ocean mist had become thick and oppressive, the surf thunderous as it pounded against the mouth of the cove.

Don't stop, don't stop, she thought desperately, chanting the mantra with each stroke.

A swell crashed over them, plunging their frozen bodies into darkness. Her foot caught on a stone. Slipped off.

Shore!

When they bobbed to the surface again, Byrna was chattering curses. But Carlette was filled with a renewed determination. Her fingers groped the water. Her eyes, half-blinded by the salt, blinked feverishly.

Another wave broke over them.

Carlette's feet hit something solid. Her knees buckled, but she managed to dig her toes into toothy rubble. Bubbles escaped her mouth in a silent scream as the toes of her boots ripped, spilling blood, but she pushed them forward, step by step. The hungry ocean fought to pull them back, but Carlette was single-minded, her whole world narrowed down to air and shore and *survival*.

Finally, the water receded.

She grabbed the stone with her free hand, hauling them up, racing the next wave. She knew that if the water reclaimed them now, she wouldn't have the energy to fight back. With Byrna limp in her arms, both of them quivering, Carlette emerged from the sea step by brutal step.

Finally, she could take no more. She fell to her knees. Byrna toppled off her shoulders, flopping against the sharp rock.

Get up, she told herself. *Keep going*.

Her body wouldn't listen.

The next wave crashed noisily behind them, water surging in, cold and heartless.

It pooled around her legs but came in no further.

They were safe.

Carlette allowed herself to breathe. A stitch drove into her side like a dagger, her palms were both an angry red, and blood dribbled down the leathers of her pants. But her head was above water and, right then, she didn't care about anything else.

Byrna was hacking beside her, water dribbling out of blue lips.

"No. More. *Flying,*" Byrna said between coughs.

Carlette laughed weakly, blinking up at the cliffs. A giddiness flushed through her. Somehow, they had survived. Tuk's plan had worked, delivering them right to the edge of Commercant Bay. The bobbing ships stretched out before her, illuminated by lanterns and the warm glow of a noisy city.

But her laugh died as soon as it came.

The Ceillan sky chariots had the bay surrounded, reminding Carlette of the price they had payed. Even now the Featherhands could be torturing Tuk, prying information out of him like nails from wood. Would they kill him right away? Demand his help in dominating the skies? Were they, like everyone else, also hunting for Caika?

Carlette didn't know and wouldn't find out anytime soon, not until she stopped Yokan.

She hoped he would survive that long.

Teetering on feet so cold they felt more like wood than like limbs, Carlette stumbled to her feet. She coughed and steadied herself against the nearest boulder, trying to consolidate the last of her warmth. They had to act quickly.

"What was Yokan's plan?" Carlette asked, pulling Byrna away from the water. The Moian girl moaned in pain. "They were going to sneak the pup into the bay. How?"

"On… a dinghy," Byrna panted. "They were… ordered to leave it docked by one of the larger… freighters so no one would notice."

Carlette supported Byrna to a small, dry ledge, eyes tracking the horizon. Above them, the Magistrate's house would be teeming with activity; his soldiers preparing to march down the Rae du Ora with the young prince in tow. Settlers would be lining the street, waving banners and anticipating the regal parade.

Her gut twisted. She grabbed Byrna's arm and hauled them both upright.

"We need to find a boat," she said, helping Byrna hobble forward.

"And… do what? Kill… the little beast… ourselves?"

"The only way to stop the she-wolf is to return her baby," Carlette said, feeling the full certainty of her words even as she said them. She alone had touched that vast mind. She, better than anyone, knew what this creature would do to save her infant.

Or avenge it.

"And how do you plan to do that?" Byrna hissed as they rounded a corner. "I'm not sure… about you, but I can't carry an Amonoux pup… like this."

"Let's just find it first," Carlette snapped, her temper stretched to the breaking point.

They were running out of time. She knew the Ebonal hunters were already in place, Yokan's plan already in motion. They might be too late…

Carlette's sharp eyes fell on a nearby clump of jagged shapes, almost invisible in the encroaching shadows. Her heart stuttered. Was it a guard? A wolf? An Ebonal hunter?

But no, it was a pile of debris washed in from the bay, shunted into a small culvert where the waves swirled in. Carlette squinted, barely making out the snapped wood, the sloping masts.

Was that… a rowboat?

She sped up, yanking a protesting Byrna along with her. Together they lurched toward the junkpile, rocks shifting beneath them, making it even more difficult to walk.

"What are you—?"

"I think that one's intact," Carlette said, interrupting Byrna.

But when they were close enough to make out the details, Carlette's hope deflated.

"First the airship, now this?" Byrna grumbled.

Carlette didn't blame her. Calling the dilapidated thing in front of them a boat was generous to the point of stupidity. The rolling waves and salty air had left this ancient fishing vessel less a means of transportation and more a pile of wet kindling.

But in the distance, she could hear the celebrations starting, the trumpets of a parade.

They had to do something.

"Help me flip it over," Carlette said, releasing Byrna.

Byrna fell over twice as she tried to help Carlette detach the wood from the stone. Seaweed and barnacles had all but cemented its edge to the serrated ground. But with three grunting tugs they were able to break it free. It creaked and groaned, but Carlette didn't pause to see if it could handle the abuse.

With a mighty heave she shoved it upright and let it topple into the water.

Byrna found the algae-covered mooring rope and together they watched the little boat bob in the relative calm of Commercant Bay. Water leaked through a multitude of holes, filling the base of the vessel in moments. But Carlette fished around the bow—breathing through her mouth to avoid the odor of rot and decaying fish—and found a bucket.

"Get in," Carlette said, thrusting the bucket at Byrna.

"You know, maybe a few kids dying isn't the worst thing—"

"Get. In."

Byrna tried to slide into the ship but ended up catching her broken leg and tumbling into the boat with a crash and a shout. Carlette cursed inwardly and scanned the cliff. No guards yet but there were enemies on all sides.

They needed to be careful.

"Aren't Moians supposed to be good at *hiding*?" Carlette hissed, shoving them off the coast with half a broken oar.

"I'd be happy to break *your* leg and see how *you* do," Byrna hissed back.

The tiny boat leaked like the Magistrate's purse. Byrna's efforts with the rusted-out bucket were barely enough to keep them afloat, not to mention noisy. Carlette winced with each grunt and splash, but the howling wind of the oncoming storm was enough to cover their approach.

She glared into the shadows.

Unlike the mountainous waves in the open sea, the waters of Commercant Bay were calmer. Not pristine, but Carlette was able to guide them over the tiny swells. Gently swaying masts rose around them in a forest and a few shapes moved on the ships, but Carlette knew those men wouldn't be paying much attention. These were the sailors who had drawn the short stick and been left to stand guard. With the pirates floating just outside the bay, the captains would have left more than the usual security. So the extra men would play cards, get drunk, gripe about missing the fun, and feel up whatever woman was unlucky enough to be chartered to that crew: hoods, cooks, the occasional female sailor.

Carlette kept her head low, wishing her hair was as dark as Byrna's.

As they moved through the ships, doing their best to keep quiet, Carlette probed the bay. She could feel the steady undercurrent of human minds, brushing her senses like branches scraping against a closed window. And, of course, the thrum of the ocean that she'd only just begun to appreciate.

But no Amonoux pup.

Her instincts prickled.

"Something's not right," Carlette said.

There was a stirring below her, alien and strange. She tried to puzzle through it, head aching as she sifted through the deluge of information. Her power settled, as it usually did, on the most ferocious minds, the most violent thoughts.

Sharks.

Carlette zeroed in, strained to see through the animal's murky mind.

It tasted blood in the water.

She drew out of the creature with a snap and began to paddle more fiercely. Byrna asked a question, but Carlette didn't hear it. Fear pulsed through her, alive and hissing and desperate.

Please, she prayed to her ancestors. Please no. Let me be wrong.

Their pathetic little fishing vessel rounded the hull of a three-masted schooner and Carlette's throat caught. She knew. Tears blurred her vision, but she didn't slow until they had reached it.

"Well," Byrna said, lowering the bucket. "Shit."

Drifting in the gentle currents of the bay was a massive white shape, almost the size of their boat. The pup's throat had been slit and blood leaked out like an oil spill. Water was beginning to churn around it, ocean creatures rushing up for an easy meal. But the body was still intact. Carlette could even smell the lingering stink of its fear.

They were too late.

The pup was dead.

"What now, larva girl?" Byrna asked in a low, sad voice.

Carlette opened her mouth without having any idea what she planned to say. They'd failed. Tuk had been captured for nothing. Of course the Bloody Paws had killed the pup, why wouldn't they? It was too much trouble to keep it alive. Too much to ask for mercy…

"I don't—"

But Carlette was interrupted by sound, so distant and soft that, if not for their shocked silence, she would have missed it entirely.

A furious, agonized howl.

CHAPTER THIRTY-THREE

✳ SACRIFICE ✳

Carlette guided their fishing dinghy under the docks, cringing at Byrna's rasping breath. It would take so little—nothing more than a badly timed gasp—to end their journey right there in the mud. Boots thundered overhead, the excited sound of men and women who would kill them without hesitation. Byrna's pale face was a moon in the viscous darkness, eyes tracking the noise.

"These prissy settlers wouldn't last a heartbeat in the forest," Byrna mumbled, shaking her head in disgust.

Carlette shot her a wide-eyed look filled with a single command. Quiet!

The fishing boat bumped against one of the dock posts with a wooden *thunk*. Carlette waited, breath held, to see if the sound had betrayed them. But in the symphony of raised voices, crashing waves, howling wind, and the distant, cheerful sound of instruments, no one seemed to notice the small dinghy quickly sinking below their feet.

"Now what?" Byrna whispered, half-swimming to the stern.

Carlette had turned things over in her head again and again.

There was no other way.

"Now I go and warn the prince," she said in a low voice, not meeting Byrna's eyes as she dragged the beetle-speaker to shore.

Carlette had known since they'd found the dead pup. It was as if a lantern had been ignited, lighting her path. The Magistrate wouldn't listen—he'd probably have Carlette shot on sight.

But Dirlen…

Despite the young prince's acerbic sarcasm, Carlette had sensed an openness in him. Maybe he would listen, if only to protect his people.

It was the best idea she could think of.

"You're mad," Byrna hissed. "No one will hear what a hood has to say."

"The prince will," Carlette said with confidence she did not feel.

Byrna snorted. "And I thought you were just getting started with Tuk."

"We don't have a choice," Carlette snapped, crouching in the shallows. A guard dog whuffled, its claws scraping the deck above them. Carlette gently pushed the hound to ignore their pungent, telltale scent.

"Bullshit. Listen to me, larva-girl, we need to get out of here. This whole city is going to be bloodier than childbirth in a few minutes."

"If we leave them, what does that make us?"

"Alive."

"If your idea of a better world involves standing back as hundreds of innocents die, then I want no part of it."

Byrna sighed. "You and your damn honor."

"Use your power from here. Watch for Yokan. Wait for things to break before exposing yourself. And send me a signal when she's close."

Byrna looked at Carlette for a long moment, her white-rimmed eyes shimmering in the darkness.

272

"Tell me, larva-girl," Byrna said, and Carlette felt the weight of her words. "Are you worth all this?"

Carlette faced the Moian, forced herself to hold Byrna's gaze.

It was like holding lightning.

"I don't know," Carlette replied. "I'm no leader. I don't think I'm anything like Voka. But I believe we can do better. Be better." She paused, looking at her scarred and bleeding hands. "I won't ask you to die for me, beetle-speaker. But if you examine what's in your heart, I think we're fighting for the same cause."

Byrna's mouth twisted into a wicked grin. "And if I don't have a heart?"

Carlette couldn't help smiling back. She hadn't been sure of Byrna before, had always second-guessed the girl's loyalty. Moian, Bloody Paw, beetle-speaker, Ferrenese. She wore too many labels, each of them a shifting target.

But as Byrna extended one hand and Carlette reached out to grasp it, an understanding settled between them.

"To your better fucking path," Byrna said.

Carlette nodded, squeezed Byrna's hand, and slid out from beneath the dock like a ghost into the windblown night.

It was easy for her to sneak along the rooftops, hiding in chimney shadows and climbing turrets as the Gaulday celebrations spread out before her like a carpet of laughter and sweet-smelling foods. She felt eight years old again, just a rascal sneaking around town.

But the looming presence in her mind kept her rooted in the present.

The Amonoux pack was there, brushing against her consciousness, growing ever closer. They crashed through the forest on their way to Tuleaux as quickly and lethally as the thunderheads wafting over the open ocean.

No one could feel them but her, so Carlette kept moving.

She had to reach the prince, had to make him evacuate the city. With any luck, the young and old could be saved, funneled into the tunnels, hidden in the cliffs. The city would recover, could rebuild, but if the children died...

Carlette would never forgive herself.

Guilt and frustration braided in taut vines around her ribs. This was all her fault. The letter, her hood; without them Yokan would still be in the mountains. If Carlette had held herself together, maintained control in that first Bloody Paw attack on the Iron Bridge, she would have been down there, dancing and celebrating with the rest.

And Tuk?

Carlette shook her head. She couldn't think about Tuk, not strapped to Erebus's table, not captured on the pirate ship behind her.

Now, more than ever, she needed to concentrate.

Carlette found a good vantage point over the main square, hidden in the shadow of a gigantic spire. The Church of the Hand's bells rang merrily in her ear, almost deafening at this height. Scanning the crowd, Carlette felt her fear swell with every familiar face.

Mya, ruddy-cheeked and laughing.

Mileen, standing apart from the other orphans with a determined, stubborn expression.

The pinched-mouth Magistrate and his voluminous wife.

The Woodsman and his guard of hoods.

The shopkeepers who had always grinned at her and Quaina as they sprinted down the Rae du Ora.

The prince.

Carlette leaned out, examining the raised platform where the young royal sat in a place of honor, above even the Magistrate himself. Prince Dirlen looked as wry as ever, his mouth quirked as he watched the church choir sing Delasir's anthem. It was as if the entire night was a good joke and he alone understood it.

Carlette wondered how the source of so much gossip could appear so comfortable in front of a crowd.

Six guards flanked the prince, three on either side. The crowned anchor emblem of the royal palace glimmered gold and purple on their chests. Their full regalia drew the eyes of settlers who hadn't seen such opulence since leaving their home nation, if at all. But Dirlen wore a simple tunic and breeches, one booted foot hanging off the armrest of his throne-like chair.

Carlette needed a distraction.

She swept the area, wracking her brain for ideas.

Think, think, think...

And then, from somewhere in the distance, she felt that familiar presence, tainted by something horribly wrong.

Grand Mera was approaching the main gates.

Carlette swallowed.

She'd run out of time for an elegant approach.

Clenching her jaw, Carlette scanned her power over the choir and dove into the easiest mind. A young girl. Carlette enhabited her in an instant, doing her best not to hurt the youthful consciousness.

She tugged.

The girl's scream pierced the night.

Panic rose, immediate and swift. Every guard grabbed their weapon, snapping to attention. The little girl was convulsing, falling to the ground. All attention was on the choir, on the pretty child now flailing like a fish.

In the chaos, Carlette slid down the wall of the church and sprinted around the edge of the Chantiere. She grabbed a hanging jacket, wrapped it around her, pulled up the fur-lined cowl. It smelled of sweat and ocean, but at least it hid her face.

Guards stepped in front of Dirlen, bristling against the hidden threat.

Carlette slipped under the hanging backdrop and grabbed the prince's shoulder.

"What—?"

Carlette slapped a hand over his mouth. She had only seconds.

275

"The Bloody Paws are about to attack this city," she muttered, the words tumbling out of her in a desperate barrage. "Don't ask me how I know this. Please, you need to evacuate or everyone is going to die."

"You," said the prince as his guards turned, their faces twisted with fury as they barreled toward Carlette. "You're that hood that went missing. The one transporting our Nuri spy!"

Strong hands clamped down on Carlette's arms, hauling her back. She kicked out.

"*Please*, sir, you need to listen. Everyone here is in danger."

She could feel the eyes, the minds, turning their attention to the raised platform like notched arrows. The Magistrate was on his feet, his wife's mouth open in shock. The Woodsman strode toward them, his entourage close behind. Their power swirled around her, closing in, ready to take her down.

Mya was staring helplessly at Carlette, as if the worst had finally come to pass.

But Carlette kept her attention on Prince Dirlen, willing him, *begging* him, to understand. "Your Majesty, I can explain everything, I promise, but there's no *time*. They're on their way right now!"

"Stop," Dirlen said, slicing one hand. The air itself seemed to freeze. Dirlen stepped forward, eyes narrow, the click of his boots on the platform the only sound in the square. He was taller than Carlette but not by much. He glared at her, his face more serious than she had ever seen it.

"Our fences are strong," he said in a low voice. "I've seen them myself. The Bloody Paws have never breeched them before."

Carlette shook her head.

"It's not the Bloody Paws. It's the Amonoux pack. The rebels have baited them into the city. They'll be here in minutes."

Dirlen frowned.

In the corner of her eye, Carlette saw a moth fluttering by the prince's head.

Byrna.

"How could you know this?" the prince asked.

Carlette pursed her lips, ignoring the squeezing pain of hands around her arms. What could she possibly say in answer? That she was a deserter? That she'd lost faith in the cause and discovered herself along the way? That she might have fallen in love with a Nuri spy, not only breaking the rules of Jemelle but the very laws of Delasir?

That she was a Furix?

The moth fluttered more insistently, circling around the guards. One of the huge men swatted at it.

Carlette met the Prince's gaze.

"I was captured by the rebels. I overheard their plan," she said, wondering if he could sense the half-truths in her voice. "You have to listen to me, I'm on your side. I fight to defend this city."

That, at least, was true.

Prince Dirlen frowned.

Moths were batting against Carlette's ears now. A haze of insects was slowly filling the square, tiny feather-light wings stirring the crisp autumn night.

"Please," Carlette pleaded. "I can't watch anyone else die."

For a single moment, Carlette thought the prince might listen. She could see the wheels in his head turning, the temptation to sound the alarm growing. She leaned forward, willing him to *do it*.

But before he could speak, a voice called out from the other side of the Chantiere.

"Well, well, well," Grand Mera said, so cold it made the ocean spray seem like bathwater. "What have we here?"

CHAPTER THIRTY-FOUR

❋ GRAND PLANS ❋

Carlette struggled helplessly against the guards, but it was no use. Grand Mera had arrived, resplendent in a sweeping cloak and hat pulled low over her eyes. In all the years Carlette had known the old woman, she'd never seen Grand Mera dress up for anyone.

Surely someone would suspect...

But a sigh of relief billowed up from the crowd. The hoods were here. The Bloody Paws wouldn't dare attack the fences with the entirety of Jemelle inside.

Carlette struggled, snarled, but Dirlen had already turned to face the tall figure.

"Don't listen to her!" she spat, probing with her mind, reaching for leverage. There was a horrible *wrongness* scattered among the trainees.

Hidden rebels in stolen hoods.

"No!" Carlette said, but the Woodsman threw her a disdainful look, waving his hand in dismissal.

"Blindfold her and take her to the cells," he snapped. And then he shook his head. "You showed so much promise."

"Please, it's her!" Carlette said as a strip of fabric was tied around her face, weakening her power. "It's Yokan!"

"Fanciful, isn't she," came Grand Mera's voice. Closer. She'd reached the middle of the square, cutting through the crowd like butter. Carlette sensed a wave of unease roll through her fingertips, Mya's confusion, Mileen's instinctual distrust.

Even the surrounding settlers seemed to sense something wasn't quite right.

"Grand Mera, I welcome you to Tuleaux," said Prince Dirlen, somewhat uneasily.

"Thank you, your highness," came Yokan's twisted words from Grand Mera's throat. "But it is I who must welcome *you* to our island. How fortuitous that you chose to join us for this Gaulday celebration."

"It has been a pleasant experience."

"Too bad it won't have a pleasant end."

There was a pregnant, horrible pause.

"I'm not sure what you mean, ma'am."

Dirlen's voice was tense. Whispers rose like air escaping Tuk's balloon. Even the hands on Carlette loosened, their attention elsewhere.

"It's not her!" Carlette shouted, kicking out, not caring who heard her. "She's enhabited! You have to save her!"

Grand Mera's deep-throated chuckle was chilling, the satisfaction of a predator licking its chops.

"There's no saving her, little girl. There's no saving any of you."

"Ma'am, if you don't explain yourself, I'm afraid I will have to—
"

"What? Kill me? But you've already done so much worse than that. You've butchered my people, raped my lands, destroyed the

279

balance of our peace. But do you know what makes me *laugh*, little prince? Despite all that, you've only made us *stronger*."

A chair scraped, clattered as it was thrown back.

"Seize her," commanded the Magistrate.

There was the icy sound of swords being drawn. A gunshot echoed in the square.

A woman screamed.

The guards released Carlette and she fell to her knees, ripping off her blindfold.

Grand Mera stood in the center of the crowd, her face in shadow. All around her, fights were breaking out, her fellow rebels surging forward to defend her, kill for her. The Woodsman crashed forward, his massive battleaxe cutting through the invaders like a scythe. People shrieked and shouted. Settlers crowded into the alleyways, fleeing toward the fences.

Not that way, Carlette thought helplessly as she stretched out her power, scanning for Yokan.

She had to save Grand Mera. To the guards, Mera was just the strange old bachelorette who ran Jemelle. The embodiment of a necessary curse. Disposable. The shields of Tuleaux didn't care if she was enhabited, acting against her will.

All they saw was an enemy to cut down.

Carlette reached out for Grand Mera's enhabited mind. She found Yokan's connection, climbed recklessly up it.

Let her go.

Carlette's grip on Yokan's mind was razor-sharp and ox-strong. There was no point concealing her power anymore, no reason to hold back. Swarms of bugs were emerging from beneath the square, surging out around the platform she stood on. One Bloody Paw fell, shrieking, covered in ants.

But Carlette focused all her energy on Yokan's mind.

She clenched tighter.

A red hood in the back screamed.

There.

280

The Woodsman had elbowed through, throwing settlers aside. He pulled back his axe just as Grand Mera turned to face him, grinning, eyes glowing white.

She's all yours, Yokan said through their mental tether.

And, just like that, Yokan severed her connection with Grand Mera. It felt like stepping off an unexpected ledge, like a snapped rope whipping back at her. Carlette was left to tumble into the old woman's mind, disoriented, out of control.

For a brief instant, Carlette saw the world through Grand Mera's eyes.

She felt the clockwork mind of Jemelle's headmistress, breathed through her rasping lungs. In the single heartbeat it took to fill the edges of Grand Mera's consciousness, Carlette realized she was already half-dead, weak and broken under Yokan's control. There would be no bringing her back. No saving her. Blotches of darkness were already spreading, places that Carlette could not touch.

Places where the tissue of her brain had become nothing more than meat.

Carlette inhaled a sob, holding tight to what was left of the woman she'd loved.

By the time she realized her mistake, it was too late.

The Woodsman's axe came down like a cleaver on Grand Mera's chest, caving it in half. Pain and death reverberated up Carlette's connection, sudden, sickening. It crashed over her like a tsunami. Carlette collapsed onto all fours, vomiting all over the platform.

"It's her!" someone shouted.

"She's behind this!"

"Stop her!"

"Kill her!"

Cries for vengeance and shrieks of terror swirled around her like spooked birds. Through watering eyes, Carlette saw Yokan smiling at her from beneath her own stolen hood. The rebel leader was a rock in the rushing river of people, motionless against the panicked current.

Guards rushed toward Carlette, closing in.

She steeled herself, ready to fight.

But Byrna saved her with another wave of insects swarming up their legs, amplifying their screams.

Carlette staggered to her feet, using the prince's chair for support. He was there, alone and stock-still, watching her with an unreadable frown.

"Please, Your Majesty," Carlette wheezed, wiping her mouth. "You must evacuate."

Dirlen's eyes narrowed.

"Whether I am a traitor or not," Carlette said, struggling to keep her voice steady. "I am telling you now that if you do nothing, everyone here will die."

"And if this is a trap? Some trick to force us all into the mountain?"

Carlette stared at the chaos in front of them, her heartbeat ragged. Grand Mera's mind was still a tendril of smoke, curling into the starry sky. She wondered where Mya was in the crowd. Shielding her orphans, perhaps, or fighting to escape the square?

Did she know yet that her sister was dead?

Carlette turned to the prince, ready to get on her knees and beg. For Mileen's sake. For Mya. For all the people she'd already failed.

But before she could say anything, the turmoil was broken by a single, reverberating *crash*.

It was too late.

The Amonoux pack had arrived.

CHAPTER THIRTY-FIVE

❆ CARNAGE ❆

"Get women and children into the caves," Dirlen barked. "Gather the soldiers."

Carlette wanted to cry with relief as Prince Dirlen and the Magistrate began to organize. But the panic had already rolled well out of their control. Citizens of Tuleaux sprinted every which way, knocking into one another, falling to Bloody Paw weapons. The Chantiere was stained red, cobblestones outlined by rivulets of blood.

The prince grabbed Carlette's shoulder.

"You say you're on our side," he said. "Prove it."

Carlette nodded once and dove into the chaos. The crowd battered her like driftwood, and the fog of terror was worse. It filled the air like Byrna's insects, making it impossible to think straight.

There was no time to reach the tunnels…

"To the ships!" Carlette screamed, fighting the tide of civilians. "To the ships!"

Carlette grabbed a little girl around the waist to stop her from being trampled. The mother shrieked and began to beat at Carlette's head, but Carlette stopped her with a flicker of power.

"Take her to the docks and get on a ship," she said, infusing her words with commanding magic.

Blank-faced, the woman accepted her child and disappeared into the darkness, heading to the boatyard.

That's two…

Suddenly, bugs swarmed up Carlette's legs, concentrating around her in a whirlpool of movement. She tried not to panic, took a deep breath as the insects fluttered around her. The moths arranged themselves in a halo.

"Listen to me!" Carlette shouted, and those around her paused, mouths open in awe. "Get to the docks! You'll be safe in the water!"

She hoped.

Finally, the settlers seemed listen. The people around her turned, sprinted toward the water.

It wasn't enough.

Panic had become the most powerful enhabiter in the city. Even the trained guards and soldiers wore it on their faces. Bodies crammed the alleys, the crowd flattening everything in its path.

Carlette ground her teeth as she waded through.

Where was Yokan?

A fight had coagulated around the Prince. Carlette glimpsed six Bloody Paws fighting to reach him, snapping and biting and enhabiting their way through the shield of soldiers. Birds scraped at the guards' arms, fighting swarms of horseflies. Deep barks signaled that a few hounds had joined the fray.

Carlette plunged in.

Snapping her hands forward, she swiped out with the snow-snake spines on her arms. Half were missing and the rest were bent and frayed.

But with any luck, a few might have poison left.

Snarling like a mountain stag, Carlette slashed out with both hands. A Bloody Paw screamed. Another fell, his mind crippled by Carlette's crushing grip. Insects swarmed a third. The soldiers backed away, shouting, as the Sibilese warrior shrieked, clawing at the ants and flies that stuck to his skin like spilled oil.

Something tapped insistently against Carlette's mind.

A warning.

She spun around, brought her arm up.

Yokan's bladed bow sank into the leather on her arm, its decorative bones jangling.

"Well aren't you full of surprises?" said Yokan, her voice the unsettling mix of a growl and a laugh.

Carlette ducked, swept her leg out. Yokan leapt over it easily.

"Powerful enough to stop me," Yokan said, bringing her bow down again. Carlette dodged it, felt it snag on her stolen coat. "Strong enough to bodywalk my rebels without breaking your stride."

"These people," Carlette snarled, swiping out at Yokan, "are *innocent*."

The rebel leader leapt backwards with sinuous grace.

Bugs clouded around them.

"No one in this city is innocent, girl," Yokan growled, striking with enough force for her bow to chip the cobblestones. "They deserve what they get."

"They say the same thing about *you*," Carlette snarled, whipping her arm at Yokan's head. She felt skin catch. Blood spurted. "Where does it end? When do you stop?"

"When we're free."

Yokan's left cheek dripped blood, scratched by one of Carlette's spikes. She wiped it, examining the crimson stain.

With an almost obscene smile, she put her fingers in her mouth.

Carlette fought the urge to gag.

Yokan stalked forward, still grinning. "Ebonal children are raised to tolerate *nathair* poison. It's how we remove their *weakness*."

285

Carlette deflected her blow, twisting around to punch at Yokan's side.

In the distance, the screams were sharpening, rising to a fever pitch. Snarls ripped through the night. The sounds of collapsing buildings and crashing bodies had become almost deafening.

All around them, people died.

"How can you justify this?" Carlette said, knocked back by the bridge of the bow.

"You would not understand, girl." Yokan darted forward, jabbing at where Carlette's leg had been a moment before. "Delasir's taint runs in your blood. You are the illness I seek to cure."

Carlette flicked her mind at Yokan, grabbed hold. "Say that again."

Yokan's chuckle was strangled as Carlette squeezed.

"You make a mockery of our people," she wheezed. "Look at you. You cannot do what needs to be done. You could have killed me, and yet here we are."

Her grin was spectral, taunting.

Carlette's gut twisted. She told herself that it didn't mean anything. She could kill this woman, do the thing she had been trained to do since she was nine years old. It would be as easy as taking a breath. With just a little pressure, Yokan would be nothing more than a husk on the ground.

Like Grand Mera.

A soldier cried out nearby, clawing at insects, and Carlette knew she couldn't do it.

She wasn't a weapon.

Not anymore.

With a jab of power, Carlette stole Yokan's breath and shut down her brain. It took more energy than killing her, but in a few heartbeats, Yokan collapsed onto the gory cobblestones.

Unconscious, but alive.

Filled with conflict and self-loathing, Carlette embraced the fury that washed through her. Allowed herself to ride its full strength. With a casual flick, she took down a Bloody Paw. Another. A guard tried to strike her down and he fell with a strangled cry. Men were backing away, but not quickly enough.

Carlette was a lit wildfire and the men around her fell like leaves.

She wondered if this was how Yokan lived every day. Furious. Sparkling.

Animal.

Prince Dirlen watched her make her way through the mess, his expression carved from stone. For an instant, their eyes met. Beneath his emotionless gaze—an expression cultivated by the vicious Beraselle courts—Carlette could taste his fear. And in that moment, reflected in the bastard prince's eyes, Carlette saw herself.

She was goddess.

She was a monster.

What am I doing? she thought, recoiling from this feral edge she'd never known existed. *What have I become?*

But a new sound rose, breaking through her worry.

Mileen's scream.

Byrna leaned against the docks, watching settlers and soldiers race for the bobbing ships. Her eyes glowed but no one seemed to care. It was a sign of their panic that no one noticed the paw tattoo or the near-black Moian hair. Byrna was out in the open—an uncomfortable place for a beetle-speaker of the Hanging City. Her power flowed, pure and delicious, and no one stopped her.

It wouldn't be enough.

She could sense it through the feelers of her insects. Death approached. The thousands of minds she touched hummed with excitement at the prospect. To them, death was food. A place to lay eggs.

Life.

To Byrna, though...

How many innocents would die this night? How many children? It was one thing to plan an attack in a deserted mining tunnel, fueled by rage and vengeance. It was quite another to see the fear, to taste it. These people were far from blameless. But that didn't make them evil. Watching them flee for their lives, fight for survival, Byrna couldn't help but notice the similarities between these settlers and the men and women forced to abandon the Moian capitol under the pursuit of Nuri Zanburs.

She watched with a cocked head and a heavy heart.

It was frightening how close she'd been to becoming the very thing her father had always hated. Was her mother watching from the Great Forest, shaking her head in shame?

Someone tapped her on the shoulder.

Byrna spun around, her hold on the insects snapping like a thousand tiny threads.

"What the...?"

It was Tuk, looking disheveled and exhausted but otherwise unhurt.

"Well if it isn't the daisy himself," she said, folding her arms and grinning. "I must admit, I'm surprised to see you with all your fingers."

"Byrna, I made a deal. To get us all out of here. But we need to go, *now*."

Byrna's smile widened.

"You made a deal with the *Featherhands*?" She cackled. "And I thought Carlette kept you around just for fun."

"Yes, but it only works if we get out of here!"

Tuk grabbed Byrna's arm, pulling it over his shoulder.

"What's the deal?" she asked as they hobbled up the beach.

"You'll like it," Tuk said, half-lifting Byrna onto the docks. "I promise."

Carlette's world was a vortex of violence. Guns cracked. Swords clanged. Screams echoed. Death was everywhere, viscous and pungent. And layered over all of it were the Amonoux, howling against the night, ripping through Tuleaux like a city made of paper.

She ran, trying to ignore the horrifying images as they hit her like cannonballs.

A woman's body torn in half, intestines spilling onto the street.

An Amonoux pouncing on a screaming soldier and his horse.

A group of orphans shaking in the shadows.

That drunkard Eylon, sprinting toward the broken fences, his bloodshot eyes wide with terror.

The Amonoux had plunged into the heart of Tuleaux, leaving a trail of wreckage in their wake. Settlers fought to reach the caves, but the wolf pack had wedged themselves between the city and the relative shelter of the mountain. With the fences broken, other animals had leaked inside too, eager for food. Three enormous forest spiders scuttled over the rooftops, dropping sticky residue behind them. Hungry foxes swooped through the air, silent and deadly. Mountain stags galloped through the streets, their fangs wet with blood.

The rebels had succeeded.

Tuleaux, as they'd known it, was gone.

All Carlette could do now was find Mya and Mileen and the other orphans. She couldn't lose them too.

A body knocked into her.

Carlette twisted to see a black-haired Sibilese woman cocking back a spear, bearing down on her. *Not now.* She ducked around an upturned carriage, unwilling to waste any time. But then, suddenly, a long writhing *something* was wrapping around her ankles, tripping her. She crashed into a hay cart with a strangled gasp, rolling over to see what it was.

It was a desert snake, about to plunge its fangs into her thigh.

Carlette tried to gather her frantic thoughts, reached out for the Sibilese woman's mind. But before she could act, a shadow moved. The rebel was lifted into the air as if by magic.

Carlette squinted.

No, not magic.

A long, black feeler.

Tabis.

The snake around Carlette's calves loosened. With a shove, she kicked herself free and stumbled to her feet just as the kicking rebel was whipped against the nearest wall with bone-breaking force.

Carlette looked up.

Hanging in the alley like a nightmare brought to life, the cairog was draped between two grimy buildings. It clicked at her, as if in greeting. Carlette nodded thanks before diving beneath its innumerable legs, making for the Rae du Ora. She braced herself, held her breath.

But nothing could have prepared her for the slaughter.

The street overflowed with terrified soldiers, pouncing Amonoux, shouting Bloody Paws on bloodstained mounts. The Woodsman directed his hoods, barking orders and wielding a massive battleaxe. A horse-sized spider came out of nowhere, tackling the nearest city guard to the ground.

Another shriek rose, Mileen's broken voice pounding into Carlette's skull.

"Help!"

She turned.

"Mya!" Carlette screamed, almost toppling over as she rushed into the melee.

There, framed in an alley like a creature from an ancient story, was the she-wolf.

All seven of her eyes glittered with power. She radiated anger, frustration, impotence, loss. Carlette could feel her, feel the pain in her. But even that couldn't drown out Carlette's own terror as she recognized the two figures the Amonoux was bearing down on, her next two victims.

Mya, leg trapped beneath a heavy wooden beam, and Mileen standing over her, legs splayed wide, as if the brave little girl could stop a legend.

"NO!" Carlette shrieked.

She lashed out with her power, grabbing hold of Quaina's thread. It was easier to find this time, but harder to hold. She clutched it with everything she had. She was a dinghy in a hurricane, an airship in a storm. Carlette had never felt so much *power*. Instinctual and raw, the she-wolf's mind was crackling like Carlette's had been only moments before, but so much stronger. Carlette held on, desperately gripping her link to the Amonoux as if there was nothing else in the world.

No! she thought as that vast consciousness threatened to consume her, drag her into unknowable depths.

The wolf's rage swept toward her like wind whistling over the desert.

I'm sorry, Carlette thought, barely aware of the sobs building in her chest. *I'm so sorry. But you have to stop.*

Carlette shoved things at the she-wolf. The image of her pup, bleeding in the bay. The Bloody Paws, carrying him over the mountains in the toboggan. The vague, human concept of a trap.

This, she understood.

They want you to do this, Carlette tried to say without words, struggling to make this animal understand things that were so horribly, dreadfully human. *They're using you. Please, turn back. There are pups here too.*

Carlette offered up images of orphans running down the now-ruined street. She thought of Mya, a different kind of matriarch.

Please, turn back. Don't meet their darkness with more darkness.

That great, alien mind shifted, softened.

Darkness... the wolf thought, and Carlette could almost see the understanding form.

The Amonoux couldn't grasp evil, for what in nature is? But she knew a loss that went deeper than death. A hunger that wasn't natural. There was a black emptiness that pocked her lands, shaded trails her pack no longer walked.

A strange sense of kinship flooded through Carlette, unexpected and overwhelming. The she-wolf was Voka, in her own way; a wild force, a leader, displaced by the march of civilization. Carlette could understand, all too clearly, how the pack felt about these *humans,* driving deeper into their mountains, eroding the freedom they'd once known.

It's a cycle that never stops, Carlette thought hopelessly, sharing the she-wolf's longing. *A path that never ends.*

Until someone steps forward to end it, said a small voice in Carlette's heart. Quaina's thread glowed.

Help me change things, Carlette thought, throwing open the shields around her mind.

Slowly, the wolf's hackles settled. Her lips closed, covering fangs. Carlette could feel that seventh and most mysterious eye peering into her, appraising her very soul.

She was too exhausted to care what the she-wolf saw.

After a long moment, the gigantic queen of the Amonoux pack threw back her head and howled. But this was a different sound. Filled with mourning, laced with sadness, it echoed off the mountains like a funeral dirge. Carlette sensed more than saw the stillness as it crept over the city.

Thank you, Carlette thought, brushing Quaina's thread one last time before letting it slip away.

She opened her eyes.

Like a ship angling into the horizon, the she-wolf and her pack were turning, melting into the darkness, allowing themselves to be swallowed by forest shadows. Carlette knew that the Bloody paws would sense the change. They were warriors, not soldiers. Discipline would fail them. Even now, she could feel their beasts scrambling to reach the Giant's Wood, to disappear.

Body swaying with exhaustion, Carlette took one, teetering step forward. Mileen turned, at first with a curious frown and then with gaping horror.

"Look out!"

Something hard hit the back of Carlette's head.

Her eyes crossed. Her knees hit the ground.

As her consciousness leaked away like water through cupped hands, Carlette thought of Quaina.

For you, my friend.

And then the world dissolved.

Chapter Thirty-Six

❋ QUEEN OF NOTHING ❋

Carlette woke with a start, head throbbing. She jerked. Her numb shoulder slapped against stone. Her eyes snapped open, but it made no difference. The world was black and cold and dark. Something was dripping. Something else shifted to her right.

Instinctually, Carlette stretched out with her mind to find the life she could sense nearby. But her eyes were covered. She tried to flex her fingers and found them balled in a fist. She brought her wrists together and heard a metallic clink.

Iron gloves.

Her heart sank.

She knew where she was, although the understanding brought no relief. The cold, the damp, the muffled rumble of the sea. It all made sense.

She was in the mountain cells beneath the Geldrue, trapped in the cliffs.

Carlette began to piece things together. She remembered the Amonoux, remembered touching that vast mind and speaking to the she-wolf like an equal, almost like a friend. But as the puzzle slotted into place, she also remembered the faces of those around her. Mya's agonized dismay, Mileen's gaping mouth.

And, somewhere behind her, the commander of the King's Axe watching as a suspected deserter brought an Amonoux to a halt.

The Woodsman had done this.

Pain radiated from the base of her neck where the grip of his axe had hit her. She'd seen it before, a soldier sneaking up behind a rogue hood or prisoner and bringing the butt of their gun down where the spine meets the skull. It was enough to shock the enhabiter, stop their magic, and—if wielded with enough force—knock them unconscious.

Carlette rubbed one fisted hand against the lump, grimacing at the scrape of metal against the cold skin of her neck. She shivered and pressed herself against the stone wall.

This was the end. The Woodsman had watched her enhabit an Amonoux. She would likely be executed by nightfall. It would be a public affair, a warning to hoods and Ferrenese alike.

Stinks like Voka.

Carlette pictured the girl she'd seen hanging from the fences, a frayed rope around her neck, harsh words scrawled on cheap wood. Soon it would be her own body hanging in that place of dishonor until the crows and insects ripped her down.

She shivered again, curled up.

It doesn't matter, she told herself, gathering the remnants of her courage. You saved them. You stopped the worst of the attack. Tuleaux will repair itself and life will go on. You did what you came to do.

But the platitudes rang hollow even as she thought them. Just hours ago, Carlette had been brimming with hope. Standing beside a Nuri mechanic and a Moian warrior, a better world had been visible. Maybe even possible. But then that huge, beautiful, *wonderful* dream had been smashed to pieces, broken on the shore of her reality. And of course it had, why wouldn't it be?

Delicate things didn't last long in Ferren.

She felt like a child.

Carlette shifted, rolled her shoulders, wishing she could see the last room she'd ever be in. At least she'd meet death with her head held high. By the elders, she'd faced it enough times in the past few days to be sure.

Perhaps there were only so many times one could cheat the underworld.

She sighed.

"You're awake. I was wondering if they'd killed you."

Carlette jumped at the sudden voice. It was harsh, a hoarse female lilt that had clearly once been strong. A voice used to shouting commands and barking orders, made rusty from screaming.

She knew immediately who it belonged to.

"The Pirate Queen," Carlette said. It wasn't a question.

A chuckle echoed around the damp stone.

"Call me Iara," said the woman, moving noisily. "No point in formality down here."

Carlette's senses zeroed in on the scuffle of her chains.

"I heard them bring you in," Iara rasped. "Damn soldiers ran out of here so fast I thought you might be rigged to blow. I figured maybe they wanted to kill me at last, make it look like some kind of mining accident."

Carlette didn't answer.

"What did you do, to make grown men sprint away like little girls?"

Carlette swallowed.

Was there any point in keeping secrets, this close to the end?

"I enhabited an Amonoux," she said, hating how the small words mangled the grand complexity of her encounter with the she-wolf. "I'm a Furix."

The Ceillan woman's laugh turned into a hacking cough.

"Damn," Iara said at last. Stone shifted and Carlette caught the pungent smell of an unwashed body. "I thought you were just a hood one of them fucked."

Carlette leaned against the obsidian. She could smell salt breeze in the distance, hear crashing waves and seagulls. The sound of freedom, so close and yet so far away, made her blood curdle.

After a moment, Iara spoke again. "They're going to execute you in the morning. Heard one of the boys say it."

"I know."

"You seem calm. Not every day a woman meets her end."

Carlette snorted, leaned her head back. "I envy those women."

Iara waited in silence and Carlette felt as if the words were being tugged out of her. They squirmed in her chest, desperate to be released. With hours left in her life, she had to talk to someone, speak her dreams aloud, or else they may as well have never existed. She wanted, *needed* to be heard, if only for a moment.

And, at this point, Iara was the best audience she could hope to get.

"I'm not afraid of death," Carlette said at last, her voice small. "But I wish I could have done more. Seen more. I never lived, not really. I was a cog in their war-machine, trained for eight years to forget my own humanity." Tears prickled in her eyes, absorbed by the blindfold. "A whole life was stolen from me and I regret that I won't get to steal it back."

Tuk's face bloomed in her mind's eye. He was grinning, his aviator cap tilted to the side as if it was about to fall off. As usual, his hair had all the tidiness of tossed straw and his chin was smeared with oil. But Carlette would have given anything to touch that smudge of grease, run her fingers through that nest of hair.

With fierce regret, she remembered every time the two of them had been alone, every time she could have acted. She'd created excuses, pushed him away. She'd had orders, a mission, duty, training.

All that was meaningless now.

"The settlers hold their own ideas about civilization and progress," Iara said with disgust. "I suppose one has to respect their industry. You've never seen the Bladed City, I assume, but I've been to Revinburg. I've seen the reasons they do what they do. Trust me when I say, it was never personal."

"You sound like you admire them?" Carlette said.

"I do, in a way. I've studied them my whole life. It's my duty to understand the enemies of my people, after all." Iara chuckled again. "And besides, they're not nearly as mysterious as they think they are. The Nuri are a far more complex society."

Carlette's heart twisted.

"And you?" she asked to change the subject. "Don't you fear your own death?"

"Oh, they can't kill me," Iara said with a lazy confidence. "My men will rip their precious harbor to shreds. I've lost a few fingers to this adventure, but I won't be here forever."

"You plan to escape?"

"*I* don't plan to do anything. My Featherhands won't abandon me."

"You place a lot of trust in pirates."

"Pirates, my dear, are the most honest people in the world. Keep them fed and give them a cause to kill for and they'll follow you to Hyba's doorstep."

"And what cause do your men kill for?"

Iara shifted, chains clanking.

"The same thing any person does. Freedom. The right to love and live and make your own way. We fight hard for such a privilege."

"I thought the Ceilan Isles were safe."

"In this world, nowhere is safe." Carlette could hear the wry smile in Iara's voice, the bitterness. "We've been in this war far longer than you, my miserable friend. Our sky chariots have been breaking against Delasir ships and Nuri stormriders since before Tuleaux was named. You think you've seen the worst of it out there in the mountains?" Iara laughed. "You have no idea."

298

Carlette didn't know what to say. She wondered if she should be insulted, but Iara's words were true. Her own insignificance and ignorance had already roped around her, barbed with shame. How could she have believed that her power was enough to unite the tribes? What chance did one Furix stand against all the blood and pain and suffering out there? Carlette had bought into Byrna's image of her like a starving cat swallowing a fish, and now she was sick from it.

"I've heard about the Featherhands," Carlette said to distract herself from her own humiliation.

"Good things, I hope."

Carlette laughed. "Hardly. But impressive stories."

"I aim to entertain."

Carlette leaned back, imagining the squalling ocean and salty breeze beyond the stone behind her. "I wish I could have seen them."

"If I'd ever met you on the open sea, the only prison-mates you'd know would be fish."

Carlette snorted. She liked Iara.

Yet another enemy who felt like a friend.

Footsteps echoed toward them. Even with her powers muffled, Carlette could feel a familiar mind, accompanied by two others.

The bastard-prince, flanked by armored guards.

Carlette tried to sit up straighter, using her fists to push onto her knees. She would be strong and meet whatever came without flinching.

The footsteps stopped right in front of her cell. Water continued to drip and Carlette heard the rustle of capes. She waited for the prince to address her. When he finally did, his voice was unexpectedly light.

"We've seen better days here in Tuleaux, Miss Carlette."

She was silent, braced against his dry acidity.

He heaved a heavy, exasperated sigh. "Hard to believe one person could be responsible for so much damage."

"I wasn't responsible, Your Highness, but I did try to stop it. I apologize that I didn't do so in time."

Iara scoffed but they all ignored her. The prince was quiet for a long moment. Carlette could feel him thinking, making decisions.

She waited, her neck straining as fought to keep herself upright.

"Leave us."

The guards hesitated, their doubt palpable. But they couldn't ignore a direct order from a member of the royal family. Carlette felt them depart, oozing frustration, their boots squeaking against the damp obsidian floor.

There was a rustle as someone moved. Carlette sensed the Prince, closer this time. Crouching in front of her, perhaps? He smelled of flowers and clean fabric and perfumed hair.

"I was sent an anonymous message that I should come and speak to you in private. About some dangerous secret. It's a waste of time, if you ask me, but I don't like to leave loose ends."

"Are we in private, your majesty?"

"What is the secret?" Dirlen asked, ignoring her sarcasm.

"Why should I help you? You're going to have me executed."

Dirlen took a long moment to respond. "The Magistrate believes you're dangerous."

"And you don't?"

"I believe you were as overwhelmed in that fiasco as any of us. You just happened to know more. So tell me, what else do you know?"

Carlette's chin lifted even higher. She imagined meeting his eyes through the blindfold.

"I know, *your majesty*, that Delasir's monsters are worse than Ferren's. I know that there is beauty on this island, beauty that your people try to beat out and burn down. And I know that no matter what I'm accused of, I wouldn't take any of it back."

"Ah, spirit," the prince said dryly. "Awfully troublesome thing, but ever so infectious. I can see why the Magistrate wants you dead."

"I'm sorry for what happened," Carlette said. "And I'm sorry for the people that died. But I wasn't behind the attack."

"It seems you misunderstand me. That's not why the Magistrate is planning to have you killed. He believes you're some kind of legendary demon or something. An ancestor of a famous rebel. Is he wrong?"

Carlette pursed her lips and remained silent.

Dirlen laughed again, more derisive this time.

"These settlers are so quaint, aren't they? Imagine growing up with such fanciful stories. I can see why they get superstitious. Take this Voka character; she sounds like a bad bedtime story. A wolf-rider with blood in her hair? Honestly, how imaginative."

"Voka was real," Carlette said. "And she was every bit as powerful as the stories say."

"So you met this woman? Saw her somewhere out there in the wild?"

Carlette bit the inside of her lip. Dirlen was taunting her, trying to get her to confess. And why shouldn't she? No amount of pleading would save her now. Why bother hiding anymore?

"I know because she was my ancestor," Carlette said, her words ringing. "I am Voka's descendant. Her blood runs in my veins."

When Dirlen's voice came, it was closer than ever.

"So you can ride wolves and speak to spirits?"

"I stopped the Amonoux pack from destroying this city. If that's a crime—"

"Tell me, how did you hide it? All those years in the Convent and then in Jemelle. How could you possibly control such a gift?"

Carlette swallowed. Grand Mera was dead, but Mya was still out there. Sheltering a deadly secret.

"I was born in Tuleaux," she said. "Not in the Convent. My mother and I begged on the streets until she died. I survived, and when I was eight years old, Grand Mera found me." Carlette's throat constricted. "She protected me."

There was a pause. Then Dirlen clucked his tongue.

"Now what am I supposed to do with that? To think I was expecting a brave warrior, raised by animals or some nonsense. Instead I find a street rat with a powerful mentor. Legend indeed."

Carlette's lips twisted. "Sorry to be such a disappointment, Your Majesty."

Dirlen shifted again, stepping back. "I'm a bastard son. I'm used to disappointment."

Carlette grabbed hold of her courage, taking a deep breath. The prince was here, listening to her. There would be no better time.

"Don't you think," she asked, leaning forward, "that life doesn't have to be like this? What if the war could end? What if there was a future without all this?"

"A rebel with a dream? That's new."

Carlette deflated, hanging her head. "No newer than a pampered prince too comfortable to change."

"Very philosophical. But I'm afraid I must return to my duties. I have an important role you know. Lots of *learning* to do."

Carlette heard Dirlen's cape swoosh and his boots click back another step, but she wasn't listening. Something was crawling up her pants, scratching at the skin of her calf. Insistent. Urgent.

Warning.

"Best of luck in the City of Souls, Miss Carlette," Dirlen said. "As interesting as you are, I'm afraid I can't stop the Magistrate from killing you. But never fear, I'll—"

What the prince would do, Carlette would never know. Because at that moment, the entire side of the mountain exploded in a hail of gunpowder and beetles.

Chapter Thirty-Seven

❋ BY GROUND AND SKY ❋

Carlette curled into a ball as stones rained down around her. Explosions and dust filled the air. Metal crashed. Stone tumbled. Carlette threw her arms over her head, felt the iron bruise her forehead. Another blast tossed her into the corner, slamming her against the wall like a sack of flour.

Then everything stopped.

For a moment, Carlette thought she'd died. Her ears rang, a high squeaking note that pierced through any attempt to think. Her muscles felt detached from her body. There was pain, so much pain.

As the agony subsided, she realized that tiny legs were scratching at her spine, climbing the column of her neck.

With a half-shriek, Carlette tried to knock the beetles off. Her fist crunched one insect against her neck, but three more crawled up her shirt. Her hearing returned, muffled and foggy. Raised voices echoed in the mountain tunnels. Everywhere was the scrape and scuffle of insects.

Or was that just a single scraping noise, very close to her ear?

Carlette froze.

The snapping, crunching sound grew as the ringing faded. Iara was laughing. Male voices were shouting over the crackle of breaking rock.

Carlette's blindfold fell away, half-eaten by beetles.

Information rushed at her in a kaleidoscope of sound and noise. She was in a mountain cell, or at least the remnants of one. Black stone littered the ground, sprinkled with bent iron bars. The air was thick with rock dust, sharp and slicing. Somewhere nearby the wind howled.

Carlette blinked against the darkness.

But it wasn't darkness.

A distant red glow filtered in through the haze.

It couldn't be...

Ocean spray whipped at her face.

Tentatively, hardly daring to believe it was real, Carlette used one gloved fist to push herself upright. She stumbled, limping on a bruised leg, but the pain barely registered. Because an entire wall of her cell had been blown off. The mountain was now open to the tumultuous sea. Thick storm clouds swirled, tumbling toward Tuleaux, and through the thunderheads Carlette could see the distant hopeful light of dawn.

Her mouth fell open.

What happened...?

Everywhere around her, beetles lay twitching. Dying. She gaped at them, understanding slowly breaching through her shock.

Byrna.

The beetle-speaker had told her about the plan to trap the Amonoux cub. Beetles coated in gunpowder. Carlette shook her head, a fanatical grin spreading over her face. It was impossible, unbelievable, but somehow her friends had come back for her.

A voice broke through her amazement.

"Carlette," Iara barked.

Carlette whirled to see the Pirate Queen tossing aside her own blindfold. The fabric fluttered to the ground like a lost message. Her cell had burst outward, bars scattered down the hallway like broken toothpicks. Carlette gaped in wonder. Even emaciated and dirty and wearing Iron Gloves, Iara was an imposing woman. Her braided hair fell almost to her waist and her eyes flashed like lightning. She stood, feet apart, with the air of a commander about to march into battle.

Dirlen lay at her feet, bleeding from a gaping cut on his forehead.

"Help me," Iara said. Her voice was urgent but calm.

Guards were still shouting from beyond where the blast had collapsed the tunnel. The sounds of boulders rolling away reverberated through Carlette's feet. They had minutes, maybe less, before the frantic men reached their fallen prince.

With no time to think about the weight of her decision, Carlette nodded.

Stumbling forward, head still swimming, Carlette felt like she was underwater. Iara had already managed to pull one of the prince's arms over her shoulders. She was using the strength of her legs to pull him up. Carlette struggled, her fists clumsy and ineffective as she grasped Dirlen's other arm.

"Where are we going?" Carlette asked.

"The air."

"*What*?"

"Move!"

Stone shifted and voices rose, closer this time. Carlette glanced over her shoulder as she and Iara limped to the gaping hole. The guards had created an opening. A glint of black metal appeared, the dark eye of a barrel pointing right at them.

"Duck!" Carlette screamed, yanking their three bodies forward.

They tumbled, sprawling on the debris of the explosion. A bullet pinged off the obsidian. Carlette heard a shout.

"No, stop! You might hit the prince!"

"We'll never survive the fall," Carlette said, panic rising as she and Iara struggled to their feet again, irreverently hauling Dirlen's body over the debris.

"We only need to survive the leap."

"What are you talking about? We'll die!"

Iara grinned savagely.

"Ah, but we'll go with the wind beneath our wings."

"We don't have wings!" Carlette shouted, wondering if prison had driven the woman mad.

But then she heard a sound from outside, a familiar, sharp scree. Carlette felt more than heard the thump of giant wings.

"Our rescue arrives, wolf-rider," Iara said with a wink, hauling Dirlen another few feet.

Of course...

Trying not to think about leaping into a furious storm, Carlette doubled her efforts. The guards had widened the opening behind them, creating an almost human-sized crawl space. Carlette twisted to glance over one shoulder, but a stone shifted beneath her foot. She fell, crying out as her knee was sliced open.

The prince spilled to the side.

Iara stumbled.

They were close to the opening. Carlette could see immense shadows moving in the clouds, the Featherhands raptors calling to them.

"Grab his legs," Iara commanded, wheezing.

Carlette obeyed, wrapping her arms around Dirlen's knees as best she could. Together, she and Iara lifted his body and shimmied to the hole. Carlette's head spun as she peered out. The waves were crashing and violent and so very far beneath them. Birds swooped like gods of lighting and thunder. She heard another caw, felt its power resonate in her bones.

Suddenly, Iara threw back her head and cawed in return, the sound a fierce campaign against the night. Carlette jerked in surprise.

"Ready?" Iara asked, her smile impossibly wide and wild.

306

"No!"

"On three."

Before Carlette could try to argue against the insanity of their plan, Dirlen's body was swinging.

"One."

Another bullet pinged, this one closer to Carlette's ear.

"Two."

Someone was stretching through the tunnel. A uniformed torso grasped at broken rocks, face twisted in a snarl.

"Stop in the name of the king!"

"Three!"

Carlette released Dirlen's legs. His body sailed through the opening, caught by the wind, spinning into the near darkness. Carlette watched the bastard prince disappear.

"You're mad!"

"Thank you!"

And then the Pirate Queen linked her iron glove through Carlette's elbow and pulled her bodily into the open air.

Carlette's scream was swallowed by the shrieking wind. She was tumbling, hair whipping, heart pounding. Iara's arm slipped out of hers and she heard the unsettling sound of feral laughter. The world tilted; the sky blurred. She couldn't tell where the ocean ended and the horizon began. Red streaks of dawn light made everything look ripped and bloody.

Something snagged against her leg, not quite grabbing hold. She spun. Jerked. Thick bands of steel closed over her chest, stopping her tumble. But they weren't steel. They were talons, as long as she was tall. Oily black hooks curled around her body, cradling her against the protruding toe-joints of the raptor. Carlette scrabbled helplessly with her useless hands, frantic for something solid to hold. Wings thumped. The air hummed. A victorious caw broke through the storm, echoed by three other birds.

Carlette gaped up at her rescuer. She couldn't see the pirate, but the raptor itself was monstrous. Iridescent blue wings beat at the air as the great beast cut through the maelstrom, undaunted by the tempest.

Tuleaux vanished below them.

For a moment, Carlette couldn't see. The air turned grey and dark and so thick that Carlette felt like she could reach out and grab it. Cold filled her, numbed her. Ice crystals scraped her throat.

Finally, the raptors broke through the clouds with a burst of blinding sunlight.

Carlette gasped.

It was beauty like she had never seen before, a sweeping ocean of white and gray. She soaked in red sunlight and midnight blue sky and the sensation of a great and open emptiness that you could explore your whole life and never fully understand.

All at once, Carlette understood Tuk's love of flying.

The raptors sliced through the sky with powerful, confident strokes. Carlette strained to see where they were going. *There.* Dark shapes moved in the distance, growing larger. She blinked, frozen tears making her eyelids stick together.

When she realized what they were approaching, Carlette fought the urge to laugh.

The pirate blockade had taken flight. Six chariots cut through the air, sailing on the clouds, each pulled by two raptors. Long wooden arms reached out on either side with fabric stretched between them to keep the ships aloft. They were painted in elaborate blues and golds to match the birds, with the largest and most beautiful soaring right in the middle. It was huge, pulled by four raptors, teeming with activity, and flying the Featherhands emblem.

A skull over crossed blue feathers.

Both animal and human voices rose as the rescue party approached. Birds shrieked with pleasure. Men shouted orders. Carlette braced herself, wondering what kind of welcome awaited her on Iara's flagship. The talons shifted and clicked around her, adjusting. Her raptor swooped closer to the crowded deck. Crew members grouped below her, but she couldn't make out their expressions, just the noise of a bustling, celebrating people.

Abruptly, the raptor released her. She fell, shouting, only to land hard on the deck. The chariot dipped once and then leveled out. Carlette panted, bent over on hands and knees, trying to swallow air that felt strangely insufficient. Two other bodies thumped down next to her, making the whole ship wobble again.

"Hook up the birds," Iara shouted without missing a beat. "Full flock, on the double!"

There was a scuffle of footsteps and a strangled sound of excitement. A hand grabbed Carlette's arm. She made to yank herself away, but someone taller and less exhausted dragged her into a hug.

"It worked!" Tuk shouted as he squeezed Carlette's bruised ribcage. "I can't believe it worked!"

"The daisy doubted me," came Byrna's acerbic voice. "His first mistake."

Carlette drew back, drinking in Tuk's smile, his bright expression. He was backlit by the sunrise, dark skin glowing, hair oily and wet. She blinked against water, not knowing or caring if it was rain or tears.

"You saved me," she whispered.

"Well really, they saved *her*," Byrna said, jerking a thumb at Iara. "You were just in the way."

Tuk rolled his eyes, still grinning. "Of course we saved you," he said, loosening his grip. "I couldn't leave you behind."

Emotion rose in Carlette's chest like a tidal wave. For the first time in her life, she allowed herself to ride it, feel it wash through her body and set fire to her blood. A girlish blush spread over her cheeks and she didn't do a damn thing to hide it.

With hands still bound into tight fists, Carlette snaked her arms around Tuk's neck.

He released a small, breathless "Oh!" before she leaned in and pressed her lips to his. A flicker of surprise batted against her mind, brief, unsteady, before his arms tightened around her waist and his mouth opened to hers and suddenly, he was welding together her broken pieces with a glorious, earth-shattering heat.

It was the kind of magic she'd never known, had only dreamed of.

But made so much sense.

Carlette felt the sizzle around them, waves of it, pushing away the rain and wind and cold. It could have been a sunny summer day or the winter solstice and she wouldn't have noticed either way. A terrifying, liberated voice sang in her chest and she didn't bother to silence it.

All she could think was that it was a tragedy she hadn't done this sooner.

When she pulled away, Carlette felt the minds and eyes of the ship on her. She didn't care. She wasn't afraid or ashamed anymore.

She never would be again.

Byrna leaned against the edge of the chariot, smirking and gripping Prince Dirlen's arm as if he were a naughty child and not a semi-conscious royal. All around them pirates sniggered, but Carlette was immune to whatever they were thinking.

Instead, she stepped back and addressed their queen.

"You saved us. Thank you."

Iara cocked her head as a crewmate picked the locks on her wrist. One manacle clinked off, thudding against the wood. The deckhand began to work on the other one.

"What you said back there," Iara answered as if nothing had happened. "In the cells about a better future. Did you mean it?"

The other manacle fell off.

"Every word."

Iara looked at her for a long moment, flexing fingers tattooed with iridescent feathers. Carlette noticed that the Pirate Queen's eyes were hawk-yellow and twice as piercing. She felt like her heart dangled out of her chest, vulnerable and open for all to see.

Let them.

Finally, Iara's lips pulled into a sly grin. She nodded to the deckhand who'd freed her.

"Well? What are you waiting for? Get her loose."

As the young pirate began—more than a little nervously—to work on Carlette, Iara stepped forward, her stride graceful and balanced despite the shifting of the chariot.

"It appears, my new friend," Iara said as the heavy gloves fell away, "that we're on the same side after all."

Carlette flexed her own fingers, savoring the rush as her power came back in full force.

"It appears we are."

The Pirate Queen offered her hand. "Welcome aboard the *Last Shadow*."

Carlette accepted without hesitation.

Iara's strong grip had the confidence of a ruler, the certainty of a free woman, and Carlette wondered how much she could learn from this creature of the sky. Hope bubbled inside her, infectious, raw, impossible to resist. Standing there above the clouds, surrounded by people she barely knew but deeply loved, the whole world felt like a promise.

Carlette grinned back.

Iara leaned in close, winking.

"But let's try to keep the kissing to a minimum, eh? I've got a ship to run."

EPILOGUE

❋ EYLON'S CURSE ❋

Commander Invitas had always hated Ferren. It wasn't the black magic or the Delasir settlers or even the deadly creatures that constantly ripped his squadrons apart.

It was the stink of death.

Persistent, inescapable, it seemed to settle over the whole island like a cloud. No matter how many times he sent his uniform away for cleaning, it reeked of smoke. Even in the pristine glass halls of Caika, overlooking the mountain tips and clouds, he could still smell the Moian city burning, feel death the way he'd been told the witches felt life.

No matter how unnatural and threatening the native magic was, it had never gotten any easier to murder children.

The commander sighed as he glared out at the view, absorbing none of its splendor. When he first arrived, he'd stared at that behemoth mountain range for hours, wondering how close he could get to it, how much of it he could fly over without being sucked into the sky. He smiled to himself. It was that kind of thinking that had drawn him to the air corps in the first place.

Boots thundered behind him.

He turned, brushing a stray lock of salted black hair off his face.

Two men strode in, their uniforms torn. One bled freely from a slice on his arm, another wore a bruise on his cheek like a rebel tattoo. Between them hung the sorriest creature Commander Invitas had ever seen: a fat, balding, middle-aged man who slumped like a dead fish. To the casual observer, he looked worse than useless.

But the Delasir anchor on his neck spoke differently.

Commander Invitas swept his sharp gaze over the bruised men. These were the unit leaders he had sent to investigate the possible attack on Tuleaux. A captured Bloody Paw had suggested—between screams—that the Gaulday celebrations might not go as planned. Judging by his men's appearance, the commander thought that might have been an understatement.

"Report," he snapped.

One of them stepped forward as the other supported the stranger, whose head lolled to one side, bleary eyes crossing.

Was he... drunk?

"Our suspicions were correct, sir. The Bloody Paws attacked Tuleaux. It seems they baited an entire Amonoux pack into the settlement. Their fences collapsed and half the city is destroyed, but a good number of civilians survived. Somehow, they managed to turn back the wolves and the Bloody Paws all at once, although the details remain unclear. There are rumors about a Furix, but it's probably just terrified colonists imagining things."

Commander Invitas nodded, his gaze flickering to the half-conscious man. Ideas bloomed in his head, one after another, but he kept his face schooled and impassive. Invitas had been entrusted with this station for more than just his impressive military heritage. His mind was made of strategy, of violence. Opportunities to honor the Emperor came as easily to him as breathing. So he saw the opening before them like a paved road. This was the perfect chance to press their advantage and take vengeance on their enemy.

"What of Jemelle?" the commander asked as his thoughts hummed.

"No immediate news. Students are back, although their ranks are diminished. Some witnesses said that the headmistress was in the main square when the attack started. We have no idea if she survived or not."

Commander Invitas jerked his chin at the stranger.

"And him?"

To his surprise, the soldier's expression split into a wide, triumphant grin. It was the kind of smile that a soldier would never wear in front of his commanding officer.

Unless he couldn't help himself.

"We found this one wandering through the woods, drunk as a Ziggurat lady on her birthday," said the man, trying and failing to control his glee. "Calls himself Eylon. I think you should speak to him, sir. He's an… interesting person."

The commander's eyes narrowed. He took a step forward, boots clicking on the tile. The drunk man raised his head and it took everything Invitas had not to express his surprise.

Rather than white, this man had bright red circles around his pupils.

"Who are you?" the commander asked in perfect Delarese, voice crisp and cutting.

"Was wonderin' when you were gonna' speak my language," Eylon said, his head tipping back.

Invitas's lip curled against the stink of body odor and stale whiskey. "You will answer the question, witch, or I will have my men extract the answer from you."

"I'm jus' a hood, sir," said the man, his speech slurred almost beyond comprehension. "Don' have anythin' t'hide."

"Your eyes. Why are they red?"

Eylon tilted his head in a clumsy, curious movement.

"I'd love t'help you, sir. Really. Don' have much loyalty t' the king, if ye know what I mean. But I need… reassurances."

"Like what?"

The man shook himself free of the soldier supporting him. He swayed for a moment, spreading his fingers.

Why hadn't they put gloves on him?

"I think we can help each other," the stranger said, enunciating with obvious effort. "But not if you kill me."

"Keep evading my questions and I'll kill you anyway."

Eylon smiled, as if the idea of death was little more than an irritation.

"*Tell me*," Commander Invitas said, dropping each word with the weight of a gavel. "Why are your eyes red?"

"Because, sir," Eylon answered with a leering smile. "I'm exactly what you've been lookin' for."

The commander was struck by the sudden impression of a rapidly approaching wind change that would alter their course. Perhaps their world.

He leaned in to ask, "And how would you know what I'm looking for?"

Eylon smiled, breath rancid.

"I… can cure magic."

For a moment Commander Invitas could do nothing but silently absorb the implication of his words.

Cure magic?

Is that even possible?

His men smirked; his mind buzzed.

And then Eylon the Null fell to his knees and vomited all over the Commander's polished leather boots.

To be continued…

GLOSSARY OF TERMS

Adenai: one of the two tallest mountains in the Shadow Peaks and the Ebonal goddess of life.

Amonoux: the large, seven-eyed wolves who prowl the Shadow Peaks and sometimes come down from the mountains to feed. According to legend, the seventh and most magical eye sees the invisible power that binds the world together and is fueled by the souls of their victims. Considered sacred in Ebonal lore.

Aurok: native to the Wihach Plains, these are large, horned grazing mammals, most often used by the Raebus people as beasts of burden or raised for milk and meat.

Avc Maisan: the street in Tuleaux known for its brothels and orphanages.

Ayurai: a wealthy seaside trading port in Nurkaij.

Beraselle: a Delarese city where the royal family spends their summers, located in the protected northern reaches of the peninsula. Considered the most beautiful city in Delasir.

Bloody Paws, the: the main rebel group on Ferren, led by Yokan. Their goal is to purge the island of all foreign influence and destroy the Delasir invaders.

Bodywalking: the Ferrenese term for enhabiting a human being and controlling their body. Considered a great social taboo, this power is used only in the most desperate of situations.

Brime: a Ceillan drink based on palm alcohol.

Caika: the secret base of operations used by the Nuri Stormriders to strengthen their hold on the island.

Cairog: also called forest beetles, these are long, many-legged insects that are found in the Giant's Wood and mining caves around it. Difficult to enhabit and feared for their terrifying visage, they are considered to be one of the worst monsters of Ferren.

Cerise Tower: a school of Jemelle also known as the Tower of Blood, this is the main dorm of red hoods, also known as Prederaux, who enhabit predators.

Ceillan Isles, the: homeland of the Ceillan people, consisting of a group of stony islands that float over the ocean. Believed to be held aloft by some power of the trees that grow there. Also known as The Floating Isles.

Ceillan People, the: Inhabitants of the Ceillan Isles, this Ferrenese tribe is known for riding raptors and guarding the oceans around Ferren. These people see themselves as the rightful guardians of the island and are currently led by the Pirate Queen, Iara.

Chantiere: main square in Tuleaux, most commonly used for festivals, announcements, markets, and executions.

Chevin Tower: a school of Jemelle also known as the Tower of the Steed, this is the main dorm of brown hoods who enhabit horses, farm animals, and beasts of burden.

Church of the Hand: a form of ancestor-worship that has become the main religious denomination in Delasir, popular among the settlers. Also called the **Church of Elders**, it represents the five 'fingers' of a person's foundation (father, mother, maternal grandparents, paternal grandparents, and self, represented by the thumb). Its members believe that the dead go to the **City of Souls** and that each individual is protected not only by their deceased family but also by their loyalty and accomplishments in life.

Collectors: the men assigned by the Delasir magistrate to bring back Ferrenese women of child-bearing age to produce half-Ferrenese magic-users for the Order of the Hood.

Commercant Bay: the main port of trade used by the Delarese settlers, leading into Tuleaux.

Convent of Others: an underground monastery of sorts, located inside the Tuleaux cliffs, where the captured Ferrenese women are kept and forced to bear the children who will one day become hoods.

Delasir: a far-north kingdom on the continent, known for its bleak weather and poor soil. In order to support a growing population, the people of this nation struck out to claim more resources, originally to fuel their factories and then to fuel their effort to steal territory from their southern neighbor, Nurkaij. With several established settlements and a long history on Ferren, they believe themselves to have successfully colonized the island.

Durchemin (also called the Iron Road): a cage-like hanging road that traverses the mountains between Jemelle and Tuleaux. Supported by thick iron bars nailed into the obsidian rock of the Shadow Peaks and carefully fenced in to protect against animals and rebels alike, it is the safest way to travel through the heartland of Ferren. Overlooks the Giant's Wood.

Ebonal Tribe, the: the northernmost people of Ferren who live in and above the main mountain range, often feared for their brutality, ruthlessness, and proficiency with magic. Known to ride Mountain

Stags, they are believed to be the most powerful of the Ferrenese tribes because of their proximity to the Shadow Peaks.

Enhabitation (to enhabit): the magic possessed only by the island people of Ferren that allows them, using the power of their minds, to control the bodies of other living creatures. Since it is highly dependent on touch and sight, this power can be impeded almost entirely using blindfolds and wrapping the user's hands. This is why hoods are mandated to wear gloves unless instructed by a supervisor to use their magic, and also the purpose of Iron Gloves (see below).

Exolar: a nation to the west of Delasir, known for its violent raiding parties and frequent revolutions.

Faclan Islands: an archipelago connected to the tropical jungle occupying the southwest of the island, occupied by the Faclan tribe.

Faclan Tribe: a group of people living in the southwest of Ferren, commonly known for their blue tattoos, facial piercings, and familiarity with poisons.

Featherhands, the: a group of pirates/warriors led by the Ceillan queen, famous for destroying Delarese and Nuri ships alike in their mission to protect the island of Ferren. Every member is marked with tattooed feathers on each of their fingers.

Ferren: the mysterious island first colonized for its abundance in iron and then claimed for the magical power displayed by the island people.

Fethidi: also called forest spiders, these are the large, venomous arachnids who live in the Giant's Wood.

Feur: capital of the Raebus clans, located on the east side of the island.

Furix: one who can enhabit an Amonoux.

Gaulday: the biggest festival in Tuleaux, designed to celebrate Micros Gaul who originally discovered Ferren. Often a time for official events such as the testing and appointment of new hoods, showcasing royal visitors, and celebrating notable achievements.

Geldrue: the high cliff plateau that overlooks the city of Tuleaux, home to the wealthiest settlers and the Magistrate's fortress.

Giant's Wood, the: a forested area filled with enormous Goddeau trees and the main homeland of the Moian tribe. Often feared for the size of the creatures living there.

Goddeau trees: the trees of the Giant's Wood, famous for their size and red-tinted wood. The sap of these trees is toxic and can cause severe infections if it gets into a human's bloodstream.

Great Forest, the: the Moian afterlife.

Guerison: a hospital of sorts, run by the Church of Elders and located in Tuleaux. Doctors, healers, and Skin Smiths are trained here

Hanging City, The: the capital city of the Moian tribe, located in the heart of the Giant's Wood.

Hasach, the: also called the **Endless Sands**, homeland of the Sibilese people located in the southeast corner of Ferren.

Haute Sea, the: the ocean surrounding Ferren, made dangerous by Nuri Stormriders and Ceillan pirates.

Haya Sahar: capital of the Sibilese people. Translates roughly to 'life city.'

Hisanan Plains: a grassy stretch of land in the middle of Nurkaij, occupied by wild horses and farming settlements.

Howl: the tavern halfway between Jemelle and Tuleaux, built into the mountain. A common place for travelers on Durchemin to stop for a meal.

Hyba: the second of the two tallest mountains in the Shadow Peaks and the Ebonal goddess of death.

Ice Plains, the: homeland of the Ebonal people.

Iron Gloves: metal contraptions that encase a prisoner's whole fist, blocking off the magic of enhabitation. When paired with a blindfold, these will effectively neutralize Ferrenese magic.

Iron Road, the: see Durchemin.

Jemelle: a fortress located in the Shadow Peaks and main base/school for the Order of the Hood. A common waypoint for traders on their way through the mountains via the Wandering Pass.

Kammunuk: a Nuri city close to the border of Delasir that was famously razed in the war between the two nations. It is now a wasteland that is intermittently won or lost by either side.

Kamora: a large Nuri district in the south, recently conquered by the emperor and notoriously difficult to cross due to insurgent activity.

King's Axe, the: an elite group of hoods, led by a non-magical commander called the Woodsman. They are often sent to the front lines of battle and invited to royal events, despite Delasir's general bias against Ferrenese people.

Lumach: also called rock lizards, these are the long, sinuous reptiles who live in the Endless Sands, often used by the Sibilese people in battle or for long journeys.

Mioux: also called the **Weave**, translates to 'everything' or 'the energy that holds the world together'.

Moian Tribe, the: a forest people who live in the Giant's Wood, specifically the Hanging City. Known to ride Sionach into battle.

Mountain Stags: the favored mounts of the Ebonal tribe, these are large, carnivorous mammals with long fangs and multi-pronged horns. Violent, territorial, and difficult to enhabit, they are rarely used outside the Shadow Peaks.

Narrows, the: colloquial term for the war zone located between Nurkaij and Delasir. Known for its inhospitable cliffs, lifeless landscape, and unpredictable storms, it's generally considered to be one of the most brutal environments known to man. Because it is difficult to traverse without the assistance of animals, airships, or raptors, it only became crossable after Delasir discovered Ferren and began to use hoods in battle.

Nathair: see Snow Snakes.

Norjay: a songbird native to the Giant's Wood, roughly the size of a human toddler, with a needle-sharp beak used to fish large insects out of cracked bark. Common prey of forest spiders and sionach.

Northernists: a group of rebels in Nurkaij that support the Delasir ideas of state control and elimination of wasteful luxury. Namely a movement that seeks revenge against the rich and privileged.

Nurkaij: home of the Nuri people and most dangerous enemy of Delasir. Ruled by an emperor, they are known for their travel via hot air balloons (see **Stormriders**) and using elephants in war.

Oeil Tower: a school of Jemelle also known as the Tower of the Eye, this is the main dorm of yellow hoods who enhabit birds and flying creatures.

Order of the Hood: an organization formed by the Delarese Magistrate designed to train half-Ferrenese children in the practice of enhabitation, specifically for the purpose of fighting in the war against Nurkaij.

Prederaux: also known as red hoods, these are the members of the Order trained to enhabit predators.

322

Raebus Clans, the: a group of people who live in the Wihach Plains on the east side of the island, known for their red hair and peaceful temperament. They tend to live in ground dwellings dug out of the hills.

Rae du Ora: translated to the Golden Avenue, this is the main street in Tuleaux where the merchants sell their wares.

Raptors: also called death birds, these are the huge, hawk-like, flying creatures who hunt the skies around Ferren. The adult birds are used by the Ceillan people to pull their flying sky chariots (see below). As juveniles, they are often used as individual mounts to either defend the Ceillan convoys or fight against invaders.

Requin Tower: a school of Jemelle also known as the Tower of the Shark, this is the main dorm of blue hoods who enhabit ocean-dwelling creatures.

Revinburg: also known as the Bladed City, where the King of Delasir resides with his closest advisors. Capital and main trade port of Delasir.

Rianaman Plateau: an area in the Narrows where the fighting is the thickest due to its flat, open nature. Alternatively under the control of either Delasir or Nurkaij, depending on the day.

Riders of Hyba: a once-sacred group of Ebonal warriors who protected the mountains and then the rebel-leader Voka. All were killed in, or executed soon after, her final stand against Tuleaux.

Rock Lizard: the large reptiles Sibilese warriors ride into battle, famous for their colorful head fringes, sharp claws, fast speeds, and paralytic saliva.

Sago: a drug sourced from the Ferrenese mountains that causes hallucinations and inspires so-called 'connection with nature.' It has become popular in the Nuri workforce, particularly as a way for merchants to keep commoners controlled.

Sandfang: the official title of a warrior from Haya Sahar, defender of the Sibilese tribe.

Scara Tower: a school of Jemelle also known as the Tower of the Eye, this is the main dorm of black hoods who enhabit insects.

Seminary, The: A compound in the mountains where the scientists of Nurkaij study and live.

Sibilese People, the: inhabitants of the desert lands in the southeast of Ferren, mostly nomadic and known for their black hair, tan skin, and proficiency with spears. Often seen riding the large and venomous rock lizards.

Sionach: also called flying foxes, these are large mammals with webbing between their front and back limbs that allows them to glide between the tress of the Giant's Wood. Often used as mounts for the Sibilese people, they are also the favorite food of forest spiders.

Shadow Peaks, the: also called the **Ombramont**, this is the main mountain range that breaks up the island of Ferren. Commonly believed by the island's inhabitants to be the source of their magic, it is also rich in iron and therefore run through with many abandoned mines.

Shohan: a nation to the west, located between Nurkaij and Exolar, known for its beautiful art and peaceful society.

Skin Smiths: half-Ferrenese practitioners of magic who are trained to enhabit humans for the purposes of torture and coercion. They are the most feared and reviled of the hoods. Sometimes called a silver hood.

Sky Chariots: the flying ships used by the Ceillans, pulled by trained, often-enhabited raptors. The ships are believed to be made of a lightweight wood that only grows on the Ceillan Isles and has magical buoyant properties.

Slants, the: slang term for the poor, crowded residential area in Tuleaux between the docks and the cliffs. Popular area for sailors to find food and entertainment.

Snow Snakes (also called **Nathair** by the Ebonal tribe): rarely seen, these are warm-blooded reptiles who live beneath the deep snow of the Shadow Peaks. They are known for having extremely poisonous spines that paralyze their prey and cause terrifying hallucinations. Their white, lustrous skin has lately come into fashion in Delasir, driving hunters to seek out these dangerous creatures.

Steppingstone: the only bar and tavern in Jemelle, notorious for the unsavory quality of its clientele.

Stormriders: Nuri battalions of hot air balloons, often armed with flamethrowers. The highest rank in the Nuri military, also called the air corps.

Tathirs: a Nuri sect of religious zealots who want to purge all magic from the world.

Tierre Tower: a school of Jemelle also known as the Tower of the Ground, this is the main dorm of green hoods who enhabit creatures of the forest, excepting predators.

Triumvirate: the symbol of the Nuri belief system, also referring to the association of temples and priests who represent it. Three snakes twisted into a triangle represent past, present, and future, encompassing everything.

Tuleaux: the main Delarese settlement in Ferren, home of the island's Magistrate and most of its settlers. Surrounded by high walls and protected on one side by natural cliffs, it is generally accepted to be the safest place for colonists to live.

Wandering Pass, the: the main route through the Shadow Peaks, connecting Tuleaux and the Wihach Plains. Often traveled by scouts, traders, or the Collectors who bring back Ferrenese captives to breed hoods.

Weave, the: see Mioux.

Wihach Plains: home of the Raebus people, known for its rolling green hills and lack of trees. A generally peaceful land.

Windseekers: a group of rebels, mostly consisting of Stormrider deserters and ex-Nuri military.

Woodsman, the: a title given to the current leader of the King's Axe. The position is royally appointed and considered a great honor, although most nobles don't see it as such due to the social prejudice against hoods.

Vaijan: capital and main trade port of Nurkaij. Also the location of the Ziggurat.

Voka: an infamous rebel who led the most successful attack against Tuleaux that almost resulted in the destruction of the city. She was the last known Furix, famous for riding an Amonoux into battle, and was defeated only when one of her closest warriors betrayed her, leading to her capture and subsequent execution.

Zanbur: a specific kind of airship used by Nuri Stormriders, known for being small and swift. Can't travel far without the support of a larger ship, but nimble enough to navigate mountains and Goddeau trees.

Ziggurat, the: where the emperor of Nurkaij lives, along with his most esteemed nobles and advisors.

THANKS FOR READING!

If you enjoyed this book and would like to support the author, please consider leaving a review or sharing it with your friends.

Subscribe at aawoodsbooks.com for news about upcoming releases, giveaways, and much, much more!

A. A. Woods is a Boston-based writer of science fiction and fantasy. She's lived in Montana, Costa Rica, Vermont, and Scotland, which has given her a soul-deep wanderlust that she treats by exploring her own imagination. Her deepest ambition is to make people think.

Find out more at **aawoodsbooks.com**.

328

Keep reading for a teaser of

SEVERED

A. A. WOODS

SEVERED
BOOK TWO
"A gripping, mesmerizing tale!"

CHAPTER ONE

❋ THE DIVE ❋

Carlette would never get used to freefall.

She could feel Tuk's vibrating excitement behind her, sense his longing to call out a whoop of joy. The enormous raptor they were riding—a borrowed Ceillan mount named Star—radiated a similar wild euphoria as it did what it had been born and bred to do. All around Carlette, the Featherhands scythed through the air like shooting stars; silent, deadly, haloed by the corona of the sun as they bulleted toward their enemy below. Like any predator, Carlette felt the anticipation of the hunt. She could join their enthusiasm for a righteous fight.

But she'd never quite *enjoy* the roaring wind beating her face and the ocean racing up to meet them like a deadly wall.

Below them, closing in faster than Carlette was comfortable with, the Delarese freighter exhaled steam and smoke into the sky. More cover for the pirates. Carlette squinted through Star's keen eyes, scanning the deck. The sailors were pale and dark-haired, plain uniforms stamped with the Delasir anchor. They scurried below, little more than ants in the churn of a day's work. Were they excited to return home? Happy to be charting a course back to the Bladed City? Or relieved to be leaving the wild island of Ferren behind?

Carlette wondered how many of them knew what dreadful cargo they carried.

A soldier of the king looked up, squinting against the noon sun.

Even from this distance, Star could make out the man's eyes widening. His mouth opening.

He shouted an alarm.

Too late.

Iara's raptor let out a ferocious *scree*, releasing the rest of the pirates from their silence. War-cries filled the air, drowning out the panicked scatter of the deckhands.

"Aw yeah!" Tuk called, letting go of Carlette's waist to raise his fist in the air.

Carlette's budding grin was wiped off her face as Star snapped her wings out and tilted to the side. She swallowed hard, gathering her courage.

Just like you practiced, she reminded herself.

"Ready?" she screamed over one shoulder, pulling her boots in beneath her.

She glanced back to find Tuk grinning like a madman.

"Always," he said.

And then launched himself off the raptor's saddle and into open air.

His natural habitat.

In the millisecond Carlette had to watch his trajectory, she marveled yet against at his grace. Tuk joked that he was born with the sky in his veins, a remark that seemed fanciful to anyone who had not yet seen him in it. He was fearless in the open, bold in the emptiness, his clothing catching the wind like so many tiny sails, as if nature herself aimed to welcome him home.

332

She'd never get tired of watching him.

But today, there was no time.

"Dammit," Carlette muttered as Star swerved, too fast, twisting so as not to hit the ship's massive smokestacks. They plunged through a cloud of steam, moving quickly up the ship. There wasn't room for hesitation, but she hated this part. No matter how much discomfort her training in the Order of the Hood had prepared her for, she still preferred keeping something solid beneath her feet, even if it was just a raptor's back.

Gritting her teeth, Carlette closed her eyes, coiled her muscles. She imagined the verbal beating Iara's crew would give her if she backed out of this mission. The taunts would be merciless. Imagine: their famous red hood, forged by Jemelle and brutalized by Delasir's soldiers, failing to take part in a simple rescue mission because she was *scared*?

Besides, this one was personal.

Shrieking like an osprey, Carlette threw herself off Star at the last possible second, jerking out her arms to stabilize her course. For a moment, her world was brackish wind and the horrible gut-drop sensation of falling.

How can Tuk enjoy this?

Then she landed.

Hard.

Her knees buckled, body rolling instinctively. It had taken many hours of training to learn the art of boarding, especially drawing her curved Ceillan blade quickly while not impaling herself in the tumble. But Iara had been a patient teacher, and now Carlette bucked herself upright, sword in hand, ready to join the fray.

She stopped.

The giddy relief of landing in one piece almost made her burst out laughing.

The fray had started without her.

Iara and Koro stood in the middle of the deck, back-to-back with swords in both hands, fighting off the soldiers closing in on them like

333

a blood clot. Malistar, huge and muscled, tossed yet more sailors into the water as easily as if they were dolls. Carlette didn't want to think of the horrors Eri was bringing up from the depths to meet them. Tuk brandished a flamethrower, stolen off a captured Nuri vessel, as he tried to clear a path to the lower decks that had locked up under the attack.

Carlette saw a thin, vicious-looking sailor edging around the battle, coming up behind Tuk.

She surged forward, planting her foot on the railing around the bow and hurling herself over the main knot of fighting. This time landing with more control, she let her momentum carry her into the sailor's back, using her magic on him at the same time. The white rings around her eyes glowed. Her bare hands, one tight around the sword grip, the other clenched in a fist, tangled into the life that swirled around her like a second layer of the world.

She focused on the sailor about to strike Tuk.

With a feral snarl, she tightened her mental grip.

The man froze, knife stuck in the air.

Making an effort not to kill him—an effort Iara would have mocked her for—Carlette shoved his consciousness into sleep. He fell with a *thump* that was barely audible over the raucous fighting.

Tuk spun, grinning and almost getting cleaved in half by another soldier's battleaxe.

Lifting her free hand, Carlette stopped the arc of the weapon and forced the woman to tumble backwards over the railing.

She winced at the splash and tried to ignore the brief sensation of cold water spilling into the woman's throat.

"Hey, thanks," Tuk said with a bright smile. "That's two more I owe you."

"Be more careful please," she panted. "Or you might never make it up—"

She was interrupted by something hitting her side, knocking her over. Slavering teeth snapped, too close to her face. She glimpsed wild eyes ringed with white, under control.

Hounds.

"Carlette!" Tuk shouted, surging toward her, his flamethrower useless against this new enemy.

But she was already dominating the canine minds, even as more of them were released. She wrested control with savage efficiency, skittering up the connection to whoever held them. A hood, of course, their power cold and focused. Carlette wrapped around that more complicated human mind easily, recognizing it, strangling it. Memories flickered spasmodically through the link, of Jemelle, of Ferren. Carlette shared some of them, but this wasn't a person she knew.

Small mercies.

"Get the door," Carlette growled as she heaved the now-docile dogs off her, shoving the hood into oblivion. Silently, she prayed that their body had fallen somewhere safe.

"Right!" Tuk flung the hose of the flamethrower over his shoulder and lunged forward, grabbing the iron handle. It was locked, of course. Delasir had to protect the delicate sensibilities of the high-born men and women below, not to mention keep a certain prisoner from getting out at an inconvenient time...

Luckily, they had an expert on hand.

Guarding Tuk while he worked on the lock, Carlette thought about what had brought them here. A whisper of horrific news, the wafting, noxious fumes of war coming off the island. *Her* island. Things in Ferren had been escalating steadily since she'd enhabited the she-wolf last fall. Whole battalions of Delarese soldiers had been sent to hunt for her, scouring the landscape, interrogating hoods, the situation exacerbated by gruesome confrontations with the Bloody Paws. Rumor had it that the top Delarese general, a mysterious General Gulon, had arrived to oversee the reconstruction of Tuleaux himself. Nuri airships were behaving erratically, attacking unpredictably. And worse. There was no denying that a boulder had been set into motion. The attack on Tuleaux had initiated something that could not be undone.

Carlette tried not to think of her role in that.

Or lack thereof, as Byrna would sneer.

Half-watching Tuk work, Carlette turned to the deck. The battle had shifted. Iara and her pirates were gaining a clear advantage over the soldiers, pushing them into corners where they were rapidly subdued. But the fight hadn't quite gone out of them yet. The King's men had been blindsided, not as armed as they should have been. But that didn't mean they planned to surrender control, especially not to the Featherhands.

Enough, Carlette thought, sheathing her sword.

She glared at the melee, holding her hands out in front of her. It was difficult to enhabit so many minds at once. A normal hood could hardly hope to hold a single human being, much less the dozens aboard the ship. But Carlette wasn't normal. She wasn't just a hood.

Even if she wished she was.

With a steady exhale, Carlette shot her power out like loosed arrows, embedding herself into the consciousnesses of the Delarese sailors and soldiers. They all froze. It was easier to just hold them still than bend their bodies and minds to her will, but she still shook with the effort.

For a moment, nothing moved.

Swords dipped toward the deck, held loose in confused hands.

Then Iara straightened, cocking her head with the avian grace that was so typical of the Ceillan people. "About time, Furix," she said, spinning her blades before sliding them into the twin sheaths on her back. "Tie 'em up, quickly now! Don't want our traitor to run out of steam."

Carlette winced at the jab.

As the Featherhands set about following Iara's command, the Pirate Queen came up to Carlette, slapping her on the shoulder. "Wasn't sure you'd make it off Star."

Carlette only growled in answer.

Iara winked. "You're right, how foolish of me to doubt the Furix."

"Almost done," called Koro, the head of the Ceillan Queensguard. He glanced at Carlette, eyes darting between the two women as if he could sense their tension even from that distance.

"I can hold it," Carlette said in answer, speaking through gritted teeth.

Iara folded her arms. "Of course you can."

"Aha!" came Tuk's victorious shout from behind them, accompanied by the grating of unhappy gears. "Their engineers couldn't outsmart *me*."

"Very good," Iara said dryly, gesturing to the twins. "Explosives first."

Alma grinned. Alex saluted. "Aye aye Captain," they said together before hurrying into the shadows belowdecks.

"Have fun," Iara called.

Carlette had been with Iara's crew almost five months, from the events of last autumn to the fresh glow of spring. But even after dozens of missions, hundreds of hours of training, and endless meals and evenings together, she found herself surprised by the strange dynamic of the Pirate Queen's crew. They were at once obedient and unruly, wild and contained. They fought with a feral viciousness Carlette had only ever seen in the Bloody Paws, but there was a contentedness among the Ceillan warriors that confused Carlette. Almost as if they were... enjoying themselves.

It was a concept she was still learning to appreciate.

"Alright," Iara said after a few seconds, pulling Carlette out of her musings. "Let's go ruffle some feathers."

Following the twins, Iara stepped into the shadow and onto a landing at the top of the iron stairs. Carlette watched with apprehensive curiosity, even as she continued to hold the soldiers and sailors being bound by the pirates. The inside of the steamship was a marvel to her, every bit as grand and lifeless as the magistrate's home back in Tuleaux. Metal walls, grated steps, and a steady relentless chugging that sounded like the lungs of a giant beast. She would have been afraid, if not for the knowledge that those around her did this all the time.

Clearing her throat, Iara lifted a cone-shaped amplifier from its hook on the wall. She threw them a sly grin.

Then, enunciating clearly, she spoke to the ship. "This is Queen Iara of the Ceillan Isles. You might have heard that your vessel is under attack. I'm here to inform you that the situation has shifted. Your men are subdued, your deck has been claimed, and your ship will soon be incapacitated. If you are a passenger traveling home, I advise you to stay in your quarters. My crew has orders—and inclinations—to kill anyone they meet in the halls, armed or not. Keep your heads and you might just to keep your lives too." She leaned in. "And to anyone in the cargo hold, I recommend you get the hell out."

Ending with a caw-like laugh, Iara hung the amplifier back in its spot and turned to them. "Think they got the message?"

Next to Carlette, Koro let out a longsuffering sigh. "It would have been easier if you didn't warn every damn sailor belowdecks what we're up to."

"Ah, but what fun would that be?"

"Done!" called a pirate from the deck.

At Iara's nod, Carlette released her hold on the sailors and soldiers, sagging against the doorframe. Tuk caught her around the waist, but she waved him off. It was more the shock of returning entirely to her own mind than the exhaustion that made her stagger. Peering out at the deck, Carlette saw men and women struggling against their bonds, eyes wide with surprise and fear and helplessness.

She didn't have to imagine how they felt.

"Koro?" Iara said, stepping aside and bowing with a flourish. "If you will?"

"You won't do anything stupid, will you?" he asked.

Iara feigned indignation. "Do I ever?"

With another sigh, Koro gestured to Malistar. "Round 'em up!"

Iara, Carlette, and Tuk stepped back as the bulk of Iara's crew surged through the door, swords and pistols drawn, wearing hungry

338

expressions. Koro would lead them to the cargo hold, set them lose to take what plunder they could carry. Jewels and silks and weapons and food. Who knew what such a large ship, with so many rich passengers, might hide?

And if one prisoner disappeared in the raid, who would think it anything but an accident?

When all but a few lookouts had disappeared into the corridor, Iara jerked her head, suddenly more serious. "Let's go."

And then the three of them were plunging into darkness.

It was one thing to imagine the narrow halls and humid air of a Delarese steamship, to hear the stories and prepare for the worst. It was quite another to feel those metal walls closing in, reverberating with the strange language of a giant seafaring machine. Tuk probably understood what all those hisses and rumblings meant, but not her. To Carlette, it felt like being surrounded by very noisy demons. She could sense Iara's discomfort as well.

Ceillans didn't take well to closed spaces.

Carlette moved quickly, following Iara through the snaking halls. It was dark, the flickering sconces doing little to light their way. Tuk was a warm presence behind her, but the noises of battle reverberated around them, carried by the same announcement system Iara had used. Shouts. Shots. The clang of bullets against metal.

One thing was certain.

They didn't have much time.

Pausing at a carpeted intersection, Iara looked to Carlette. "Your turn, Furix."

Keep reading at https://www.amazon.com/dp/B098W8RP5N

www.ingramcontent.com/pod-product-compliance
Lightning Source LLC
Chambersburg PA
CBHW030413180626
46812CB00005B/1993